DUNOVAN CASTLE

Tracey L. Fischer

PublishAmerica
Baltimore

First printing

ISBN: 1-4137-0369-0
PUBLISHED BY PUBLISHAMERICA, LLLP
www.publishamerica.com
Baltimore

Printed in the United States of America

This novel is dedicated to my grandmother,
Mrs. Georgette M. Moser,
whom I love very dearly.

Chapter One

Darkness came early on January first, 1800, for the Fitzpatricks. It was only four o'clock when brothers Michael and Matthew came home from working in the fields. Their mother, graying hair tied tightly in a bun, away from the once beautiful face, was setting the table for dinner. She looked up in surprise to see her two sons home so early.

"Michael, is something wrong?" she said worriedly. "You are home a little early, aren't you?"

Home is not what I would call it, the handsome black-haired young man thought, looking around the small sparsely furnished cottage.

Although small, his mother and younger sister, sixteen-year-old Beth, named Elizabeth for her mother, tried to keep the cottage clean with white curtains and a vase of daisies. He knew his sister had picked the daises from Lord William's gardens, trying to make the house cheerful. Michael had lived all his twenty years in the little cottage on the emerald rolling hills of Ireland, but he would never call it home.

"No, Mama, nothing is wrong," golden-brown-haired Matthew answered, sitting down and starting to pile the corned beef and potatoes on his dish. "Lord Dunovan gave word to Henry, his overseer, to let us have the rest of the day off, it being the first of the year and all."

"Also, since it looks like a storm is coming, the honorable Lord William does not want to be blamed for another death like old Gerald O'Conner," Michael said bitterly.

"Michael," Beth said, "can't you keep your mouth shut? You know Mr. O'Conner was like a second father to me. His being the father of Gabrielle, my best friend, we were always close." Michael was startled. Beth had never snapped at him before. Sure, he knew she and Gerald were close, but Gerald had died almost two years ago. Something else had to be wrong.

"Beth, what is the matter with you?" Michael asked alarmed when he saw the tears on her cheeks.

"Now, see what you've done, Michael Fitzpatrick!" his mother scolded. "And for Pete's sake, Matthew, would you stop inhaling the corned beef and cabbage before your hardworking father gets home. We haven't even said grace yet!" Elizabeth went over to where Beth was standing in front of the fire, trying to pull herself together before her father John came home.

"Beth?" her mother questioned. "Beth, look at me. I want to know…" The request was cut off when the tired looking John burst through the door. "What in the Lord's name is going on here?" he thundered, taking in the sights of Matthew stuffing his face. Michael looked as though he wanted to be any place but here – which he probably did, knowing how much he hated their little cottage and poverty and his daughter sobbing by the fire with his wife looking at her with worry. John slammed the door and stomped into the little cottage, throwing his hat and scarf on one of the few chairs they had and went toward the fire.

"Lizzie, what in the hell is going on here?" he demanded of his wife using the affectionate pet name he had given her years ago. Elizabeth moved from Beth's side to give her husband a peck on the cheek, steering him away from the sobbing Beth and toward the dinner table. "How was the bar, dear? Crowded?" she asked, referring to Dunovan Bar where he worked as a bartender. He did this instead of working the fields because of his limp – where he got shot in a brawl many years ago.

"That's not what I asked! What is the matter with everyone? It looks like a wake in here!" He moved a chair closer to the fire to warm up his leg. It was giving him trouble again.

"I asked Gabrielle to marry me!" Matthew said, pausing for a moment from his food. Silence greeted this declaration. Elizabeth and John turned around to face him, stunned and speechless. Beth started to cry harder.

Michael broke the silence by saying, "How do you expect to take care of Gabrielle? We only have three bedrooms as it is, barely enough room for the five of us, much less another person and probably a baby in less than a year!"

"Son," John said, "why don't you wait a year or two to marry the lass? She is only sixteen."

"Matthew, don't you think you're both a little young to marry. You are only eighteen," Elizabeth stated logically.

"Why can't anyone in this blasted house be happy for me?" Matthew shouted. "All anyone does in this house is complain. No one is ever happy!"

"Matthew, would you please clean up that mess?" Elizabeth said quietly. The mess she was referring to was the cabbage and corned beef that Matthew spilt when he had his temper flare up.

"Sorry, Mum," Matthew said and went about cleaning it up.

Beth was still crying by the fire. She was beginning to get on John's nerves, that and coming home to a family broken by poverty and arguing. He sat down on the rug by the fireplace and sighed. "Shut up, Beth," he said as gently as possible. "Family," he continued, ignoring the hurt expression on Beth's face, "come sit down by the fire so we can have a discussion. Yes, Michael, you have to come too." John said this because he knew that Michael would complain as he always had about the family tradition to pour out their feelings on the little wool rug in front of a warm fire. Sometimes he worried about the boy. He knew that Michael had lost all hope of becoming a doctor. There was no money to put him through school. He had some education, like Matthew, but he aspired to take care of the sick. The few years the boys had at the village school was not enough to know about the body and what ails it. John knew that Michael was hateful toward the English, especially Lord William Dunovan. Michael hated Lord Dunovan because he was English, but also because of his family. Many years ago, as the legend went, Lord Dunovan's great-grandfather, Henry Dunovan, insulted the royal family. Instead of being executed like an Irishman would, Henry was banished from England to rule twenty square miles of Irish land. Why wasn't Henry executed? Well, there were many rumors about that. One was that the Dunovans had always been in the king's court and were highly respected nobility. The king could not just kill off nobility, or he might be in danger from his people as well as his court. The other rumor was that Henry had an affair with the queen and her majesty ruled the kingdom from behind the king. Without her, the king would be in a war with the whole world. This is why Lord Henry was spared death and sent off to Ireland. John realized that Michael was being irrational about the whole matter. All of this, if it did happen, happened over one hundred years ago. He had told Michael over and over again that it was old news and he should find some lass to marry, have children, and farm. Maybe he could earn enough money to leave the reign of Lord Dunovan and go somewhere, where he would be happy. Michael, being stubborn, which he was sure came from Lizzie's side of the family, wouldn't listen. As soon as his family had sat down by him, he started the speech they had all heard many times before. Elizabeth knew it had been a while since the famous speech was told, just as she knew her children probably needed to hear the story one more time. She just wished it would not take so long. She started to knit; maybe this sweater for Beth would be halfway finished tonight. Beth blew her nose in her handkerchief; she really did not feel like hearing the speech again. Maybe if she started to cry again, he

7

wouldn't go into it. She certainly could cry some more. She looked up; her mother shook her head no, as if she knew what Beth was thinking. Beth looked down at her hands, twisting the hankie, and blushed. Sometimes she wished her mother did not know her so well.

Matthew was sorry he had yelled and thrown a fit, but if his family had been happy for him, he would have told them the good news – not as good as marrying Gabrielle, but good. Now Papa had to go into his lecture one more time. He shifted into a more comfortable sitting position and put an interested expression on his face, while thinking about how happy Gabrielle was about the proposal. She had looked at him with her big green eyes and threw herself into his arms, mindless of the sweat on his shirt. He had put his hands in the corn silk-colored hair and turned her face upwards. He looked down and asked in mock seriousness, "Is that a yes or no?"

"Oh, Matthew, it's a yes! Yes a thousand times. Yes!" she shouted.

"Now are you sure?" he asked jokingly. Then he ducked as she punched him in the chest.

"Lass, are you going to be a husband beater?"

Gabrielle pretended to think it over before she replied, "Maybe."

"Oh really?" Matthew asked before he started to tickle her on the sides of her body and under her chin. She was laughing so hard she collapsed on the mossy hill. Matthew followed her. Finally, as they both knew he would, he captured her mouth with his own. However, Sean Denhey, one of Matthew's co-workers, interrupted them. "Hey, Fitzpatrick, lunch is over. Time to get back to work!"

"Matthew, do you have to go back to work?"

"If you want to get married, I have to earn money." He stood up, then held out his hand to help Gabrielle to her feet and said softly, "You are sure you want to marry me, aren't you?"

"Matthew, I want to marry you more than anything else in the world."

"Matthew, come on, lover boy. Time to get back to work, or you'll loose that new position of yours," Sean called.

"Coming," he replied before kissing Gabrielle one more time.

"Matthew, what new position?" she asked, grabbing his sleeve.

"I'll tell you later," Matthew promised.

"No, tell me now," Gabrielle demanded.

"I can't now…" He was unable to finish, when Gabrielle punched him again. "Oh, Gabrielle, stop that. I'll tell you tonight."

"You're coming over?" Gabrielle asked.

"Yes, to ask your mother for your hand in marriage right after I tell my family," Matthew replied.

"Let me tell Beth, please. She is my best friend, and I want her to be my maid of honor," Gabrielle pleaded.

"Fine. Listen I have to go." Matthew ran up the mossy hill back to the fields; he felt that he was the happiest man alive. Well, that feeling was certainly gone, thanks to the reaction he had received from his family. He tried to concentrate on what his father was saying.

John was explaining the history of the Fitzpatrick's of Ireland. "As you all know, our family, Fitzpatrick, goes way back to the beginning of Ireland – the beginning when we had kings and queens. Our people were the ones who lived in the castles, owned the land we now farm, with the products to be sold by the Irish and the profits for the Irish." John paused to say, "Lizzie darling, would you get me some ale before I continue?"

She got up to get what her husband requested, glad to move. Her foot was asleep. Michael wished he did not have to listen to this again; he had to go out. He needed to go to Donovan's Bar to see Doctor McKay. No one knew that he was still planning to be a doctor – that he was trying to get the doctor to let him be his apprentice. After enough experience, he would go to London and set up a clinic. It would mean to serve the English, but they were the ones who had money. He watched as his mother handed over the tin cup with the white foam almost brimming over the sides. John reached up to take it and drank like he was dying of thrust. When he was halfway finished, he set the cup on the floor and made a motion with his hand toward Elizabeth to sit down. "Ah, thank you, Lizzie darling. Now where was I?"

"The Irish ruling the Irish," Michael said sarcastically.

"Thank you, son," John said, ignoring the sarcasm. Michael sighed loudly while John continued on with his story. "The English and the Irish never got along, but things were fine for awhile. We minded our business; the English minded their own business – until the English got greedy. They wanted more land, we fought, and they won. They took the Irish land." At an attempt at humor, he added, "St. Patrick got rid of all the snakes but couldn't do anything with the English. Makes one wonder what the English are." The humorous remark was met with silence. John coughed and continued on. "I tell the history of our Irish heritage to remind you that the Fitzpatricks have always, through war, through famine…well, just about anything, stuck together. This is why I was amazed to come home to find my family on the beginning of a New Year – hell, a new century – looking as though they wanted to kill each other. Now to begin with, Beth, what is the matter with you?"

Beth looked at her father with the dark blue eyes that was the Fitzpatricks characteristic, except for Matthew. Matthew had inherited his mother's soft brown eyes.

"Come on, lassie, out with it!"

"Well, it was Dutch O'Brien; he does not want to marry me," Beth declared, naming the golden-haired, blue-eyed, wide shouldered, muscular, potato farmer who had his cottage down the dirt road from the Fitzpatricks. Beth had always loved him since she was a little girl. A year older than Matthew, they were the best of friends, which made it easy for young Beth to tail along. Of course Dutch had always thought of Beth as a little girl, only as Matthew's little sister. But that was before the harvest dance. In the fall, when all the spring-planted potatoes, cabbages and whatever else could grow was finished being picked, the town of Dunovan celebrated. The young girls bought new skirts, swirling skirts that just reached the ankles, in bright greens, reds and blues. They bought new stockings in the shade darker or lighter than the skirt itself. The men wore white shirts with billow sleeves and dark pants. The celebration was a time of happiness. They looked forward to every year. But for, Beth this year was different; she had finally turned sixteen and had grown into quite a beauty. Medium height, long curly black hair, good figure, deep blue eyes and a rosy complexion completed the picture. Dutch O'Brien was amazed that little Bethie, as he always called her, could look so pretty and grown up. It was beyond his control when he asked her to dance. They fell in love at that dance, and Dutch had promised her marriage when Matthew asked Gabrielle. Dutch wanted a double wedding. Everything was set; all Matthew had to do was ask Gabrielle to marry him. Today when Gabrielle caught Beth returning from the ten mile horseback ride, on a horse she borrowed from a nearby farmer to pick daisies, to tell her the good news, she was ecstatic. Beth ran to the O'Brien cottage to tell Dutch that they could get married. But when she reached him and told him, he looked at her with no emotion and said that he couldn't marry her. After the statement, he stomped into the cottage and slammed the door.

"Beth," her mother asked alarmed, "did Dutch do something to you that he should marry you?"

"Of course not, Mum!" Beth replied as she stood up to close the curtains.

It was thundering and raining outside, and it sounded like the earth was exploding.

"Then why would he ask you to marry him?" Michael asked. He wished things would hurry up. This evening was dragging. Beth explained her situation. Michael rolled his eyes heavenward. He liked it better when his sister was plain and had no romantic problems. Elizabeth tried to assure her that Dutch would change his mind. Maybe she just took him by surprise.

John, like Michael, was bored with Beth's problems and moved on to Matthew. "Matthew son, what Michael said earlier about us having no room here, you know that it true. Why did you ask Gabrielle to marry you?"

Now, Matthew thought, was the time to tell them his good news. He started by saying, "I have worked very hard in the fields since I was twelve. Unlike some people in our family who have always had to work in the fields because we are not wealthy, I enjoy being a farmer. Also, unlike Michael, I have never had a higher ambition than farming Lord Dunovan's land. This past year I have been able to produce more food and wool than anyone else has on Lord Dunovan's land. That is why today I received this letter." He pulled a carefully folded piece of paper out of his belt. "It is from Lord Dunovan, saying that I am to be the new assistant overseer. This new position means that I get a wage increase and my own cottage. This is why I thought it was time to ask Gabrielle to marry me."

John was the first to answer Matthew's statement. "Well, lad, that is wonderful news. Did Gabrielle say yes?"

"Of course she said yes," Beth declared. "She would be idiotic to say no!"

"Pa, I have to go and ask her mother for her hand. I won't be long."

"Matthew, it is storming pretty bad outside," his mother said worriedly.

"I won't be long, Mama, and the O'Connor cottage is just down the road." Matthew got up and got his old brown cape off the wooden peg on the wall.

"Matthew, wait a minute," John said getting up and going to his room he shared with his wife. They heard rumbling; then John came back out with a small wooden box.

"Matthew, this ring was my great-grandmother's. I want you to give it to Gabrielle. I would have given it to Lizzie, but I was too proud. I had to buy her my own ring." He looked at this wife of almost thirty years with tenderness and love. He remembered working long hours in the Dunovan fields, before his leg injury, to pay for the ring with the two diamonds intertwined with yellow gold. The box he now handed to Matthew contained a small square cut emerald set in white gold. The emerald was perfect and had that rare blue-green quality when you looked deep into it.

Matthew closed the box gently and hugged his father, saying, "Pa, I don't know what to say."

John just replied, "Gabrielle O'Conner is a lovely girl. Take care of her, son, and give me a grandson."

Matthew happily hugged his father and planted a kiss on his mother's and sister's heads before he reached Michael. Matthew knew his brother thought he could do better than just an assistant overseer, but he just did not have the need to do anything else with his life.

"Michael, I want you to be my best man. Will you?"

"Of course. You better go before it gets too late." He could hear the tightness in his brother's voice. He did not approve of the engagement, but at least did not give him a lecture on what he should do with his life. He left the cottage and went out into the dark stormy night. In the warmth of the Fitzpatrick cottage, the small wooden clock chimed seven times. Elizabeth stood and went to the table where Matthew had left something, not a lot, but something, for the rest of the family to eat. John and Beth rushed to the table, famished, not having eaten since noon time, sat down and got ready to say grace. Being Irish, they were Catholic and thought God would help them and not allow the English to continue to rule them unfairly. Elizabeth was serving the cabbage and potatoes when she looked up to see Michael take his black cape and swing it over his broad shoulders and fasten it around his collar bone.

"Michael, are you going out?" Beth asked.

"Yes, Beth, that is what one usually does when they put their cape on."

"You don't have to be so sarcastic," Beth pouted.

"Son, where are you going? Don't you want to eat why your mother has cooked for us?"

"No, I am not hungry. I'm going out to Dunovan Bar to celebrate the New Year and my bright future," he said sarcastically.

With this, he yanked the door open and stormed out of the cottage into the night. Elizabeth started to get up to run after her son. There must be something she could do; it hurt her to she her eldest son in pain. John touched her arm, saying, "Lass, let him go. He needs to be alone."

"Michael seems to be restless lately," Beth observed, stuffing a large piece of corned beef in her mouth.

Elizabeth exhaled loudly and said, "Michael is my oldest son, but I could never understand him."

It was true; Elizabeth had always tried to be supportive of her three cherished children, always tried to help them. But Michael was different.

Although all her children were beautiful, Michael was handsome beyond compare. Tall, muscular, black hair, deep blue eyes that were different from Beth's somehow, and perfect features made him the envy of many men and the fantasy of many girls. She knew of his hope to be a doctor, but there was nothing more she could do beside what she did. She now felt guilty about going to Doctor McKay to ask him to take Michael on as his apprentice. The doctor did it as a favor to her and informed her that Michael was very happy and was one of the most caring youngsters he had ever met. She knew it was wrong to mess in her son's life, but if it made him happy, she was happy. She looked wistfully at the firmly closed door.

John covered her hand with his and said, "Elizabeth, don't worry. Michael can take care of himself. He'll be back." He took his hand back and pointed to her plate where her untouched food sat.

"Now, eat your food and try not to worry." Elizabeth sighed and picked up her fork and said, "He is my child. I will always worry."

* * * * * * *

Michael walked the two miles to Dunovan town quickly in the fierce storm. As soon a he walked out, his midnight-colored hair was plastered around his head. He wished he had a horse instead of walking everywhere. He loved horses. When he was young, he had learned to ride on Whirlwind, the family horse. He remembered crying for a day when his father had to shoot the beautiful brown beast with the big brown eyes. Whirlwind was sick and had to be put down, and the family couldn't afford to buy a new one.

The tragedy of Whirlwind was many years ago, and that was not what bothered Michael now. His frustration now was his family. He loved his family very much, but sometimes they seemed too caught up in their own lives to help him. Oh, they seemed concerned, but Beth was always caught up in her appearance, and his parents never seemed to want him to excel in life. It wasn't his fault he wanted better for himself than being a farmer. He wanted something better than raising half a dozen children in the same cottage his family had occupied for over two hundred years. Matthew…well, Matthew would always be happy serving others. He liked Gabrielle, well enough, but this marriage meant that Matthew would stay in this God forsaken country all his life raising children, then being buried without a trace that he had existed, like all the other Fitzpatricks buried in the cemetery. Matthew would never change, Michael decided as he yanked open the wooden door of

Dunovan Bar.

Michael walked in and unfastened his cape, hanging it up on the back wall. He saw Doctor McKay on the stool talking to the bartender. He walked up to him and ordered a whiskey.

"Hello, Doctor," he said cheerfully. He was the only man besides his father that he truly admired.

"Well hello, Michael lad. You remember my daughter Colleen?" he said reintroducing the pretty strawberry blonde nineteen-year-old with the hazel eyes.

"Hi, Michael," she said shyly.

"Hi, Colleen," he answered. "How are you?"

"Fine."

"Good. Doctor, I wanted to know if I could go on your rounds with you tomorrow?"

"If the storm lets up."

"Here you go, Fitzpatrick," the bartender said, pushing the mug across to him.

"Thanks." He took a swig.

"Hey, Michael," Luke Flanagan said coming and sitting next to him.

Luke was a plain looking young man with wheat-colored hair and gray eyes. Michael knew he loved Beth but was too shy to go near her.

"Hello, Luke. How are you?"

"Fine. How is…" He swallowed. "How is Beth?"

"Beth is fine."

"I heard Beth was going to marry Dutch O'Brien," Colleen said.

"That is what she wants," Michael said noncommittally.

"He's not good enough for her," Luke declared.

Oh no. He did not, Michael thought. *He did not tell Dutch that Beth was too good for him.*

Michael looked over at Luke, who was drinking his ale and maybe looking a little smug. He did tell him that.

"Luke, can I talk to you in the corner?"

"Sure," he said nervously. Luke was frightened of Michael. Michael was bigger than he was, and he was overprotective of his sister. What if he found out that he told Dutch that Beth did not like him? Would Michael hurt him? Luke walked over to the corner where Michael was sitting with his arms folded across his chest. Michael was amused with Luke. Only a person who was totally in love would insult Dutch O'Brien. Beth would never love

14

someone like Luke, but he knew someone who would. "Luke, I know you are in love with my sister, but she is in love with Dutch. You want her to be happy, don't you?"

"I suppose." *Just not with Dutch*, he added silently.

"Good. She wants you to be happy too." A little lie, but no one would know. "And I know someone who has a fondness for you."

"Really?" Luke knew he was no prize in the looks department, but he was dependable.

"Yes, Colleen McKay would love for you to escort he to my brother's wedding." This was true. He saw how Colleen had watched Luke during the harvest dance.

"Your brother is getting married?"

"Yes, to Gabrielle O'Connor."

"That's great, Michael. Wonderful news for Matthew."

"I suppose." He heard the clock strike nine o'clock. He better leave before it got too late.

"Luke, I have to go. Talk to Colleen."

"Bye, Michael."

Michael got his cape and left. He was glad everything was settled with Beth. He liked Dutch; he was a good man. He would treat his sister well. He walked home through the pouring rain, feeling a little depressed. Everyone he knew was happy the way things were. Maybe there was something wrong with him. He did not even have a girlfriend. Oh, there were plenty of girls he could date or even have a tumble in the hay with, but none of these girls understood him. He reached the door of his home and walked in to see his family gathered around the fire once again. Matthew was home looking extremely happy. Michael decided he should try to be happy for Matthew. After all, it was his life; he should live however he wanted to.

"Matthew, did Gabrielle's mother say, yes, you could have her hand in marriage?" he asked as he sat down.

"Yes, she did, and she—" Matthew was interrupted by scratch on the door.

"What is that noise?" John asked.

"Maybe it's a tree," Beth said.

"Beth darling, we don't have trees in our yard," John said.

The scratching continued, until there was a loud bang on the door.

"What could that be?" John asked.

"Why don't we find out?" Elizabeth said, walking towards the door. She opened it and gasped.

"John, could you come here?" she called in alarm. John jumped up to what the problem was. He saw the young girl with bruises and blood on her face, and she was unconscious. John bent down to lift her gently into his arms, as to not hurt her anymore, and laid her on Beth's bed.

"What in the hell happened to her?" Michael asked.

"Who is she?" Matthew asked. The rest of the family had run into Beth's room to see the girl with red hair, ripped clothes and a bloody face.

Beth looked at her and said, "Why that's Kathleen Dunovan!"

The Fitzpatricks were shocked. What was Kathleen Dunovan, daughter of Lord William Dunovan, doing in their cottage all beaten up with ripped clothes and unconscious?

Chapter Two

Dunovan Castle was alive with laughter, music and bright lantern light. It was the best party of the year, or so all the guests said. To Mary Dunovan, it was the most hideous evening of her life. She sank down on one of the overstuffed chairs in the library, moving her voluminous ball gown so it would not get crushed. Mary Dunovan, wife of Lord William Dunovan, mother of Kathleen Dunovan, sat alone in the library with one lone candle proving her light. At thirty-six, the red-haired, sea green eye colored woman was still admired for her stunning beauty. Her beauty was not the reason Mary sat alone in the dimly lit room. Although all of William's friends' drooling and trying to get a good look at her cleavage was a good excuse to avoid the party. The reason Mary was alone was because of what took place earlier in her bedchambers. She and William slept apart because, after having Kathleen, she was unable to have anymore children. William had stormed into her room after making the usual rounds of his fields, clearly upset. Mary could tell that he was drunk, his usual state these days. She was at her dresser with a lantern, brushing her hair. She was a little frightened at his appearance – gray hair sticking up, collar askew, coat ripped and gray eyes flashing. She had never seen him so disheveled. She tried to remain calm and continued to brush her hair. To show fear would be a weakness, and she had learned many years ago never to show fear to any man. William stomped over to her, grabbed the brush out of her hand and flung it to the ground. Grabbing a hand full of curly red hair, he yanked her out of the chair and through her to the ground.

"Now," he shouted, "who did you tell?"

Mary was getting to her knees. "Tell? Tell what to whom?" She was on her feet now facing the ranting William. He lifted his arm and smacked open-palmed across her jaw. The blow caused her to reel back in pain, falling over her bed. She tried to get up, but William pushed her back down on the bed and pinned her down by holding her shoulders.

He leaned over, bringing his face close to hers and said, "Whom did you tell?"

Mary moved her jaw; there would be a bruise. "I do not know what you are talking about."

William grabbed her shoulders, lifted her off the bed and started to shake her, yelling, "Whom did you tell, stupid slut?"

Mary yelled back, repeating, "I don't know what you are talking about!"

William looked down at her, released her shoulders and stood up. She sat up gingerly and rubbed her shoulders gently. Silence greeted the couple whose eyes were locked. Both had hatred in their eyes. Both wondered who would break the silence. It was William who spoke first, saying, "You know, Mary, today is Kathleen's sixteenth birthday. She is old enough to know her true heritage."

Mary gasped. He could not make her tell. "Oh yes, Mary, it is time to tell your beloved daughter the truth."

"But why, William?" At this point, Mary was sobbing. What had she done to upset William so much? What had brought up the past?

"Why? I'll tell you why. Today Henry, my overseer, told me to tell Kathleen happy birthday. Then he mentioned that he saw Kathleen once and noticed that she looks nothing like me."

Mary still did not understand. "William, that does not mean anything!"

He took two quick strides over to Mary and smacked her again. "Yes, it does. Now everyone knows that my loving wife," he said sarcastically, "is a loose wench!"

Mary knew he was behaving irrationally, so she said nothing. "Tonight at dear Kathleen's birthday ball, you will tell her the truth of your immoral and disgusting affair."

"All this because some Irish peasant told you Kathleen did not resemble you!"

"Oh, Mary," he laughed dryly, "how stupid can you be? Henry is cousin to Webster O'Leary's mother. He found out, and now will spread it to all Dunovan town tenants. Those Irish spread gossip almost as fast as they breed. The truth of your torrid affair will come from your mouth to your daughter's ears." With this he left Mary alone in her room, slamming the door as he went.

What was she to tell Kathleen about her birth? Would she wind up hating her? Mary thought back seventeen years ago when she first saw the golden-haired, golden-eyed Webster O'Leary. What she had with him was not torrid or disgusting; it was…wonderful. Lost in memories, Mary relived the year when she turned nineteen, which she had spent in Ireland.

18

Chapter Three

It was the year of 1783, when Mary St. John got off the horse-drawn carriage and dragged her carpetbag down off her seat.

"Do you need help, lass?" a white-haired man with light, almost colorless blue eyes asked kindly.

"No, I do not need help," Mary replied with hostility.

The old man shrugged and walked on. He was soon lost in the busy crowd. Mary looked around at the crowded town of distaste. She hated Ireland on sight, when she first rode through on the nasty bumpy carriage. Her father, George St. John, Prime Minister of England, had sent her here to Ireland as a birthday gift, or so he claimed. She had good reason to believe that her father was tired of her. Ever since her mother Jessica died, her father had been very cold toward her. He looked at her with a pained expression on his face. When she came into the room, he walked out. She knew it was because she was the spitting image of her mother. Blue-green eyes, long, curly golden-red hair, fairly tall and thin but with the proper curves in the right places were all inherited from her deceased mother. Jessica St. John had been sick for many months. It started out as a cold, then escalated to typhoid, then finally turning into consumption. Consumption was what finally killed her, almost four months ago, in early December. Of course Mary was distraught and mourned many weeks over Jessica's death. But George was hit the hardest. She knew her parents were very much in love, even after twenty years of marriage. They both had come from middle class English families. They had met when Jessica had her coming out ball when she turned eighteen. George was a student at the university, where he studied politics. They fell in love and stayed faithful for twenty years. So when Jessica died, George was crushed and ignored his daughter as well as his friends and associates, retreating into a world of his own. When Mary had turned nineteen, he decided to give her a vacation to Ireland. She would stay with the family of his best friend Adam O'Leary. She had only once met the big, white-haired, black-eyed Irishman. He was nice enough, but she did not understand why her father, a respected Englishman, could be friends with a dirty Irishman. Not that Adam was dirty, but he was Irish. And the Irish were mostly farmers, messing in the dirt all the time. Mary pulled herself out of her memories when she heard a deep voice call into the crowed, "Mary St. John? Is there a lass named Mary St. John?"

Mary searched the people, looking for the owner of the booming voice. She saw a tall, blonde-haired, golden-brown-eyed young man who looked like a Greek god. Her breath caught in her throat; he was the most handsome man she had ever seen. Then she scolded herself, remembering that this was Ireland not England. And this man was an Irishman, a horrible dirty Irishman. She waved her hand, which caught the young man's attention. He jogged gracefully over to her and took her bag saying, "You must be Mary St. John. I'm Webster O'Leary, the oldest of Adam's sons. Pa was unable to come to greet you because he has been sick and is still too weak to make the trip to Ashimori. I was told to come fetch you. I hope you can ride. Can you?"

"Can I what?" Mary had been trying to figure out how his arm muscles got so developed.

"Can you ride?" Webster repeated.

He looked down at her. Even though she was tall for a girl, Webster O'Leary had to be at least six foot two, with amusement in his brown eyes. To Mary, the amusement obviously showed that he had many girls lose their train of thought around him. She would have to watch herself. It would not do to fall in love with an Irishman. Mary had been taught to hate the Irish; they were the ones who stole the English land. She knew the Irish had the stupid idea that the English got greedy and took over their land. She knew the truth; her father had always said this to her. Why would he lie? But she also wondered why Adam, the Irish farmer, was his best friend. The adult world was stupid, she decided. Twenty-two-year-old Webster O'Leary led the very beautiful Mary St. John to the two waiting horses. He had bought the horses with the money he earned working as a tenant farmer on Lord Dunovan's land. He stood in front of the two brown horses, then turned suddenly, almost knocking over Mary. She stepped back and blushed. She had been walking very close to Webster.

"Sorry," she mumbled, blushing deeper.

He wondered if she might be an Irish descendant. She had the strangest colored red hair he had ever seen. It wasn't merely red, like Katie O'Neil's or Maureen Macdonald's. It was a deep auburn with gold highlights; it hung in loose ringlets, forming a soft cloud around her head. Her hair hung around a perfect round face, with skin as smooth as porcelain with a touch of apricot color on her cheeks, and her eyes, well, they were the prettiest blue he had ever seen. No, not blue, they were the color of the sea, a deep blue mixed with green. Webster's gaze wondered over the long neck down to the swell of her breasts that were just peeping over her black gown down to the tiny waist to the slight swell of her hips. She was still in mourning for her mother.

Mary watched him do this; she caught her breath, then let it out angrily. Just what did this man think she was? "Mr. O'Leary, are you going to stand there all day? I would like to get to your home this year." Her sassiness amused Webster; she was the only person of the opposite sex who dared talk to him like that, besides his mother. God rest her soul.

"Sorry, lass, but you never answered my question. Do you ride?"

"Of course I ride," she declared haughtily. "But isn't your house here in Ashimori?"

"No, lass. Our cottage is in the town of Dunovan."

"How far is it to this town of yours?" she asked. She had a feeling she wasn't going to like the answer. Webster smiled at the worried look on her face.

"From here to Dunovan it is twenty miles, about a day's ride, but we will try to stop over at an inn."

She sighed and lifted herself up on the horse Webster had drawn closer to her. As soon as she was on the horse securely, Webster threw her carpetbag to her. She watched as it glided by to hit the dirt.

"Not much of a catch, lassie," Webster observed, jogging over to pick it up and hand it to her.

Mary reached out and grabbed it from him, tucking it in between her front and the horse's neck. "You could have warned me before hurling that thing viscously at me."

Webster hid a smile and climbed onto his own horse. Mary St. John was, as he suspected, a spoiled English girl who did not know what real life was about. *She probably never did a lick of work in her life*, he thought. She's also probably never had a man before. Maybe he could change both situations. He clicked his horse on in the direction of Dunovan town. Mary followed, after choking on Webster's dust. She knew it was going to be a long ride and an extremely long vacation.

* * * * * * *

Mary's behind hurt. She and Webster had been riding for hours. After a day's travel on the boat, then the long carriage ride for two days, and then riding for another six hours, it was no wonder she was numb from the waist down. She and Webster had ridden in silence since they had left the main tow of Ashimori. She was tired and bored. If Webster had come to her home, she would have at least talked to him. But this man rode out in front of her and kept riding, not looking once behind him. She glared at his back and tried to find a more comfortable position.

Webster was surprised that Mary had not come to ride next to him. He remembered meeting her father many years ago. George St. John was one of the friendliest people in the world, for an Englishman. Webster had never really felt resentment or hate toward the English, even though they took over the land that had rightfully belonged to the Irish. But he felt that one day things would work out, and the English and Irish would get along.

The two rode on in silence, passing the rolling hills and the black earth with fields of cabbage, potatoes and lettuce growing up from the ground. Many castles dotted the green countryside, old and crumbling. Mary could imagine a time when lords and ladies roomed those great halls in long, flowing gowns – a time when men treated ladies with respect and chivalry, unlike today when men put a woman on a horse like a sack of meal and left it alone.

Mary urged her horse to go faster, until she came up beside Webster. She looked over at him and was again amazed by his perfect features. She wondered if his fair skin goes bronze in the sun during the summer or if his blonde hair got lighter. She shook her head and told herself, *Why should I care?* That strange feeling in her chest and the shortness of her breath had nothing to do with Webster O'Leary. It was because she was tired, she told herself firmly.

"Something wrong, lass?" Webster asked, noticing how she was studying him with great intent.

"No, I was just wondering when would we stop for the night?"

"In about another hour or so," he replied offhandedly.

In an hour or so? Mary fumed. *Who does this man think he is?*

"Mr. O'Leary," she started to complain, "I'll have you know I have been on that disgusting carriage for two days to get to this blasted country, after a days journey on a boat. And now you so carelessly inform me that we will be riding for another hour? I have been on this old hag for over six hours."

Webster watched as her sea-colored eyes became a darker green with anger. He liked how her cheeks were flushed again.

Mary watched as a slow smile lit up his face. It infuriated her. "And just what is so funny?"

"Here's the inn where we will be stopping for the night."

Mary's mouth opened and hung so that she looked like a landed fish. Webster had told her the story of having to ride another hour to see what her reaction would be.

The man was obviously having fun at seeing her flustered. She sighed and slid off the horse following Webster into the little inn. They walked in to find an elderly, white-haired lady sitting behind a desk. She rose as she saw the couple walk in. In all of the fifty years Josie O'Hara had been running the O'Hara Inn, she had never seen a more perfect match. She had known Webster O'Leary since birth. She was the midwife who brought him into the world. He was the most handsome man in Dunovan town. She saw him there often enough to know that many of the young girls had already set their caps for him, but he had not settled down yet. Josie switched her gaze to the young girl. She was exquisite. Perfect. She had never seen anyone so beautiful in her life. Those eyes blue with the faint green in them. The long, curly hair that hung to her waist, a golden red that was very rare.

"Webster, lad, how very nice to see you," she said in a thick Irish accent. "And what brings you to my humble inn?" she added, knowing full well that her inn was the biggest, cleanest, most traveled to in this part of Ireland.

Webster smiled and said, "Josie, we need a room for the night."

Mary watched as Josie's face lit up and said, "Oh, then you two are married?"

Mary choked and quickly turned her head in Webster's direction. The smile was gone now, and there was something unreadable in his golden brown eyes.

"Josie, you misunderstood," he said motioning towards Mary with his hand. "This is Miss St. John. Her father is Pa's best friend; I had to get her from the station in Ashimori. She's from England."

"Then you two aren't married?"

"No."

"'Tis a shame then." Josie cleared her throat and walked toward Mary, holding out her hand and saying, "I am pleased to meet you, Miss St. John."

Mary hesitated to take the older woman's hand. Touching commoners was not something she was used to.

"Thank you, uh…what is your name?"

"Mrs. O'Hara, but you may call me Josie, lass."

"Then you may call me Mary," she replied rather stiffly.

Josie lifted her eyebrows at this but said nothing. *An English brat*, she thought, *but there must be something more to her for Webster O'Leary to fall in love with her*. She saw that look in his eyes; it was unmistakable.

"Well, then I suppose you are hungry. Just sit down at the table, and I'll fetch you some beef stew and ale."

"No others today, Josie?" Webster questioned.

"Not tonight. A storm's coming."

"Really? I hadn't heard – a bad one?" Webster asked as he stuffed the first bite of stew in his mouth.

"Well, according to John Fitzpatrick, who rode in today to get something for that little son of his. He said he heard that the old witch predicted a doosy."

"The witch?" Mary questioned.

"Lass, the witch is an old woman who lives in the woods. She knows many things, but a witch, I am not sure of," Webster said.

Mary was amazed at how he could say all this while having food in his mouth. Her own food sat untouched. She found that she was too exhausted to eat.

"Mary darling, how long has it been since you have slept?" Josie asked.

Mary felt ashamed that she showed her fatigue. Her mother could stay up for a straight week, then throw the most talked about ball of London without sleeping.

"I have not slept in over two days."

"Webster," she scolded, "why didn't you tell me? Poor thing. No wonder why she almost fell into my good beef stew."

Webster looked at Mary. "Why didn't you tell me you're tired?"

"And why should she? Lad, you know a proper lady never complains, especially since she's a guest."

"Oh, she complained fast enough when I teased her about your inn being another hour or two away."

Mary flushed at the tantrum she had made. She must have look like a spoiled brat.

"Webster, enough. Now get off your backside and take the girl to her room."

Webster stuffed one more mouthful of stew into his mouth and stood up, scraping his chair across the floor. "Which one is hers?"

"The first one on the left as you up the stairs. And take her bag with you."

Josie sighed; maybe she had made a mistake about those two. No, that could not be it. She was never wrong about affairs of the heart. Webster walked ahead of Mary with her carpetbag under his arm. When he reached the door to her assigned room, he waited for her to reach him and handed the bag to her.

"Thank you," she mumbled.

"Lass, why did you come here?" It was a question that had been bothering him all day. He folded his arms across his broad chest and leaned back on the door, waiting for an answer.

Mary blushed again. Webster was the only person who had ever been so direct with her.

"My mother died a few months ago, and father was tired of me." Mary was surprised that she was very close to tears. She thought the inside mourning for her mother was over.

"Your father was tired of you?" Webster questioned softly.

"Yes," she replied as a tear rolled down her cheek.

Webster stepped closer and gently wiped the tears off her cheeks. She looked at him with big round eyes.

"And so he sent you here to Ireland."

"Yes," she whispered hoarsely.

She watched as his golden eyes caught hers and his head bent down to hers. The kiss was gentle and soft like rain. They both stood apart, not touching, except his large callused hands holding her flushed cheeks. They broke the kiss and gazed into each other's eyes. Mary dropped her bag as he pulled her closer to him, placing a strong arm around her waist and the other gently holding her head. Her arms automatically went around his neck, as the kiss became deeper. Vaguely she remembered who she was and who he was and pulled away.

"I…" she faltered. "Excuse me, Mr. O'Leary. I'm extremely tired."

Webster bent over to pick up her bag and handed it to her. She snatched it from him and escaped into her room, slamming the door firmly in his face.

"Good night, lass," he said softly. He then turned with a faint smile on his lips and went down to finish his dinner. He was suddenly ravenous, but he had a feeling he needed something besides food.

Mary was furious. That man had a lot of nerve taking advantage of her like that. Just because she was upset, he had no right to kiss her. *And another thing*, she scolded herself, *why did I start crying? Mother has been gone for a while.* She climbed into bed, ignoring the feeling in her stomach, the fluttering feeling she got as soon as Webster had first touched his lips to hers. She rubbed her bruised lips with gentle fingers. She had not liked the kiss, she told herself firmly. She pulled her nightgown over her head and climbed into bed. "I have no feelings for you, Webster O'Leary," she whispered into the night. Mary fell asleep knowing it was a lie.

* * * * * * *

Webster woke the next day feeling ashamed of himself. He had never had a kiss so intimate with someone he barely knew. Sure, he had many girls, some of them as wealthy and well known as Mary St. John, but none so beautiful. He knew that he should not have taken advantage of her last night, but she had looked so forlorn, he couldn't help himself. He finally got up out of bed and pulled on his black breeches and white shirt from the day before. The comment Josie had made about Mary and him being married had shocked him.

Had she seen that marriage to Mary was what he wanted? As soon as he saw those perfect features and that golden-red hair, he knew she was the one for him. But he could tell that she thought the Irish were beneath her. Maybe he could explain to her what a hardworking person he was.

He went down the few stairs and walked in the room where he had eaten the night before to find Josie and Mary sharing a cup of tea. He waved her down with his hand.

"Stay seated, Josie. I can grab a cup o' tea for myself."

Mary was telling the kind Josie about herself when Webster walked in. Now she looked down and studied her hands, afraid to look at him. She thought back to earlier that morning, while Webster and Josie engaged into a conversation about the storm.

Mary had woken at the crack of dawn, unable to keep up the pretense of trying to sleep any longer. She put on a different dress than she wore yesterday. It was simpler, but still black, with a high collar and buttons that traveled to her waist. The only decoration she wore was her mother's cameo. She piled her hair on top of her head in a loose bun and went down stairs. She hoped everyone was awake so that she could finish this vacation up as soon as possible. She prayed that no one would be up. She wanted to remember the warmth and sweetness of Webster's kiss. No matter how hard she tried, she could not forget what those few moments had done to her. She would have to bury those feelings inside while she was in Ireland; it would not do to fall in love. But falling in love is what she was doing, not that she was an expert at it or anything. She had no romance at all because of her strict upbringing. She had read enough books to know that the lightheaded feeling, and the strange sensation she felt in her stomach had something to do with love. She entered the room where Webster had inhaled the food, to find Josie O'Hara adding long columns of figures. Josie was so engrossed that she did not see her come in. Mary cleared her throat and said, "Uh…good morning, Josie."

Josie O'Hara quickly stacked the papers and stood up. "Good morning, dear. You are up early. Did you sleep well?" Josie took one look at Mary's blue-green eyes with the dark shadows beneath them and her pale skin with blotches of red in them and knew the answer. "Mary darling, sit right down while I gather up tea and biscuits."

Mary sat down, grateful for Josie's kindness.

Josie came over and placed the tea and biscuits in front of her, taking a seat across from her. "Now, why don't you tell me what's wrong?"

"Why, nothing's wrong," Mary said, avoiding Josie's eyes.

"Nothing, eh?" Mary nodded weakly. "Then why the red eyes? And don't you dare tell me it's a cold." Mary remained silent. "Come on, lass. Tell me," Josie gently probed.

With the gentle coaxing, Mary's story broke free from where she had kept it bottled up for so long. The way her parents had kept her sheltered from the world. Her beloved mothers' death. Her father turning cold and distant, finally sending her to Ireland. And at last the subject of Webster O'Leary. Had it really only been yesterday since they first met? It seemed so much longer. She told Josie of her blooming love for him, but how those feelings would never fully develop because he was Irish.

At this, Josie interrupted, "And just what is wrong with the Irish? And just where did you learn such nonsense?"

"Everyone knows that the Irish took the English land, and then when we took it back, they were bitter, therefore causing a war."

"Darling child, that isn't the truth. We Irish have ruled this land for thousands of years before the English took over."

Mary believed her. She didn't know why, but there was something about Josie O'Hara that made one believe.

"Now that we have the unpleasant business settled, let's talk about Webster O'Leary. What happened between the two of you?"

Mary blushed. She was doing that a lot lately. She told Josie about how Webster had asked her why she was in Ireland, how she told him about the death of her mother and her father being tired of her, and finally about the embrace.

"How do you feel about him, Mary? Do you really think you love him? Or is it just lust?"

Such a direct question needed an honest answer. What could she say? She had never felt like this about anyone before. Then again, she just met him. Was it lust or love? Before she could answer or even decide, Webster had come down the stairs. Just to look at him made her nervous and excited. So, she chose to avoid him and study her hands, not that he was paying any attention to her. He and Josie were rambling on about the wicked storm they were about to have.

"When do you think it will hit?" Webster asked. He also was ignoring the person who had caused him to have no sleep last night.

"Sometime today, lad. You might want to take Mary here to your home after breakfast so you don't get caught in the storm."

It was at these words that their eyes met. Blue-green met golden-brown, both filled with wonder and question. Both held the hint of something else.

"Lass, are you finished with breakfast?"

"Yes," she answered shyly.

"Let me pay Josie for the night. Why don't you go gather your things." He turned to Josie and said, "How much do I owe you?"

Josie told him the amount, and he gasped, "Josie, that's highway robbery!"

"Aye," she agreed. Then she said, "With all that food you wolfed down last night, the price is nothing."

Webster took the pouch he had around his neck and gave it to Josie. It was the last of his money he had saved from the winter. Mary, who had not yet obeyed Webster's command to get her things, viewed this exchange with interest. She ran up to her room, ravaged through her carpetbag until she found what she needed. She ran back down stairs, almost colliding with Webster. She stepped back a few feet before she said, "Mr. O'Leary, why don't you take this?" She offered him a gold shiny coin. Her father had given her a pouch full of them for her vacation. Webster looked down at the coin in her hand with disgust.

"No thank you, Miss St. John, but I have plenty of money. Now would you please go get your things so we can leave today!"

Mary recoiled from the hatred in his voice and ran to her room.

"Webster lad, you don't need to take your frustrations out on her," Josie scolded gently.

"Who does she think she is, thinking I can't take care of a simple inn bill? Maybe Aaron was right. Maybe all English are stuck up, thinking they are better than us."

"Now, lad, you know your brother blames William Dunovan for your ma's and his wife's deaths. Not all Englishmen are like Lord Dunovan, who can dispose of people without thinking." Webster regarded her in stony silence. It was easy for her not to hate the English. All she did was run an inn. He had tried to forgive the English and think of them as people, but he could never forget the way his lovely, gentle mother was shot down in cold blood. And why? Because she had taken a single rose from William Dunovan's garden. He realized that all he did was despise Lord Dunovan, not all English. It was just easier to lash out at Mary.

"Mr. O'Leary, I...I'm ready to leave if you are?"

He turned to Mary who was standing at the foot of the stairs grasping the carpetbag tightly in her hands.

Webster was ashamed at himself for snapping at her. He realized that she was just trying to help. A low rumble of thunder sounded in the distance. The storm was coming, and if they did not hurry, they would be caught in it.

"Webster, why don't you go get the horses ready while I say good bye to Mary. Maybe we will pack you some food in case you want to stop."

"But I can not pay for that."

"Lad, it's a gift from me, an old friend. Now go before I give you a swift kick in the rear and send you out."

Webster left, slamming the door.

Josie turned to Mary and said, "Come, darling. Help me make sandwiches to take with you. Now don't mind Webster; he has violent mood swings. Has ever since his mother was killed."

"Killed?"

"Yes, but you ask him about it. He doesn't like people talking about him. And don't worry. Everything will work out fine. Here, take this." Josie handed her a basket filled with sandwiches of corned beef with a bottle of ale. Mary took the basket with her free hand, the one without her bag.

"Thank you, Josie."

"Mary, do not worry about Webster. He has a fondness for you, I feel."

Mary turned to leave, wondering how Josie was so smart. Webster was sitting on his horse waiting impatiently for Mary to come out. He would apologize to her for reacting so suddenly at the offer of money. But he had always been taught to take care of the woman, and the offer had hurt his pride. As he was thinking of this, Mary came out of the inn. She walked over to her horse and put her bag and the basket on the seat, then climbed up.

"Are you ready, lass?"

She looked shyly up at him. What was going on in those golden-brown eyes? Did he care for her? Did she want him to? Yes, she decided. Yes, she did want him to love her. It wasn't just lust; it was more.

"Yes, I'm ready!" she shouted up at him.

"Good." He urged his horse to go. Webster heard her horse come closer to him. He turned his head and looked back at her. "Lass, would you come ride beside me?"

What does he want? Mary thought as she urged her horse faster. She looked at him wearily.

"I am sorry about this morning. It was my damned pride. I thank you for your kindness."

"You are welcome. I'm sorry I hurt your pride."

"About last night…I think we should talk about it."

"Nothing happened last night. I was upset, and you tried to comfort me; that was all. I overreacted anyway."

"All right, if that's how you feel," Webster replied coldly. He turned his head as he saw the sea-colored eyes cloud with tears. He urged his horse to move faster. *Damn, this is going to be a long summer*, he thought.

* * * * * * *

It was a week later after Mary had arrived at the O'Leary's cottage, when Webster suggested that she meet him for a picnic at noon. She was very surprised that he should make such a request. He had not talked to her much since the day they had ridden from Josie's. Mary was astonished that she found Ireland so charming. It really was a beautiful country. She loved the bright clothes, and the people were very friendly. Adam O'Leary was extremely nice and kind. He seemed to be happy that she was there. She had experienced some hostility from some of the other girls she had met, but Mary suspected that it was because she was in the same house as Webster and Aaron O'Leary, not that they should be jealous or anything. If Webster went out of his way to avoid her, then Aaron went just as far out of his way to make rude comments to her – comments about how the English were heartless killers, how the English were bloodsucking vultures that wanted to destroy the Irish. Last night at dinner, Aaron was asking her if she enjoyed eating the food the Irish had sweated and died over. That was the last draw.

"What about you, Mr. O'Leary? Where does your food come from?" she retorted.

Aaron had flushed at these words and had not said another word to her, but the hatred was still evident. That morning when Webster said to her, "Lass, maybe at lunch today you could come join me for a picnic. I'll take you around the countryside," Aaron had been ready to leave, but at those words, he turned around and said," I would not eat anything from her. She'll probably poison it!"

"Don't be ridiculous, son. Mary doesn't know where to get poison," Adam O'Leary had said logically.

Aaron glared at his father and stomped out of the door. Nothing else was said about Aaron.

Webster cleared his throat and said, "Well, lass, how about it? Lunch today?"

"All right."

"Good. Meet me in the field where I showed you the first day you came." He turned away from her towards his father. "Pa, you ready?"

"Aye."

Mary had watched as they left. She wondered why Webster had invited her for lunch. Maybe he was going to ask her to leave. Well, she supposed she would find out soon enough. She grabbed the basket where she had made lamb sandwiches with carrot and celery sticks and the ever-present bottle of ale. She didn't know how these people could drink so much of this stuff; it was bitter. She started to make the half-mile walk to the appointed field, swinging the basket in her left hand.

Webster had stopped working ten minutes before. Now he was waiting at the end of the field, trying to straighten his hair the best he could. What was taking her so long? He had to talk to her. Even though it was never mentioned again, the kiss still hung between them. It was very tense whenever either one of them were in the same room. The embrace had to be discussed whether she liked it or not. He felt there was more to it than just her being upset that night. At least for him it was. It was not comfort he wanted to give her; it was love. But she had to want it too. He would not force himself on her. Webster watched as he saw her form coming over the green hill that separates the O'Leary cottage from the fields where the O'Leary men worked. She wore her golden-red hair loose around her head like the first day they met. Today, instead of a proper English gown, she wore a black swirling Irish peasant skirt and a black button-down shirt with ruffles on the sleeves. He wished she would wear colors instead of black, but he knew she was still in mourning. Mary saw him at the edge of the field. She waved and walked faster to reach him. Webster looked so handsome standing there with his white shirt unbuttoned to reveal the smooth, bronzed, muscular chest. She was right; his hair did get lighter in the sun. It was a light blonde now, which set off his tanned face and warm eyes to perfection. She reached him, and he took the basket from her.

"What's in here, lass, boulders?"

"No, just sandwiches and ale."

"It feels heavy." Mary had no reply to this, so she said, "Well, where is a good place to eat?"

Webster guided her over to an area shaded by trees. Mary reached inside the basket and pulled out a blanket she had taken off the bed so they wouldn't have to sit in the dirt. Webster helped her set up the sandwiches and vegetable sticks, then leaned back on the tree, tucking a knee under his chin. He took a bite out of his sandwich and said, "Lass, you've improved in your cooking." He remembered that the first night she came, she burned the beef stew.

"I am not used to cooking, but now that I have to, I enjoy it."

"Well, I enjoy eating it. Even Aaron said it was better than anything I could scrounge together."

Mary chose to ignore the remark about Aaron and said, "You cook?"

"Aye, I'm not as helpless as I look."

"You look far from helpless."

"Really, how?"

"What do you mean, how?" They both knew they were avoiding what they really wanted to say to each other, but they didn't know how to start. Webster decided to plunge right in and speak his mind.

"Lass, I wanted to talk about things."

"Why do you call me lass and not Mary?" she asked suddenly.

He knew she was sidestepping the issue. That was all right. They could play this game a little. "Why don't you call me Webster?"

Mary did not have an answer for that; she rarely called him anything. "If I called you Webster, would you call me Mary?"

"No."

"No. Why not?"

"Because if I were to call you Mary, it would change everything."

"Change what?"

32

They were finally getting to the point. "Lass, the first day I saw you, the first instant, I knew, I felt you were the one – the one I wanted to marry. You seemed different than the others. You are prettier, more elegant somehow. It might be from your upbringing that you're different, but I think it's from you inside. Most people, like you, would come to Ireland and sulk. But you, you came her and learned how to cook."

Mary interrupted, "I learned to cook because you would not take my money."

"Damn it, woman! Aren't you listening to me?" Webster had moved closer to her and was standing on his knees, holding her by the shoulders. "I love you. I am not sure how it happened, but it's true, and I want you to marry me."

Mary gasped. She was not sure where this conversation had come from; all she wanted to know was why he never used her real name, although she was quite fond of lass now. She looked into his eyes and saw that what he had said was the truth. She wanted to tell him that she also loved him, but before she could, a crack of thunder sounded above, lightening flashed, and a cold forceful wave of rain covered them both.

Webster was quick to his feet shouting something at her she could not hear. He put his hand out and helped her to her feet. Mary guessed he had tried to tell her that they needed to run for shelter. She grabbed the basket that now only contained the bottle of ale and began to run, holding Webster's hand.

Mary had always heard that the summer storms in Ireland were deadly. She remembered when she was a young girl and her father had gone to Ireland, the country had suffered from storms that washed out trees, lightening that had started huge fires, destroying homes and villages. After recollecting this, she knew why Webster had taken on that look of alarm and rushed her to her feet.

Webster was holding on to Mary's hand for dear life. He wanted to reach the little cave, where Aaron and he used to play as children. It would be safe until the storm passed. He felt Mary stumble and fall. He turned back to see her sprawled on the wet grass.

"Can you walk, lass?" he shouted.

"No, I think I twisted my ankle."

He grabbed her, lifting her up and carried her in his arms. Mary put her arms around his neck, burying her face into his warm chest. His shirt was opened halfway down his chest. Mary was surprised he felt so warm, considering the rain was as cold as ice. They finally reached the tiny little cave, which had moss covered walls. It felt warm and dry inside. He gently laid Mary down on the hard, mud-packed ground. The cave was quiet.

He asked Mary, "Lass, are you all right?"

"My ankle hurts."

"Why don't you let me look at it?" Webster gently took her foot and untied her black boot that just covered her ankle. She winced as he removed the shoe, but did not say anything. "Can you move it?" Mary slowly rotated her foot, it hurt but she could move it. "Good, that means it's not broken," Webster said as he pulled his shirt out of his pants and began to tear the bottom edge off.

"What are you doing?" The sight of him pulling his shirt out of his paints startled her.

"I'm making a bandage for your foot. Why? What did you think I was doing?"

What on earth had she thought? She wasn't sure what was going on. She was feeling nervous and not thinking straight.

"Lass, would you take off your stockings?"

"What?" Mary wasn't sure she heard him right.

"Take off your stockings."

"What for?" Just because he said he loved her that did not mean she was going to take a roll on the floor with him. She still wasn't that sure of her feelings, anyway.

"So, I can wrap this bandage around your ankle," Webster explained. What was wrong with her? He wasn't going to attack her. He gently lifted her bare ankle and tightly wrapped the torn fabric around her swollen ankle. "That should hold you for a while." Webster took off his shirt and his pants.

She looked at him with wide round eyes and exclaimed, "What are you doing?"

"I'm taking off my clothes."

"I see that, but why?"

"They are wet, and I don't want to die of pneumonia. You also should get out of your wet things. I'll start a fire so we can stay warm."

"Take off my clothes!"

"Oh, come now. I won't look. And besides, don't you wear a chemise or something?"

"Yes, but…" She was unable to finish. It sounded stupid just to sit there and catch cold. She began to unbutton her cotton shirt as Webster started the fire. She was easing out of her skirt when she asked, "Webster, is what you said true?"

He looked at her. Even with her hair wet and hanging limply around the flushed face with the big questioning eyes, she was beautiful. He knew what she was asking. "Yes, lass, I do love you. I've never loved anyone else like this before."

"I love you too, Webster!"

Webster looked away from the fire and moved toward her, still in his woolen shorts. He took the face that had haunted his every waking thought in his hands. He made her meet his eyes and said, "Lass, are you sure?"

She nodded. Webster brought his mouth over hers, kissing her hungrily. He felt her shiver, pulled back and said, "You're cold."

"No, no, I am just excited," she said and put her arms around his neck.

The kiss made Webster's body wake with heat and passion. He moaned and pulled away again.

"Webster?" Mary questioned, opening her eyes.

"Lass, if I don't stop now, I won't be able to after…"

"After what?"

She's so young and naïve, Webster thought. "If I don't stop now, I'm going to take you now here on the ground."

Mary knew what he meant. "I don't mind," she said timidly.

He looked at her sharply. "Do you understand what I mean?"

She nodded. "Make love to me, Webster. Show me how to be a woman."

He watched as she began to untie the bow that held the chemise together. He moved toward her, taking her mouth once again with his own. He moved her hands off the undergarment. "Let me," he whispered hoarsely. She untied the last bow and revealed her creamy flesh. He kissed her shoulder, marveling over the smoothness of it. He stood up to remove his shorts, but before he did, he asked, "Are you sure?" She nodded. He kicked his underwear, and they skidded across the cave. He went to her, kissing her soft warm mouth. His mouth moved down her neck, hesitated over one soft full breast. Then he kissed it gently. She gasped and pushed him closer. He moaned, then moved to make her his.

* * * * * * *

A month after the storm, Mary was starting to worry. The problem had to do with Webster. They were getting along very well and talked about marriage every day at lunch when she brought the basket. At night, they went for long walks, stopping sometimes to make love on the grassy hillside. Mary even suspected Webster had told Aaron about them because he had stopped making snide remarks. She heard the cottage door and Webster call out, "Lass, I'm home. Let's go for a walk."

She ran out of her room to give Webster a hug. "How was your day?" she asked.

"Fine. Would you like to go for a walk?"

"No, Webster...I ...would you sit down? We need to talk."

He did as she asked, alarmed by her pale skin and bright eyes. "Lass, what is it?"

"Do you remember when you told me if you called me Mary, things would be different?"

He nodded slowly.

"Well, I finally figured out what you meant by that. What you were trying to tell me was if you thought of me like an Irish peasant, everything was fine. You could forget my English background."

"What are you talking about? Do you want me to call you Mary?"

"Webster, I'm...well, I'm pregnant," she blurted out.

Webster's mouth dropped open. Then he closed it and jumped up to enfold her in his arms. "Oh, lass, you've made me the happiest man in Ireland. Hell, the whole damn world."

"You're not mad that the baby will be half English?"

"No, that little bit will give it class," he said kissing her. In the background, she heard the door to the kitchen slam. She chose to ignore it, basking in the warm happiness of Webster.

"Will you call me Mary?" she asked.

"Darlin', I'll call you what ever you want."

* * * * * * *

Two weeks later, Webster was walking Mary home after she met him for lunch.

"How are you feeling?" he asked worriedly.

"Fine."

"Are you sure?"

"Webster, you've asked me that three hundred times. I feel fine, wonderful in fact. I've never felt better in my life. I—"

Webster grabbed her in a bear hug. "All right, I get the idea. Can I help it if I'm worried?"

"Try!" She decided to change the subject. "Where did Aaron go?"

"I think Pa said he had some business in London."

"Oh."

They walked hand in hand back to the little cottage. When they walked in the door, George St. John smacked his daughter across the cheek.

"Whore! What would your mother say if she were alive?"

"Father, what is it?" Mary asked holding her hand to her cheek.

"Don't speak to me. You couldn't be trusted, could you? You had to go lay with some Irish peasant. You had to ruin my good name, didn't you?"

George's gaze went to Webster. "Just who in the hell are you?"

"Sir, I love...uh, Mary, and I am going to marry her."

"Oh, so you're the one who violated my daughter. Well, listen here, you filthy Irish scum. After I beat you, I will see that you hang for rape."

At this time, Adam O'Leary walked in. "Why hello, George. What are you doing here?"

"Your son has raped my daughter!"

"What? Aaron, do you know anything about this?" Adam asked, seeing his youngest son lounging in the doorway with his arms folded across his chest and a satisfied look on his tanned face.

"Aye," he said, nodding his dark blonde head. "I wanted to get Webster away from that English temptress, so when I heard that she was pregnant, I went to tell Mr. St. John, myself!"

"Bastard." Webster shouted.

"No, boy, that's what my daughter is carrying, thanks to you."

"I am going to marry her."

"You will never see her again or your child," George said, yanking Mary by the arm and pushing her out the door.

"Webster," she cried. Mary ran out chasing them, but stopped when he saw George pull out his pistol.

"You come near me or Mary ever again, and I'll blow your head off."

He saw George ride off with the crying Mary. Webster ran into the cottage and grabbed his brother by the collar. "How could you?"

"She wasn't good enough for you."

"She is the girl I love."

"She was the girl who seduced you. Do you think she could marry you, an Irish farmer?"

"She's the mother of my unborn child."

"How long do you think she'll keep that child?"

"Aaron, Webster! That's enough," Adam shouted. "Aaron, how could you do that to your brother?"

"She was wrong for him!"

"Because she is English?"

"Yes!"

"Not all Englishmen are bad."

"Oh, no? What about your good friend George St. John? He was only your friend because you saved his life."

"That's not true!" Adam cried.

"Yes, it is. Hook how fast he turned when he knew his precious daughter was implanted with the seed of a dirty Irishman."

Silence greeted Aaron's accusations.

"Aaron, you should leave," Adam said his voice shaking with rage.

"This house was never a home for me anyway. Not since ma and Susan died," he said.

An English soldier, a soldier who worked for Lord Dunovan, shot his wife.

After Aaron left, Adam said, "Do you suppose we'll ever seen him again?"

"I hope not. I'll kill him if I do," Webster vowed.

* * * * * * *

For Mary, the next few months were a nightmare. Her father confined her to her room. After a tearful trip home from Ireland, George ordered her to her room, not even allowing her to come down to take her meals. The night she returned to the English manor, she begged her father not to kill Webster. The only way he would agree to her request was for her to marry whom he told her to marry. She had not seen her father for weeks. Had he forgotten about her? Did he mean to make her mad, pacing in her locked room? Just when she was considering climbing out her window, which was fifteen feet off the ground, or slashing her wrists, her father burst into her room.

"Sit down," he commanded. "And do not say a word."

Mary eased her body on the bed. She had put on quite a bit of weight. She had calculated that the baby would be due in late December or early January. Would her father make her stay in her room for the next two months or so?

"This summer I sent you to Ireland to get over your mother's death.

38

Obviously, you had other things on your mind. Now that you are about to have your Irish brat, I want you out of my house. I've found you a husband, and it wasn't easy. But at least I'll never have to see you again. Your new home will be in Ireland."

Was he going to let her marry Webster? She looked at him hopefully.

"You will marry Lord William Dunovan. You will pack your things and leave tonight." With his orders delivered, George left Mary to deal with the shocking statements.

William Dunovan – the man who killed Webster's mother! Webster finally told her one day during lunch after Mary kept probing him for the story. She had been curious ever since Josie had mentioned it to her weeks prior. George must have known. This was his revenge. She began to pack her things. She realized that most of the things she owned were black. She was still in mourning for her mother. And now she could mourn for herself and her lost life. Mary went down with her packed bags. She met the man she would marry. Lord William Dunovan was a tall, slender man with gray hair and gray eyes. He was not handsome, but somewhat pleasant looking, if one liked that large nose and ruddy-cheeked look. Mary did not; she hated him on sight. He looked old and was probably cruel.

"Ah, this must be Mary," William said.

"Yes," she replied unemotionally. She would deal with this with no reaction.

"And how old are you?"

"I'll be twenty next month."

"Well, enough small talk. Get to know each other on the boat ride to that smelly country," George said, anxious to get rid of them.

Mary turned to look at her father. She would never forgive him, but she understood. "Good bye, Father!" She turned and walked out of her childhood home.

On the three-day journey to Dunovan Castle, William laid down the law.

"I only married you as a favor to your father, in return for more land. I too was forced to Ireland, because of some smart aleck relative. I'll tell you about that another time. As my wife, you will obey me. You will stay in the castle and not venture farther than the five acres the castle stands on. You will not talk to anyone other than those I allow you to. In exchange for this, I will provide everything you need. I will give your child my name and take care of it. But if there is ever a hint of the truth of its origin, you will tell it. Do we understand each other?"

She nodded. What else could she do, but agree?

They had arrived at the Dunovan Castle. It loomed gray and lonely. Mary followed William up the many stairs until he stopped in front of the door. "This will be your room," he said, opening the door to a large room decorated in gold and beige.

"My room?"

"Yes, when the child is born, you will be ready to take me as your husband." He laughed as he saw her shutter in repugnance. "Oh, yes. That's the only reason I married you. Good night, lass," he said cruelly.

Her father must have told him about Webster's pet name for her. She heard the door shut behind her. Tears streamed down her cheeks. She threw herself in the bed, devastated with her predicament. Where was Webster? Would she ever see him again?

* * * * * * *

For months, Webster had tried to find Mary. He didn't have money to travel to England, and his father said to forget about her, but he just couldn't. He had heard that Lord Dunovan had taken a young, beautiful, red-haired English girl. Rumor had it her name was Mary or Meredith. Webster had an off feeling the new wife was his Mary. He had to find out but had no time to make the ten-mile trip to Dunovan Castle. On New Year's Eve, when a message was sent that he was needed at the Dunovan Castle, Webster did not hesitate to borrow a horse to get there. He reached the castle and went inside several hours later. He heard the pain-induced screams; it was Mary. As he started to go up the stairs to follow the screaming sounds, Lord Dunovan met him.

"You must be Webster," he said calmly as Mary let out another ear-piercing howl.

"Yes. You sent for me?"

"That I did. Would you like a cigar?"

Did the man ask him there to torture him with Mary's cries? "No, thank you," he said, looking anxiously up the stairs.

William saw the look and said, "You may go see the wench."

Webster tore past him running up the stairs and threw the door open. What he saw shocked and alarmed him. Mary lay on the bed deathly pale. The bed she laid on was soaked with her blood. She stopped writhing long enough to see Webster filling the doorway.

40

"Webster," she whispered.

"Aye, lass, it's me," he said tenderly, crossing the room to kneel beside her bed.

The midwife said something about getting water, but Mary and Webster didn't hear her.

"Lass, how do you feel?"

"Like death," she answered truthfully. She grasped his hand tightly as another pain went through her.

He went almost as pale as she did when he saw more blood gush out onto the bed. "Lass, what can I do to help?"

"Nothing. Just stay with me and call me Mary," she joked.

"As you wish."

* * * * * * *

Several hours later, on the stroke of a new day and year, Mary had a girl with golden-red hair and golden-brown eyes.

"Lass, what will you name her?" Webster asked, cradling the sleeping newborn in his arms.

"Kathleen."

"After my mother?"

Mary nodded her head. "It's for my marriage to William."

"Why did you marry him?"

"My father forced me to."

"Because of me?"

She nodded weakly hating to see the pain in her lover's eyes.

"Oh, lass, I'm sorry," he said, his voice full of sorrow.

"Don't be. I'll always love you."

"What a touching scene." William's voice gave Webster a chill.

"William, I had a daughter," Mary said, vaguely gesturing toward Webster who still had the sleeping Kathleen.

"That's what the midwife said. Mr. O'Leary, it's time for you to leave."

"May I say goodbye to my lass?"

"Lass?" William asked, pretending not to understand.

"Mary," Webster clarified.

"Of course, then I want to never see your face again."

"What about the child?"

"She is not your concern." William made a motion to the maid to take

Kathleen away. He walked out, followed by the maid and a crying Kathleen.

"Will you be alright?" Webster was sitting on the edge of her bed, pushing the damp hairs off her forehead.

"I think so. We have an agreement. He'll take care of Kathleen."

"She's beautiful."

"Yes, she has your brown eyes."

"And your red hair." At a loss for words Webster stood bent down to give Mary a tender kiss and then said, "Good bye, lass. I love you." He left so he wouldn't have to see her tears and so she wouldn't have to see his. He left Dunovan Castle, going out into the dark stormy night. Webster vowed that he would never return again, for if he did, he would kill Lord William Dunovan, and his child needed someone to take care of her.

* * * * * * *

Mary heard a door slam, which pulled her thoughts from the golden summer she had spent in Ireland. She had never seen Webster again after that stormy night, on which Kathleen was born. Even though she had never seen Webster again, he was always in her thoughts. Every time she saw Kathleen, she was reminded of him. But Kathleen trusted her. How was she going to tell her of her true heritage without Kathleen hating her? The question loomed before her in the silent darkness of the library.

Chapter Four

It was the evening of the new century and her sixteenth birthday, as beautiful Kathleen Dunovan, clad in a navy blue, scooped neckline, billowing, velvet ball gown, hid under the stairs. With her stunning deep brown eyes that shown with their own light, a tiny upturned nose, a mouth that held a small smile always, a petite statue with a high full bosom, rounded hips and long, wavy, brown hair that held just a touch of red, Kathleen was much sought after, a thing she despised. She hated the boys who came from good families with old money; they only had one thing on their mind. Although she was not allowed to go outside the castle boundaries, her parents had hosted enough balls for her to know that men only wanted a good tumble in bed. It was at these balls that girls her own age spotted a man they liked, danced, flirted, then went outside or to an unoccupied room, not to return for hours. She heard someone coming her way, and she moved quietly out from under the stairs. She grabbed the sides of her dress in both hands and went towards the library, hoping to find seclusion. As she opened the heavy paneled door leading into the library, she saw her mother sitting in the chair near the fireplace.

"Kathleen?" Mary asking, squinting.

"Yes, Mamma."

"Shut the door."

"But it's dark in here."

"Kathleen, please come in here and shut the door."

Kathleen did as she was told, a little wary of the alarm in her mother's voice. She sat down across from her mother. She wondered what her mother would say to her.

Mary lit a candle, and Kathleen gasped, for she saw the black and blue marks across her mother's jaw and cheekbones. She suspected the bruises came from her father. She had noticed that he had been drinking a lot lately. As a result of the excess drinking, her parents had been fighting, but this is the first sign she had seen of physical brutality, although she thought there might have been other beatings.

"Kathleen, I want you to listen very carefully to what I am about to say. During this time, you are to say nothing. Do you understand?"

Kathleen nodded. Maybe she would tell her why her father hit her.

Mary had thought long and hard during her somber time alone in the library. She began her story. Mary started out by telling Kathleen about her parents, her mother and father being married for so long, then the tragic illness and death of her mother. After the death, her father had turned cold and sent her to Ireland for her nineteenth birthday. She explained how she was to stay with her father's best friend, Adam O'Leary. She was not happy with going to Ireland, she told Kathleen, because of the hatred between the Irish and English. But when she got there, she met Webster O'Leary. Kathleen watched as her mother's face and eyes took on a special glow when she mentioned Webster O'Leary's name. She wondered who he was; her mother had broken off the explanation of who Webster O'Leary was.

"Mama, who was Webster O'Leary?" Kathleen's question was greeted with silence from her mother.

"Yes, Mama, just who was Webster O'Leary?" William asked mockingly. He had opened the door to the library so he could hear what Mary was saying.

Kathleen jumped at her father's voice and turned around to see him standing in the doorway. How much had he heard of her mother's story? Did he know about Webster O'Leary?

"William, I am handling this my own way. Please leave."

"You are handling it your own way? Just like you handled Webster O'Leary?" he said viscously.

Mary's eyes flashed with anger. All these years she had obeyed William's rules and tried to be a good wife. But Kathleen was her daughter, not his. She would tell her the way she felt was best.

"William just leave!"

William walked into the library to stand behind Mary's chair, touching her head gently. Mary shuddered as William rubbed her hair and said, "Mary, you sound agitated."

Kathleen watched as her father left her mother to stand in front of her.

"Kathleen, Ryan Winchester tells me you left him in the middle of a dance." He shook his head at her and asked, "Is that the way I taught you to behave?"

"No."

"Then why did you?"

"Ryan Winchester is the biggest oaf I ever met. Oh sure, he's nice and comes from a good family, but when you have someone dancing all over your feet, it is not politeness I want to give him. It's a good swift kick in the—"

Kathleen broke off when her mother exclaimed, "Kathleen, please watch your tongue, especially about your betrothed.

"My what?"

In answer to Kathleen's shocked question, William said, "What do you expect of an Irish brat?"

"Mother, what's going on here? What are you talking about 'betrothed'? What does father mean, Irish brat?"

Mary slowly explained that in return for a business favor, Lord William promised that Kathleen would marry Ryan Winchester.

"But that's unfair! I don't love Ryan," Kathleen cried.

"In my life, I've learned that love causes trouble. Is that not right, Mary?"

Mary turned white as William continued with, "You had to marry me because of your lurid affair with Webster O'Leary."

"It was not lurid!"

Kathleen sat in shocked silence. William wasn't her father? She was part Irish? The same Irish who work for William?

William looked over at Kathleen's white, disbelieving face. It was about time he caught the little brat offguard, he thought, for William had always disliked her. Not just because she was made up of a race of creatures who did not have a purpose except to serve the English. He didn't hate her because she wasn't his daughter, although it was unfair that she took his name when he was no relation to her. He hated Mary's daughter for her beauty, for Kathleen was a hundred times more beautiful than Mary was. And she was so damned cold to him, like she knew he hated her.

Kathleen finally broke the silence by saying, "My real father is Webster O'Leary?"

"Yes," Mary answered. "I never wanted to tell you, at least not like this. I met your father—"

"I don't want to hear this!" Kathleen shouted, standing up and bolting for the door only to be stopped by William grabbing her hair. He yanked her hard and threw her to the ground. Kathleen fell, hitting her head on the arm of the chair.

"I understand how you feel," he said with false sympathy, "but you should listen to your mother's feeble explanation.

Kathleen sat up and said, "Whatever her reason was, I really don't care. I'm just glad that you are not my father."

"Kathleen!" Mary scolded.

"Well, it's true mother. I've always hated him. The way he beats you up, drinks, hurts the animals, and mistreats the Irish workers. I'm glad he is no relation to me."

William received Kathleen's declaration by kicking her in the side. She lay on her side gasping for breath, as he mother said, "William, there is no need for violence."

"Shut up, you stupid whore! Your Irish brat is under my roof. I shall treat her however I please." William bent down grabbing a fistful of golden-red hair, bringing Kathleen to her knees, then forced her to stand in front of him.

"I raised you as my own daughter, and you will not speak to me in that manner." He grabbed her under her chin and forced her to look at him before continuing. "You will obey me and marry Ryan Winchester, or you can leave this house right now."

Kathleen, who was bleeding from her fall against the chair, bruised on her face from William grabbing her, and in pain from the mighty kick he gave her, looked her once thought father in the eye and spat in his face. William, who was surprised by her actions, let go of Kathleen's shoulders long enough for her to escape to the door and out of the library. Even through the hall, Kathleen could still hear the band playing for her birthday party. She ran past the ballroom, reaching the front door of Dunovan Castle safely. Or so she thought, for William, although stunned, had regained his composure and raced out after her. Once again he grabbed her by the hair, turning her around to face him.

"If you leave this house, you will never come back again," he warned.

"That's exactly what I had in mind!"

He smacked her hard across the face, slamming her against the wooden door. Kathleen reopened the wound on her head when she fell against the door. William then shoved her out the door into the dark cold night. Thunder rumbled in the background as William shouted after her, "Begone with you then, you Irish bitch." This statement was followed by the bang of the door.

Kathleen stumbled away from the castle and fell onto the soft green grass, ripping her dress in the process. She was in pain from the many blows William had given her. She touched her forehead and saw the blood for the first time. Before she was too preoccupied with getting away from William. As the rain started, Kathleen got to her feet, shaking, and began to walk. Blackness loomed before her, leading her into areas she did not know. Kathleen felt as though she had been walking for hours. Many times throughout the night she had slipped and fallen in the slick, dark mud, adding to her many abrasions and scratches. Finally her dream was answered when she saw the tiny cottage with the firelight shining through the window. She fell again and had to crawl toward the door. She brought one shaky hand up to the wooden door and feebly scratched at it. She waited a few minutes, and when there was no answer, Kathleen Dunovan gathered all her strength and banged on the door before fainting.

Chapter Five

As always in Ireland after a storm, the hills are greener, the flowers are brighter, the cottages are whiter, and a sense of peace covers the country. It was a sunny beautiful day with the birds singing in harmony, the day after the storm. When Beth woke to the sound of the birds, it was almost as if last night had never occurred, almost but not quite. Beth, as she started the fire to warm the cottage, thought back to the previous evening. After identifying the unconscious body as Kathleen Dunovan, John declared that they would take her back to her home immediately, but Elizabeth stopped him by saying that they did not know how she got into her present situation and that they should take care of her. Of course, this statement was received badly by Michael. Beth remembered his sapphire-colored eyes blaze with anger as he shouted, "I don't want any English spoiled brat in my house!"

"Michael, this is not your house. 'Tis my house, and if your mother thinks she should stay, then she shall. Michael, you will examine the poor lass and treat her wounds." John's voice left no room for argument.

Beth had watched as Michael asked her to get fresh water to clean Kathleen's wounds. After cleaning her and putting bandages on the deeper cuts, Michael had pronounced that she would live and all she needed was rest. Beth was interrupted from her reverie when she heard a gentle knock at the door. *Who could it be this early in the morning?* she thought as the knock sounded again, but louder this time. She hurried to the door, not noticing that she was in her white night dress with her hair hanging in a limp braid. She hoped it wasn't anyone involving Kathleen coming to blame them for her beating.

Beth opened the door to see Dutch O'Brien, looking as handsome as ever. How could someone that good-looking break her heart so easily?

Dutch looked at Beth, wondering if she knew that all that covered her was a night shirt that barely reached her knees and said, "Beth, I have something to ask you."

She looked over at him with worry. Dutch caught that look and swallowed, cursing himself to have caused her so much pain because of his stupidity.

How could he have believed Luke Flanagan? He had known deep down that Beth loved him, but he had always wondered why. She could have anyone.

"Dutch, is there something that you desire from me?"

Only one thing, he thought to himself, looking at her form through the nightdress. Out loud he said, "Yes, there is something I want."

"What is it?" she asked.

Beth watched as Dutch grabbed her hand in his and went down on one knee. Dutch pulled out a golden band and placed it on her finger and said, "Beth, I want you to be my wife." It was said simply, but Beth could hear the emotion in his voice. He really loved her, she thought joyously.

"Yes, Dutch, I will be your wife!"

The smile on Dutch's face was a match for Beth's as he stood up and gave her a kiss that promised a world of love and happiness.

Kathleen Dunovan opened her eyes to find herself in a place she had never seen before. She wondered how she got there, then remembered as she tried to sit up and felt a shot of pain go through her head. She sank back in the soft bed, letting out a moan. She thought back to what had happened the night before. Not born to William? Born to an Irishman? It was too confusing for Kathleen to think about. Kathleen sat back up again, bracing herself for the pain. It wasn't as bad this time as she climbed out of the strange bed. She stumbled out of the room she slept in and wondered cautiously into the living room. She wondered slowly around the sparsely furnished area. *Whoever lives here must be very poor*, Kathleen thought to herself, as her golden eyes took in the sight of a ragged sofa, the sagging, beat up chair and the almost threadbare rug by the fireplace. She wondered over to the pot that was simmering over the low fire and was about to lift the lid when she heard a deep male voice behind her say with a touch of sarcasm, "Please make yourself comfortable."

Kathleen turned quickly around, almost colliding with a tall, tousled black hair, muscular, bare chested young man glaring down at her with the bluest eyes she had ever seen.

"Um, hello?"

"Did you want something?" Michael asked, as he wandered over to the fire to warm up.

"I was sort of wondering how I wound up in your cottage. It is your cottage, is it not?"

Although Kathleen remembered that she had run away from William, she was still bit fuzzy on how she got to the strange cottage.

"Of course it's my cottage, my family's cottage. I wouldn't be here if it wasn't."

"Well, it's not my cottage, and I'm here."

Michael turned slowly around away from the fire to face Kathleen standing before him with her arms folded across her chest. He looked at her thoroughly for the first time. Last night he was so angry at everything – Matthew for giving in so easily, his unfulfilled dream to be a doctor, the English for controlling him. He really had no chance to get a good look at her. She was simply beautiful. She had the prettiest eyes he had ever seen. They weren't merely brown, but golden, like they had an inner fire. Her hair was amazing, falling almost to her waist in cascading golden auburn curls. She was perfect in every way, except that she was English. She felt herself blush under Michael's intense gaze.

"Could I ask you why you're starring at me?"

A tad snobbish, isn't she? Well, he could fix that. After all, he saved her life last night. She should be grateful.

"Perhaps you would like to tell me how you came to be in my home beat up and half naked."

"Perhaps you would like to tell me who you are?" Kathleen said, using the same condescending tone he used on her. Kathleen's eyes grew darker as he stepped closer to her. Frightened, she brought her hands up to fend him off. As Beth strolled through the front door humming, that was how she found them, looking like two roosters ready to attack each other.

"Good morning," Beth said.

Michael and Kathleen jumped and turned toward Beth.

"Where were you, Beth, in your nightgown?" Michael asked, glad that there was someone else in the room. He was surprised the girl had thought he was gong to hit her. What had happened to her to make her feel so freighted? Why did he care?

"I was outside," Beth answered.

"Doing what?" Michael asked, getting aggravated with the vague answers.

"Dutch came by."

"For what?" he asked.

"Did you not sleep well?" Beth decided to ask when she saw Michael getting ready to throttle her. "He came to ask me to marry him," she finished excitedly.

"You went out to see him in your nightgown?"

"Michael, you are talking to a strange girl you don't know bare-chested, and she is in her nightgown," Beth answered, agitation in her voice. She was tired of Michael's attitude. What was the matter with him?

Kathleen was sitting on the sofa watching Beth and Michael argue back and forth. She was glad to know the first names of the people who helped her. Thinking back once again to the attack on her by William, she should have been more grateful to Michael. But what was his problem? Her thoughts were invaded when Beth came in front of her and said, "I bet my overly friendly brother failed to introduce himself. Hello, I'm Beth Fitzpatrick, and this is my brother Michael."

Beth held out her hand, which Kathleen shook shyly.

"My name is—" She faltered, not sure if she should tell these people who she actually was. What if they made her go back home to a person who wasn't even her father? At least here in the Fitzpatricks' cottage, she was among her people. Sort of. Well, she was half-Irish.

"I know who you are, Miss Dunovan," Beth said.

"How do you know my name? Who I am?"

"I only know you because I go to Dunovan Castle to pick flowers from your garden. The Lord knows you never come down here."

"That's right. We're Irish, and you're English. Much too good for us, aren't you?" Michael asked mockingly.

Kathleen blushed and said, "No, it's just my...Lord Dunovan never let me come down here. He always said I had no business with the Irish workers." *He didn't want me to meet my real father,* she added silently.

"Good morning," Elizabeth called, coming in with John, with Matthew training behind putting on his shirt.

"Mama, Dutch asked me to marry him!" Beth exclaimed, running up and thrusting her hand in front of her mother.

"That's nice, dear," John said, patting her head as he walked to where Kathleen was sitting.

"Well, lass, how are you feeling this morning?" he asked kindly.

"Fine, thank you."

"Would you like to tell us how you came to be on our doorstep, dear?" Elizabeth asked after hugging and congratulating Beth.

"I'm not really sure, but I would like to thank you for helping me, Mrs. Fitzpatrick."

"Well, you should be thanking Michael, lass. He was the one who cleaned your wounds and put a bandage on your head, which you seemed to have lost. Maybe Michael can make you a new one, hey, Michael?" John asked.

Kathleen looked over to the fireplace where Michael was standing, now clad in a dark blue shirt. "You're the one who helped me? she asked, shocked.

"Of course he helped you; he's our resident doctor," Matthew joked.

"Who are you?" Kathleen asked confused.

"I'm Michael's younger brother Matthew, and who might you be?" he asked pleasantly.

"Yes, dear, we were all very curious last night as to who you might be. Beth had this crazy notion that you were Kathleen Dunovan," Elizabeth said.

Kathleen swallowed and said, "She was right. I…I am Kathleen Dunovan."

"Are you sure?" Matthew asked.

Matthew, what kind of question is that?" Beth asked.

"Well, she was beat up pretty bad. Maybe she's not all together," Matthew said, tapping his forehead.

"I have seen Kathleen Dunovan, and that's her," Beth declared.

"Listen, Matthew and I have to get to work, or we won't be paid by the overly generous Lord Dunovan," Michael said, pointing to Kathleen, who flushed. "If Miss Dunovan would like to come outside with me, I'll change her bandages."

Feeling a little out of control of the situation, John said, "Wait, before anyone moves, I want to make a few things clear." He waited while everyone sat down. He ignored the sighs and the eyes rolling heavenward by his family and said, "Miss Dunovan is our guest, and I'm guessing that she does not want anyone to know that she is here. Am I right?"

Kathleen nodded her head.

"Then you may stay here a long as you like."

"Pa!" Michael exclaimed.

"Michael, it's my house, and what I say goes. Kathleen will stay with us, and no one else is to know."

"John dear, we can't keep the poor child in all the time. What do we say about her?" Elizabeth asked worriedly.

"She's your brother's daughter, Kathleen O'Riley from Scotland. Is that all right with you, Kathleen?"

Kathleen, who was on the verge of tears, stood up and hugged John, then Elizabeth, saying, "Thank you. Thank you so much. No one has ever been so kind to me before, Mr. and Mrs. Fitzpatrick."

"No, dear, it's Uncle John and Aunt Elizabeth, or if you're not comfortable with that, John and Elizabeth will be fine," Elizabeth said kindly. "And, Kathleen dear, anytime you want to talk to me about anything, feel free to, okay?"

Kathleen caught her meaning and said, "Thank you, but right now, I'd like to keep it to myself."

"Does this mean she's staying?"

"Yes, Beth," John said.

"Good, she can help me plan a double wedding with Gabrielle."

Upon hearing these words, Michael stormed out of the cottage, forgetting about Kathleen's bandages.

"Stay here, Kathleen," Matthew commanded as he went after Michael, leaving her near the watering pump.

Michael, who was angrily walking towards the plowing fields to do his work, stopped abruptly as he heard Matthew call his name. He waited impatiently until Matthew caught up to him before asking, "What is it, Matthew?"

"You forgot to change Kathleen's bandages," he said, gesturing to where Kathleen was standing.

"And your point is what?" he asked coldly.

"She could get an infection."

"So? Matthew, I don't give a damn what happens to her."

"Because she's English?"

"Very good, Matthew, how did you guess? Could it have been my resentment to our poverty? Or maybe my dashed hopes to be a doctor?" Michael asked sarcastically.

"Well, letting Kathleen die from an infection is sure a good way to prove yourself as a doctor, isn't it?" Matthew watched Michael's face as he realized that what he said was the truth.

"You can understand how I feel about having an English girl in our home, especially Lord Dunovan's daughter. That man keeps us where we are today and everyday."

"I've never had the deep hate you hold for the English, Michael. I enjoy working in the fields. I don't like the numbers or trying to take care of complaints. I'm happy just as I am, assistant overseer and engaged to the most wonderful girl in the world. It sounds kind of pathetic that I don't want anything else, doesn't it?"

"No, Matthew, I wish my life were that simple."

"I have to go to the field now. Assistant overseer and all, I don't want to be late."

Matthew turned to leave then turned back around to see Michael walking toward Kathleen. He wondered what had happened to her and if she would tell them. Probably not, but that wasn't his main concern. Now getting to work was. He took another look at Michael and Kathleen, thinking they made a nice looking couple and ran up the hill. Kathleen had watched as the two brothers exchanged words. She sensed that Michael did not want her to stay in his home. She would have to be pretty stupid not to see his hatred he had for her. *But why does he hate me?* she wondered as she saw Michael heading for her. Outside in the daylight she noticed how dark his hair was, and his eyes were not merely blue but a deep sapphire color. And how tall and broad shouldered he was. She had never seen anyone so handsome. She bet he too was engaged like his sister or at least had someone he was courting. Why did she care? Aside from his good looks, he was very rude, and he hated her a lot.

"I have come to check on your wounds and rebandage them."

"Thank you," Kathleen said, moving closer to Michael.

"Why don't you sit on the ground while I get some fresh water." It took Michael several minutes to get a steady stream of clear water to pump into the bucket. He was distracted momentarily as Kathleen ran her hands through her hair, which in the sunlight was not only brown but had a red-gold tint running through the disorderly curls. He moved the bucket beside her and sat down, his body facing her side. "You have a deep cut on your head. You may have a scar," he said as he ripped part of his shirt to use as a wash cloth to clean the cut. He noticed her wince as he gently moved the damp cloth over the wound. "Do you feel any dizziness?"

"Some."

"You might have had a concussion. You also have a swollen cheek bone. Does it hurt to talk?"

"Not really. Is there a bruise?"

"Yes, but no cut," Michael said as he looked into her brown eyes. They had gold in them that rivaled the sun's golden rays. She really was beautiful.

Kathleen blushed under Michael's intense gaze and broke the silence by saying, "Are you a doctor?"

"No," he answered shortly.

"Why then did Matthew call you a doctor?" she asked in confusion.

"He was kidding." Changing the subject, which was none of her business anyway, he said, "I have to go to work. You don't need another bandage on your head. Just don't bump it again or you will reopen the wound." Michael got up to leave. He stopped when he heard Kathleen say, "Thank you. I am very sorry you're not happy with my staying her. I'll leave as soon as possible."

Michael looked down at her looking up at him. "It would be for the best."

"Why do you hate me so much? You do not even know me!"

"I know your kind. Your father is the reason I am stuck in this lice infested cottage. The reason why I am not a doctor is because of the English who don't want the Irish to be educated."

Kathleen was shocked. She never knew her father took part in keeping the Irish uneducated. At parties, she had heard William's friends say that the Irish taught themselves. *What else have William and my mother lied to me about?* "Michael, I am sorry."

He heard the sincerity in her voice and saw it in her face, but he knew she was lying. Why would she feel sorrow for him? Besides, he didn't need her sympathy.

"Just leave as soon as possible!" he said curtly and walked swiftly up the glisten with dew hill, leaving Kathleen alone.

* * * * * * *

"Would you like some tea, Kathleen?" Ella O'Connor, Gabrielle's dark blonde-haired mother asked. She moved the silver teapot toward Kathleen.

"No thank you, Mrs. O'Connor," Kathleen answered pleasantly. She looked around the O'Connor cottage, which was not much different from the Fitzpatricks', and thought back to earlier that day. After the disaster with Michael, she went back in the tell John and Elizabeth that it was kind of them to offer their home to her but it would be best if she left. Where she would go, she wasn't sure, but she knew that she couldn't stay with the way Michael felt about her. Go back to Dunovan Castle? Never! What would William do to her if she went back?

She remembered how she went back through the wooden door to see John and Elizabeth in an embrace, obviously still very much in love even after all these years of marriage. John left saying that he had to go to work. After his departure, Beth gave her a green skirt and a white blouse to wear and told her that they were going to Gabrielle O'Connor's house to plan for the wedding. When Kathleen, Beth and Elizabeth got to the O'Connor's cottage; Kathleen was introduced to the beautiful Gabrielle and her mother Ella. Kathleen was told that Gerald O'Connor was killed working in William's fields. Although there was no implication of blame on her, she still felt guilty. Slowly, as she brought herself back to the present, she realized that everyone was looking at her. Gabrielle noticed that she had not heard her mother ask, "Are you married, Kathleen?"

"No, ma'am."

"Engaged?"

"No, ma'am"

"A pretty young thing like yourself?" Ella stated, amazed.

"I've not found anyone I want to marry yet."

"Elizabeth, couldn't your brother's wife find someone for her?" Ella asked, having been told the story that Kathleen was Elizabeth's niece from Scotland. Elizabeth flustered at what to say.

Kathleen answered for herself, "You want to know something, Mrs. O'Connor?"

"Ella, please."

"Well, Ella, I would never marry anyone that I didn't want to marry. I know someone who was once deeply in love, but she had to give him up because he came from a hated country of her father's. Her father then forced her to marry someone who she despised. Never would I let that happen to me."

"Independent, isn't she?" Ella asked Elizabeth.

"Ma, Beth and I don't have that problem. Matthew and Dutch love us, so there is no problem," Gabrielle said and smiled at Kathleen who shot her a grateful look.

"So, when should we have the wedding?" Elizabeth asked.

"Maybe we should ask Matthew and Dutch?" Beth suggested.

"Are you simple child? You don't leave wedding plans up to men! They would get together and forget what they were planning and wind up in Dunovan Bar," Ella exclaimed.

"Ma, are men really that uncaring?" Beth asked fearfully.

"Not if they love you."

"I think we should have the ceremonies next month," Gabrielle stated. She wanted this gathering to be over. She was bored. She also saw that Kathleen was not really enjoying herself.

"Yes, next month would be fine. Are you still going to be here, Kathleen?" Ella asked.

Kathleen looked over at Elizabeth and said, "I'm really not sure."

"Well, if she does stay, she can be Beth's maid of honor."

"Really?" Kathleen asked happily.

"Why of course, dear," Elizabeth said. "And who will be your maid of honor Gabrielle?"

"I guess I'll ask Eva Harris," Gabrielle said, naming the raven-haired holly green-eyed girl who was the daughter of John's best friend and fellow co-worker, Fenton Harris.

"Gabrielle, do you think that's a good idea? She and Michael haven't spoken since last May when they broke off the engagement."

"Michael was engaged?" Kathleen asked.

"Yes, for almost a year, but then they broke it off," Beth said.

"Why?" Kathleen asked curiously.

"They just weren't right for one another," Ella said.

"It might also have something to do with Eva cheating on him with Bartholomew McKnight," Gabrielle said. "I'm just surprised Michael never found anyone else. He's so handsome."

"Bartholomew McKnight, Lord Dunovan's tax collector?" Kathleen asked.

"Why, yes, how did you know?" Ella inquired.

"I guess someone must have told me," Kathleen mumbled, avoiding Ella's eyes.

"I think we should have the wedding March the fifteenth," Beth declared before Ella could ask anymore questions about Kathleen and Bartholomew's relationship.

"Beth, that would be lovely," Gabrielle said.

"Ma? Ella? Is that all right?"

"Yes, that's fine dear," Elizabeth said.

"Fine, I hope you will be able to stay, Kathleen, and see a real Irish celebration," Ella said. "I'm sure you do things differently in Scotland."

"Yes, we do." *March the fifteenth*, Kathleen thought to herself. That was over three months away. Could she stay here this long without anyone discovering who she was.

Chapter Six

The month of February came and went with very little significance. In Ireland the weather started to warm as a prelude to spring. The first few blooms of the new season started with the sweet smell of heather in the highlands. Spring is the season of love throughout the world, and it was no different as the double wedding came closer for Matthew, Dutch, Beth and Gabrielle. Beth and Gabrielle went all the way to Ashimori to have their wedding dresses made. Elizabeth had wanted Beth to wear her dress, but since Gabrielle could not wear her mother's dress, the two girls decided to have identical dresses made. Beth and Gabrielle both neglected their chores, which were taken up by Ella and Kathleen. She was more than happy to help Beth. She and Beth had become very close, often talking about how happy Beth was to finally marry Dutch. Kathleen had met the wheat color haired Dutch O'Brien with the clear blue eyes and knew Beth was indeed lucky to be marrying him, for Kathleen saw that Dutch was kind and caring as well as handsome. She really loved Ireland. Ireland was beautiful with rolling green hills and the occasional shower, which made everything look greener and brighter. She didn't like the country just because it was beautiful; it was because of the people. The people she had met were all very friendly and accepted her as a Fitzpatrick and as an Irish descendant. Her home with the Fitzpatricks was the only place that actually felt like a home to her. Unlike Dunovan Castle, where her opinions did not count, nor did she have a choice of her future, the Fitzpatrick's cottage was a place where she had a say. She helped decide what to fix for meals, although cabbage and potatoes was what the meals mainly consisting of. Nevertheless she was treated like a member of the family by everyone. That is everyone but Michael. Michael ignored her entirely or made a sarcastic remark to her about her background. When he was throwing around obviously hateful comments, Kathleen wanted to tell him the truth about herself, that she too was Irish and hated Lord Dunovan. But Kathleen held her tongue and kept her secrets to herself, for she was sure Michael would not believe her. Even if he did, what could he do for her?

If Kathleen was feeling unwelcome in the Fitzpatrick home and thought it was because of Michael, she was correct. Instead of the month of February being a prelude to spring, it was a prelude to hell for Michael. Besides his disdain about having an English girl in his home, he was not exactly happy about the wedding coming up in March. He still felt it was wrong of Matthew to be happy and settle down working in the English lord's fields.

Not that he denied Matthew happiness. He loved his brother and wished him whatever he wanted; he just wished that Matthew's happiness was not in Ireland. Matthew was not the only member of Michael's family he was unhappy with. He was mad with his parents for letting Kathleen stay in his home, which he made evident at every opportunity. Beth also was not in his good graces at this moment. Michael knew there were not very many opportunities for women of the peasant situations to marry rich, but he felt that with Beth's beauty, she could have married a little higher than Dutch O'Brien. Also the situation with which everyone was accepting Kathleen into the family like she actually was a cousin made him want to punch a wall. Beth had asked Kathleen to be her bride's maid much to Michael's dismay. How could Beth ask an absolute stranger to be her bride's maid? Not that he really disliked Kathleen personally. Michael thought that Kathleen was the most beautiful girl he had ever seen, and if she were actually Irish or even Scottish, he knew she would be the only girl for him, not only because of her beauty, but because she was kind and thoughtful. He couldn't tell if that was actually her true personality or if she was just trying to stay on their good side to keep living with them. Michael also noticed that Kathleen tried to avoid him as much as possible, which was fine with him. He didn't have time to have a romance even if he wanted to. Besides, he wasn't sure that Kathleen was avoiding him because she did not want to bother him or if she hated him. But there was one thing that he couldn't get out of his mind – the fact that she never mentioned either her family or what happened that night she ended up on their doorstep.

How did Kathleen feel about Michael? Out of all the men she knew from her father's acquaintance, Michael was the only one she would consider marrying. Kathleen didn't like Michael just for his good looks, although that certainly helped. She liked him because he was a good person. Anytime someone was hurt or in need of help, Michael always dropped what he was doing to assist in anyway he could. Again, Kathleen kept her feelings to herself because she knew Michael hated her. He hated her for what she stood for. She knew one day she would have to tell the truth about herself or go back to Dunovan Castle. She wondered if she was greatly missed.

* * * * * * *

"Your wife has lost a great deal of blood, Lord Dunovan," the kind, elderly Dr. Richard Lander stated, closing his black bag. "How did she come to have these injuries?"

"Dr. Lander, I called you here to help my wife, not to be questioning me about her injuries!" Lord Dunovan stated coldly.

"I'm sure I didn't mean anything by it. I was just concerned for Lady Dunovan."

"Yes, well, that will be all."

Lord Dunovan waited to see the doctor leave before going in to see Mary, who was lying on the bed with bruises, cuts and possibly a few broken ribs. She appeared to be asleep but stirred when William walked into her room.

"Mary, where is Kathleen?" he shouted. "You better tell me where Kathleen is if you want to live." Silence greeted his threats. "All right, you lie there, but mark my words, I will find the little whore, and she is going to be a lot worse off than you." William left slamming the door.

Mary winced. She knew what was going on; she only pretended to be simpleminded. She did not, however, know where Kathleen was, but she hoped her daughter found a place far away from Dunovan Castle.

Mary faded into blackness, weak from William's recent beatings. She was surprised that William had bothered to call Dr. Lander. She wondered what the purpose was.

As Mary went to sleep, her thoughts were of a thousand years ago when she was nineteen and totally in love with Webster – a time of happiness that she would never regain again. She only wished that she had was that she laid eyes on Kathleen and Webster one last time. Then she could die and end her long sorrowful life at last and go to a better place than Earth. A place where it didn't matter what country you were born in or who your parents were.

Chapter Seven

The saying, March comes in like a lion and goes out like a lamb, was true in some ways for the Fitzpatrick family of the year 1800. The month came in with a burst of hot air that was rare for the mild weather of Ireland. March was also a month of great joy and anticipation for some, and frustration, waiting and longing for others. It was the month for the long awaited wedding. Planes have been made, elaborated on, and some had been dismissed completely. Beth and Gabrielle were both going to wear white and carry wild flowers from the fields, with white lilies in their hair. Their wedding dresses both had lacy tops and full-skirted bottoms that came just below their ankles. Matthew and Dutch were paying for everything except the gowns. The wedding would be held in the middle of town for all to see and then would be accompanied by a feast and party. Matthew and Dutch thought that since they were going to pay for the wedding, they deserved to anticipate their wedding night. This was one of the wedding plans that was rejected. Another failed plan was not to have a wedding at all, which of course was provided by Michael. Kathleen's suggestion to decorate the path from the Fitzpatrick cottage (both Beth and Gabrielle would get ready there) with flowers was taken with great enthusiasm. Everyone just hoped that the flowers bloomed in time. It looked like they would, since the hot weather came in. It was the custom for the men to get together before the wedding to discuss their plans and futures, and no matter how much the groom loved his bride-to-be, they drank to the loss of their bachelorhood.

On March the fifth, ten days before the wedding, the men of the town were toasting Matthew and Dutch.

"Congratulations, Dutch! Congratulations, Matthew!" Christopher O'Hara said. "When I married Mary-Margaret two springs ago, it was the happiest day of my life. I hope you two have as much joy also!" Christopher's toast was greeted with a loud cheer.

"Drinks all around on me!" Bartholomew McKnight said as he walked over to Michael, who was sitting in a corner trying his hardest to get drunk. "Hey, Michael, what are you doing in the corner alone?"

"Drinking."

"Aren't you happy to see your brother getting married?"

"Ecstatic," Michael replied sarcastically.

"I hear you're the best man."

"Correct."

"Who are you going to take to the wedding?"

"Don't know."

"I am going to take Eva," Bartholomew said snidely, knowing that Michael was still sore on the subject. Whatever he could do to bother Michael, he did. Bartholomew had always had a strong jealousy toward Michael, for Michael had always done what he wanted. Michael didn't have to bow down in front of the Irish-hating, stuck up Lord Dunovan.

"You're going with Eva?"

"Yes."

"That's nice."

"Well, I'm going to go join the party."

Good, he's finally gone, Michael thought. Now he could get back to his drinking. He was upset that night for more than Matthew's wedding; it was what had happened earlier that day with Kathleen. He took another swallow of whiskey as he thought back to the morning.

* * * * * * *

So close to the wedding, everyone had a place to go except Kathleen. Kathleen declined to go with Beth and Elizabeth for the last fitting before the wedding. When Kathleen woke up, both John and Matthew were gone, so she assumed Michael had also left. She was very surprised and startled when she heard the deep voice ask, "Where is everyone?" Kathleen jumped out of her seat where she was resting after Elizabeth and Beth had departed.

"Your mother and sister went to town, and your father and Matthew went to work."

"Why are you still here?" Michael asked while pulling on an old brown shirt.

"I did not feel like going. Why are you so late getting up?"

"I was helping the doctor with Maureen O'Flary and the birth of her child."

"What did she have?"

"A boy."

"Wonderful!"

"Wonderful? It would be best to have been a girl or born dead."

Kathleen recoiled from the bitterness in Michael's voice. Living in the same house with him had not enlightened her any on why Michael was so bitter.

"How can you say that? The birth of a child is supposed to be a blessed occasion."

"A baby has no right to be born to poor impoverished people who can barely afford to feed themselves, much less a baby."

"So, why is a baby better off a girl?"

"A pretty girl can always marry above her class."

"What about a good looking man?" Kathleen asked curiously.

Where on earth did she come up with that question? Michael asked himself. He looked into her golden eyes and saw only curiosity. He was half hoping that she might have meant him and her getting married, because his infatuation with her beauty was developing into something Michael had never felt before. Something was different than what he felt with Eva. That was only good old-fashioned lust. With Kathleen, it was a feeling he had never felt before. He couldn't keep her out of his mind no matter how hard he tried. Michael often missed dinner just so he wouldn't have to look at her. He tried to forget about her. A relationship would never work.

"Well, can an attractive man marry higher than his class?"

"Would you marry me?"

Kathleen's eyes grew wide as she asked, "Pardon me?"

"Would you, for the sake of argument, marry someone like me?"

"You mean, for the sake of argument, would I marry you?"

He nodded slowly.

Kathleen saw a strange light enter his dark blue eyes. "No."

"No what?"

"No, I would not marry you."

"Why not?" Michael demanded, forgetting the promise he made to himself to keep their relationship neutral.

At this point, Kathleen was dishing out breakfast porridge on a plate, her back to Michael. When she didn't respond to him, he grabbed her by the arm, causing her to whirl around and drop the plate on his shirt.

"God damn it!" he swore.

"I am sorry, but you grabbed my arm."

"So, this is my fault?" Michael asked as he angrily tried to clean his shirt with a linen napkin with jerky motions.

"Well, why did you grab my arm?"

"Why wouldn't you answer the question?"

"What question?" Kathleen asked confused.

"Why wouldn't you marry me? If you think a man can marry up, why not you and me?"

"It would never work."

"You mean you're too good for me, don't you?"

"Michael, why don't you go to work? I'll get you a new shirt," Kathleen said, trying to change the subject. She moved to the basket where the clean clothes had been taken in from the laundry line outside. Michael's strong arms pulling her against his bare muscular chest stopped her, however.

"I'm not good enough for you, am I?" he asked as he turned Kathleen around and crushed his mouth to hers.

It was a kiss that brought out all the frustrations and feelings that they both been feeling for so long. For Kathleen, the kiss was a feeling of joy and hope – a gesture that said to her that maybe she could have happiness. For Michael, the embrace was a symbol of what could never be. Michael broke away from her, gently removing his hands from the mass of curly auburn hair and quickly found another shirt to wear.

"I told you it was easier for a girl to marry a higher family than a man," he said mockingly.

"For some people, it could work, just not for us."

"Forget about it, Kathleen. I know I'm not good enough for you. You should really leave after the wedding. It would be best," Michael said and walked toward the door, finally leaving for work.

He was stopped by Kathleen's voice which pleading said, "Michael, wait."

"What?" he asked without turning around.

"It's not me who is too good for you. It is you who are too good for me."

* * * * * * *

Michael thought back to his encounter with Kathleen while he sat drinking without getting drunk, much to his disappointment. He wondered what she could have meant by her statement. He was too good for her? What in God's name did she mean by that?

Michael was pulled out of his thoughts when he heard a deep voice say, "Fitzpatrick, why aren't you with your brother celebrating?"

He looked up to see the silent Webster O'Leary standing before him.

"I don't feel like celebrating."

"I know how you feel. Mind if I join you?"

Webster shrugged and said, "Sure go ahead."

Michael, as well as everyone else who lived in the realm of Lord Dunovan's rule, respected Webster O'Leary. He was a bachelor of thirty-nine who lived on the outskirts of town who worked hard, and although he didn't socialize much, he could always be counted on to lend a helping hand.

"I haven't seen you for a while, Webster. What have you been up to?"

"I've been traveling around Ireland to see what the Irish army is up to." He coughed.

It was well known that Webster, who owned his own land, often traveled to see if he could find his brother Aaron. It was rumored that about twenty years before, they had a falling out. Older members of the community said it had to do something with a girl. The story says that Webster was once in love and Aaron didn't approve, so he did something to get rid of her. Aaron left his family to join the Irish army. That was the last time anyone had seen or heard from him. But Webster never forgot and wanted revenge. He could tell that the young Fitzpatrick was uncomfortable with the topic, so he changed the subject by asking, "Are you still engaged to Eva?"

"No, we broke it off last year. It was not love, at least not on my part. We just were not meant to be together. We are too different. She never understood my wanting to be better than a farmer." *Not to mention the fact that she is evil*, he said silently.

"Still trying to be a doctor?"

"Yes, but look what good it's doing for me."

"Have you ever thought about getting married? Maybe settling down?"

"I want something better than to marry some peasant girl who would give me nothing but problems and children. Why didn't you ever marry?"

"You know the rumors. I fell in love with a very special girl, but she was taken away from me."

Michael could hear the sadness in his voice. "She must have been something for you to still feel for her."

"Yes, she was."

"Do you know what happened to her?"

"She married someone wealthy and had my child. Before she was taken away, she got pregnant with my daughter."

"You never saw her?"

"Yes, once. When my daughter was born, I was there."

"The girl you love, is she alive?"

"Yes."

"Irish?"

"English."

"Why would you get involved with someone English? You know all they do is give us problems."

"I loved her; it did not matter what she was. When you fall in love, you will understand." Webster got up to leave. "I better go. Take care of yourself and try to realize that some things you can't change. You have to accept things."

"Have you accepted things, Webster?"

The question caught Webster offguard. Had he accepted the way things were? No. he hadn't. but he could tell that young Fitzpatrick needed reassurance. "I have accepted some things."

"Oh, Webster. By the way, what was your daughter's name?"

Telling Michael her name could not hurt anything; he would never meet her. "Kathleen."

"Kathleen…her name is Kathleen?"

"Yes, she was named after my mother."

He left Michael alone to wonder if Webster's Kathleen was his Kathleen. Was that why she left home? Was she ashamed of being half-Irish? If she was, what did she mean that he was too good for her?

* * * * * * *

The days that followed Matthew and Dutch's celebration, Michael and Kathleen avoided each other like one would avoid the plague. After Michael talked with Webster, he watched her secretly for any resemblance to Webster. As far as he could see, they looked nothing alike – except the eyes. Webster had brown eyes with golden light in them…but how many people had brown eyes? No, Kathleen Dunovan was one hundred percent English, much to Michael's dismay. If Michael was confused, Kathleen was mystified beyond her imagination.

The day before the wedding was hectic with last minute preparations, which Kathleen helped out with by calming Beth down. Kathleen had never seen anyone so hyperactive before in her life. Beth was a nervous wreck, spitting questions out at Kathleen non-stop. "Does my hair need a trim? Should I wear it on top of my head or flowing down my back? Flowers? Are you sure about my dress? Maybe I should wear the outfit I met Dutch in? What flowers should I carry? Should Gabrielle and I carry the same kinds of flowers?" and on and on. Elizabeth finally told Beth to take a walk – a long walk, while she prepared Beth's wedding gift from the family, which gave Kathleen a chance to rest and think. She thought about Michael and what happened two weeks ago. She still wasn't sure what had happened that day with Michael. They had gone from talking about impoverished children to him asking her to marry him. And when she said no, he seemed very upset. Could he perhaps like her? No, that was completely out of the question. Michael had not talked to her for days. He couldn't possibly have feelings for her…but what about that kiss? A man who actually knew what he was doing had never kissed her before. She remembered Ryan Winchester and Edward Ridgemont trying to kiss her. They wound up slobbering all over her trying to rip her dress off. Because of their rude, ill-fated attempts at love making, they came away with a little limp from a good swift kick. Michael was…well, Michael. Kathleen's thoughts were stopped as she heard the front door slam.

"Who's there?" Elizabeth called from her room.

"It's me, Ma!"

"Michael? What are you doing home so early?"

"I finished early. Besides, it looks like rain." He ignored Kathleen, who was sitting by the dormant fire on the old rug, completely.

Elizabeth came out and said, "Why don't you take Kathleen to pick flowers for the wedding tomorrow?"

"I don't think that I should have to pick flowers," Michael said, watching Kathleen's face turn red.

"Yes, Michael, you should do something for your brother's and sister's weddings. Kathleen, you can use the old wicker basket."

"I…I can go by myself," Kathleen stammered, rising to fetch the basket.

"Nonsense! Michael will go with you. Run along while I finish Beth's gift. Make sure the flowers are in full bloom, and get some heather also and maybe some violets."

Michael went out in front of Kathleen, not bothering to hold the door or helping with the basket. As soon as they walked out, Michael briskly walked ahead muttering, "We can go over to those hills," gesturing to a group of rolling hills with multicolored flowers about half a mile away. Michael began to walk but was stopped short by Kathleen's voice saying, "You don't have to help if you don't want to." He ignored her and continued with his fast paced stride.

Kathleen sighed and followed him. No word was spoken or uttered between them until they reached the desired hills, when Kathleen declared," After tomorrow, you will never have to see me again."

"Going home?" Michael asked, as he started to pick the sweet smelling heather and throwing it into the basket, which Kathleen had put on the ground.

"No."

"If you're not going home, where do you plan on going?"

"I don't know"

"Kathleen, what happened that night you came to our house?"

"I cannot tell you," she said, continuing to pick flowers.

"Why not?"

"It's none of your business." *And you don't care,* she added silently.

Michael stomped over to where she was kneeling, trying to find the best flowers, grabbing her by the shoulders and hurling her to her feet, causing the flowers to scatter across the ground.

"What the hell do you mean, it is none of my business?" he demanded, shaking her shoulders, forcing her to look at him.

She made a futile attempt to free herself, but failed, so she said, "Alright, Michael Fitzpatrick, you want my story. I'll tell you my story!"

Michael was a little stunned and released Kathleen, who in turn sat down.

She looked up at Michael and said, "Please sit." She gestured to the spot in front of her. "What do you want to know?

"Everything."

"I really am Kathleen Dunovan…sort of." How could she tell him the truth? What would he think of her?

He sensed her hesitation and reached for her hand, which was damp with moisture, showing her nervousness. He knew he should let her stop, that he knew he should totally forget about it – about her – but he could not. No matter how wrong it was for him, it was right. "Kathleen, whatever your problem is, you can tell me."

She looked into Michael's blue eyes, which reflected only concern.

"Mary, my mother, got involved with an Irishman one summer. They really did love each other, or so she tells me," Kathleen said with a trace of bitterness. "Anyway, her relationship was dissolved by her father, although not before she was pregnant with me. Her father forced her to marry Lord Dunovan. I know he owns this land that you farm and live on. I know he charges too much and takes too much profit out of your hard work, but at least you don't and will never have to live with him. He is a cruel, unfeeling man. Many times when he was drunk, or not even, he would come home and beat my mother. He did it without any feeling whatsoever."

"Was he the one who hurt you?" Michael asked, gripping her hands between his.

"That day I come to you I was running away from William. You see, New Year's Day was my birthday, my sixteenth birthday. William had decided it was time for me to know my true heritage. He wanted me to marry this man I didn't want to, so I rebelled, and he beat me. I escaped before he could kill me. There was no way that my life was going to end up like my mother's. Trapped in a loveless marriage."

Michael was speechless. Kathleen had endured so much, much more than anyone should have to go through in a dozen lifetimes. So she must really be Webster's O'Leary's daughter. He wondered how she felt about being Irish.

Kathleen mistook Michael's silence for disgust. He must be silent because she and her Mother repulsed him. Then she began to get angry. Just who did he think he was to judge her? She broke free from his grasp, standing up.

"Well, now you know. Are you happy that you're better than an English lord's daughter? Are you satisfied in knowing that an English girl had an affair with an Irishman, having an illegitimate child? You will be happy to know that I will be leaving tomorrow after the wedding. I would leave sooner, but I promised Beth and Gabrielle." Kathleen began running away from Michael.

Michael, after getting over his initial shock at her words and accusations, got up to chase her. Kathleen was fast but no match for Michael's long, powerful legs. He caught up with her, quickly grabbing her from behind around her waist. He brought her down to the ground and rolled on top of her squirming body.

"Let me go!" she yelled, beating him with clenched fists on his hard chest.

Michael grabbed her fists in his own, holding them on either side of her head. They lay stretched out, body upon body, until Kathleen calmed down and began to cry deep, heart-wrenching sobs that tore Michael's heart in two. "Shush, Kathleen. Stop. It's alright," he whispered softly, kissing her forehead.

"You don't have to go home tomorrow. You can stay with us, and I will protect you."

"You will?"

"Yes."

"Why?"

"Because I think I love you."

"But I..."

"Hush, Kathleen, don't say anything. It's alright. Will you go to the wedding with me tomorrow?"

She looked into Michael's perfect sapphire blue eyes and simply said, "Yes, Michael, I will."

Chapter Eight

The day of March the fifteenth burst upon Lord Donovan's town with bright rays of sunlight that compared to the king of England's treasures. It was a perfect day to have a wedding, Kathleen decided. She had only gotten a few hours sleep, which made her able, for the first time, to see dawn break across Ireland. To see the mass of rolling green hills slowly become visible in the light took Kathleen's breath away. Kathleen was still amazed about what had happened yesterday. The scene with Michael in the fields had left her emotionally as well as physically exhausted. Although tired, she could not have slept if her life depended on it. Besides her excitement that Michael said he loved her, Beth and Elizabeth had stayed up all hours of the night preparing for the wedding. Kathleen had stayed up to help, so when they finally went to sleep, she was wide awake. She tossed and turned, finally falling into a restless sleep. Kathleen sat outside on the little mat in front of the cottage door so she would not wake anyone up. That was how Michael found her, sitting with her legs out in front of her, crossed at the ankles, her long hair hanging unbound down her back. She was supporting herself with her arms behind her. She wore the white shirt and green skirt that Beth had given her the first day she was there. Michael had never seen her or anything else look so beautiful. Kathleen looked like she was deep in thought when he went outside. He didn't want to disturb her, but he needed to talk to her. Michael gently closed the door, as to not to startle her, but she jumped and turned around, quickly standing up when she saw Michael. Each time she saw him, she was amazed by his beauty. This morning he had put on black pants and a flowing black shirt with large sleeves that tapered at his wrists. The front of his shirt was tied with a loose black cord that allowed his smooth muscular chest to show. Dressing in black showed off Michael's dark hair that almost matched the color of his clothes. His eyes were the only color he needed in Kathleen's opinion.

"Good morning," Michael said softly, coming closer to her so that he stood in front of her for the first time.

She noticed that he carried a large, rectangular-shaped, white box with a ribbon around it that matched his eyes.

"Good morning," Kathleen said shyly, unable to meet his eyes.

"What are you doing up so early?"

"I did not sleep very well last night."

"Do you feel sick?" Michael asked, touching her forehead with the back of his hand.

"No, I feel fine."

"Would you like to go for a walk?"

"Sure."

They walked in silence, not touching but standing very close.

Michael broke the silence by saying, "Kathleen, let's stop here. I need to talk to you."

They sat down in the wet, dewy grass. Kathleen looked up at Michael, who had sat next to her. Was he sorry about yesterday when he told her he loved her? Was he going to tell her that she should leave to go home? Was he not going to take her to the wedding?

"What do you need to tell me, Michael?" she asked fearfully.

Michael heard the fear in her voice and gently touched her cheek with his hand, trying to put her at ease. Kathleen jerked her head back as though his touch had burned her.

"Kathleen, about yesterday…"

"Yes?" she asked coldly.

"I just wanted you to know that I won't tell anyone what you told me that happened to you."

"Thank you."

He nodded his head and reached for the box and said, "I …Kathleen, I noticed that you did not have anything for the ceremony today. To wear, I mean…" He handed her the box.

She took it and laid it on her lap where she saw a piece of paper with writing on it.

"What is it?" she asked, holding the paper up.

"It is my letter to you. I wrote it last night. I did not sleep very well either."

Kathleen sat staring at the paper far a long moment before Michael noticed she was not reading it.

"Are you going to read it?"

She kept her head down and shook her head no.

"Why not?"

"I can not," she replied, still keeping her head down.

"Kathleen, look at me…why…? Kathleen, look at me. Why won't you read my letter?" Michael watched as her face got flushed and tears filled her eyes.

"I can not read or write," she said with shame in her voice.

Kathleen can't read or write? Michael thought with dismay.

"Why can't you?"

"William does not think women should be educated. I know no math or foreign languages either. I only know what my name looks like."

Michael was angry. What kind of man was Lord Dunovan? The Irish taught themselves, those who wanted to learn. His father had made sure his children knew the basic math and how to read. Even though none of them expect Michael took to it, at least they all knew how to read and write. Even Beth could read a whole book, if she wanted to, but she did not care to read.

"I know you must think I am stupid, but if I could learn to read, I would."

"I don't think you're stupid, just deprived." That sounded odd to Michael. Kathleen lived in a castle, was considered English, never had to work a day in her life, yet she was the one who was deprived. An idea formed in his mind. It would be fun if she agreed. "Would you like to learn how to read?"

Kathleen nodded.

"I could teach you if you wanted me to."

Kathleen's face lit with joy. "Really?"

"Yes."

She moved and hugged Michael around the neck. The sudden gesture caused him to fall on his back.

"I guess you accept my offer," he said teasingly, looking up at her face.

Kathleen blushed and moved off of him. She stood up and brushed her skirt off.

Michael still lay in the grass looking up at Kathleen. "Where are you going?"

"Back to the cottage."

"Wait. You haven't opened your gift. Aren't your curious about what's inside?"

Kathleen sat back down and took the box from him. "What about your note? Will you read it to me?"

"No, you keep it, and when I teach you to read, you can read it to yourself." Michael thought he had handled that well as he watched Kathleen pull at the ribbon. He could not have read the note in front of her; he was a little embarrassed of what he wrote. He had never told a girl that he loved her more than anything else.

Kathleen opened the box to find a beautiful white shirt with embroidery of a brown deer on the back that seemed lost in the thick forest of green. She gently touched the deer, feeling the silk of the thread. It was the most beautiful piece of clothing anyone had ever given her. He watched as Kathleen gently touched the deer. He had bought the shirt for her a few weeks after she came in Ashimori. The deer with its large brown eyes and almost haunted look had reminded him of Kathleen so much that it caused him to buy it on impulse.

Now he cursed his impulsiveness. How could he have been so stupid as to think this girl who had everything would be happy with a handmade shirt by some Irish worker? He reached to take the shirt back, saying rather stiffly, "I'll take it back. I'm sorry that I tried to give you this. I know…"

"What?"

"What do you mean what?"

"You mean to tell me your going to take the shirt you gave me away? That is not a very nice thing to do." Kathleen knew that Michael thought the garment insulted her.

"You want it?"

"Why of course I want it! It is the most beautiful thing I have ever seen. Imagine a person giving you something, then taking it away from you. Honestly, Michael, you are—"

Kathleen was interrupted by Michael moving closer to her and kissing her. It was a different kiss than the first kiss; this one was slow and gentle. Gone was the urgency of Michael trying to show how wrong they were for each other. Now Michael showed her how perfect they were together. Michael broke it off when she subconsciously pressed her body closer to his. It would be wrong for him to go any further at a time when she was still vulnerable. Although he had told her that he loved her, she had not shared her feelings.

He held out his hand to Kathleen and said, "Maybe we should start to get back before they miss us."

Kathleen picked up her box that contained her new shirt and put her hand in his. Standing next to Michael made Kathleen feel very small and fragile. She looked up at him and said, "Thank you for my shirt, Michael."

"You are welcome, Kathleen."

* * * * * * *

Gabrielle O'Connor woke on the clear, cool, day of her wedding with a dilemma. Her problem had nothing to do with the wedding. Marrying Matthew. No, that was not the problem, for marrying Matthew was the only thing she had ever wanted in life. From the moment she met him, she knew that he was the one for her. It went much deeper than physical attraction. *But all that is beside the point*, Gabrielle thought as she went out her cottage door to go see Beth. What was she going to do when Father O'Boyal asked who giveth this woman? Her father was dead, and it just was not proper for her mother to give her away. She sighed and continued her walk towards the Fitzpatricks'. As she approached the little cottage, she noticed Michael and Kathleen walking hand in hand. She wondered what was going on. She thought they hated each other. She waited until they went into the cottage to knock on the door, which was answered by Michael. "Good morning, lass," he said cheerfully.

"Good morning, Michael," Gabrielle said cautiously, as she had never seen him in such a good mood before. "Beth and Matthew are still asleep. But you could help Kathleen get the flowers set up on the path to the center of town."

"Beth is not up yet?"

Michael shook his head. "Well, that's alright. I don't want to see Matthew before the wedding anyway, you know, because of the bad luck and all. Where's Kathleen?"

"In the kitchen, I believe."

"Is she really your cousin?"

"Why do you ask?" Michael said as he nervously watched the door leading to the kitchen.

"It just does not seem like you're related, especially after seeing you holding hands," she added softly.

"She's just a friend of the family, who needed help. Do not tell anyone though."

"You care about her, don't you, Michael?"

Michael answered, "Yes."

Kathleen came out of the kitchen with a hot pot of porridge. "Good morning, Gabrielle. Excited?"

"Oh, yes."

"Beth is still sleeping."

"I know. Michael told me. But I do need help with something."

Kathleen put a generous helping of porridge into a wooden bowl and handed it to Michael.

"Thank you," Michael said, catching Kathleen's eyes with his own.

"You're welcome." Kathleen tore her gaze away from Michael and said, "What do you need help with, Gabrielle?"

"I do not have anyone to give me away."

"Ah…no…maybe my father could give you away…" Michael said, getting Gabrielle's hint.

"Beth wouldn't want John to give me away too, Michael."

Kathleen walked over to Michael. "Michael, it would be nice for you to participate in the wedding."

"Oh, alright, Gabrielle, I will give you to Matthew."

"Thank you," Gabrielle cried, kissing Michael on the cheek.

"Gabrielle, who is your bride's maid?" Michael asked.

"Eva Harris."

Michael stopped eating. "Would you repeat that please?"

"Eva's going to be my bride's maid."

"Why?"

"Because she's my friend. My god, Michael, what is wrong with you?"

"Nothing," he mumbled, avoiding Kathleen's curious glance toward him.

Beth came out of the room she shared with Kathleen wearing a plain shirt and skirt. "Good morning. Gabrielle, what are you doing here so early, and where is your dress?"

"I just needed to come over and ask Michael something. He has decided to give me away."

"That's nice. Kathleen, I was thinking of what are you going to wear?" Kathleen crossed over to pick up the discarded box with her beautiful shirt in it.

"Oh, Kathleen, that's gorgeous. Where did you get it?"

"Michael gave it to me."

"Michael? Michael gave it to you?" Beth asked in shock.

"Yes."

"Kathleen, why don't we go lay out the flowers?" Michael said before Beth could ask anymore questions.

"I thought I was going to help Kathleen with the flowers," Gabrielle said, somewhat amused at seeing Michael nervous.

"You can help Beth get ready at your house." Michael stood up from the table, leaving his bowl half full. Grabbing Kathleen by the arm, he hurled her out the door.

"What is wrong with him? Beth asked puzzled.

Before Gabrielle could answer, Kathleen came back in blushing a deep red and said, "We forgot the flowers."

Beth and Gabrielle, amused, avoided each other's eyes as they watched Kathleen grab the basket and exit the cottage once again. They waited until Kathleen was safely out the door before they burst into laughter.

"Oh my, Michael has it bad for her. Beth, why didn't you tell me?"

"I didn't know. Who would have thought Michael would fall in love with Lord Dunovan's daughter?"

"Whose daughter?"

Beth, realizing what she had said, tried to deny it, but Gabrielle wouldn't let her off the hook so easily.

"This morning, Michael said she is a good friend of the family, but she is Lord Dunovan's daughter? Why is she staying here?"

"Gabrielle, do not tell anyone and don't tell Kathleen that you know, but she came here one night beaten up pretty badly. We do not know who beat her, and we never asked…maybe Michael knows."

"Poor Kathleen," Gabrielle said softly.

"She is alright now, though." To break the silence, Beth suggested waking her mother and going to Gabrielle's to get ready.

"No, let her sleep. I noticed she has a cough."

"Fine, we can do it ourselves and leave a note for her to come meet us later." They left the cottage walking along the short path to Gabrielle's home. As they got closer they encountered Kathleen and Michael having a heated discussion on the dirt road leading to the center of town.

"What in the hell are you looking at?" Michael yelled in aggravation when he saw the two girls stop to stare at them. Michael watched as Beth and Gabrielle continued walking, ignoring his outburst. He was mad. Mad at Gabrielle for bringing up Eva. Mad at Kathleen for asking about her. When they left the cottage together, Kathleen had yanked her arm out of his grasp.

"How dare you drag me out as if I were a side of meat!" she had yelled at him.

Michael had grabbed her arm as she stomped by him, causing her to whirl around and crash into his hard muscular chest.

Kathleen looked up at his face and said, "Let me go, Michael."

"No."

"Why not?"

"I will not let you go until I explain why I took you out of that room."

"I do not want to hear it. Besides, are we not supposed to be decorating the path for the wedding?"

Michael had released her while she went to get the basket full of flowers they had picked yesterday. When she walked out the door, she had begun to put the flowers on the side of the path, ignoring Michael. He had stood watching her place the flowers artistically on the ground for several minutes until he got annoyed and stomped over to her.

"Kathleen. Kathleen, put those damn flowers down and look at me before I knock them on the ground."

Kathleen placed the flowers down and stiffly turned around to face him, arms folded tightly against her chest. "Why did you embarrass me in front of Beth and Gabrielle?" she accused.

"I did not mean to. I was trying to save you from their questions."

"Well, next time you can mind your own business."

Before Michael could come up with a retort, he saw his sister and Gabrielle gaping at them, causing him to take out his frustrations over Kathleen with them. Sighing, he took a deep breath and looked back at Kathleen.

"Kathleen, believe me please. Gossip spreads like wild fire. Do you want Lord Dunovan to find out you're here?"

Kathleen realized that Michael was telling the truth, looked up at him and whispered, "I am sorry."

"It is all right, Kathleen. Now let's get back to what we came out here to do."

They worked in compatible silence until Kathleen, feeling extremely curious, asked, "Michael, who is Eva?"

"Why do you ask?"

"I saw the way you reacted to Gabrielle when she mentioned her name."

"She was my fiancée," he said shortly.

Kathleen knew by the tone of his voice that she should stop this line of questioning. But she couldn't. "I remember Beth telling me one day at tea that you had a fiancée. You broke up with her. Why?"

"We were not meant to be together."

"Did you love her?"

"Kathleen, is this line of questioning necessary?"

"No."

Once finished with the flowers, they went their separate ways to get ready for the noon wedding. Kathleen got her new shirt from Michael and went to Gabrielle's cottage. Michael went to his cottage to help Matthew.

Beautiful black-haired, cat green-eyed Eva Harris put on her best shirt and skirt and left for Gabrielle's cottage. When she arrived, the little cottage was in chaos. Beth, who Eva couldn't stand, was running around asking if she looked all right, which, Eva had to grudgingly admit, she looked beautiful. She walked toward Ella and asked what she could do to help.

Ella stared back at the girl in shock. "What are you wearing?"

"My best outfit for the wedding."

"You call that your best outfit?"

"It's the one that makes me look the best."

At this point the chatter, the nervous movements had stopped. Everything was quiet, as everyone looked at Eva. Eva wore scarlet from head to toe. The blouse was open very wide at the neck, revealing quite a lot of her ample chest. Kathleen blushed seeing Michael's former fiancée for the first time in such a provocative outfit. Kathleen admired her boldness at wearing such an outfit. No wonder Michael asked her to marry him; she was beautiful. Kathleen felt very plain in her new shirt and long white skirt. Compared to Eva, she felt like a mud hen next to a peacock.

"Eva, how nice it was of you to come early to help with the wedding preparations," said Gabrielle, steering her away from her mother's evil glare.

"You and Beth have the same wedding dress," Eva observed. "I am not her maid of honor too, am I?"

"No, oh! I forgot you never met Kathleen, Beth's uh…"

Overhearing the conversation, Kathleen stepped in with, "Cousin, I am Beth's cousin."

"Michael never mentioned a cousin." *Especially not one so breathtakingly beautiful*, Eva thought, looking Kathleen over from head to toe.

"Well, we know how Michael is preoccupied with his doctor's work," Gabrielle stated. "I never understood why Michael wanted to be a doctor."

"Maybe he wants to help people," Kathleen said.

"One should help themselves before they help others," Eva retorted.

"Is that why you and Michael broke off the engagement?"

Eva glared at Kathleen. Just who did this girl think she was. No one talked to Eva Harris that way. Before Eva could retort, Beth's mother announced that it was time to head toward town. The mothers and friends of the brides were to walk along the path spreading more flowers, with the maids of honor following. Then the brides followed behind the maids of honor in step with each other. At the edge of town was where Michael and John Fitzpatrick would escort the brides to the center of town with Matthew and Dutch escorting the bridesmaids. Everyone left the cottage except Eva and Kathleen, who were the last in the wedding march and had to wait a few minutes to go out. The two girls eyed each other warily in silence until finally Eva said, "You do not look like any of the Fitzpatricks, Kathryn."

"Kathleen."

"What?"

"My name is Kathleen, and you are right. I do not look like the Fitzpatricks, because I am just a friend of Beth's passing through Ireland."

"No one's ever mentioned you before."

Kathleen ignored Eva's statement and asked what she had been wondering ever since she met her. "Why did Michael break off your engagement?"

"You know I was engaged to Michael?"

Kathleen nodded her head.

Eva looked closely at Kathleen and saw much more than friendly curiosity. "You're interested in him, aren't you?" Kathleen blushed and Eva continued. "Your interest in him is pointless, Kathleen, because we will be married." At that statement, Eva turned in a blur of scarlet away from Kathleen, slamming the door.

For the ceremony, the town of Dunovan celebrated in their ancestors' style, with music, dancing, drinking, eating and whatever merriment they could find. Kathleen and Michael had just finished their fifth reel when he looked down at her laughing face and said, "Kathleen, we need to talk."

Kathleen looked frightened at the urgency of his voice but said, "All right, where?"

"Let's go to those hills so we will not be overheard."

Kathleen and Michael's departure from the wedding party went unnoticed by all except for Eva. Eva had been watching the two of them all day, dancing, eating, laughing. It made her want to rip Kathleen's golden red hair out of her head. Just who was this girl? Everyone knew that she and Michael were meant to be together. It didn't matter that Michael had told her he did not love her. They would be married. Strong arms pulling her around the waist from behind against someone's strong chest interrupted Eva. She turned to see Bartholomew McKnight, her date. She struggled to be let go, but failed.

In irritation, she said, "What do you want, Bart?"

"I thought we could go over to the barn and you know…" He let his voice trail off suggestively.

"No," Eva said, trying to see where Michael was taking Kathleen.

"Why not?"

"I am not in the mood," Eva snapped, breaking away from him.

Bartholomew grabbed her by the arm, causing her to stop and turn around to glare at him. "You're not in the mood? Why not? You were the other day when I asked you to this stupid wedding." He stopped his ranting when he saw where Eva's gaze was. "Still interested in Fitzpatrick? Obviously he wants nothing to do with you now that he has the princess of this rat infested town."

"What?"

"Michael Fitzpatrick wants nothing to do with you. You should have known better than to give yourself without being married. You—"

He was stopped by Eva's hard smack across his cheek.

"What the hell did you do that for? Does the truth hurt?"

"Shut up! What did you mean by, now that Michael has the princess of Dunovan?"

"You do not know that girl with the red hair is?"

"She said her name was Kathleen, a friend of the family. Beth and Gabrielle said she was a Fitzpatrick cousin, but she looks nothing like them."

Bartholomew let out a snort of contempt. "If that girl has a drop of Irish blood in her, than I am the King of England."

"Bart, stop playing games with me and tell me who she is," Eva said in frustration.

"What will you give me?"

"Whatever you want."

"I will hold you to that promise," he warned her.

"Just tell me!"

"That girl is none other than Kathleen Dunovan, Lord William Donovan's daughter."

"Are you sure?" Eva asked in disbelief.

"Of course I am sure. I collect taxes for Lord Dunovan, don't I? Now time for my reward," he said reaching for her.

She batted his hands away. "Stop that. I'm thinking how we can use this information to our advantage."

"Against Kathleen and Michael?" he asked with interest.

"Who else?"

"You are a conniving little wench, aren't you?"

"Of course."

As Bart and Eva plotted against Michael and Kathleen, they did not notice a lone figure in back ease away from their conversation. Webster O'Leary wondered how he was going to warn his daughter without frightening her away. How much had Mary told her? He looked toward Michael and Kathleen setting themselves down on the hill not far from the wedding festival.

As Michael sat down, he wondered how to begin. He had never told anyone what he was about to tell Kathleen. He had no reason to, because he had never felt this way about anyone before, not even Eva. To this day, he really did not even remember proposing to her. He never loved her or any other person for that matter, except his family, until…

Until today when he was walking down the wedding path with Gabrielle, it was not Gabrielle he was holding but Kathleen. In his mind he saw Kathleen with her long, wavy, golden-auburn hair flowing freely down her back, topped on her head a wreath of white roses. She was in all white, nothing fancy, just a regular shirt with a long lacy skirt, looking so beautiful, and she was his. The vision of Kathleen was so blinding to Michael that when Father O'Boyal asked, "Who giveth this woman?" he did not even hear him. The father had to ask him again with a pinch on the arm from Gabrielle for him to realize that he was supposed to give Gabrielle to Matthew and stand next to Eva. Standing next to Eva in her scarlet outfit did nothing for Michael as he gazed across the path at Kathleen. Eva had tried to ask him something, but he did not hear her. At the end of the ceremony he went directly to Kathleen, meaning to talk to her then and there, but he was sidetracked by Matthew and Dutch, who asked him to make a toast, and after that, there were more toasts. Then the lamb was brought out. After the meal, Kathleen had begged him to teach her how to dance the Irish reels. At first, Michael tried to talk her out of dancing. He had never enjoyed taking part in any of the traditional Irish customs. One look from Kathleen's golden brown eyes had made him forget all his ancestral prejudices. He had fun, much to his surprise. Kathleen was a quick learner and was able to pick up the most complicated Irish dances in no time. The time had gone by so fast with Kathleen in his arms, faster than he had wanted. Soon he had to go back to his cottage, but this time he would not have his brother and sister with him. They had grown up, made lives for themselves, and now it was time for him to make a life for himself with Kathleen.

Kathleen was watching and waiting for Michael to begin. She wondered what was wrong now; the day had turned out very well, despite Eva's threats. Michael had not gone near Eva, spending all his time with her. Maybe he wanted to tell her that he was going to go back to Eva though, tell her that he was just being nice to her today. Kathleen had to find out. She wished Michael would hurry up and say what he had to say. She saw him take a deep breath before he began, which made her even more apprehensive.

"Kathleen…"

"Yes?"

"Kathleen, I…" Michael trailed off, seeing that she was gazing at something beyond his shoulder. "Kathleen, what is it?"

"That man, who is he?" she asked curiously of the man who had been watching them for some time at the bottom of the hill.

He turned around to see Webster O'Leary watching them intently. Michael had not realized that he had been at the wedding. Michael brought his hand up in a wave, which Webster turned away from, embarrassed at being caught looking at them.

"That's strange," Michael mumbled to himself, over Webster's behavior.

"Michael, who was that?"

"Webster O'Leary."

"Webster O'Leary?"

"Yes, he is a friend of mine, sort of."

"Oh." Kathleen had turned very pale at learning Webster's name, Michael noticed. "Is he married?"

"No, Kathleen he is not. He was too much in love with your mother to ever marry."

"You knew?"

Michael shook his head. "Not until you told me about your mother was I sure. Webster told me he fell in love with the most beautiful girl in the world and had a baby girl with her. He was unable to marry her because she was taken away by her father who forced her to marry a heartless man." Michael reached out to hold Kathleen as she started crying.

She pulled back only for enough to look at his face to ask, "Did he ever see his child?"

"Once. When she was born, Webster was there."

"Why? Why did my mother's father take them away from each other? Why, Michael, why?"

It practically tore Michael's heart in two as he heard the pleading in Kathleen's voice. He had no answer for her though, so he held her until she calmed down.

"I must talk to him."

"Who?"

"Webster O'Leary, my true father."

"After I talk to you."

"No, please, Michael, I need to hear him tell me he loved my mother. I need him to tell me that she was taken away from him, that he did not abandon her because she became pregnant with me. Please take me to him," Kathleen begged.

Michael stood up held out his hand to help hoist Kathleen to her feet and said, "All right, Kathleen, our talk can wait."

* * * * * * *

"You should not have brought her here, Fitzpatrick," Webster O'Leary reprimanded from the darkness of his cottage.

After seeing his daughter again so many years following her birth, he went back to his cottage and began to drink. Seeing Kathleen reminded him of Mary so much it brought all the memories he had tried to forget but never really could over the sixteen years he and Mary had been apart.

"Didn't you want to meet me?" Kathleen softly said, trying to make out her father's form in the darkness."

"I did meet you once long ago. The night you were born, I was there."

"Why did you leave? Why didn't you just take my mother and go?"

"Go? Go where, lassie? Your mother's father threatened me with rape charges. Do you know what would have happened? I would have been killed; Mary would have been disgraced, unable to marry anyone. What would have happened to you? I could not let Mary try to take care of you alone. I had to do what I did."

"But William Dunovan does not care about her or me. The night of my sixteenth birthday he beat me and turned me out of the Dunovan Castle."

"Michael, is this true?" Webster stood up to light a lantern.

Michael winced slightly at the sudden brightness and said, "Aye, 'tis true. On the first day of the year, she was at our doorstep knocked unconscious. Lord only knows how she made it to our house without dying. If you remember, we had a pretty bad storm that night, too."

"What about Mary? You left Mary, my Mary, alone with that monster?" he accused Kathleen.

"He threw me out."

"And you never went back?"

"No."

"You have to. You have to save your mother."

84

"I can not go back. He will kill me if I do."

"He'll kill Mary if you do not."

"What do you care? You never tried to see me or her."

Webster grabbed Kathleen by the arm. "I could not go back. I would have killed Lord Dunovan and been hanged for the act. My daughter was not going to grow up without a father."

Silence loomed after Webster's words. Kathleen broke free from her father's grasp and ran out the door.

"Not a happy reunion, uh?" Michael asked sympathetically.

"Damn Lord William Dunovan to the deepest hell for laying a finger on her," Webster swore collapsing into a chair.

"Webster, I better go find Kathleen. Do not do anything stupid," he warned.

"Michael, wait."

"What?"

"You care about her, I can see that. Try to make her find out if Mary is safe, please. Be careful. Eva and Bartholomew found out who she is, and they are scheming to do something."

"Dammit! Thanks for the warning." Michael turned to leave.

"Oh, Michael?"

"Yes?" he asked, turning around.

"Take care of her for me, would you?"

"I will."

Michael ran down the hill back to the wedding festivities looking for Kathleen. He found his sister and Gabrielle talking and laughing gaily.

"Michael, hello," Gabrielle greeted, breaking off her conversation with his sister upon seeing him.

"Have you seen Kathleen?" he demanded.

"Why, Michael, didn't you ever learn any manners?"

"Beth, you better tell me if you have seen Kathleen before I rip out all your hair." Michael spoke calmly and slowly so that his sister understood him.

Beth sensed something was wrong; she had never seen Michael this angry before. "Kathleen ran by a few minutes ago. She went back to the cottage saying she was not feeling well."

Michael ran the mile from the center of town to his family's home, not thinking of anything except Kathleen. He slammed opened the door and found Kathleen huddled up in front of the dormant fireplace in a little ball. He bent down and scooped her up in his arms, ignoring the protests to leave her alone, and carried her to his room. It was almost bare now that Matthew had moved out.

Michael sat down on his bed and rocked Kathleen in his arms until she was only crying softly. They stayed in this position for a long while, until Kathleen finally spoke.

"He was right, Michael. I should go back."

"You can not."

"Why not? I'm healed. Beth's married. You do not need an extra mouth to feed, and you don't need me here any longer."

"Wrong, Kathleen. I need you. You will not leave until we celebrate our wedding." Kathleen leaped out of Michael's arms, went over to Matthew's bed, and sat down.

"What do you mean our wedding?"

"If you go back now, I will never see you again. Lord Donovan would probably kill you, and I can not loose you, Kathleen."

"What about Eva?"

"I never loved her. We got engaged because I felt I had to get engaged."

Realization dawned on Kathleen, as she understood what Michael was saying.

"Kathleen, believe me, please. I love you! It was clear today when you walked down the center of town…I had a dream of us…you were so pretty…" He trailed off. "Please, Kathleen!"

Kathleen threw herself into Michael's arms. He held her tightly for awhile until he heard her crying again. He pushed her back to look down at her face. He gently wiped away her tears.

"Kathleen, stop crying. Everything will be fine."

"Will it, Michael? Will it really?"

"Yes, I promise." Michael leaned his face over hers. "Trust me, Kathleen. I will take care of you."

Kathleen leaned her head back for Michael's gentle kiss.

"Say it, Kathleen. Say you love me too! Tell me you will marry me."

Kathleen looked into his eyes, Michael's beautiful blue eyes. She opened her mouth to speak but was unable to when she heard a loud bang and then, "Michael, lad! You're mother, she's fainted."

Michael bolted at his father's words, leaving Kathleen alone. Michael ran out to see his beloved mother deathly pale in his father's arms.

"Save her, Michael, please," were his father's only words to his son as he laid his wife's limp form on the old sofa. Michael prayed to the high heavens that he could grant his father's request.

Chapter Nine

After suffering from pain and delirium for over a month, the life of Elizabeth Fitzpatrick, loving wife, mother and caring friend, was mercifully over.

The day of her funeral was appropriately gray and dismal to greet the tears and solemn faces of her loved ones. Elizabeth's sons, husband and son-in-law, dressed in black, carried her coffin through town. Elizabeth was to be buried by the sea. The beach with its rocky surface looking over toward the deep blue water was a place she had always loved.

By the beach was the place she had met her beloved John when she was a young girl of fifteen. His family's cottage had been perched on a cliff overlooking the stone sculptured strip of sand with the white foamy waters crashing against the sand. Elizabeth had watched the young John Fitzpatrick come to the water everyday for almost a year before he had bothered to talk to her. She had made sure that she could be seen from where he stood, gathering the shellfish that littered the sand. John Fitzpatrick, at eighteen, was well aware of the beautiful Lizzie. Lizzie was how he thought of her, but he was shy, so he stayed away. He was sure that the McNeils had already found Lizzie a husband, a suitable mate for the strawberry blonde, velvet brown-eyed girl that he would want for himself, but sure that he was not good enough to have for himself. For a year, John and Elizabeth watched each other from afar, each sure that the other did not want to be sociable one another. Then one day Elizabeth, at the ripe old age of sixteen, decided that she did not want to be an old maid, went down and asked John to dinner with her family. John accepted, and thus began a courtship that lasted six months, after which John felt they had had a proper amount of time to know each other, so he proposed to her on the rocky beach. Their marriage had been perfect in every way. They talked, enjoyed each other's company and stayed in love for their entire thirty years of marriage. They produced three healthy, beautiful children who obeyed their rules for the most part. They had just married two of their children, and the oldest had seemed to be settling down, learning to accept things for what they were.

So, why had God taken her away just when things were perfect? Why, is what John had asked himself since Michael told him that Lizzie had a lung disease. He asked himself the question every time he heard her go into one of her fits of coughing that never failed to bring up specks of blood on the handkerchief that Lizzie held to her lips. He asked God why every time he saw Michael give her a spoon full of syrup, which could only help her pain, not cure her. Each night, John had asked God why he took his Lizzie from him after she told him that it was time for her to leave Earth.

Elizabeth had asked Kathleen to get John for her. She told Kathleen to do it quickly, for it was time. Kathleen, with tears in her eyes, had run to get John from Dunovan Bar. He had run all the way home, knowing from Kathleen's pale face that his Lizzie was about to leave him. He got on his knees by the sofa where she laid and gently held her weak hand in his.

"John…"

He bent his head toward hers so he could hear her.

Elizabeth struggled to be heard. "John…love you. Tell…Matthew… Beth…love. Michael…"

John, seeing that she was stalling, asked, "What about Michael, Lizzie?"

"Michael…will be a doctor. Michael, my first child…love him most. Worry…"

"Do not worry, darling. Rest, please." John had tears streaming down his face.

"No, I must tell Kathleen…take care of Michael. He loves her." Finally saying her peace, Elizabeth Fitzpatrick went limp and left her beloved husband, home and country.

After kissing his wife's cherished face, telling her that he would be with her again one day, John went outside the cottage to find Michael roaring drunk and yelling at Kathleen.

"Ever since you came, nothing but trouble has followed."

"Michael, that's not true!" Kathleen cried.

"It is, and you know it. I wish you would leave." Michael turned away from her, starting to walk back to town but stopped when he heard his father call his name.

"Ma?"

"Yes, Michael, she just passed away."

"It is my fault. I could not save her."

John put his hand on this son's shoulder. "'Tis not your fault, son. God took her away."

"God gave me the chance to save her." Michael turned and started toward town.

"Michael, where are you going?" Kathleen called.

"To get a drink."

"Mr. Fitzpatrick…John, stop him, please. He can not go on like this," Kathleen pleaded with him.

Ever since Elizabeth had taken ill, Michael had been drowning his sorrows in drink. Every night after giving his mother medicine that barely helped her pain, he went to Dunovan Bar to get drunk. He blamed himself for his mother's sickness. He could do nothing for her, and as of lately, Michael's blame had turned toward Kathleen. He once again blamed her for being related to Lord Dunovan, who kept the Irish as farmers, not giving them an education. Kathleen was the only one he could lay his guilt on.

John reached out and gently wiped the tears off of Kathleen's smooth cheek. "You love my son, lass?"

"Yes."

"Lizzie said he loved you right before she died. She told me to tell you to take care of him."

"How can I when he will not let me?"

"I do not know, but Michael does love you."

"No. He said I was the cause of his problems."

"That was the drink talking. Go to him. He needs you."

"I love him so much. It hurts to see him like this."

John had watched as she began walking towards town. He hoped she could save his son.

As the funeral march reached the strip of land where Elizabeth was to be buried, John looked toward Kathleen where she stood in black, with her hair pulled away from her face, next to Beth and Gabrielle. John wondered what had happened between them last night. He dismissed the thought from his mind as Father O'Boyal began the prayers.

Dutch held Beth's hand as the prayers began.

Kathleen could not concentrate on what was being said. Her thoughts were of last night.

After saying that she loved Michael out loud for the first time, she had gone to find him. Upon arriving at Dunovan Bar, she found him just entering the tavern.

"Michael, wait." She ran up and gently touched his arm but recoiled when she saw the coldness in his eyes.

"What do you want, Kathleen?" Michael's voice was as cold as his eyes.

"I…I am sorry about your mother."

"Are you?"

"Yes, of course. She treaded me like a daughter."

"Well, you at least have another mother to go to, so why don't you?"

"Michael! Why are you doing this to me? To yourself? Why do you blame yourself for your mother's death? You did everything you could. You need to gather yourself together and help save others."

"I could never go back to trying to be a doctor. Don't you see, I failed! Now go away and leave me alone." He turned away from her.

"That's right, Michael Fitzpatrick. Go drink your sorrows away. But don't you dare blame me for your failures. You have a chance to help others, a chance that only you can either take or walk away from. If you walk away, you will be a failure, and you are not a failure because I could never fall in love with a failure."

Kathleen brought herself to the present as Father O'Boyal finished, and it was time for the family to grab a hand full of soil to throw on the coffin.

"Kathleen, I can not," Beth cried, clutching Kathleen's sleeve.

"Yes, you have to," Kathleen said, bending down to grab a hand full of rich black moist soil. She tried to give it to her, but Beth refused. Beth turned and stumbled, trying to get away from the loss and sadness. Dutch went after her to hold her in his arms as she sobbed. He said something to her, and she shook her head no. Kathleen felt a knot form in her throat as she watched Dutch walk Beth to the beach and sit down and hold her. Dutch loved her so much. It reminded her of Michael holding her the night of their wedding. But no, he hated her because she was considered Lord Dunovan's daughter. After declaring her love to him for the first time last night, Michael had turned from her, slamming the bar's door in her face.

"Kathleen." Gabrielle touched her arm.

"Hello, Gabrielle."

"Beth would want you to throw her fist of dirt for her."

"Oh no, I can not."

"Yes, Elizabeth thought of you as another daughter." Gabrielle gently pushed her towards Elizabeth's grave.

Kathleen looked up at Michael watching her intently. She could not tell what he was thinking; she looked down and tossed the damp dirt over Elizabeth's plain pine coffin.

After the funeral, Kathleen searched for Michael and found him throwing shells into the ocean. She watched as the wind whipped around him, causing his black hair to look as unruly as his clothes. His shirt hung loosely on him since it was united at the throat and hung out from his pants. She saw the torment on his face and turned away not wanting to disturb him.

* * * * * * *

May the first was celebrated with the farmers planting their new harvest early in the morning, while the women of the town set up the may pole, cooked lunch, set up games for the children and decorated the town with flowers and ribbons. It was a time to celebrate a new beginning, a new time of life. A new time of life was what Michael was looking for. Since his mother's death, he had been very withdrawn not talking to anyone. He had gone back to doctoring not too long ago and stopped drinking.

He had been shook up the night Kathleen had called him a failure. No one expect his mother had ever told him that his life was in his hands. If he succeeded, it was up to him; if he failed, it would be his fault. Then she had told him that she loved him for the first time. The words he needed to hear from her, she finally said them, and what did he do? He turned away from her, angry at hearing the truth. The truth, of him becoming nothing but a farmer. He looked for her in the crowd of people knowing that it was time to talk her. He began to walk toward Kathleen, who was sitting next to Webster O'Leary.

"Kathleen, I wanted to tell you that I was sorry for yelling at you that night you and Fitzpatrick came by."

"You were right. I should have stayed."

"No, Kathleen, you were right to leave. It was wrong of me to get angry at you for saying the truth that has haunted me for years."

"Truth?" Kathleen questioned.

"I should have tried to save Mary. I should have taken her away from Ireland. From England. We could have gone away. France maybe. We could have gotten lost in France. I could have farmed."

Kathleen waited a while, watching Webster get lost in a fantasy that could never have happened, before she said, "When was the last time you saw her?"

"The night you were born. Lord Dunovan sent for me to be with lass," he said, using the name he had always called her. "She almost died giving birth to you. We said goodbye the night you were born, for Lord Dunovan told me that if he ever saw me again, he would kill me. My daughter needed a father. I'm sorry I made the wrong choice." Webster held his daughter for the first time in over sixteen years. "I loved your mother. I still do. I love her so much."

Kathleen held him tighter as he cried. "Father, I will go back tonight to save my mother."

"No, Kathleen, you will not."

Kathleen broke free of her father's grasp to see Michael Fitzpatrick looming over her with his arms folded across his chest.

"What do you want, Michael?" Kathleen asked warily. It was the first time he had spoken to her since the night before Elizabeth's funeral.

"I need to talk to you," he said urgently.

"You go with Fitzpatrick. We'll talk later," Webster said, seeing that she was about to protest. He left the two alone.

Kathleen sighed and looked up at Michael expectantly. Michael saw Gabrielle and Beth coming toward them.

"Kathleen, let's go for a walk."

"Michael, I don't think that is such a good idea."

"Why not?"

"I am not very happy with you right now, and I do not want to be alone with you." Kathleen saw the hurt in Michael's face, but he had hurt her too.

"Please, Kathleen. I need you so much."

"Why hello, Michael. Kathleen," Beth said cheerfully. "Are you having fun?"

"Of course. Loads of fun," Michael said sarcastically.

"Hello, Beth. Where is Dutch?" Kathleen asked, ignoring Michael.

Beth rolled her eyes and said, "He and my older stupider brother are seeing who can climb the may pole faster."

Kathleen laughed. "Sounds like fun. Maybe I should go see."

"What about our talk, Kathleen?"

"You go ahead, Beth, while I talk to Michael. I'll catch up with you later. Say hi to Gabrielle for me."

"Sure. Bye you two," Beth said gaily trotting off towards the celebration.

Kathleen watched.

"Kathleen?"

"Where do you want to go, Michael?"

"I know the place beyond those hills," he said, pointing to a group of trees about two miles away.

"That is far, Michael," Kathleen said, getting up to stand beside him.

"Please, Kathleen."

She looked into Michael's eyes and saw the need reflecting in them. "All right, Michael."

As they began walking, Michael knew he had to convince her that he really did love her. He had not realized that he hurt her so much. After all, she had been through with Lord Dunovan and her mother – how could he hurt her like that? He had taken all his frustrations out on her. He had promised he would never hurt her, that he would take care of her, protect her. He said a quick prayer to God, to help him make Kathleen believe that he loved her. He hoped God helped him this time. He took away his mother from him. Standing next to Michael, Kathleen was lost in her own thoughts. What could Michael possibly say to her? He had made his feelings clear to her the night he told her she was nothing but a spoiled English brat. The death of Elizabeth was all her fault, he had said. Reliving those words brought tears to her eyes. John had told her that it was the alcohol talking, not Michael. But if that were true – and she hoped it was – why had he not talked to her before today?

"Michael, how much farther?" Kathleen asked as they reached the forest's edge.

"Just a little farther."

Upon arriving at Michael's place, Kathleen gasped. "My God! Michael, this is the most beautiful piece of nature I have ever seen." Kathleen looked at the sparkling waterfall that ran from glossy gray rocks covered with moss. The water ran into a pool of clear water which was surrounded by exotic looking flowers of all colors. All was nestled in a bridge of large trees. "Michael, it's Eden. Paradise. I never knew such a place existed."

Michael had watched Kathleen's face light up with joy at the beauty of the wilderness. He was glad that he could finally make her happy again. He reached out and pulled her into his arms, kissing her eyes, nose, cheekbones and finally her mouth. She tasted so sweet, like honey. She felt so good against him, soft, pliant. He held her closer, angling her body with his.

"No, Michael," she protested weakly.

"Yes, my love," he whispered against her mouth, then began kissing her warm soft neck. "You're so beautiful, Kathleen. So perfect. Like porcelain.

"Michael, please," she whimpered.

"What, Kathleen? What is it?"

"I thought you want to talk."

He buried his face in her hair, which felt like silk. "I am sorry, Kathleen. So sorry. I was full of grief over my mother. I could not do anything to help her, I felt guilty. I took it out on you. I am sorry. Please will you for give me?" Michael gently kissed her cheek and felt the dampness. He licked at a tear, tasting its saltiness, before he said, "Kathleen, don't cry. Please don't cry."

"Michael, I love you," she cried, pressing her face against his shoulder.

"I love you, too. Kathleen, stop crying please," he pleaded with her.

"Michael, I… I am sorry too for calling you a failure. You are not a failure. You're the one who is perfect," Kathleen said, slowly opening his shirt to reveal smooth warm chest and kiss his warm flesh. Michael groaned and lifted her up in his strong arms, carrying her over and laying her down gently beneath a willow tree. He stood looking down at her. She was wonderful. She loved him.

"Michael?" Kathleen questioned, sitting up, placing her arms behind her for support.

Michael took off his shirt throwing it down on the ground. He gently pushed Kathleen down as he laid his long body on top of hers. He kissed her warm inviting mouth, her long graceful neck. He heard her make a low moan in her throat when he unbuttoned her blouse and palmed one smooth breast. She was not wearing anything under her shirt, much to his pleasure. He brought his mouth down to her flushed aroused breast.

"Michael, no." She breathed raggedly.

Michael stopped and leaned his face over hers. "What is it? What is wrong, Kathleen?"

"We should not. It's not right."

"It is. I love you, Kathleen. I won't hurt you. I'll never hurt you again. I swear." Michael began to kiss her again, moving down to take as much of that perfect globe in his as possible.

Kathleen felt desire run through her body. She had never known such pleasure, and it was caused by Michael. Her Michael. Her love.

"Michael, please," she begged, arching her body against his.

"Tell me you love me."

"I love you, Michael Fitzpatrick, more than anything else in the world," she cried.

He slowly and gently took her. Her saw her wince with momentary pain and then sigh with pleasure. He had never known it could be like this with a woman. Kathleen was perfect in every way possible.

"My love."

He sighed as her legs wrapped around him naturally. How perfect this place was for them, he thought as he moved to make her his and his alone.

When it was over, Kathleen lay next to Michael, secured against his chest by his strong arms. She kissed his chest.

"Kathleen," he whispered, nodding her face to look at him. "I love you so much."

"I know. I love you too."

"You're not sorry, are you?"

Kathleen shook her head no.

"Did I hurt you?" he asked worriedly.

She smiled. "Not much. You hurt me more when you told me to go away."

He held her tighter. "I am sorry. Do you forgive me?"

"Yes, of course." After a moment's silence, she asked, "Do you think it was like this between my mother and father?"

"No."

"No?"

"No two people have ever loved each other like we love each other, Kathleen."

"Michael, I have to go back."

"No, you can not leave me. Why even say such foolish words at a time like this?"

"Don't get angry. I have to make sure my mother is all right."

"Not until we're married. Lord Dunovan can't do anything to us once we're married." He looked down at her. "You will marry me, won't you?"

"Hmm...yes, of course." She snuggled against his warm chest.

"We'll have such beautiful children." He stroked her soft hair, thinking of his future. His future with Kathleen. Her mother could come and live with them. Maybe she'd be reunited with Webster. He moved Kathleen's head to his shoulder while she slept and snuggled closer to her. He went to sleep next to her. The most peaceful sleep he had had in a long time.

* * * * * * *

Lord Dunovan looked at his wife's sleeping form. He smiled at the news he had for her.

"Mary. Wake up," he commanded loudly.

She weakly opened her eyes. What did he want now?

"I know where your daughter is. Do you hear me? I know where Kathleen is. I'm going to bring her home to watch you die."

"Kathleen?" Mary whispered.

"Yes. I'm bringing her home to watch you die. Then I'm going to force her to marry Ryan Winchester. If he'll have her now that she's been infested with the dirty Irish."

"No..." Mary protested weakly.

"Oh yes. And if Winchester won't have her, I'll beat her just like I beat you." He laughed cruelly at Mary's white face and left her alone.

Kathleen was alive and still in Ireland? William was going to kill her if she came home. *No, it couldn't be true,* Mary thought before lapsing into darkness. But somehow deep inside her she did know it was true. What could she do to save her daughter? Her beloved daughter. Mary slept and dreamt of Webster. Her love. Her life. She would not die before she saw him again. She could not. If only God would grant her that one wish, then she would die happy.

Chapter Ten

"Michael!" Kathleen exclaimed as he put his arms around her waist bringing her against his solid chest. He moved her heavy mane of hair off her neck so he could kiss it.

"Michael, stop that."

"Why?"

"You'll be late for work."

"I just wanted to say good morning, Kathleen," Michael said releasing her. He moved around so that he stood in front of her. "Don't you want to say good morning to me?"

"Good morning, Michael." He smiled and yanked her toward him, causing her to collide with his chest.

"Good morning, love." He bent his head to give her a kiss.

Kathleen waited until the kiss was over to gently push him away from her. "Go to work, Michael."

"I was not done yet," he protested playfully.

"By the time you're done, you will be a week late for work. Now put on your shirt and go to work."

"So this is what I chose to marry." He addressed the ceiling of the cottage, thrusting his arms through the shirtsleeves. "A woman who gets rid of me when I have a present for her."

"What kind of present are you referring to?"

He smiled at the caution he heard in her voice.

"A real gift, love."

"In a box?" she asked warily.

He chuckled and then said, "Kathleen what do you think I am?"

"Well, you attacked me."

"You like being attacked, as you call it, and you damned well know it. Remember that day last week?" he asked softly, gently biting her ear as he gathered her in his arms once again. "You brought me lunch. I fed it to you bite by tender bite. Afterward, we made love on the hill. Do you remember, Kathleen? Your body rolled on the flowers causing their scent to escape and blow through the air. Do you remember, love?" Michael whispered tenderly into her ear.

Kathleen nodded her head, as she recalled the warm day last week when she thought it would be nice to pack lunch and surprise Michael. Kathleen and Michael had not been able to spend much time together since celebrating May Day. With summer approaching, Michael had said he liked to try to get all his planting done so all he had to do was water his part of the fields during the hot weather.

"Yes, Michael, I do vaguely recall something of that nature happening," Kathleen said in a bored English accent. "Might I have my present now?"

"Stuck up English brat," he said, swatting her bottom and handing her a tiny white box.

Michael stood in front of Kathleen as she sat down on the sofa and opened the box. She gasped when she saw the two gold rings inside. Quickly, she looked up to see Michael's tense, anxious face watching her. Gone was the teasing light from his blue eyes. It was replaced by the look of fear. The look was the same one that she had seen the day he had given her the shirt with the deer. He loved her, she thought wildly. He really did want to marry her.

Michael watched as Kathleen's eyes clouded with tears and her hands began to tremble violently. He knelt down in front of her. "Kathleen what is it?" he asked worriedly.

She shook her head, too full of emotion to speak. She handed him the box with the rings, afraid that she would drop them. Michael took it and placed it next to her on the sofa, then gently took her face in his.

"Kathleen, look at me. Why are you crying? Don't you want to marry me?" Michael waited impatiently for her answer. Had she changed her mind? Was she lying when she told him she loved him?

Kathleen put all his fears to rest when she swallowed and said, "Michael, I want to marry you more than anything else in the world."

"Then why the tears, love?"

"I have never in my life seen rings so beautiful. So perfect for us. I…I was not sure you still wanted to marry me," she finished softly.

Michael held her tightly against his chest. "Oh, Kathleen. Love. Never doubt my love for you. I will always love you, forever." He took the ring with the tiny roses carved into gold and got down on one knee holding her right hand.

"Kathleen Dunovan, will you be my wife?"

"Always. Always and forever." Michael put the ring on her and sealed it with a kiss. He gently lifted her up in his arms.

"Wait, Michael."

"What?" he asked, looking down into her face.

"What about your ring?"

He put her down so she could place his ring on his finger. "Are you happy now?"

"Yes."

He scooped her up in his arms once again and started to walk to his room. Again she stopped him.

"What is it, Kathleen?" he asked impatiently.

"What about work?"

"To hell with it."

"I was hoping you would say that," she replied, bringing her face up for his deep kiss that told her he was hers and she was his alone.

* * * * * * *

Summer, like spring, came early for the tenants of the town of Lord Dunovan. But summer in Ireland was not like summer any other place on earth. Ireland's summer was perfect. It was warm during the day, but rarely did it get unbearable. Often it showered late in the afternoons or early in the morning, leaving the land green and ripe, like a jewel. Summer was the perfect time for a wedding, or mourning over a lost love, as Webster O'Leary was doing the day Michael went to Dunovan Bar to ask for Kathleen's hand in marriage. He had thought it was proper, since Webster was her father and obviously the one who loved her. He was amazed that no one from Dunovan Castle had tried to find her. Not even her mother. That day when she asked him when they would marry so she could go see about her mother, he had said, "Kathleen, don't you think she would have contacted you by now?"

"Maybe she's sick."

"Someone would have contacted you if that were true."

Kathleen's temper had snapped. "She is the only one at that damn castle who loves me. I have to go see about her."

Michael shook his head as he strode toward Webster; someone would have contacted her if they worried about her. Especially now since so many people had guessed that she was not a relative. Word would have gotten to Dunovan Castle that a golden redhead named Kathleen was staying with the Fitzpatricks.

"Webster, hello," Michael said quietly as to not startle him.

"Hello, Michael, how are you?" Webster looked tired, Michael observed, and older. Since meeting his daughter, he had given up searching for his brother. *He seems to have given up on life,* Michael thought. Michael sat down across Webster.

"I want to marry Kathleen," he blurted.

Webster took a long swallow from his glass, waiting for Michael to continue.

"I want to ask your permission to marry her."

"You love her then, do you?"

"More than anything else. I will take good care of her. I'll never let anyone hurt her. I'll never hurt her. I…" He was rambling desperately in his need to convince Webster to let him marry Kathleen.

"Michael, please stop. Why are you asking me for Kathleen's hand in marriage?"

"Why? My God, man, you're her father. Who else should I ask?"

What's wrong with him? Maybe he's had too much to drink, Michael thought.

"Why not ask Lord Dunovan or her mother?"

"Why should I? They have not even tried to find her." Michael was getting angry. "Webster, look, I only asked you out of respect since you are her father." Michael stood up. "But no matter what you say, I will marry Kathleen."

"Michael, lad, sit down. You may marry Kathleen. I was just surprised. Have you asked her yet?"

"Yes. She was so happy. She says she loves me."

"You sound a little stunned over that," Webster observed, amused over Michael's bewilderment.

"I guess…I never thought that I would find true love. And especially not with an English girl."

"She's half Irish, you know."

"I know. But she was raised—"

Michael was cut short when a sudden loud bang sounded. He looked up to see Kathleen running toward him. She collapsed against him out of breath.

"Kathleen?" he questioned shaking her gently.

"Michael…it's your father." She stopped to take in a large amount of air.

"What about him?" Michael gripped her arms, shaking her harder, when he saw the tears roll down her cheeks. "Kathleen, what is it?"

"He got thrown from a horse. He was visiting your mother's grave when the horse saw something that frightened it."

"Pa. Is he—" Michael swallowed unable to say the word.

"Yes, he died. I am sorry, Michael. His friend Joseph Bennigan came by with the news. I came as fast as I could. Michael, I'm sorry," Kathleen said, hoping that he would not retreat into himself again.

Michael reached for Kathleen, looking for comfort. He felt her hesitate before wrapping her arms around his neck. He held her for several minutes before burying his face in her soft hair and began to weep.

* * * * * * *

The next few days were extremely difficult for Michael. He felt lost and alone. Both of his parents were dead, and his brother and sister, although grief stricken over their father's death, had their own lives to lead. Without Kathleen, Michael was sure he would have done something drastic. No one since his mother had cared and worried about him like Kathleen did. She made him meals, washed his clothes and held him close to her when he wept over his loss. A couple of days ago at John's funeral, she had stood by him, tightly gripping his hand while the mass was held. She had walked with him while he threw the required clump of dirt into the grave. After the funeral, they walked together to lay a rose on Elizabeth's grave, which was next to John's. Before Michael and Kathleen could walk home, they were stopped by Eva and Bartholomew.

"Hello, Michael. I am so sorry," she said with false sympathy.

"Thank you," Michael said, pulling Kathleen to stand next to him.

"What will you do now, Fitzpatrick?" Bartholomew asked.

"Work," Michael replied shortly.

"What about you, Kathy, where will you go?"

"Her name is Kathleen, and she will stay with me," Michael snapped.

"Not for long," Eva said, when she thought Michael and Kathleen were out of earshot. But Eva was wrong. Kathleen heard her threat, but she kept it to herself, not wanting to worry Michael. A few days after the funeral of his father, Michael woke up to find Kathleen cooking breakfast with tears streaming down her face.

"Kathleen?" She jumped, quickly wiping the tears off her face then turning to face Michael.

"Good morning, Michael. Here sit down," she said, pulling out a chair for him. "I'll get you some breakfast." She began to put fruit and cream on the table in front of him.

"Kathleen."

"Yes?" she asked, avoiding his eyes.

"Kathleen, what's wrong? Why were you crying?"

"It was nothing."

"Look at me and tell me nothing is wrong," he demanded.

"Michael, what happens now?"

"You tell me what is wrong with you, then I try to fix it."

"No, Michael. I meant, what happens between us?"

"Now that my parents are both gone, you mean?"

Kathleen looked down and nodded her head.

"We get married, Kathleen."

The room was silent for a long while. Finally, Kathleen brought her golden eyes up to Michael's brilliant blue ones. Kathleen saw the honesty in his eyes and almost leaped for joy. Perhaps she could have happiness. She had been worried that he would blame her for his father's death now that the initial pain of loss was over.

"You still want to marry me, don't you?" Michael asked worriedly.

"Oh yes, Michael. Of course I do." Michael sighed and held open his arms. "Come here, Kathleen." Michael buried his face in her soft luxuriant hair. "What brought all this on?"

"I was afraid."

"Afraid? Afraid of what?"

"That you would blame me for your father's death. That you would shut me out of your life, send me back to Dunovan Castle. Go back to drinking again."

"Kathleen, look at me. Never would I do that do you again. I love you. What would it take for you to completely trust me again?"

"I trust you, Michael," Kathleen said weakly.

Michael sighed, "Obviously you do not, or you would not doubt me or my intentions. I know things have not always been smooth with us, but I do love you."

Kathleen moved away from Michael's lap and sat down in a chair facing him. It was too easy to listen to him and believe what he was saying when she was so close to him. She knew things needed to be said. She looked up at Michael watching her, waiting for her to begin.

"Michael," she started, "I know that you are not happy about living here in this cottage as a farmer for an English lord. I know that you would rather be a doctor, and you should."

"Kathleen, we have been over this before, my dream to be a doctor. It is a dream that can not be realized. There is nothing more that I can do about it. It is my fate. I help Doctor McKay; that is all I am able to accomplish. What has my being a doctor have anything to do with your not being able to trust me?"

"Michael, please just listen I'm trying to make a point. You do not like your home much or Ireland. I understand it is because of the centuries of unfairness that the English have controlled you in your own home. You are right to feel this way; it is wrong that people try to control others just for land."

"Thank you for your sympathy," Michael said with mild sarcasm.

Kathleen continued on ignoring him. "You see, being raised as an English girl, an heiress, I thought nothing of how you, the Irish, were being treated. Sure, I had some notion that the way Lord Dunovan treated his tenants was wrong, but who was I to say anything? I thought we were better. Lord Dunovan never let me go past the castle gates, and mom and I spent the season in England. I never knew that he worked you like dogs just to keep me in finery."

"Kathleen, you say you had some idea we were not well treated. What did that mean to you, not having dinner on gold plates, not being able to have a new dress of velvet made?"

Kathleen heard the bitterness in his voice. She knew there were still feelings of hate from Michael. He had it all wrong though. Kathleen laughed without humor. "You think that it how it is at Dunovan Castle, Michael, gold plates, new clothes everyday? I suppose you would think it was wonderful for me there? I guess you would have loved to be raised in a castle."

"Better than a cold dirt floor with barely enough food."

"No, Michael. I would rather have been raised in this cottage where there was love. You think I had anything in that castle. Well, I did not. A few weeks ago when you told me that if someone actually cared about me, they would have tried to find me. That hurt, Michael. Deep down, I knew it was the truth though. Even if my mother were hurt or dying, Lord Dunovan would have found me and dragged me back to see her die and suffer. Everything you think I had is nothing compared to what you have, love. I am sure my mother loved me, but not enough. Even though your parents are dead, you still have your brother and sister. What do I have?"

"You have me, Kathleen."

"Do I? Do I really? For how long? Until you decide that I am not worthy of you? Until you decide that we are not meant to be together?" Kathleen's questions were met with silence. "For how long Michael?" she asked again urgently.

"Forever, Kathleen."

"I love you, Michael, so much it scares me."

"Scares you why?" Michael longed to hold her in his arms, but he did not, knowing that she had to let out her fears.

"Everything I have ever loved has been taken away from me. I loved your parents, Michael. You may find that hard to believe, but I did. They were the most kind, giving people I have ever met.

"They did not force me to be any different than what I was. They did not try to make me marry someone I did not want to. They were taken away from me just when I thought I could have true happiness." Kathleen paused to swallow the lump that had formed in her throat and wipe her tears. Then she continued, "And you, Michael Fitzpatrick. I came here hurt, and you saved my life. But you hated me for where I came from. You tried to hide your feelings from me behind your hate for the English. You insulted me, blamed me for your poverty, and your mother's death too. You never did look all the way at my heritage. That is not even real. You never saw me. Even after that day that seems so long ago, when you first kissed me. You told me it would never work for us. Then the day before Matthew and Beth's wedding, I finally told you what happened the night I came here. You told me you loved me.

"But now I know that you did not really hear me. I told you Lord Donovan beat my mother without a moment hesitation. And today you asked me what I thought unfair was.

"Not having dinner on gold plates. That is not what unfair is. Unfair is growing up a lie. Believing your parents is one thing, then finding out they were something different. Unfair is living in a home without love. Unfair is knowing the person you love the most in life will someday somehow be taken away from you."

"Is that why you do not trust me, Kathleen? You think I will stop loving you. I did hear you that day when you told me about Lord Donovan, but you have to understand. Anything would have been better for me than this," he said sweeping his hand to indicate the squeaky cottage. "When you came here, you were all the things I could never have. The first time we kissed was a symbol of the difference between us. We could never marry. I was not good enough for you. That day you told me that you were not good enough for me, that had me puzzled until you told me about your mother and Webster O'Leary. Then I knew you meant. You thought you were inferior to me."

"Didn't you?"

"No, Kathleen, I felt sorry for you and something that I had been trying to deny, love. You are different than anyone I have ever met before. You're kind, compassionate and helpful. I loved you before you told me about the night you came. That you trusted me enough that day proved to me that we could have a relationship if you trusted me. But I was not going to force you. You had to know for yourself. The night my mother died, you finally said the words I had hoped for you to say, that you loved me."

"I also called you a failure," Kathleen said at an attempt of humor.

"You were right. I had to stop blaming others. My life is in my hands. What I do is my fault, not yours not Lord Donovan's, but mine. I could never give you what you had at Donovan's castle."

"I should certainly hope not."

"Kathleen, I'm serious. I could never give you jewels, clothes, whatever else you had there."

"No gold plates?" Kathleen said with a twinkle in her eye.

"No gold plates, Kathleen. But I could give you something you have never had and something I never did give very easily."

"What would that be?" she asked breathlessly.

"Love, Kathleen. I will give you all the love in the world plus more. You have to believe me. Trust me, Kathleen, and we can be happy."

Kathleen walked into Michael's outstretched arms with no hesitation this time.

She believed him. They could be happy together. "Michael, I love you."

"My love, my life, my only one, nothing now could come between us. I promise."

Kathleen felt his arms tighten around her. They could be happy together.

"Do you want breakfast, Michael?"

"Only if you join me." Kathleen smiled into his handsome face and kissed his jaw.

"Yes, Michael, I will join you." Michael smiled as he heard the promise in her voice for much more than breakfast.

* * * * * * *

"Michael is a man in love, Beth," Gabrielle said as she watched Michael and Kathleen play like children in the grass.

"I like Kathleen, and so does Matthew. We will more than welcome her as a sister-in-law," Beth said.

Watching as Kathleen tried to outrun Michael, she laughed as Michael dropped her down on the grass and rolled on top of her.

It was several weeks after Michael and Kathleen had their heart-searching discussion. They had been invited to be with Beth, Dutch, Matthew, and Gabrielle for dinner. Michael could not have been happier. Every night, Kathleen waited for him after work with dinner waiting. Every chance she got, she told him she loved him. But it was the little things she did – having fresh flowers at mealtime, mending his shirts, washing them, and she never complained or talked about her mother at Donovan Castle.

Michael looked down into her laughing face and softly kissed her forehead.

"Happy?" he asked huskily.

"Yes, Michael. I am very happy."

"Good."

"Michael."

"Hmm?" he asked as he kissed his way around her face then down her throat.

"Don't you think I should go help Beth and Gabrielle?"

"No." He began unbuttoning her blouse.

Both were startled to hear, "Unhand her, you viscous scoundrel!"

Michael quickly rolled off of Kathleen. Sitting up, he saw his brother looking down at him.

"Do not fear, lovely princess. I will save you from this toad."

Kathleen laughed as Michael helped her to her feet.

"God damn it, Matthew. You scared the hell out of me."

"Good. You looked as though you would have eaten her instead of my wife's delicious meal."

Matthew walked over to Kathleen. "Hello, Kathleen, how are you?"

"Fine, and yourself?" Kathleen asked, blushing at being caught with Michael.

"I am fine. Dutch, can you believe that the fair Kathleen has agreed to marry Michael?"

"Surprises never cease. Hello, Kathleen."

"Hello, Dutch. How is Beth?"

"She is fine." Matthew laughed as Dutch ran into his cottage throwing his arms around Kathleen's shoulders.

"You really want to marry, my brother?"

"Yes."

"Why?"

"Now listen here, Matthew," Michael said threateningly

"I was only playing, Michael. You must give him a sense of humor, Kathleen," he whispered in her ear.

"I'm going to eat Beth's food, aren't I?" Michael said, overhearing Matthew's comments.

"Be nice, Michael," Kathleen pleaded.

"Kathleen, come here for a minute, will you?" Michael said.

"No, Kathleen. Do not go near that man-eating plant."

"Shut your mouth, Matthew."

"Shut my mouth?! How rude. Kathleen darling, manners. You must teach him manners, as well as a sense of humor."

"His manners are fine, Matthew."

"Maybe his bedside manners, lass," Matthew said winking.

Kathleen blushed.

"Matthew, stop tormenting them and come help me," Gabrielle called from the front door of Dutch and Beth's cottage.

Matthew went off mumbling, "Work, work, work. That is all I do, and what thanks do I get."

"Kathleen love, wait." Michael grabbed her arm as she started to head to the cottage.

"What?"

"You have to uh…re-button your blouse."

Kathleen turned red as she looked down to see a lot of her chest and chemise revealed. She quickly re-buttoned her blouse.

"What would your brother think?"

"That I was anticipating our wedding night," he stated innocently.

"Michael!"

"Come on, Kathleen love. Let's go in."

"Will your brother think ill of me?"

"No, Kathleen," he reassured her.

Kathleen placed her hand into Michael's as they walked into Dutch's cottage. Beth, giving them both a hug, greeted them.

"Beth, what a lovely cottage," Kathleen exclaimed as she looked at the blue curtains and tablecloth, the white sofa and throw rug, and the fire that Dutch was setting in the fireplace.

"Thank you, Kathleen," Beth said, her voice full of pride.

"They never compliment the husband, do they, Matthew? The one who works for the lovely cottage," Dutch said, putting an arm around Beth's waist.

She pushed him saying, "Dutch, when I first moved here, it looked like a pigsty, and you know it."

Dutch hung his blond head. "You are right of course. I was nothing but an animal in human's clothing. You have reformed me, lovely one."

Matthew laughed at his sister's and husband's exchange. "I, of course, was perfect to begin with. I did not need to be changed."

Gabrielle raised an eyebrow at him. "Perfect?"

"But, of course."

"I finally got you to put your clothes in a neat pile instead of throwing them all over the place."

"But I was trying to take them off in order to get to you. Why just last night you commanded me to kiss you and then—"

"Matthew! Please stop this," Gabrielle pleaded. Matthew grabbed her and laid her down on his lap.

"Admit that I am perfect," he said, tickling her sides.

"Stop, Matthew. Please," she moaned.

"Tell me I'm perfect," he commanded, tickling her harder as she tried to get away.

"You are perfect, Matthew. Now let me up."

"And you want to marry his brother," Gabrielle said as she finally got off her husband's lap.

Kathleen looked at Michael, who sat next to her on the white rug, rubbing her neck with one hand.

"I love Michael. He does not need to be changed."

"Michael not have to be changed?" Beth asked before going off into a fit of laughter.

"Beth," he warned.

Matthew took up where Beth left off. "Have you seen Michael eat? He shoves the food in without stopping."

"Wasn't that you, Matthew?" Beth asked sweetly. She ignored her brother's glare and said, "No, Michael was the one who always forgot to replace the soap by the tub. The one who always left the dishes on the table, mysteriously having something else to do."

"On the subject of changing," Michael said. "What about you, little sister?"

"What about me? Women are perfect."

"Perfect? Weren't you the one who always used someone else's bath water?

Instead of drawing your own from the well and warming it up, you were always in my tub.

"I needed to bathe, Michael," she said primly.

"After I sweated and worked hard in the fields and needed a long soak in the tub, you took my water.

"Michael, please, you sweated all day. A little more never hurt to help your one and only sister."

"You did do that though, Beth," Dutch said.

"Did? How did you change her, Dutch?" Michael asked as he absentmindedly played with Kathleen's hair.

"Why she scrubs my back, and I share my bath water with her."

Beth smacked Dutch on the head, stood up and announced that it was time for dinner. Michael stood and helped Kathleen to her feet. They headed to the table where Michael held out a wool chair for Kathleen to sit in.

Before sitting, Kathleen asked, "Beth, is there anything I can do to help?"

"No no. Sit down, Kathleen. You are our guest."

"Are you sure?" Kathleen hesitated.

"Of course. You are here to enjoy yourself."

Kathleen sat down next to Michael.

"Have you decided when the wedding will be?" Dutch asked after they had all sat down.

"Soon. Very soon," Michael said softly as he tenderly gazed over at Kathleen.

"Who do you want to be your bridesmaid, Kathleen?" Gabrielle asked.

"I had not really thought about it," Kathleen admitted. "But I think the proper person would be Beth if she wants to."

Beth smiled. "Of course, Kathleen."

"Where will you live, Michael?" Matthew asked.

"I do not really know. I can not afford—"

Kathleen broke in, "I like where we live now, Michael."

"Michael, Beth and I could help pay for your wedding," Dutch offered.

"Thank you, Dutch, but I have money plenty to pay for our wedding. Just as long as Kathleen here does not want to go to London to have her wedding dress made," Michael teased.

"I thought I would wear my shirt you gave me, Michael, the one with a deer and a long white skirt," Kathleen said, knowing of Michael's dream of their wedding.

"Why, Kathleen, that would be lovely," Matthew said, stuffing a large piece of ham into his mouth. "Beth is there anymore—"

Beth hid a smirk and said, "There is more in the kitchen."

Beth watched as Matthew sat there looking at her. "The kitchen is over there, Matthew."

Matthew grunted and got up.

"Gabrielle, how do you put up with him?"

"I love him, Beth, believe it or not. The big cow."

Matthew came back in with a biscuit in his mouth and pulled on Gabrielle's blond braid.

"I love you too, Gabrielle."

"Are you positive that you want to marry into our crazy family, Kathleen," Beth asked.

"Watch who you call crazy, brat," Matthew said as he helped himself to his wife's potatoes.

"I love you and your family, Beth. I've never known such happiness." Kathleen knew that Michael never revealed her secret of the night so long ago, but she knew that Beth and the others knew that she never wanted to talk of Donovan Castle again.

"Matthew, there is more food that Beth and I prepared," Gabrielle said as he scooped ham off her plate and into his mouth.

"Michael, maybe we better go. I think I heard thunder."

"Thunder? Matthew, we should leave also."

"I want some dessert first."

"There is more, you hog. You leave my house," Beth said with mock anger.

"Beth, what about that apple pie in the window sill?"

Beth shot her husband a withering glance as she went to go retrieve the apple pie.

Kathleen got up, taking her plate and Michael's into the kitchen.

"Kathleen, what did I tell you? You are a guest. Go sit down," Beth said.

"At least let me help with the pie."

Beth smiled and handed her the dish. "Thank you, Kathleen. You know I always wanted another sister. I'm happy that you will be joining our family."

Kathleen put the pie down on the counter and hugged Beth.

"I have always wanted to have a sister," she said with tears in her eyes.

"Kathleen, stop that," Beth said sniffing. "Don't you know crying is contagious?"

"Kathleen. Beth," Gabrielle called before coming in. "Matthew is grumbling about pie. Wat are you doing?"

"Welcoming Kathleen into our family. You'll be her sister-in-law too, Gabrielle."

"How lucky I am." Kathleen sighed. "A whole family with just two words – I do."

Kathleen walked back out with the pie. Matthew got up to be around her and the pie.

"Matthew," she chuckled, "doesn't Gabrielle feed you?"

"Feed him?" Gabrielle asked incredulously as she walked in with Beth following her carrying dishes. "He eats more food in one meal than I do in a week. All I do is cook for him."

"I am a growing boy. I need nutrition," Matthew said.

"I do not think you are considered a boy anymore, Matthew," Michael stated as he pulled Kathleen down to sit next to him on the white rug.

"The doctor speaks."

"Matthew, one day I really am going to hurt you."

"Watch out, Kathleen. Michael has a violent streak," Dutch warned.

"And how would you, Dutch O'Brian, know if I have a violent streak or not?"

"The first time I kissed Beth, you almost killed me."

"I was protecting my sister's innocence."

"And who will protect Kathleen's innocence from you Michael?" Matthew asked remembering the two earlier in the grass.

Kathleen blushed. "I don't need anyone to protect me."

"See, Matthew. Kathleen's more than willing."

"Michael!" Kathleen cried, punching him in the chest.

"She is a hitter too? Gabrielle beats me black and blue"

"No more than you deserve."

"Ungrateful wench," Matthew said, smacking her solidly on her bottom as she took their plates to the kitchen.

Michael got up, hauling Kathleen to her feet. "Beth, Dutch, it was nice of you to have us over. Thank you." Michael hugged his sister and shook hands with Dutch.

"Yes, thank you, Beth. When Michael and I are married, we'll have you over one night for dinner," Kathleen said, hugging Dutch and Beth.

"Will you have us over too?" Matthew asked.

Kathleen laughed. "Yes, of course. We will start gathering food now though to feed you."

Matthew grinned and grabbed Kathleen in a bear hug. "Welcome to the family, little one."

"Thank you, Matthew."

"Michael, Gabrielle and I will walk you home."

"All right," Michael agreed, putting an arm around Kathleen's shoulders.

Once the two couples were outside, Matthew sent Gabrielle ahead, wanting to talk to his brother. Matthew waited until Gabrielle and Kathleen had put some distance between them to say, "Michael, are you happy?"

"With Kathleen, you mean?"

Matthew nodded his head.

"Yes, Matthew, I have finally found happiness. I truly do love Kathleen, and she loves me too."

"I like Kathleen, Michael."

"As long as you approve," Michael teased as they reached the cottage where Kathleen and Gabrielle waited.

"She's good for you, Michael. She makes you laugh. I have never seen you totally relaxed."

"She makes me happy."

"I'm glad," Matthew said as he put an arm around his wife and kissed her head. "Now this one gives me more trouble than she is worth."

Gabrielle gently bit his neck. "Oh, Gabrielle. Didn't you eat enough?"

"You inhaled most of my food, Matthew."

Thunder broke the gentle laughter, causing Michael to say, "We'd better go."

"Goodnight, Kathleen."

"Goodnight, Matthew."

"Take care of her, Michael," he said, embracing his brother as Gabrielle and Kathleen said good night.

Michael held open the door for Kathleen, waited for her to step inside, then scooped her into his arms.

"Michael, what are you doing?"

"Finishing what we started earlier," he said as he gently laid her down on his bed.

"Michael, your family is so nice to me."

"It is easy to be nice to someone who is nice, love."

As they kissed, Michael undid the buttons of her blouse, and Kathleen helped him take off his shirt.

"Michael?"

112

"What?"

"I love you."

"Oh, Kathleen, me too, love. I love you too so much." He sighed as he gently caressed her breast.

"Michael, you make me happy. Thank you."

"For what, loving you? It could never be anything else for us, Kathleen. We were meant to be together. Forever."

* * * * * * *

"You know exactly whose my daughter is, Mr. Midnight?" Lord William Dunovan asked Bartholomew McKnight.

Bartholomew took a drink of whiskey. "Yes, I do know where she is."

"How much?"

"What?"

"How much do you want to tell me the precise location?" William waited as Bartholomew's eyes assessed the surroundings of Dunovan Castle.

"How much is it worth to you?"

"I will pay anything to have my daughter back where she is safe in her home."

"Five hundred pounds."

"What?"

"I want five hundred pounds," Bartholomew replied.

"Done," William said.

Bartholomew heard a scream that startled him. "What was that?"

"That is my wife."

"What is wrong with her?"

"My wife, although not your concern, is dying. Now about Kathleen, you have information or not?"

"She is staying at the Fitzpatrick cottage."

"Fitzpatrick?" William thought aloud. "Aren't they the ones who lost the mother and father?"

"Yes, but Kathleen is staying with the oldest, Michael."

"You do not like him much, do you?" William asked hearing the bitterness in Bartholomew's voice.

"I hate the ground he walks on."

William smiled. "Maybe we could work something out to punish him for keeping my daughter."

Bartholomew smiled cruelly. Maybe without Michael Fitzpatrick around, Eva would forget about him and concentrate on him.

He leaned over to listen intently as William explained his thoughts.

* * * * * * *

"Kathleen love, I'm home," Michael called as he walked through the cottage door. Silence greeted his announcement. Where was she? She usually ran out to greet him as soon as he walked through the door.

"Kathleen?" he called again.

"I am in here, Michael," she yelled from his bedroom that they now shared.

He walked in to find her sitting on the floor with her hair in a bun, in one of his old shirts, in a pile of old papers and books.

"What are you doing, Kathleen?"

"I am cleaning," she said proudly. He knelt down in front of her, wiping a smudge of dirt off her nose.

"You do not have to clean this old trunk out, love."

"I want to."

"Wouldn't you rather stand up to great me properly?"

"No. This is fun."

Michael turned her nose and stood up to remove his shirt that was damp with sweat.

"Fun, she says," he said talking to himself as he put on a clean shirt.

"Cleaning is fun. Don't let Beth or Gabrielle hear you say that. I'll never see you again." Michael spun around to see Kathleen leaning with a book, smiling casually. "Did you hit me, Kathleen?"

"Yes."

"Why?" he asked, heading down and piling her up to his arms.

"I wanted to know what this book was," she said holding up a battered copy of his favorite book.

"That is *Hamlet*, by William Shakespeare," he said, placing his hands on her waist.

"What is it about?"

"What?" he asked distractedly as he ran his hands up her sides past the gentle swell of her breasts and into her hair, which he loosened to form a soft cloud around her face.

"The book, *Hamlet*, what's it about?"

"A prince," he said, bending down to kiss her nose.

"What does he do?"

"Kathleen love, let's not talk about this now. Let's go eat dinner."

Kathleen paled and dropped the book. She pressed her face against his solid chest.

"Kathleen?" He grabbed her as he smoothed her hair.

"Oh, Michael, I forgot dinner."

Michael forced her to look at him. "You forgot dinner, lass?" he asked sternly.

"I'm sorry, Michael."

Michael looked down into her worried troubled face and hid the smile that crossed his face. "I work all day long to earn money to put a meal on the table that I expect to find on the table when I get home. And what do I come home to? A mess all over my bedroom and no food."

"I'm sorry, Michael," Kathleen said, taking herself away from Michael. "I'll see what is left over from lunch."

Michael grabbed her, spinning around; she crashed into his chest.

"I'll forgive you on one condition."

Now that Kathleen saw the amusement on his face, she sighed in relief that he was not angry with her.

"What condition would that be?"

"That you clean up this mess and—"

"And? You said one condition," Kathleen reminded him.

"And," he said ignoring her, "you meet me for lunch tomorrow by that piece of land in the woods that you know so well."

"So you can take advantage of my innocence?" she asked as she remembered Matthew's comments last week at dinner.

"Yes," he replied without blinking.

"Michael, I have a condition for you."

"Do you think you should be offering conditions? You are the one who forgot my dinner."

"How about we go share some bath water? I'll let you scrub my back while you tell me about *Hamlet*."

"No, love, you scrub my back while I tell you about *Hamlet*."

Michael laughed as she pretended to try to get away from him again. He crushed her solidly against him and brought his mouth down to hers. The kiss left Kathleen weak, limply laying her head against his chest. Michael lifted her up in his arms.

"Michael, what are you doing?"

"We are going to share some bath water like you suggested."

"What about the mess?" she protested weakly.

"It can wait."

* * * * * * *

The next morning, Kathleen woke up in Michael's bed with a smile on her face. She turned over and reached for Michael, groaning when she realized he was gone, left already for work. She felt guilty; he had let her sleep while he went to work, probably forgetting about breakfast. She sighed as she rolled out of bed pulling on Michael's shirt over her head, which feel to her knees. She smiled, happy for the first time in her life. Kathleen wandered out of the room and into the living room. She looked up at the mantle of the fireplace. Seeing that it was almost lunch time, she went into the kitchen to gather bread, fruit, and leftover lamb from the other night. She put everything plus a pint of ale into the wicker basket she and Michael had used to pick flowers for the wedding. She went into Michael's room to get dressed.

Michael had bought her several shirts and skirts to wear, claiming he was tired of her wearing Beth's borrowed clothes. But she knew that Michael was trying to give her what he thought she would miss later on once they married. She smiled at the gold bowl he had made for her, calling in a favor from the towns goldsmith. Michael had told her how he had saved his son once from death. She remembered when Michael had come home that day; she was waiting for him outside. It was dark that day, and she had been startled when Michael came out of the mist dressed in a dark gray shirt.

"Hello, Kathleen love. Sorry to have frightened you," he greeted her.

"How was your day?" she questioned, wrapping an arm around his waist as he put his arm around her shoulder and led her to the door.

"It was fine. Kathleen love, remember that morning when I told you I could never give you all the things you had at Dunovan Castle?"

She nodded. "You promised me something I never had before, love and happiness, a family."

"Yes, I love you and want to make you happy always and have a family with you. But just to make sure you never leave me…" he said, pulling out from behind his back a tiny gold bowl about three inches in diameter. She had taken the bowl from him, feeling the carved designs in it, and said, "Michael, my gold plate?"

"Aye, love."

"You did not have to do this, Michael."

"But I wanted to."

Kathleen smiled at the sincerity of his voice and kissed his cheek and said thank you.

Kathleen pulled out of her revere, taking off Michael's shirt and putting on her shirt with the deer, touching it lovingly. She ran a brush through her hair, thinking of her wedding, which was to take place next week. Michael told her he asked Webster O'Leary for permission to marry her. She was happy that Michael did not think badly of her for being illegitimate.

Kathleen was startled to hear someone knocking at the door.

"Wait a minute," she called, pulling on a long black skirt. Kathleen paled as she opened the door to find Stuart Whitmore, Dunovan Castle's butler, standing in front of her.

Gray-haired and unsmiling as he always was, he said in a clipped English tone, "Miss Dunovan, you are to come home immediately. Your father requests your presence."

"Lord Dunovan is not my father, and I refuse to go back to that damned castle!"

"Your mother is dying," he said flatly, not looking at the girl's face. "Lord Dunovan says that if you do not return by nightfall, she will die tonight, and the…the gentleman you are staying with will be taken to England for trail."

"Trial? For what?" she cried.

"Kidnapping and rape. Please come back, miss, else he will be killed."

Kathleen swallowed. "Stuart, my mother, what's happened to her?"

"Lord Dunovan has beaten her to close to death. She is barely alive."

Kathleen held onto the doorframe for support. She felt weak, like she was going to vomit on the butler's shoes.

"Why, Stuart? Why would he do such a thing?"

"Because of you. He wanted to know where you were."

"Who told him? My mother did not know where I was."

"Bartholomew McKnight, I believe. Now I suggest you pack your things, and I will take you home."

"Please, can't you just tell him that I'm not here, that you did not find me?" Kathleen pleaded.

"What of your mother and the man you are staying with. Miss Kathleen, please think of them. Once you come home, they will be safe."

"Mother and Michael," she whispered. She had to go see Michael first. She had to say goodbye.

"Stuart, you said that I had to be home by nightfall. Well, I will get myself there. Just leave the horse, and I will be there."

"Fine. Please be careful." The butler nodded, turning his back on her and leaving.

"Oh, Stuart?"

"Yes, miss?"

"You tell Lord Dunovan to go to hell and stay there."

She ran into the cottage, slamming the door behind her. She wiped the tears from her eyes and put on her shoes. As soon as this was done, she ran out the door and blindly ran to the woods where she had Michael had first expressed their love for each other. She ran as fast as she could through the thick woods, mindless of the tears and of the tree branches scratching her face. She fell once, ripping her skirt and scraping her palms, but she continued on. She had to get to Michael.

Kathleen finally reached the clearing in the woods to see Michael standing against a tree. She ran to him, collapsing at his feet.

Michael grabbed her off the ground. "Kathleen, what in the hell is a matter with you?"

She looked up into his face pale with tears rolling down her cheeks.

"Kathleen, love, what is it? Are you hurt?" he asked, trying to see her face. She would not let him, pressing her face against his chest and holding him tightly. He held her tightly, rubbing her head with his jaw, trying to soothe her. He had no idea what could be wrong with her. "Kathleen, you have to let me help you if you are hurt," Michael said, trying to reason with her. "Kathleen, what is it? Can you speak?" he asked in alarm. She shook her head and cried some more. "Kathleen, look at me," he said, shaking her, noticing the scratches on her face for the first time. "Kathleen, what happened to you?" he asked softly, gently rubbing the scratches with his fingertips.

"Michael," she whispered achingly.

"What is it? What is wrong? Please, Kathleen, tell me," he begged as he sat down and brought her on his lap.

"I am so sorry, Michael," she cried into his chest.

"Kathleen, why are you sorry? Did you forget my lunch?" he said at attempted humor.

Kathleen swallowed and dived right in. "My mother is dying, Michael."

"What?! How do you know this?" All the time she had been here and not a word from the castle, and now this? What the hell was going on?

"Lord Dunovan sent his butler to tell me I had to return or she would die. Tonight."

"What's the matter with her? She's sick?"

"No, not sick. She's been beaten within an inch of her life. It is my fault, Michael. I should have stayed, kept my mouth shut that night, and done what he wanted. She would be alive and well today."

"Kathleen, no, don't blame yourself."

"I have to go back, Michael."

"You may not leave me," Michael stated firmly.

"Michael, please I must. I have to go back to save my mother." She would not tell him about the threat on his own life. She knew his temper. He would die before the trial.

"You may not leave me, Kathleen. You may not."

"Just who do you think you are, Michael Fitzpatrick?" she asked, getting up from his lap and standing in front of him with hands on her hips. "I must save her; she's my mother. You could not save yours, but I can save mine." Immediately she regretted the words. "Oh, Michael…"

Michael stood, grabbing her back into his arms. "What about us, Kathleen? What happens if you go back? Will you come back to me?"

"I just do not know, Michael," she replied honestly.

"Do you want to leave me, Kathleen? Do you want to go back?"

"No. But…"

"But you are going to go," he said looking down at her.

"Michael, I must go. Please try to understand."

He began to kiss her, trying to change her mind. "Don't leave me."

"Michael, no," she said, turning her face away from him.

Michael ignored her and laid her under the willow tree, that same tree that held the secrets of the first time they made love. He brought his mouth down to her again.

"Michael, stop," she said urgently, as he began to move over her.

"I can not let you go, Kathleen."

"You have to."

"Never. You are mine. Only mine. Forever."

Kathleen gripped his shoulders, digging her fingernails into his muscles as he moved on her possessively.

His breathing was ragged as he said, "You may not leave me, Kathleen love, never. Do you understand? Understand, Kathleen?"

Kathleen waited until he collapsed on her, then rolled off before she said, "Michael, if you could have saved your mother, you would have, no matter what it took."

"Not if it meant leaving the person I loved the most in the world."

"Do not lie to me, Michael. You know if there was any way to save her, you would have. You would have left me faster than a whirlwind."

"Is that why you are leaving? You don't think I love you?"

"Damn you! Listen to me," Kathleen said as fresh tears welled up in her eyes. "I have to save her."

Michael looked into her brown eyes pleading with him to understand. "Fine, you go back to that damn castle, to the people who turned you out, left you for dead and not once looked for you. You go ahead and leave." He turned his back and began to walk away.

Kathleen was after him like a flash, beating him on his broad back. "Michael, do not walk away with me. I love you, Michael. If I could, if I had a choice, I would stay with you. I have to go back, to save you, Michael. I'm going back to save you."

That caught his attention. "How in the hell is your leaving me going to save me?"

"Stuart, the castle's butler, said that if I do not come home, Lord William would take you to England for trial, for kidnapping and rape. You would be hanged, Michael."

Michael yanked her in his arms. "You would go back to save me?"

"Yes, Michael, I love you."

"I am going with you. Be damned with Lord Dunovan."

"Michael, it will be too dangerous. You don't know him. You saw what he did to me."

"I am going with you, Kathleen love," he stated, leaving no room for argument.

They walked back to the cottage in silence, both somber at what was to come. Michael stopped when he saw the black horse in front of his home and looked at Kathleen questionably.

"Stuart left the horse to be sure I would make it home by nightfall."

"I see."

"Michael, please stay here. I don't want anything to happen to you," Kathleen pleaded.

Kathleen knew what the next words cost Michael. She knew he hated the English and never wanted to see what they lived like while his family and him groveled in dirt.

"Nothing on earth can stop me from going to that castle with you. Besides, I have never seen gold plates." He tried to make it sound humorous, but it came out harshly.

"Michael, I think we should go get Webster O'Leary."

"Webster? Why should we get him?"

"He loves my mother. He should see her before she…she dies."

"Kathleen, Lord Dunovan threatened that if he ever came to the castle, he would kill him."

"He would not kill him since I am returning home. That's all he wants," Kathleen said softly.

"I will go get him. Do not leave, Kathleen," he warned.

"I will not."

Kathleen went into the small cottage and sat down on the worn sofa and thought, *Why on earth was this happening to me? Why, when I finally found happiness and love?*

"Why now?" she asked the ceiling. She of course received no answer; she had stopped believing in a higher being a long time ago. She sighed and gathered her things in a bundle. She picked up Michael's beloved *Hamlet* and put that with her things on impulse, as she remembered last night when Michael told her the story of the young prince. She was contemplating the fate of Ophelia, when she heard Michael bang open the door and call, "Kathleen, where are you?"

"In here," she said, going out to the living room with her things.

"Kathleen, I am so sorry. Maybe we can work things out once we get there," Webster O'Leary said somberly, infolding her in his arms.

"Once we get there, I should go in alone."

"I need to see my lass. I will help her. I have to save her, Kathleen. I will go get my horse."

"Maybe you could get one for me too?" Michael asked softly.

"No, I need you to ride with me. Please."

"Of course, love."

Webster returned from getting his horse to find Michael holding Kathleen tightly in his arms, not talking just standing there. He cleared his throat loudly. "If you are ready…"

Michael let go of Kathleen as he got on the black horse and held his hand out to help her up. Kathleen stood and looked up at Michael and caught her breath. He looked so handsome that she almost asked him if they could just leave. Leave Ireland forever and go somewhere safe and far away from Lord Dunovan. Maybe America. The urge was so strong that if her father was not there, she would have.

"Love, are you ready?" Michael asked.

Kathleen nodded, and against her will, she climbed up behind Michael on the horse. She gripped his waist tightly, and laying her cheek on his broad back, she began to cry.

* * * * * * *

The party of three arrived at Dunovan Castle just as darkness began to descend over the countryside. Michael felt Kathleen shudder behind him when she saw the castle.

"We are here, Kathleen love," he said gently as he slid down from the horse.

He held his arms up to help her down. She leaned down into his strong hands, which almost spanned her tiny waist. Michael brought her against his chest as she began to cry again.

"Hush, love. Please do not cry."

"Michael, go home now."

"And leave you alone? Never. What is wrong with you?"

"I have my father. He will protect me. Please, Michael, go home, or he will kill you."

"It would be better, lad. Safer," Webster said, putting an arm around his daughter's shoulders.

"Please, Michael, take the horse and leave. It would kill me to see you hurt or killed."

Michael took the beloved face in his hands and gently kissed her sweet mouth. "I love you, Kathleen."

"Me too, Michael. I love you so much. I am sorry, Michael, to have gotten you involved."

Michael wiped the tears off her cheeks with his thumbs. *How caring and sweet she really is,* he thought. "I will come back for you, love," he said kissing her again.

Kathleen waited until Michael got on the horse, handed her bundle to her, and rode off before throwing herself into her father's arms sobbing.

Webster held his daughter tightly before saying, "Kathleen darlin', it is getting late."

Kathleen pulled away from him, picked up her bundle and grasped her father's hand tightly in her own. Approaching the dark castle made them wonder what would wait for them once they got in. They walked to the door where Kathleen banged hesitantly. Receiving no answer, she had half a mind to leave right then and there, but she banged harder. This time her knocks were heard. Stuart swung open the door and said, "Welcome home, Miss Dunovan." Then under his breath added, "You are very brave."

Kathleen looked up at him and walked through the door silently. "Who are you?" she heard Stuart ask Webster behind her.

She spun around and announced, "He is my father."

Stuart digested the information without a change in expression. "Your...uh Lord Dunovan is waiting for you in the library."

Kathleen walked through her familiar former home without feeling. She spotted the inch thick dust on the furniture, the dirty carpets; obviously, there had been no parties since her birthday. She turned, sensing her father's hesitation.

"Are you coming?"

"Yes, lassie."

Kathleen took a deep breath and opened the door to the library. She walked in the dimly lit room to see Lord Dunovan sitting in front of the fireplace with a glass of clear liquid in his hands.

"Well well, if it isn't Lass's daughter and her father. Welcome home, Kathleen," he said sarcastically, holding up his glass.

"I want to see my mother," Kathleen said without wavering.

"It can wait. She is not going anywhere." William laughed cruelly as he took a swallow of what was in his glass. Webster took a step toward the gray-haired man who had hurt his love and his daughter, only to be stopped by Kathleen.

"Father, please."

"Oh, so it *is father,* is it? What did this Irish piece of scum do for you? Did he clothe you, feed you, give you a home?" William asked angrily.

"You would not let him. You and my mother's father took her away from him. And for what? Land. Because of land, you ruined many lives."

"My fault?! Ha, it was because of your mother, laying in the dirt with this, this person. Damn slut."

Webster broke free from his daughter's grasp on his arm, crossed the floor to stand in front of William.

William held up his hand and coolly said, "If you touch me, Mary will die right after she watches you die."

Webster took a step back from William's deadly calm words and said through clenched teeth, "I want to see Mary now."

"In time, you will see her, Mr. O'Leary. We have things to discuss first."

"Listen here, you sadistic bastard. You are lucky you are still alive this minute. If it had not been for Kathleen, you would have died many years ago. I want to see Lass now."

"I told you the night Kathleen was born that if you ever showed up here again I would kill you. Be grateful that you are still alive and that you will see Mary again."

Webster slumped down in a chair and looked longingly at out the library's doors to the stairs that led to Mary's rooms.

William waited until Webster sat down before he turned his gaze to Kathleen. He was taken back by how beautiful and proud she looked. Just like her mother, all those years ago. He knew how much she hated him and he relished in the thought of what he had to tell her. He would knock her down a peg or two, without even touching her. He stood up and moved slowly toward her. He lifted a hand toward her to touch her hair, but she jerked her head back from him.

"Did you have fun with the dirty Irish, Kathleen?"

"Yes."

"How much fun did you actually have?" he asked lewdly. Kathleen ignored him, and he continued with, "I heard that you were staying with a family by the name of Fitzpatrick."

"Yes."

"You were involved with the oldest son, Michael, was it?"

"Yes."

"Do you love him?"

"Yes," she said, unconsciously twisting the ring she wore on her finger. William saw the gesture and said, "I see. Do you love your mother and father, Kathleen?"

"Yes."

"Would you like to see them together again?"

"Yes," Kathleen said again, warily this time, wondering what William was up to.

"In order for your parents to see each other again, you will do what I say. You will forget about Fitzpatrick and marry Ryan Winchester. You will move with him to England and live like a lady."

"No! Please I love Michael. We were going to be married. We had plans—"

William grabbed her by the arm and forced her to look at him. "You will marry Winchester, or you and your parents die now. It is my land. I have the right."

Kathleen struggled to free herself, but it was hopeless. "You will never get away with this. Michael will—"

"If Michael ever comes near my property, I will kill him." William released her. "Will you marry Winchester?"

"No, Kathleen, don't do it," Webster said, standing up to put his hands gently on her shoulders. "Do not let him do to you what Lass' father did to us. You can leave, run away, find Fitzpatrick."

"I can not leave. He will find me, and everyone I love will die."

William smiled with satisfaction. Kathleen looked down at the ring with the delicately carved roses in it. Tears formed in her eyes as she thought of Michael, getting down on one knee and asking her to marry him.

Kathleen swallowed and looked up at her father. "Besides, I know Ryan. He is kind and gentle, a little on the slow side, but not cruel. Lord Dunovan, I will marry Ryan Winchester."

"Good. I knew you would see it my way. Ryan Winchester is upstairs now waiting for you. He has a ring or something. You will be married tomorrow."

"So soon?" Webster asked.

"The sooner the better. Kathleen's mother will die soon, and she should see her only daughter get married."

As if to confirm his statement, a maid ran down the stairs, past the green-eyed, light brown-haired man who had watched the dramatic scene unfold. The maid burst in the library.

"Beg your pardon, my lord, but Lady Dunovan had taken a turn for the worst."

"I would like to see my mother now."

"Very well. Make sure you are ready for the ceremony tomorrow," William said as he turned his back on Kathleen and her father. Kathleen and Webster ran up the stairs and burst into Mary's room to find her lying in her bed, pale with her eyes shut.

"Lass," Webster whispered.

She was still beautiful after all these years. He softly went toward the one thing that had kept him alive all the years they were apart. The hope that they would see each other again had kept him from killing himself the night Kathleen was born. He gently caressed her smooth cheek with the faint bruises along her jaw.

Mary opened her eyes and looked at him without really seeing him. "No.

Please, William. I do not know where Kathleen is." She tried to move away and winced in pain.

Webster listened and watched in horror as he realized Mary did not see him. She thought he was William coming to beat her once again.

"Lass, it is me, Webster," he said softly. Webster watched as her green-blue eyes went into focus and saw him.

"Webster? How?" She let her question trail off as she spotted Kathleen by the door. "Kathleen, you came back."

Kathleen walked closer to her mother's bed and kissed her forehead.

"Kathleen, I am sorry about everything."

"It is alright, Mother. I...I understand now what love is. Father had to see you again. I know what he went through." On a brighter note, she said, "From the time I met him, all he could talk about was you and how much he loved you."

Mary smiled weakly. "Thank you, Kathleen. I know this has cost you a lot, to bring Webster here and for you to come back. I suppose I will never know how much," she said, coughing up blood into a handkerchief.

Kathleen turned away from the tears in her mother's eyes and moved so her father could kneel down by her.

"Father, I think I am going to go out for a walk."

"Kathleen, be careful," he warned.

"I will. I will not leave the castle grounds." she promised.

Mary waited for her daughter to leave to say, "Webster, is it really you?"

Webster gently held her hand in his, thinking back to the night Kathleen was born, when she looked at him with wonder as she was now. "Aye, lass, it is me."

"I never thought I would hear you call me lass again."

"I will call you Mary if you like," he said tenderly.

Mary smiled at his teasing. "You may call me whatever you like." She gripped his hand tighter as she fought a spasm of pain.

"Lass, what happened?"

"William beat me when I told him I did not know where Kathleen was. He's obsessed with her. You have to help her. I am dying, Webster. I have many internal injuries. Plus, I have come down with the cough."

"No you can not leave me. Please, lass, stay with me."

"It will be better. We will meet again where we can be happy. You must take care of Kathleen."

Webster nodded as he swallowed the painful lump in his throat and tears blurred his vision.

"Kathleen gave up a lot to come home, didn't she? She said she found true love. What did she mean?"

"She was to marry Michael Fitzpatrick until William forced her home. She will marry Ryan Winchester tomorrow. She came home to save you and Michael."

Mary closed her eyes and said, "Tell her that I am sorry. She's quite a girl, our daughter, isn't she? Tell her I love her." Webster felt her grip on his hand loosen. "No, lass, please don't go. Not yet."

"I love you, Webster."

Webster sighed in relief when all Mary did was go into a deep sleep. He gently touched his lips to hers, then moved a chair close to her side and sat back to watch her sleep.

"I love you too, lass," he whispered.

* * * * * * *

Kathleen, after leaving her parents, decided to go for a walk outside. After promising William that she would not leave the castle grounds, she walked toward the stables. She wiped the tears from her cheeks and entered the stables. It was quiet and peaceful in the large wooden stables. It was a place for Kathleen to rest and think. She could not believe that William was forcing her to marry Ryan Winchester tomorrow. It was so soon. She barely knew Ryan; she had only seen him at parties. It was true though that he was nice and would never hurt her the way William had hurt her mother, but she did not love him.

She wanted to marry Michael. Michael, with his beautiful blue eyes and thick black hair. Michael, with his broad shoulders and muscular chest. Michael was the one who had taught her how to laugh again and given her love. Michael was the one, the only one, she wanted to marry.

Kathleen sighed as the tears formed once gain in her eyes and leaned against a wooden stall. Next week would have been her wedding. It was not to have been a large celebration, like the double wedding of Michael's siblings, but it would have been beautiful. Michael had given her money to decorate the cottage with new things. Kathleen remembered as she had protested, saying that he needed the money he earned and she was happy the way the cottage looked. Michael had ignored her and gave her the money, saying, "Kathleen love, I want you to make this your home where you could be happy for the rest of your life."

Kathleen knew that if they were to get married, she would be happy with Michael. If only she had not returned, maybe…

No, she chided herself. Her parents had to see each other again. She would have never forgiven herself if her mother had died without seeing her or Webster again. Kathleen looked up as she heard a horse snort and shift, nervous in the hay. What was wrong now? An intruder? William coming to hurt her? She picked up a pitchfork, ready to defend herself, and slowly went toward the restless horse.

"What is it, boy? What is the matter?" Kathleen asked, softly moving closer still to the black horse. Kathleen was about to chalk it up to her wild imagination when suddenly she saw a dark figure move toward her in the shadows.

"If you come near me, I am going to stab you with this fork," she threatened, holding the fork higher over her heard, acting far braver than she felt.

"Kathleen?" the dark figure asked, cautiously moving closer to her.

"Michael?" she asked incredulously.

"Aye, love, it is me. Are you planning to fill me full of holes with that fork?" he teased as he noticed her still clutching to the fork.

Kathleen threw the fork aside and flung herself into Michael's outstretched arms. She sobbed against his chest and felt his hands pull her tighter against him as his fingers dug into her back.

"You know, love, you are the only female I know who cries more tears than there are drops of water in the sea."

Kathleen looked up into his handsome face and said, "Oh, Michael, I thought I would never see you again."

"Kathleen, I told you I would come back." Michael looked down into the beautiful face that he loved so much and saw the pain in her eyes. "Kathleen love, it has been only a few hours since I saw you. What has happened?"

Had it really only been a couple of hours since she had last seen Michael? It seemed like years after all she had been through.

"Kathleen? Tell me what happened. Your mother, is she all right?"

Kathleen broke free from Michael to sit down in the hay. Michael squatted down on his heels in front of her and tried to make out her expression in the darkness, lit only by the moonlight.

"Michael, my mother is dying. Webster is with her now."

Michael gently cupped her face with his palms and forced her to meet his eyes. "I am very sorry, love. What happened?"

"I told you. William has beaten her, plus she has a cough." Kathleen swallowed and looked up at him with tears in her eyes. "She used to be so beautiful, Michael. I...I never told anyone this, but I admired her so much. She lived in that stupid castle without complaining, was always the perfect hostess, admired for her looks and manner. She always tried to make me happy. She knew I felt trapped and unloved. She let me ride my horse, Snowflake, away from the castle bounds when William was in England. I would ride and ride, wishing I never had to go back, like now. I love her, Michael, and that is why you have to understand what I have to do."

"What do you have to do, Kathleen?"

"You have to promise me that you will not get upset."

"Kathleen, please tell me."

"Do you swear not to get angry?"

"I promise! Now tell me."

"Tomorrow I am to marry Ryan Winchester."

Michael jerked his hands away from Kathleen, stood up and, glaring down at her, asked in a hoarse whisper, "Just who in the hell is Ryan Winchester?"

"My betrothed."

"Your what?!" Michael asked with shock.

"My betrothed," Kathleen repeated and hurriedly continued, as she saw Michael turn his back on her, with, "Michael, it is not what you think. I tried to explain about you, but he would not listen to me. Are you listening to me, Michael? In order for Webster to see my mother, and for you not to go to trial, I had to agree to the marriage. Michael, please, I love you. Are you listening to me?" she begged a little hysterically as the tears poured down her cheeks.

Kathleen did not see Michael move, but she felt him grab her and lift her to her feet. She fell against the hard familiar chest and sobbed.

"Kathleen," Michael whispered before lifting her face up to his and bending his head to touch her lips with his.

Kathleen kissed him back, trying to show him how much she loved him.

Michael lifted his head away from Kathleen and looked down at her. He loved her so much. How could he let her marry someone else?

"Kathleen, why don't we just leave? We could go now, right now, and no one will know."

"Michael, I can not just leave. My mother—"

"Your mother has Webster. Let's go, love. We could leave Ireland. Maybe go to that new land, America. We could have a family. There are no restrictions there; everyone has a chance…."

"Michael, stop. We can not go. William will kill Webster and my mother. He will find us and kill us too."

"Kathleen, your mother is going to die anyway, and Webster would like to be with her. I could protect you."

"I do not believe you just said that. You would allow William to kill innocent people just to have me? I thought doctors were supposed to save lives, not let people die."

Michael winced at her harsh words and knew she was right. "I am sorry, Kathleen. I just can not bear to leave you here. I have never loved anyone like I love you, Kathleen. We were meant to be together."

"I know, Michael. But we cannot. I will never stop loving you. Maybe one day we will be together." Michael held her tighter, knowing it was time to leave and not be able to do it. "Michael, I am so sorry. If I would have known what would have happened, I would never have left Dunovan Castle."

"Kathleen love, then we would never have met. Don't you know it is better to have loved and lost than never to have loved at all?"

"What will you do now, Michael?"

"Kill Lord Dunovan?" he tried to tease, but it came out hoarsely, as he knew it was what he wanted to do. "Maybe I'll go to London, maybe go to school. There is nothing left for me to stay in Ireland." *Now that we will not be married*, he added silently. Kathleen held him tighter, trying to prolong the farewell. "What are you going to do, Kathleen?"

"Lord Dunovan mentioned something about being a lady in England, but I know Ryan owns land and a home in Ireland. I would like to stay here, but I'm really not sure."

"Kathleen, I'm going to miss you so much," Michael whispered as he brought his head down for one last kiss. Kathleen kissed him back, trying to make it last as long as she could. She knew she would have to remember this kiss for a lifetime. Michael finally broke away and said, "Goodbye, Kathleen love. I love you. Never, ever forget that."

"Do you want your ring back?"

"No, you keep that, and remember that if you ever need me, I will find you."

"I love you, Michael. Don't you forget that," she said to his back as he turned and walked away. She waited until the darkness swallowed him, to sit down in the soft hay and cry.

* * * * * * *

Kathleen woke on her wedding day sick to her stomach. After vomiting into her basin, she washed her face and hair. As she was pulling her hair back away from her face, she realized why she was sick. She knew the signs from her maid last year who was married to the horse keeper. Her maid had been sick for weeks before Kathleen finally told her to see a doctor. Kathleen remembered as her maid had come home bursting with happiness, for she was with child.

"Damn!" Kathleen said softly. A baby. Michael's baby. What was she going to do? She quickly got dressed, putting on a royal blue silk dress with a full skirt and heart shaped neckline. She left her rooms and went down the hall to see her mother.

Webster was opening the door to walk out when Kathleen reached the door. He shut the door behind him and said in a grave voice, "Kathleen, your mother passed away in her sleep."

Kathleen nodded her head and held her father, but she did not cry. She had cried all the tears she was going to.

Chapter Eleven

Ryan Winchester waited patiently by a low fire in the library of Dunovan Castle for his wife. He smiled as she recalled how serene and calm Kathleen had looked that afternoon at their wedding. He had always admired Kathleen. He thought she was very brave to live with the unsavory Lord Dunovan, without complaining. The man was, in his opinion, a son of a bitch. Ryan knew Lord Dunovan would and had done anything to get his way. To live like royalty, he walked over the backs of peasants. For land he gave his daughter away. But Kathleen really was not his daughter, was she? Ryan was still confused about the scene he had witnessed yesterday. It sounded like Kathleen was illegitimate. But if that were true, why would Lord Dunovan have raised Kathleen as his own? Ryan sighed. He would have to ask her about that.

Ryan knew that Kathleen did not love him but had married him to save her mother. Ryan knew he should not have forced Kathleen to marry him. He should have let her go with Michael, whatever his name is. He just could not let her go. No matter how Kathleen felt about him, he loved her. He loved Kathleen for her courage, her sweetness, her beauty. He remembered how beautiful she had looked today with her golden auburn hair that flowed unbound down her back. How lovely she looked in her royal blue gown. She was perfect like a doll. And she was his. His wife.

She might be your wife, but she does not love you, his inner voice kept reminding him. He knew Kathleen did not love him and never would like she loved Michael. He would just have to make it work between them, no matter what it cost him. Whatever she wanted, she could have. He swung his head around as he heard the door to the library open.

Kathleen walked into the room in a plain black gown with a high neckline that covered her throat. She had pulled her hair back into a tight bun. Although she was very pale, she seemed steady as she walked towards him and sat down across from him.

"Your grace." She nodded in his direction.

Ryan hid a smile at the title she used on him. He remembered the shock on her face when the archbishop had greeted him as Duke Winchester. It was the only emotion she had showed all day. This surprised him, since her mother had just died the night before.

"Kathleen, I believe there are some issues we need to discuss." He waited for her nod before suggesting. "Would you like some wine?"

"Yes please, my lord."

Kathleen watched as Ryan got up to fetch the bottle and a glass. Good, maybe she'll get good and drunk. She had decided today that he was pleasant looking with light brown hair and holly green eyes. He was tall, not as tall as Michael was, but she only reached Ryan's shoulders. He was trim and fit and looked nice in his emerald green jacket, black trousers and knee high boots. Ryan turned and caught Kathleen assessing him. "Will I do as your husband?"

Kathleen blushed and said, "Kind of late one way or the other, is it not, my lord?"

"You are right of course. Since we are married, I would appreciate it if you call me Ryan and not 'my lord' or 'your grace.' You make me sound old, like my father. My father's dead, you know. You don't want me dead – or do you?"

"I never wanted you dead, my…er…Ryan. I just did not want to marry you."

"Ah," he said as he sat down and leaned across to hand her a glass. "This is what we need to discuss, Kathleen. I overheard you and Lord Dunovan talking yesterday. Maybe you could tell me what has taken place?"

Kathleen sighed. She supposed he should know about what had gone on. It just hurt too much to think about it. She took a sip of wine and began. She started by telling him about her birthday party. He had of course attended but never knew where she had gone after they had danced. He was stunned to learn that she had been beaten by William and thrown out of the castle. She went on to tell him about the Fitzpatricks. He questioned her about Michael after she had finished.

"Kathleen, I can see that there was something special about Michael. Please tell me about him."

Kathleen smiled when she thought of Michael and when they first met, when she was conscious of course.

"Michael did not like me very much when I arrived at his home, but the other members of his family did not mind much. They helped me, saved my life. They made me one of their family, passing me off as Elizabeth's niece. A cousin to Matthew, Michael and Beth. Beth even made me a bride's maid at her wedding."

"And Michael?" Ryan prompted when he could tell she was stalling.

"Michael wants to be a doctor. He was the one who cleaned my wounds. He is very proud. He does not like living in poverty, but he resents the rich. He resented me. We did not speak much, unless it was sarcastic remarks, until Beth's wedding. His sister Beth and his brother's fiancée were best friends and planned a double wedding. It was so beautiful, unlike…" Kathleen gasped as what she was about to say.

"Unlike ours, Kathleen?" he asked with mild sarcasm.

"You have to admit, William telling me, right before the wedding, to behave during the ceremony or he will kill Webster, does not make a happy ceremony."

"What about Webster? Who is he?" Ryan knew, but it was good for her to discuss this.

"Ryan, Webster is my real father. He met my mother years ago here in Ireland. They fell in love. They were taken away from each other, and my mother was forced to marry William. She was pregnant with me when she married."

"So you are not William's child?"

"No. I am illegitimate. Are you angry?"

Ryan hid another smile. She really was quite amusing. He said, "No, Kathleen, I am not angry. I am glad. I never did like William much. Cold hearted bastard."

Kathleen gasped. "Then why on earth would you agree to marry me?"

Ryan got on his knees in front of Kathleen. "Don't you know, Kathleen? I love you. I always have. I will be a good husband to you, and I promise I will not act too stupid for you."

Kathleen flushed. "You heard that? I am sorry. I was under a little strain yesterday."

"That is quite understandable." He leaned in to kiss her, but she moved her head, and he missed. "Kathleen, I promise I will never ever hurt you."

"That's not it, Ryan."

Ryan heard the distress in her voice. "What is it, Kathleen?"

"I love Michael so much, Ryan. We were going to get married next week."

"Did he give you that gold ring?"

"Yes. You won't make me get rid of it, will you?" she asked in alarm.

"Kathleen, I do not want to take anything away from you. Not memories, not the ring. Wear it all you like. I'll even clean it for you. All I want to do is love and protect you. All I ask in return is a little kindness, and when you feel up to it, I will take you as my wife."

"What are you saying?"

"I love you, Kathleen. I will never force you to do anything you do not want to."

"Thank you."

"You are welcome."

Kathleen made herself look at Ryan and saw the honesty and sincerity in his face. She had to tell him everything.

"Ryan, there is something else."

"What is it?" he asked softly.

Kathleen hesitated. "Michael and I...I am with child, Ryan."

Ryan sighed and stood up. He loved Kathleen, but this was getting to be a bit much. How much was he expected to take? But then he remembered what Kathleen herself had gone through living in Dunovan Castle with William as her father. No one should have to live through such hell. "I will take care of the child as if it were my own."

Kathleen stood up in front of her husband. "Thank you, Ryan, for all your kindness and understanding. I will do my best to honor your family name. I will make you a proud Duchess. And when the time is right, I will give you legitimate heirs."

Ryan held his hand out to her and smiled when she gently placed her small hand into his.

"Thank you, Kathleen."

Kathleen's warm golden eyes met Ryan's holly green ones. Both showed promise and hope. Maybe things would be all right after all.

* * * * * * *

Matthew Fitzpatrick was whistling the next weekend when he walked into his home. He smiled when he saw his lovely wife standing over the fire, stirring whatever was in the pot with a wooden spoon. He quietly walked up behind her, put his arms around her waist and presented her with one perfect red rose.

Gabrielle jumped when she felt Matthew and scolded him.

"But, sweetheart, I brought you a flower," he protested.

"Matthew, you should not sneak up on people," she said as she put the lid back on the pot then turned in his arms.

"I do not sneak up on 'people,' Gabrielle. Just you."

"You really are incorrigible, Matthew."

"Aye," he agreed good-naturedly.

"Why ever did I marry you?"

"You love me."

"Oh really? What ever gave you that idea?" she teased.

Matthew smiled as she drew her closer and brought his mouth down on hers. "I can tell you love me because you respond so well."

"Matthew!"

Matthew laughed as she struggled and moved away from him. "What's for dinner, lass?"

"Nothing for you, you beast."

Matthew reached out and pulled the plaid ribbon out of her shimmering blond hair that kept her hair out of her face.

"Now see what you did? I had that there for a reason, Matthew," she scolded, snatching the ribbon back.

"You should not insult me. Now are you going to tell me what's for dinner or am I going to have to spank you?"

Gabrielle gasped. "You would not dare!"

"Don't you bet on it," he warned, raising his hand.

Gabrielle laughed and said, "How does lamb and cabbage sound?"

"Wonderful. It's been a long day, sweetheart."

"Why don't you sit down, Matthew?"

Gabrielle dished out dinner and poured the ale before sitting down across from her husband.

"At least tomorrow is Sunday, Matthew. A day off. Maybe we could go for a picnic after mass?"

"I would love to," he said smiling at her.

They ate in compatible silence until they were both satisfied. "What did you do today, Gabrielle?"

"I had lunch with Beth."

"And what did you two clucking chickens gossip about today?"

"Matthew, please we do not gossip. We have highly intelligent conversations regarding people we know."

"What did you intelligently discuss today, darlin'?"

"Michael and Kathleen. Why, we have not seen them in such a long while. We were wondering what they could be up to."

"If I know my brother, I know what they are up to," Matthew said with a leer.

"Matthew!"

"Don't look so shocked, Gabrielle. You saw how they were at Beth and Dutch's. They really love each other. That's why they are getting married next week, remember."

"I suppose, but Beth and I really do need to finish planning the wedding with Kathleen."

Matthew got up to get more ale and cabbage. "I do know what you mean though about not seeing them. Michael did not go to work today or yesterday, and the day before, he left right after lunch."

"I guess he is all right, or we would have heard something," Gabrielle concluded. "Matthew, would you get me some more food please?"

"More food? You already had two helpings, sweetheart. Do you want to get fat?"

"Will you stop loving me if I did become fat?"

"Of course not. It is just that you usually do not eat a lot of food," he reasoned with her as he returned her plate and sat back down.

He watched as she ate her third helping without stopping. He had never seen her eat this way before.

"Do you want dessert, Matthew?" Gabrielle asked as she cleared the table.

"Sure." Matthew watched as she put a large piece of pound cake onto her plate, and an idea grew into his head. "Sweetheart, how is that virus you had a couple of months ago?"

Gabrielle paused between bites to reply, "Fine, Matthew."

"Is it all gone?"

"No."

"Really? How long will you have it?"

"About nine months," Gabrielle said with a happy smile.

"Gabrielle, why didn't you tell me?"

"I was waiting for the proper time."

"How far along are you?"

"Two months."

"And when would be the proper time to tell me?"

"Now?" she suggested.

Matthew laughed and pulled her around the table to sit her in his lap. He gently laid his palm on her still flat stomach.

"A baby. Our baby," he said with awe.

"Are you happy, Matthew?"

"Happy?" He choked. "She asks me if I'm happy." He looked into her beautiful face and smiled. "Well, actually, darlin' I am a little angry at you."

"Angry? Why?"

"I thought the happiest day of my life was when you agreed to marry me, but I was wrong. You could not have made me any happier than you have at this moment."

Gabrielle threw her arms around Matthew's neck and buried her face into his warm neck. "Matthew, I love you so much."

"Thank you, sweetheart."

"Thank you? For what?"

"For giving me a child."

"It really was not all up to me, you know. You helped – a little."

Matthew laughed, pulled her closer and kissed her. They were engrossed in their celebration when a loud knock sounded at the door. Matthew tried to ignore it, but it was persistent, and Gabrielle pulled away from him.

"Matthew, the door."

"They will come back later," he promised, reaching for her again. The knock came again.

"I really should go see who it is, Matthew."

Matthew sighed and let go of his wife. "Whoever it is better be important," he grumbled.

Gabrielle ran a hand through her hair and smoothed down her skirt before opening the door. What she saw made her gasp. It was Michael. But it did not look like him. Gabrielle had never seen him look anything but immaculate. She knew he always tried to look his best to prove that the Irish had class like the English. Tonight, however, he looked worse than the lowest potato farmer did. His eyes were bloodshot like he had not slept in days. His clothes were rumpled and worn. He smelled like whiskey, but he did not seem drunk as he stood looking down at her.

"Michael. Hello." Gabrielle stepped back from the coldness in his beautiful eyes. "How is Kathleen?" she ventured again.

Silence greeted her inquiry.

"Sweetheart, who is it?" Matthew called.

Gabrielle stepped away from Michael and went to get Matthew.

"It's your brother."

"Shut the door. I said it should be someone important," he joked.

"Matthew, something's wrong with Michael," Gabrielle whispered softly.

Matthew looked down into his wife's pale face and saw that something really was wrong.

"Gabrielle, wait here. I'll go see what it is."

Matthew went outside and was as shocked to see his brother in this shape as his wife had been. He shut the door and stepped in front of Michael.

"You look like hell, Michael," he said without preamble.

"That is exactly how I feel," Michael said icily.

"What happened? Why do you look like this?"

"Kathleen," he said softly.

"Yes, what about her? Did you have a fight?"

"No."

"Are you going to tell me what happened, or am I going to have to beat it out of you?" Matthew shouted at him.

"She's gone, Matthew," he stated softly.

The tension left as Matthew saw the pain in Michael's eyes. "What went wrong?"

"Lord Dunovan beat her mother to death. Kathleen went back so Webster could be with her mother when she died."

"Webster O'Leary? Why would he want to see Kathleen's mother?"

"He was Kathleen's father."

Matthew swallowed in surprise. "Kathleen was Irish?"

"Half Irish. Lord Dunovan was the one who had beaten her that night she came to us. He threw her out of the castle and beat her mother. But he's obsessed with her. He took her away. He took my Kathleen away."

"Maybe she will be back when her mother dies," Matthew suggested hopefully.

"She will not," Michael replied softly.

"How do you—"

"She's married," Michael cut in.

"Married?" he asked incredulously.

"She had to marry who Lord Dunovan wanted her to or Webster died. I saw Kathleen the day before yesterday. Lord Dunovan is not happy with me. My life is in danger here."

"Michael, I am so sorry. I have never seen you happier than when you were with Kathleen. What are you going to do now?"

"I am going to England."

"England? But you hate England, Michael."

"The English. I hate the English. I have never been to England."

"It is so far a way though."

"Well, I sure as hell am not staying here. Not without Kathleen. Besides, not all the English are bad."

"She was half Irish, Michael. Give her credit."

"I love her so much, Matthew."

"I know."

"I am leaving tonight. I am going to burn the cottage. Lord Dunovan will never know the difference, and the cottage has been in our family for ages. I could not bear anyone else living in it. Not after Kathleen fixed it up for us."

"I understand, Michael. Will you write to me?"

"Yes. I'll try to keep you informed."

"What should I tell Beth?"

Michael looked taken back. He had forgotten about his sister. "Tell her the truth."

Matthew reached out and embraced his brother tightly. "Take care, Michael. I know at times we have not always seen eye to eye, but I do love you."

"I love you too, Matthew."

Matthew watched as his brother turned and walked away from him. *Damn,* he thought, *why did this have to happen?* He went back into his home and grabbed Gabrielle. He held tightly to her, never wanting to let go.

"Matthew?" she questioned.

Matthew shuddered as he thought of how he would feel if Gabrielle were to be taken away from him.

"Just let me hold you, Gabrielle," he whispered tenderly.

Matthew hoped his brother could make a good life for himself in England, but he doubted it. He had no idea how Michael felt to lose Kathleen, nor did he ever want to know, he thought holding his wife tighter.

"I love you, Gabrielle."

"I love you, Matthew."

Matthew suddenly knew how he would feel if he did not have Gabrielle. He would want to die.

* * * * * * *

Death was what Michael was thinking of as he lit a match and dropped it into the hay he had spread out around the cottage. How many of his ancestors died in this cottage? Probably too many to count, he reasoned with himself. Michael watched as his family home finally caught the fire and started to blaze. He watched the fire burn and crackle while he thought of Kathleen.

The first time she had spoken to him, demanding to know who he was, despite the fact she was in his home. When he changed her bandages in the sunlight and realized how beautiful she was. The first time they kissed after the crazy fight they had about getting married. The day she had finally told him why she had left home. That was the day he finally admitted to himself he cared for her. All the times after she had showed her love for him. The way she greeted him after work, making him smile.

He had never been happier than when he was with her. He remembered how excited she was when he had given her money to decorate the cottage. They were eating Sunday dinner when he had looked up at her and caught her staring at him

"Kathleen love, what is it?"

Kathleen blushed. "I was just thinking how handsome you are."

Michael smiled. "And just how handsome am I?"

"Do not be conceited, Michael."

"But I am conceited. You remember when you called me a snob? You yelled at me when I told you to leave my home."

"Which time was that? From the minute I got here, all you've wanted to do was get rid of me."

Michael reached over the table to touch her smooth cheek. "Not anymore, love. All I want is to keep you by my side."

"Always?"

"Forever," he promised. "Kathleen, you know I can not give you everything you had at Dunovan Castle."

"Michael, please. How many times have we gone through this? All I want is you."

"Kathleen, let me finish. You know I can not move, but I would like to give you money to decorate the house they way you want it."

"Michael, you do not have—"

"I want to," he insisted.

Kathleen smiled and moved to sit on his lap. "Thank you, Michael," she said, locking her beautiful eyes with his.

"For what, love?"

"For making me happy, Michael. How am I ever going to repay you?"

"Tell me how handsome I am."

Kathleen giggled and kissed him.

Michael sighed and moved away from the fire as he remembered coming home from work everyday to find something new in the cottage and how

Kathleen had shyly asked him if he liked what she was doing with the decorations. Damn Lord Dunovan for ruining his life. How was he going to live without her?

Michael picked up his bag and turned his back on his home one final time.

* * * * * * *

Michael arrived in England two weeks later, then went to London. He hated England on sight; it was gray, wet and dreary. England was nothing like Ireland; he missed the green grass and rolling hills. But Ireland was not his home anymore, not without one beautiful golden-eyed, auburn-haired girl. Michael let out a frustrated breath of air and moved down the crowded London streets.

If Michael hated England, he loathed London more. The busy loud people pushing and shoving. London was not like his home at all. Where he came from, the people were slower, friendlier toward one another. Michael shifted the small bag he carried, continuing to walk through the crowd. He ignored the stares he received from the people passing him. Obviously, these people had never seen an Irish farmer before, he thought, and then added bitterly to himself, even though most of them live off of our sweat.

Michael did not realize that he looked nothing like and Irish farmer. Dressed in black pants and a white shirt with a small amount of lace around the collar, which was open to reveal his tanned muscular chest, he resembled an aristocrat. People could not help but stop and stare at him. No one had seen anyone more handsome or terrifying. With Michael's brilliant blue eyes flashing with anger, people could not help but stay away from him.

Michael continued walking, looking for an inn to stay in that he could afford until he found a job. A crowd gathered in the street delayed him, however. He pushed his way through the swarm of people to see what was wrong. He assessed the matter with one glance. A horse drawn carriage had turned over, managing somehow to fling its occupant out. The man now lay trapped under the wheel. The driver was shouting for a doctor.

Michael immediately dropped his bag and rushed forward.

"Are you a doctor?" the driver asked with a scowl.

"I am the closest you'll find in this crowd."

"You are Irish," he accused.

"Aye."

Michael squatted down next to the white-haired man. His eyes were closed. Michael felt for a pulse and found one. He stepped back and turned toward the unpleasant driver, who asked, "Is he dead?"

"No, he merely fainted from the pain of the fall. He probably has a few broken ribs, but he could be seriously injured if we leave the carriage on his leg."

"If you hurt the Duke, you will be hanged and flogged," the driver warned.

Michael was tired of his life being threatened. "If you do not find some men to help me remove the damned carriage off of him, he will die. And it will be your fault, not mine."

The man blanched and decided to do as he asked, yelling into the crowd. Four men appeared and quickly helped remove the weight off of the white-haired man. Michael gently moved him away from the carriage. He kneeled down beside the man and waited for him to wake; when he finally did, he tried to spring up but groaned in pain.

"Sidney, what the hell is going on?" he bellowed.

"Please calm down. You will hurt yourself," Michael said, placing his hands on the man's shoulders.

"Who the hell are you? What the hell am I doing in the damn street?" The man stopped to catch his breath. He winced in pain. "Sidney, where the hell are you? If you do not come here right this instant and explain why I am laying in the street, you can find work else where."

The driver, who was obviously the one named Sidney, stepped forward. "Yes, my lord?"

"Do not give me that 'yes, my lord' garbage. You better tell me why I am laying in the street and why this young man is hovering over me like a bee."

"We had an accident. The horses saw something that made them jump, which caused the carriage to turn over. Somehow you were thrown out and caught under a wheel. You then blacked out, and I asked the crowd for a doctor. This man came and—"

"Saved my life?" the man suggested.

"Well, yes. But you do not understand. This man is—"

"Yes, what is he?" he prompted.

"Irish," Michael provided.

"Irish?" the man questioned.

"Aye."

"Good. No one English would try to help me. Now help me up, young man. You can have dinner with me and my daughter."

"Well, I don't know," Michael protested. "You don't really know me."

"This is true. You don't know me either. I am Edward Worthington, the duke of Liverpool."

"My name is Michael Fitzpatrick, from Ireland."

"Now that we know each other, help me up."

Michael helped the man to his feet and put the man's arm around his shoulder. He walked him over to the now righted carriage.

"How should I address you?" Michael asked once Sidney had gotten the carriage moving again.

"You do not know the proper edicate to greet nobility?"

"I never had a need to learn them," Michael said bitterly.

"A farmer, are you?"

"Yes, I was."

"How did you know what was wrong with me? Sidney said I might have some broken ribs."

"I had always wanted to be a doctor," Michael stated shortly. "What shall I call you?"

"You may call me Edward, although I am not sure how long that will last though once you meet my daughter."

Michael swallowed. He had had enough of English girls. He was not looking forward to meeting any snotty English brat. Edward noticed Michael stiffen at the mention of his daughter.

"Do not worry. Clara is the sweetest girl you will ever meet. She will only be angry that you call me Edward and not Eddie, which I despise."

"How old is your daughter?" Michael feigned interest.

"Eighteen. She's unmarried, but not looking for anyone. She is not like most girls. She would rather take care of her old father than got to balls and parties." He caught Michael yawn and said, "You are not interested. That is all right."

"No...uh...Edward, it has been a long journey, and if your driver would drop me off at the nearest inn, it would be greatly appreciated."

"Nonsense, Michael, you may stay with me tonight. We have plenty of room."

"No, I think I really should stay at an inn."

"If you're worried about Clara, she will not attack you. It would mean a lot to me to let you stay at my house tonight. You saved my life."

"Only tonight," Michael warned.

Michael settled back in the deep cushions and slowly drifted off to sleep.

Edward watched the young man sleep and wondered what had made him insist he stay at his home. He wondered what or who had made Michael come to London. He was different than any man he had ever met. He was proud, intelligent, handsome and hurt. Edward knew enough about love after losing Sara, his wife, and watching Clara lose her fiancé last year to influenza. Michael had lost someone special and was deeply hurt by it; he could see it in his eyes. Maybe Michael and Clara could help each other.

Edward steeled back and made plans for his daughter and this beautiful man next to him. He would take it slowly at first, but before he died, he would see them together. He needed a son to carry on his name.

With that thought, Edward moved to a more comfortable position to ease his throbbing ribs and dozed the rest of the way home.

Chapter Twelve

"Push, Kathleen!" Ryan screamed at the writhing girl on the bed.

"Ryan, I can not. Please just let me die."

"Damn you, Kathleen! If you do not help, I am going to sit on you. I really will."

Kathleen brought her legs up and pushed as hard as she could, screaming with the effort. She never knew such pain existed. She thought she would at least pass out, but no, the damn baby wanted to come out. It had been so easy to get pregnant. Why could it not be easy to give birth?

"What can I do to help?" Webster asked Ryan.

"Use this damp cloth and wipe off her forehead," he said, handing the cloth to him and turning back to Kathleen. "Kathleen darling, think of Michael. It is his baby; he would kill himself if he knew you died in childbirth for his baby. Now push."

"Ryan…the pain…is too…much."

"God damn it, Kathleen, do not be selfish. Think of Michael."

"Michael?" she whispered, thinking of the handsome man who had given her this child.

She would hurt him the next time she saw him. Ryan she decided was right though. Michael would die if he knew that she had died in childbirth. She pushed as hard as she could.

"That's it. Kathleen. The head is coming. Push again."

Kathleen howled in pain and swore a string of oaths neither Webster nor Ryan had ever heard come out of a lady's mouth before.

Ryan swallowed a laugh. "One more, Kathleen. You can do it," Ryan coaxed nicely.

Kathleen pushed again, and finally to everyone's satisfaction, a baby's loud cry rang through the air. Kathleen lay back against the pillows exhausted and damp.

"You did it, Kathleen."

"Thank you for helping, Ryan. Sorry for the bad language. What did I have?"

"A beautiful baby girl," Ryan answered, bringing the baby toward her.

"She is precious," Kathleen said in awe, looking at down at the tiny girl. The baby opened her eyes when her mother softly kissed her head. Kathleen gasped when she saw the color of eyes. They were Michael's brilliant sapphires colored eyes. She had heard that all babies were born with blue eyes, but she knew her baby's would stay that color.

"What do you plan on naming her?" Webster asked from the corner.

"Willow. I am going to name her Willow."

"I like it, lassie," Webster said, going over to Kathleen's bedside.

Kathleen lifted the child to give to her father. "Would you take her to get cleaned while I speak with Ryan?"

Webster nodded and quietly left the room, shutting the door. Kathleen closed her eyes for a moment and reflected on the last year. It was one year ago today, January second, when she had first met Michael. Who would have thought she would be seventeen with a baby by Michael Fitzpatrick, an Irishman? She wondered where Michael was. She had missed him during her pregnancy. Ryan was very kind and supportive, especially since it was not his child. But Ryan was not Michael; it was not the same.

She missed Michael calling out to her when he came home from work, "Kathleen love, I'm home." Or his teasing words about how she was decorating the cottage, "How much money did this cost me, love?" "Kathleen love do you want us to be beggars in the street?" She wished he could have been here to see their beautiful daughter. She knew from Webster that he had left to go to England. Lord Dunovan had insisted that she and Ryan stay at Dunovan Castle. He had made Ryan his heir and business partner, which forced them to stay, since Ryan's estates were on the other side of Ireland and in England. Since William had made her stay in the castle, she insisted Webster stay with them.

Kathleen knew her father and William hated each other, but they never fought in front of her. She suspected Ryan had threatened them since she was pregnant. Webster looked like he wanted to strangle William every time they saw one another. She knew it was selfish of her, but she had needed her father with her. She had to have someone with her.

"What are you thinking about, little one?" Ryan asked, breaking into her thoughts.

"How kind you have been to me, Ryan."

Ryan moved to sit next to her and brushed her hair off of her cheek.

"You had a beautiful daughter, Kathleen. I will be proud to give her my name."

"Thank you."

Ryan watched as she stared off into space. She was exhausted from her ordeal. He was surprised when she started to laugh. "Kathleen, what is the matter with you?" Perhaps she was having a delayed reaction to the birth. "Kathleen, calm down. You will hurt yourself."

Kathleen swallowed and tried to calm herself by looking into Ryan's eyes. "Are you calm now?"

She nodded with a little giggle.

"Will you tell me what that was about?"

She swallowed another giggle and said, "When I was giving birth to Willow and not sure I would make it, you said—" She broke off laughing again. When she finally sobered, she said, "You said you were going to sit on me."

"And you found that amusing?"

Kathleen nodded her head vigorously.

"Kathleen, I think I will let you sleep now."

She realized that he thought she was crazy and started laughing again.

Ryan raised an eyebrow at her and shook his head. He bent down to kiss her on the head. "Good night, Kathleen."

"Thank you for helping with Willow, Ryan."

"It was my pleasure, Kathleen. Good night. Sit on you. I am sorry I said that."

"That's all right. It seemed to work," she said, laughing again.

Ryan closed the door and smiled to himself as she heard her happy laughter throughout the castle.

* * * * * * *

Later that same night, Webster hesitated in front of the library doors. He had been summoned by Lord Dunovan to meet him. Webster wondered what Lord Dunovan could possibly say to him. After Kathleen had laid down the law that her father was going to stay in Dunovan Castle, if she had to, Webster had tried to stay away from him as much as possible. He loathed the man, but his daughter needed him, so he made the sacrifice and agreed to stay. It was the least he could do since Kathleen had given up her happiness for her mother to see him one last time.

Webster wished Ryan had the guts to move Kathleen and now the baby away from the castle. He wanted them as far away from the evil of Lord Dunovan as possible. Ryan was a wealthy man in his own right, but being the youngest son, he was last in line to the family's wealth. So here they stayed living on edge in a madman's castle.

Webster sighed and opened the doors. As always, Lord Dunovan was sitting in a high backed leather chair drinking, with the fireplace in the background the only light.

"Good evening, Mr. O'Leary."

Webster stood by the door with his arms crossed waiting for him to begin.

"Would you like to sit down, Mr. O'Leary? Make yourself more comfortable. Have a drink or two. This is my third or fourth. You lose count." Lord Dunovan, noting that he was not going to receive any encouragement from his guest, said, "Kathleen had her brat?"

"Yes, she had a baby girl," he answered shortly.

"How nice," William said sarcastically. "A new baby girl to wallow with the Irish. Perhaps she too will have an illegitimate baby with another one of my tenants."

"There is nothing wrong with being Irish," Webster coldly interjected.

"Nothing wrong with having dozens of babies unable to really care for or feed themselves?"

"Is there something you wanted from me, or did you just call me in here to insult me and my heritage?"

"It is my castle, I will speak to you any way I see fit. And if the truth hurts, well, that's just too damn bad. Besides, you are only living here under my roof because of Kathleen who threatened to leave Ireland."

"Lord Dunovan, you hate the Irish, Mary and Kathleen. Why would you want her to stay here under your roof?"

William laughed softly and said, "Don't you know by now, after all these years?"

"Would I be asking if I knew?"

"I do not know how the mind of an uneducated Irish farmer works, Mr. O'Leary."

Webster uncrossed his arms and held his hands in tight fists, warning him not to throttle this man. "Why did you call me in here, Dunovan?"

"Before Mary died, she told me that if she was not going to see you again, she wanted you to have something."

"You waited almost a whole year before giving it to me?"

William shrugged. "Do you want it or not?"

"Yes."

William reached into his pant pocket and pulled out a small, emerald, velvet box. Webster moved away from the wall and took the box and opened it to find Mary's cherished cameo. He gently ran his fingers across the raised image. He closed his eyes and remembered the time he had asked Mary why she wore the piece of jewelry all the time. It had been a beautiful day about a week after the storm and they had been intimate with one another.

Mary had gone out to meet Webster for dinner with a picnic basket, not wanting to eat with the unpleasant Aaron. She was wearing a dark blue top with a black skirt when she found Webster under a tree waiting for her. He got up to give her a hug and kiss. They settled themselves on the plaid blanket. Webster began to open the basket and bring out the food, when he noticed Mary was fiddling with the ever-present cameo at her throat.

"How was your day, Webster?"

"Long. I missed you, lass."

"You did?" she asked with wonder.

"Of course I did. Don't you know that I love you? That you are the only thing I look forward to?"

Mary blushed and bent her head so that Webster could not see her flaming cheeks. She was not used to have love given to her so lavishly.

"Lass," he started, sensing her embarrassment and wanted to change the subject, "the brooch you wear all the time is it special to you?"

Mary looked down at the cameo. Her mother had given it to her before she died; it was all she had from her. Mary looked at Webster with tears in her eyes. "It was my mother's. She gave it to me right before she died. It had been passed down from mother to daughter for generations in my family. It reminds me of her; she was so lovely and kind."

"I am sorry to make you cry, lass. It looks like you too. You are also lovely and kind."

"Why are you so nice to me, Webster?"

"Why? What on earth do you mean, why? I love you and want to marry you. You are very special to me."

Webster moved closer to her and took off his finger a gold ring with an emerald in it. "This has been in my family for generations; it goes back to when Ireland had kings. An ancestor of mine was granted this ring and the small piece of land we live on for saving the king's life. I would like you to have it as a temporary engagement ring until I earn enough money to buy you a real one."

"Are you asking me to marry you, Webster?" she asked in astonishment.

Webster looked into her bright eyes and gently took her hand to place the ring on it. "Yes, lass, I want you to marry me."

Mary swallowed her tears and teasingly said, "Ask me properly."

Webster smiled, stood up and pulled Mary to her feet, then knelt down in front of her on one knee. "Mary, lass, would you please be my wife?"

"That was very proper," Mary said, looking down at him tenderly.

"Aye, lass. And what would your answer be?"

"Aye, Webster lad, I will marry you."

Webster stood up and held her tightly in his arms, whispering, "I love you."

"I love you too."

Webster remembered how Mary had pulled away from him and took off her cameo and placed it in his palm. He had touched the raised image and looked down at her waiting for her to say something.

"Webster, if I should die, I would want you to have this to remember me by."

"Lass, you will not die," he protested in shock.

"Please, Webster, just take it. It would mean a lot to me."

"Darlin', if anything would happen to you, I would want to have it, but you keep it for now. It's your family's."

Webster tightened his hand around the small piece of jewelry. Now he finally had it, the only thing left to him from his love, except of course Kathleen.

He looked at William and simply said, "Thank you."

William looked up at him almost as if he wanted to say something but thought better of it and said, "I have no use for it."

Webster turned and left the room, wondering what had made William such a cruel and heartless person.

* * * * * * *

Three weeks after Willow's birth, Ryan bought Kathleen a pink and white baby carriage with lace on the top and edges. She had woken up to find the gift by her bed with a note. Kathleen, upon seeing the note, was dismayed. What was wrong with men? Did they not know it was nicer to be told things verbally? Michael had never told her what was in that note he had given her with her shirt. Nevertheless, she kept it, hoping one day to be able to read it.

Kathleen went downstairs to the dining room, with Willow in her arms, to find Ryan finishing breakfast. He stood up when he saw her.

"Good morning, Kathleen. How are you feeling?" he asked as he gave her a kiss on her forehead.

"I am feeling fine, and Willow is anxious to ride in her beautiful new carriage. Thank you."

"I thought maybe you would like to travel to London for Willow's three week birthday?"

Kathleen felt her throat go dry. Michael might be in London. What if she ran into him? It was too soon to see him; the wounds were still to fresh. "Ryan, I do not think that would be such a good idea. Willow is so young. Maybe we could just go to Ishimore?"

Ryan gently rubbed his knuckles over Kathleen's smooth cheek. Something about London had worried her. "Kathleen, today is your day. We will do whatever you want."

"Thank you, Ryan."

"Come have breakfast while I hold Willow. You need to keep up your strength."

Kathleen smiled and handed him her daughter. Ryan was very understanding toward her and Willow. She was amazed at times when she woke up in the middle of the night to find him sitting by her bed rocking Willow gently. He always told her to go back to sleep, she needed her rest and not to worry.

"Ryan, I thank you so much for taking Willow as your own child. It really does go above the call of duty."

"Kathleen, I have told you many times that I love you and Willow. She's a beautiful girl, and I am proud to have her take my name. I am happy to take care of her and you."

"Ryan, I am sorry that I misjudged you when we first met. I thought you were boring, stupid, just another conceited aristocrat. I know now that I was very wrong; you are a kind and generous person."

"Thank you, Kathleen," Ryan said softly, and then to lighten the mood, he said, "Now eat your breakfast so you can feed Willow. She seems to want to eat."

Willow was chewing on his velvet jacket with her gums leaving wet sloppy patches.

Kathleen smiled and obediently ate her food.

* * * * * * *

152

Ryan and Kathleen took Willow to Ishimore in her new carriage. Kathleen was excited, having never been there before. Ryan gave her money to buy clothes, knowing how much she had enjoyed the long, brightly colored, Irish skirts. If his wife wanted to dress like a peasant, who was he to stop her?

"Kathleen, how much money do you plan to spend on clothes?" he asked mockingly when he saw the many bundles she was carrying.

Kathleen love, how much money do you think I have? Kathleen shook her head, trying to block out Michael's voice.

Ryan caught Kathleen's faraway look and gently touched her face. "Are you all right? You look a little distant."

"Yes, Ryan, I'm fine, thank you." She held the packages up to him and said, "I am ready to leave now."

"Why don't you drop these off with Stuart at the carriage house by the inn, while we get Willow's stroller and take her for a walk in this fresh, clean air."

"That sounds like fun," she said and gave her packages to him in exchange for Willow.

Ryan took over pushing Willow and suggested they take a stroll around the lake, where it would be quiet. He needed to talk to her about what her father had told him last night. Webster had located him the night before while he was signing papers in the library. Ryan's older brother had been killed, and now Ryan was to take over the family business.

"Ryan, may I speak with you a moment?"

"Of course," he replied, looking up from the document he was going over.

Webster hesitated in front of the door; he did not know his daughter's husband very well.

"Please sit down the papers can wait."

"Ryan, I am sure by now you know about Kathleen and Michael Fitzpatrick."

Ryan sighed loudly. How could he forget? Michael's ghost was always between him and Kathleen. Now with Willow, whom he loved dearly, he sensed that there was something in her features that reminded Kathleen of Michael all the time. He suspected it was her eyes, dark blue and knowing. "Yes, I know of Michael."

"Ryan, I would have been happier to see Kathleen with the man she truly loves and her baby's father. But circumstances being the way they are, I am glad that she married you."

"Thank you. I feel very touched," Ryan said with surprise and honesty. Webster never spoke to him much, staying quietly to himself, almost like he was just waiting to be gone from this earth.

"Ryan, I wanted to thank you for taking such good care of Kathleen and my granddaughter."

"I love Kathleen very much. I would never hurt her."

"I do not mean to pry, but you and Kathleen do not share the same room. Is it because of Michael?"

"Kathleen does not have those feelings for me yet. Maybe one day, but for now, I would never force her to do anything she does not want to."

"I think now that your brother is dead, you should move to your own lands on the other side of Ireland. You should also tell her that Michael is married."

"Married? How do you know?"

"Matthew, Michael's brother, told me last week. He sent word to the castle to speak with me. He thought I should tell Kathleen. It would be best for you or I to tell her and not for her to hear it from a gossiping maid or Lord Dunovan."

"I will try to break the news to her," Ryan said, seeing that Webster did not exactly relish the idea of breaking his daughter's heart again.

Now walking alongside Kathleen, Ryan was not sure how to tell her Michael was married. He did not want her to think he expected anything of her with the news. But he did think she should know. It was her right.

"Ryan, I want to thank you again for a lovely day. Willow is so happy."

"Kathleen, how many times are you going to thank me? You should know by now that making you happy is my goal. I love you." *Kathleen love, don't you understand that we were meant to be together?* Kathleen sighed. Michael was always around. She had tried to stop thinking of him but could not. He was always on her mind and in her heart. She looked at Willow with his eyes and missed him so much. It should be him here pushing his daughter around a lake, letting her chew on his finger. It should be him waking in the middle of the night to rock Willow back to sleep.

"Kathleen, you need to know something. And I'll just blurt it right out. Webster told me last night that Michael is married."

"Mary?" a white-haired old man asked her, stopping in front of the small prosession.

"What?" Kathleen asked confused. Michael married! She felt it a little piece of her shrivel up and die right there and then at those words.

"You look exactly like Mary, my daughter," the man said, peering at her closer. "Who are you?"

"My name is Kathleen Winchester. This is Ryan, my husband," Kathleen said, gesturing toward Ryan.

"Who is your mother?" the man asked urgently.

"What concern is it of yours, sir?" Ryan asked, not liking the way the man was acting. He looked a tad crazy.

The man ignored him. "Who is your mother?"

"My mother's dead. She was Mary Dunovan."

"Are you positive?"

"Yes, of course! I know who my own mother was."

"Kathleen, let's get going now," Ryan said in alarm.

The man was obviously a maniac. The man grabbed Kathleen by the arm, not roughly, but Ryan pushed him off of her. "Just who in the hell do you think you are? Leave my wife alone."

"I am George St. John, Mary's father."

Kathleen turned pale and pressed her face against Ryan's chest. "Tell him to go away."

"Kathleen, please look at me. You're my granddaughter. I know now that I was wrong. I want to make it up to you."

"Ryan, please take me home," she demanded, refusing to look at her grandfather.

"I am sorry, Mr. St. John, but she does not want to see you. I think it would be best for you to leave."

The shattered George St. John watched as his granddaughter walked away from him with her head held high. Proud, just like her mother, he thought. "Please just tell her I am sorry."

* * * * * * *

Later that night, Ryan lay in his bed alone, as usual, thinking about what had taken place at the lake earlier that day. He felt so bad for Kathleen. Nothing ever seemed to be easy for her. After returning to the carriage, she refused to speak to him or hold Willow. All she did was look at the passing scenery. She had a lot of information thrown at her all at once; her baby's father was married, and her grandfather, who was the cause of ruining her mother's life and her own, shows up out of the clear blue sky wanting to make nice with her.

Upon arriving at the castle, she went straight to her room, not bothering to say anything to Webster. Ryan had the maid leave her a tray outside of her room; he was later informed that it had not been touched. He put Willow to bed himself, as Kathleen never came back out of her room. It seemed that only bad things happened to her.

Ryan jumped to hear a soft knock at his door. Thinking it was only his valet, he told the person knocking to come in, not bothering to put on his robe over his naked chest. He lay on his bed in a loose pair of trousers when Kathleen walked through the door. She wore a long flowing white robe with her hair unbound in loose curls. She looked very pale as she walked toward him.

"Kathleen?" he questioned, softly sitting up in bed.

Kathleen untied the ribbon of her robe and let it flow to the ground, forming a soft pool of fabric at her feet. She stood before him, gloriously naked. Ryan looked at her beauty she was displaying for him unashamed.

"Kathleen, you are so beautiful," he whispered, making room for her on his bed next to him. She moved slowly, not quite sure she knew what she was doing, toward the bed and sat on the edge by Ryan.

"Kathleen?" he asked, lifting his hand to touch her soft hair.

"Ryan, please do not say anything. Just tell me you want me. Love me, Ryan, please."

Ryan lay for a long moment, looking at the ceiling, wondering what had made Kathleen come to him that night. He knew that it was because she knew Michael was married and she had lost him forever. He also knew that she felt bad for her grandfather but could not face him. She had come to him that night out of desperation to be loved, and he realized he did not care why she was here. He was just glad she was. He gently gathered her in his arms and kissed her softly.

"Kathleen, I love you," he whispered.

Kathleen wound her arms around his neck as he moved over her to enter her gently. She looked blankly over his shoulder and thought of Michael.

* * * * * * *

Dutch and Beth O'Brien went to see Matthew and Gabrielle Fitzpatrick, bringing gifts for their first child.

Matthew opened the door looking ecstatic. "What did you bring?" he demanded.

"Hello to you too, Matthew," Beth remarked, kissing her brother's unshaven cheek.

"How is Gabrielle?" Dutch asked, patting Matthew on the back as they walked into the cottage.

"Gabrielle is great! She had almost no problems, no pain. She popped out the baby like it was nothing."

"Matthew! A little graphic and lying to boot." Gabrielle yelled from their room where she had given birth to Marilyn Fitzpatrick the day before. Dutch and Beth followed Matthew to see Gabrielle sitting up in bed with Marilyn in her arms.

"She is so precious, Gabrielle. She looks exactly like you," Beth exclaimed, looking down at the little red wrinkled face.

"I think she looks like me. Her eyes are brown, so is her hair."

"Matthew, that is not hair. That is fuzz."

"But you have to admit she has brown eyes."

"Just agree, Beth. It is much easier."

"How was the birthing, Gabrielle?" Dutch asked, sitting down in a chair by the bed.

"Hard," Gabrielle replied. At the same time, Matthew said, "It was easy."

"It was easy for you maybe. You were not the one who was lying on the bed having someone yell at you to push."

"I think I am going to go get something from the kitchen," Dutch said, obviously embarrassed.

Gabrielle laughed as he made a hasty retreat to the kitchen. "What is the matter with Dutch, Beth?"

"He does not want to know of birthing babies. I am not quite sure what we will do when we have ours."

Matthew went to sit beside Gabrielle and took Marilyn from her.

"Few men are able to stand the joy of bringing a baby on earth," he announced conceitedly.

"That's easy for him to say, Beth. But when the baby started to come, he mysteriously had to leave."

Matthew smoothed Gabrielle's hair with his free hand. "I came back though."

Gabrielle smiled and kissed her husband's palm. "You were very good, Matthew. Thank you."

Dutch came back in the room with the gift Beth had picked out for Marilyn.

Gabrielle took it and thanked him. The package consisted of a white lacy gown, which Beth had made for Marilyn.

"What do I get?"

"For what, Matthew?"

"For helping birth the baby."

"You get nothing."

Matthew sighed. "I am never thanked properly for my efforts."

"Matthew, you really are a pain."

"Speaking of pain, Beth, might I have a word with you outside."

"Matthew, do not hurt my wife."

"Do not worry, Dutch. I will not harm my lovely sibling. Much. Would you like to hold Marilyn?"

Dutch started to shake his head no, but Beth answered, "Yes, he would."

Dutch gently took Marilyn from Matthew and teasingly said, "On second thought, you may hurt Beth a little."

Beth stuck her tongue out at Dutch and followed Matthew outside of the cottage. They sat down next to each other on the doorstep.

"You had a beautiful daughter, Matthew."

"Thank you. Now no one can call you the baby of the family anymore."

"Only you and Michael ever referred to me as that."

"Speaking of Michael, have you heard anything from him?"

"No not since well before he left. Have you?"

"Yes. That's why I asked you to come out here. Beth, Michael's married."

"Married? Why did he not tell us?"

"He married an English duke's daughter."

"Our Michael? Our brother?" Beth asked with disbelief.

"Aye. I received a letter from him last week. He said he married the girl as a favor to her father."

"Did you ever tell him about Kathleen?"

"Michael knows Kathleen is married; he was the one who told me."

"Did you tell him about the baby?"

"No. Why should I?"

"Matthew, you know that baby is not Ryan Winchester's."

Matthew sighed loudly. "You think the baby is Michael's?"

"Who else could be the father? Michael and Kathleen were together since May; it would be too soon for her and Ryan to have children. Besides, rumor has it she has brilliant blue sapphire eyes."

"I do not think Michael needs to know about Kathleen's child right now.

He loves Kathleen so much he would probably kill Lord Dunovan, and then he would be hanged. If that happened, Kathleen would never forgive herself."

"I feel so bad for the two of them; they were really meant to be together. Now they are both stuck with someone else, however nice they might be."

"I know what you mean, I could never imagine being with anyone else ever. It was special for the two of them; I had never seen Michael as relaxed and happy as he was with Kathleen. She was very nice and sweet, but she knew how to handle Michael when need be. When he was rude to her, she told him off; she had a backbone. That is what he needed, not people to always agree with him like we did."

"I hardly agreed to everything he said," Beth said offended.

"Yes, you did. We all did. We thought he was better than we were, and maybe he was, but with Kathleen, he was different. She looked beyond the front he put out; she found the real Michael. Not just Michael, the caring doctor, or bitter Irish farmer, but Michael, the great human being. The person who could love with his whole heart and soul. She brought out the best in him."

"What is his wife like?" she asked curiously.

"He never said. All he wrote in his letter was that she was very sweet, but she was no Kathleen."

"I hope he can find some kind of happiness with her."

"Me too, Beth. Me too," Matthew said wistfully.

Chapter Thirteen

Michael Fitzpatrick sat alone in the Liverpool House library thinking how much he hated the English springtime. In fact, he pretty much hated England all the time. It was damp, gloomy, dark. And those royals who ruled the country…well, all he could say about them was he had known animals with more morals. More than anything else in the world, he longed to be back in Ireland with his family. As much as he complained all those years about Matthew and Beth not living up to their potentials, he missed them and all their quirks. He wanted to meet Marilyn, his baby niece, and congratulate his brother and sister-in-law in person.

Most of all, he admitted to himself, he missed Kathleen. It had been a year since he had seen her, but he loved her no less. He needed her back in his life; he did not care what it took. He would go through Lord Dunovan, Ryan Winchester, or the king himself; he just wanted her so much.

Michael could not believe it had just been a year since he had seen her. It seemed like years. His beautiful Kathleen with her long golden auburn hair and amber eyes that shone like the sun. He wondered if she was all right. Did she miss him? Would he ever see her again? He just wanted to see her, hold her in his arms one last time. Feel her body against his one last time.

"Michael?" A timid voice interrupted his thoughts.

Michael looked up to see Clara standing at the door looking at him expectantly.

Damn! What did she want now? "Yes, Clara, what is it?" He sighed wearily.

"When are you coming to bed, Michael?"

"Later, Clara, later. You go on to bed now," Michael said shortly.

He watched as the honey-haired girl turned away from him with tears in her eyes. He knew he should call back to her to apologize for his rudeness, but he could not. He did not mean to hurt her feelings, he just wanted to be left alone. That's all he wanted, to be left alone with his thoughts of the past year since he had lost his Kathleen.

* * * * * * *

Michael arrived at Liverpool House and immediately knew he did not belong there, not even for one night or a meal. Liverpool House rested on acres of flat green land, with rose bushes and fountains close to the house. The house itself was almost as large as Dunovan Castle, which astonished Michael. After seeing Kathleen's home up close, he imagined all of the wealthy lived in huge rumbling castles that were dark and depressing. How wrong he was! Although Dunovan Castle had been large and extravagant, Liverpool House was almost homey looking, despite its size. It was a small chateau, with ivy growing up the sides and green shutters at the many windows.

Michael had never seen a more elegant, beautiful building; he was completely out of his element. Although he was not happy about being an Irish peasant farmer and knew he deserved better, the Duke of Liverpool's home was not where he belonged. Michael shifted in his seat and gently touched the duke's shoulder to try to stir him awake. He really must demand that the duke let him out so he could find an inn to stay in.

"Your grace…" he began, once he saw the man start to stir awake.

"I thought you did not know how to address nobility."

"I suppose I was wrong. Anyway, as I was saying, your grace…"

"Edward."

"Fine, Edward. I really do not think I can stay here. It seems a little out of my element."

"What do you mean, Michael?"

What did he mean? Was the man completely dense? "Look at me. I am an Irish farmer. I do not belong in an English manor home eating with a duke and his daughter."

"You approve of the separation of cultures of two countries on the same continent? You think the class system is proper and fair?"

"Of course not. Usually the English do not associate with the Irish, and dukes and duchesses do not break bread with farmers."

"Is that all you are protesting? Michael, you saved my life. I at least owe you dinner."

The carriage stopped, and Sidney came around to help Edward, who refused his assistance and waited for Michael's answer.

"You do not seem to understand. I am not dressed properly. I do not think I can keep up an interesting conversation with you and your daughter. We have nothing in common."

"Michael, you have nothing to worry about. You are an intelligent, handsome, young man. You could probably teach me and my daughter a thing or two."

Michael smiled at that, thinking of the day he had promised Kathleen he would teach her how to read, and how amazed he was that someone with such a privileged background could not do something he could.

Edward caught that smile and said, "So you will stay, Michael?"

"Aye. And I thank you."

"And I welcome you. Here is my home. Humble it might not be, but home it is. Help me down from this carriage."

Michael jumped out and grabbed the older man by the elbow, helping him to the ground. Once all the way out of the carriage and half way to the house, Edward leaned over to Michael whispered confidently, "Thank you, Michael. I was a little afraid Sidney might drop me, and I would break a few more ribs. He's a little long in the tooth, huh?"

Before Michael had time to comment on Edward's remarks, a young, plain, blond-haired girl in a modest gray gown ran out of the house.

"Papa, why are you so late?" she demanded of Edward.

"I had a little accident, Clara, nothing to worry about."

"An accident!" she cried in alarm. "Are you all right? What happened?"

Edward used the arm that Michael was not supporting to pat his daughter affectionately. "Princess, it was just a little accident. You know how Sidney likes to race the horses. I am just fine."

Michael used the time that Edward spent telling his daughter about the incident to assess Clara. Edward had said she was eighteen, but with her long honey-colored hair pulled back in a tight bun and that ugly gray gown, she appeared to be older. Michael watched her with her father, concern written all over her face. She was attractive, pretty maybe. She had large, pale blue-gray eyes and high cheekbones. She had that creamy complexion that English girls were famous for; she resembled a doll that you look at but do not touch. She was tall, taller than her father was; his head reached her nose. For such a tall, girl she was very thin, with none of the basic womanly curves.

Looking at Clara, he could not help but compare her to Kathleen. His beautiful Kathleen who did not even reach his shoulder, whose skin was a warm apricot color, and hair was so free and curly that he just wanted to get lost in it. His love who had all the proper curves that fit into his body like they were made for each other. He would have to learn to forget about her. She was gone and married.

Michael listened as Clara scolded her father, and it reminded him of Kathleen. Kathleen seemed fragile because of her slight built, but underneath, she had a spine of steel. Clara seemed to have that same spine as he listened to her tell her father that he was not as young anymore, he had to look out for himself, what would she do without him. Kathleen had given him that same lecture almost verbatim. *Michael, you must eat before you go to work; you should not work all those long hours then try to go help the poor; you're going to get sick. What would I do without you?* What was she doing right this minute?

"Michael, where are you?" Edward questioned, pulling him out of his thoughts.

Michael, who had fallen behind the father and daughter, caught up to them and reestablished himself under Edward's arm. "This is my daughter, Clara. Clara, this is Michael Fitzpatrick, the young man who saved my life."

"I hardly saved his life; someone would have come along that knew what he was doing," Michael said modestly, reluctantly shaking hands with Clara.

"Thank you, Mr. Fitzpatrick, for helping my father in his time in need. You are staying for dinner I hope. We are having kidneys and rice pudding."

"He will be staying the night also," Edward put in.

"Perhaps just for dinner only, Edward."

Clara looked up at Michael, startled at the first name basis; her father must really like him, she thought.

"Michael, we agreed that you would stay the night."

I do not feel comfortable in your home, Michael wanted to say, but instead said, "We will see."

"Clare and I will just have to convince you to stay," Edward said with a wink to his daughter.

Michael sighed and helped Edward walk slowly toward the house. Clara supported her father on his other side, glaring over at Michael. She did not like him; he seemed cold, arrogant. Too arrogant.

"Where are you from, Mr. Fitzpatrick?"

"Please call me Michael. I am from Ireland."

"Do you farm there?"

Michael stiffened at the question; there was something about her he did not like. "Yes, I farmed there. That is what we do."

Son of a bitch, Clara thought, that is what he was. Look at the way he walked like he was better than everyone around him. He was too proud for a person who dug in the ground for a living, who lived in a shack with dirt floors. He looked as if nothing could touch him, no one could hurt him.

163

As they reached the door to the house, Sidney ran in front of them, carrying Michael's bag over his shoulder, to open the door. After getting Edward safely through the door, Michael reached for his bag, and Clara caught sight of the gold ring he still wore on his right hand.

"Are you married, Michael?"

The questioned shook him up so bad that he dropped his bag and turned on her. "No! I am not married. What made you ask that?"

"I noticed the ring you wear."

"Clara, leave the boy alone. He wears the ring on his right hand."

"But it is a wedding band is, it not Michael?" Clara asked, ignoring her father glaring at her.

Michael did not hear the question, for he was gazing down at the ring that was supposed to be a symbol of a lasting love. He wondered if Kathleen's husband let her keep the ring he had given to her.

"Is it a wedding band, Michael?" Clara asked, hurting Michael more.

"No," Michael said in a voice that let Clara know the subject was closed. He turned away from her and took his bag from Sidney.

"Sidney, show Michael upstairs to a guest room, get me a drink, and ask the cook what's for dinner," Edward demanded, limping toward what Michael assumed was the dining room. "Michael, hurry up, drop off your things and come eat."

"Perhaps Mr. Fitzpatrick will feel more comfortable to eat with the cook in the kitchen. You know Martha is Irish," Sidney said, managing to look down at Michael even though he was shorter than the younger man was.

"Sidney, Mr. Fitzpatrick is our guest in my home. I will be the one who decides where he eats and does not eat. Michael, leave your bag here for now and come eat."

Sidney grunted and left the room; to be reprimanded in front of an inferior was uncalled for. Michael took the opportunity to look at the house closer as he followed Edward into the dining room. He passed gilded frames of what he supposed were ancestors of the duke; the floors were covered in thick red carpet, and the furniture was mahogany shined to a high gloss with small figurines littering the tops.

As they entered the dining room, he was amazed at the size of the room. The room could hold three of his cottages in it. The dining table had at least ten chairs on each side of it, not including the two end chairs. Edward sat at one and gestured for Michael to sit at his right. And of course the dishes set out for them were made of gold, and the silver had gems of the deepest blue and green set in them. Michael smiled to himself as he remembered Kathleen's face when he had given her the gold bowl. Michael scowled at himself, Kathleen, Kathleen, Kathleen. She was all he ever thought about. He had to get her out of his mind. Damn, it was hard everyone; everything reminded him of her.

"Michael, sit down."

Michael obeyed, realizing as Clara glared at him that she was the one who most likely sat at his right. She did not like him, and it seemed that Edward was trying extremely hard for them to be a family. The last thing on earth he wanted was to be related to an English noble family.

"Who will be serving dinner tonight, Clara?"

"Sidney," Clara said almost smugly, looking at Michael as she said it.

Michael exhaled loudly. The salt-and-pepper-haired, green-eyed Sidney thought he was better than he was, and Clara was after blood, it seemed. He wondered what kind of meal this was going to be.

"Michael, what brings you to England?" Clara inquired curiously.

"Nothing much."

"Than why are you here?" she demanded.

"Clara, you are worse than Sidney. Stop acting like a spoiled brat and be kind to our guest."

Clara flushed a deep red at the reprimand and mumbled, "Yes, Papa."

Michael raised an eyebrow at her and smiled.

Sidney appeared with a bottle of red wine in front of Edward and began to pour the red liquid into goblets of gold with raised stones that matched the silver. When Sidney reached him with the bottle, he missed Michael's cup and poured it into his lap. Michael grabbed the white linen napkin on the table and tried to soak up the wetness in his lap.

"I am very sorry, Mr. Fitzpatrick," he said, not sounding sorry at all and winking at Clara who tried to bury her giggles in her goblet.

"Yes, I can see that you are," Michael replied sarcastically.

"Sidney, would you please clean up the mess that you have created. And take Michael to his room to change clothes. I imagine that it must be quite uncomfortable to sit with wine in one's lap."

Clara watched as Sidney led Michael out of the dining room. He was rather good looking with all that dark hair and dark eyes.

"Princess, what do you think of Michael?"

"You mean, besides too big for his britches? I think he is not a very happy person."

"Would you be happy if you had cold wine spilled in your lap on purpose? And you should not have laughed. Do not encourage that Sidney."

"Not that, Papa. Michael does not want to stay here. You should not force him."

"Nonsense, you just do not want him here. I think he likes you though. He is a very good looking young man."

Clara glared at her father. Ever since James, her fiancé had died last year, he had been trying to find her a new husband. She thought he would have her marry Sidney if he could get a way with it. She tried to explain to him that she was happy with her memories of James. All she wanted to do was take care of him.

She remembered first meeting James, who had a little of Michael's arrogance in him, at her coming out ball. She had just turned sixteen and begged her mother to let her wear the family diamonds. She had thrown a fit until her mother caved in and let her wear them. She knew she had always been a tad selfish, but everything had always been given to her, and when something was denied her, how else was she supposed to act? She was never deliberately cruel; she just wanted what she thought she deserved.

At her coming out ball, she had worn a gown of white silk with light blue roses hand painted on the fabric. The gown had been made especially for her in Paris when she and her family had visited the fall before. It had been beautiful, with a neckline that revealed as much creamy flesh as deemed respectable by society. She knew she was to be the main attraction of her party because of her beauty. She knew she was pretty; it was a simple fact. She was not like some girls who always denied they had beauty. What was the point to deny a fact that you knew was true?

Clara had gone downstairs only after she knew most of the other guests had arrived so she could make her entrance. She recalled how she slowly walked down the winding staircase, relishing in the admiring stares. She wore her hair up off her neck with loose curls that hung around her face to frame it. As she descended the stairs, she caught sight of the most amazing gray-blue eyes she had ever seen. When she reached the bottom of the staircase, she came almost eye-to-eye with the gray-blue-eyed man.

"Hello," she greeted them coolly.

"You must be Clara," he stated in a deep voice.

"I am. What do you want?" she asked, trying to walk away from him as he leaned his arm on the banister, effectively blocking her getaway path.

He looked her up and down with his gray-blue eyes and let a small arrogant smile cross his lips. "One guess, lovely lady."

Clara ignored the remark and slowly assessed him from head to toe, taking in the blond-colored hair, the tall, muscular physique with wide shoulders, clad in a cream-colored jacket and dark pants that showed firm hard thighs.

After their initial meeting, Clara had danced all her waltzes with James Ryder, falling helplessly under his spell. He was beautiful and, much to her delight, a tad bit dangerous. He was charming, amusing, witty, and arrogant. He would not let her out of his sight or his arms. He dominated her whole evening and told her that she belonged to him that night and no one else. At the end of the evening, Clara asked him when she might see him again. He told her she would see him when she saw him.

Clara was furious at that. No one told Clara Worthington when he would see her. She had calmly and coolly told him to go to hell. He laughed at that and captured her mouth with his, passing his tongue through her mouth and pressing his body close to hers. The kiss robbed the breath from her and left her weak and wanting something – she did not know what it was. He walked away from her with a tweak to her nose and a very satisfied look on his face. Clara cursed his back and told him she hoped never to lay eyes on him again. This of course was a lie.

She was completely fascinated by him and his outlook on life. She had never met anyone of noble birth who cared nothing of money or what others thought of him. He was the son of a magistrate, and his mother was of Italian royalty. He had one brother who was older than his twenty-five years, but he had died in the navy when a pirate ship had raided his ship. Clara feared that she was much too attracted to him for knowing him such a short while, and that could be dangerous.

The next public function Clara attended, she looked for him, feeling very disappointed when she did not see him. Clara watched for him for months, going to parties, asking friends, never to find him. She decided she would have to forget about him. Obviously she had been just a passing fancy to him. She went back to flirting with every male that was under sixty and over sixteen, competing with other girls who could find the most dancing partners. She was always the belle of the party, with her charm and grace.

Unfortunately, after James, everyone seemed dull and boring. She missed James, despite his arrogance and aloofness.

Clara nodded to some remark her father was making regarding Michael and thought back to the December masquerade ball. She had worn a black and white lacy gown with diamonds and pearls sewn on it and a red half mask with sequins. She kept her eyes and nose covered with it, keeping the mask in place by a long stick that she held with one hand.

Clara dreamily remembered how a strong, firm arm had grabbed her by the waist, quickly spinning her around the dance floor and out into the cold night.

"James?" she whispered hopefully, trying to make out his form in the darkness.

"Si, cara mia, it is me," he said, drawing her closer to his hard lean body.

Clara moved away from him angrily. "Just who in the hell do you think you are? You have been gone for over three months, and you come here expecting me to fall into your arms? Ha!"

James had taken her back into his arms, ignoring her protests, removed her mask and kissed her warm mouth. She put her arms around his chest and kissed him back with all the need and longing she had felt for such a long time. He looked down into her face and smiled, seeing her closed eyes and open mouth. He gently placed his finger under her jaw to close it, which caused her eyes to open. "Did you miss me?"

"No," she defiantly replied.

"Are you so sure?" he asked before claiming her mouth once again. He made slow gentle love to her mouth, leaving her weak enough to cause her to put her head on his chest. "Tell me you missed me, cara mia," he demanded.

"Where were you?"

"Tell me you missed me, that you want me."

"Not until you tell me—" She was interrupted by James' mouth claiming hers once again.

"You missed me, you little brat, and you damn well know it," he said fiercely.

To her astonishment, Clara started to cry, soaking James' velvet jacket.

"Clara baby, please do not cry. I'm sorry. I missed you too." He held her tightly in his arms.

"Why, James, why did you go away for so long?"

"Clara, I had to. You are so young, baby. I stayed away, thinking I could forget you. I have always been against doing the proper thing. I wanted you. The proper thing would be to marry you, but I could not face that. I was so wrong though. I never meant to fall in love with you, but I have."

"James, I know we do not know each other well. I do not want to try to reform you. I want you the way you are."

"Clara." He sighed before kissing her deeply.

From that moment, Clara knew she loved him, and they were never separated again. They spent every waking moment with one another, and plans for a spring wedding were well underway when James came down with the dreaded influenza. Clara had retreated into herself, not going out, not seeing friends, when James died. She felt as if some part of her died also. She promised herself that she would die alone. After her declaration to herself she devoted her life to comforting her father, when her mother died from the same infliction. She knew her father was not happy about her decision of how to handle her life, but as she told him many times, she was happy the way things were.

As Michael walked back to his seat at the table, Clara hoped to God that her father would not force him on her.

* * * * * * *

After Michael's first night at Liverpool House, he was ready to go back to Ireland and never set foot in England again. He stayed because of Edward. He had taken a fondness to the older man, who had come down with a severe sickness that kept in bed most of the day. Michael nursed him back to health, although he was still weak. Michael and Sidney never did reconcile their differences; they hated each other equally. All they did was fight and exchange sarcastic remarks with one another. He suspected Edward enjoyed the back and forth comments, because every once in a while, he would provide a remark that would fuel the fight a little more.

Clara was another thorn under Michael's skin. Clara's dislike for him was a match for Sidney's. He did not know why the girl hated him so much; he barely looked at her, much less tried to strike up a conversation with her. She was very cold toward him, making him miss Kathleen's warm smile. He told himself Kathleen must have been different than Clara because she was half Irish.

A few weeks after Edward's sickness, he asked Michael to see him in the library. Michael wondered what he wanted as he walked into see Edward sitting in a high backed chair by the fire. Edward watched as the young man, who he now thought of as a son, strolled into the room. Edward knew it was time to let his plans that he had worked out come out in the open.

The only thing was, before his plans could be realized, he had to know Michael's story. Michael, for all his kindness as a doctor, kept his thoughts to himself. Edward knew that Michael had a painful past, he could see it in his eyes, but was unable to share it with anyone. Well, tonight Edward would force him to tell his story whether he liked it or not.

"Good evening, Michael. Please take a seat," Edward said, gesturing to the seat across from him. Michael folded his long body into an identical chair, placing his arm on the armrest, and waited for Edward to begin.

"Would you like something to drink, Michael?"

"Whiskey, if you have it."

"I do, and you are welcome to it," Edward said, motioning him toward the crystal glass decanters on a table at the back of the library. Michael got up and poured himself a large tumbler, figuring that he was going to need it for the conversation that was about to take place. Edward waited for Michael to settle himself back in his chair to ask bluntly, "Who was she, Michael?"

"Who was whom?"

"The girl who you loved, Michael. The girl you are no longer with. Who was she?"

"I do not know of whom you speak," Michael replied stiffly, taking a large swallow of his drink.

"The hell you do not! You do not even try to meet any of the girls who come by to see Clara. You do not go out. You do not even talk to the maid, and she's from your country. As for Clara, you do not speak to her." Edward thought of all the new friends Clara had discovered herself having recently. He knew it had to be because of Michael, but Michael wanted nothing to do with them. "The gold ring you wear, what is it, Michael? Is it a wedding band like Clara thought that first night you came here?"

Michael remained silent, staring stonily at Edward.

"Michael, you have to let me help you. It would be good for you to tell me about things. Open up."

Michael looked into Edward's eyes and, seeing only kindness and compassion, began his story. He started with the fact that he was an Irish farmer born into poverty and not at all happy with it. The idea he had to be a doctor, but his family could not afford university, so his mother made Doctor McKay take him under his wing. Michael knew it would have broken her heart if she knew that he had found out about her begging to take on her son. She had known how proud he was, and it was important to her to make him believe that he was good enough to go into medicine.

Michael told Edward of the night Matthew announced his engagement to Gabrielle, how he was angry at his brother for settling for a job with Lord

Dunovan, not wanting to try to better himself. Michael explained how he went out that night to Dunovan Bar and got things worked out for Beth. He finally told the story of finding Kathleen at his cottage doorstep half-dead.

This is where Edward broke in with, "This girl Kathleen was at your doorstep half-dead?"

"She was the daughter of Lord Dunovan, the man who ruled the town my family, lived in and worked for. Later, it was revealed that Lord Dunovan had beaten her and turned her out of the castle."

"My God!" Edward whispered horrified. "Why would he do that to his daughter?"

"Kathleen was not his real daughter. Kathleen was half Irish, illegitimate. She was so ashamed of the fact that she had a different father than the man her mother was married to. I had to pry it out of her."

"Did you love her?" Edward asked softly.

"Yes, and I still do. It was not easy to love her at first. Well, I take that back. It was too easy, just not easy to admit it to myself. She was English, after all. I was an Irish peasant farmer; I could not love her the daughter of the man who kept my family and friends in poverty. But Kathleen was so special, so beautiful. After discovering the joy of loving her I was happy all the time. She made my humble cottage look like a castle just by having her living it. She was tough though. She put me in my place. I need that. She knocked me down a peg or two." Michael paused to take a sip of his drink and continued with, "We were to be married. She was so excited, as was I. We had both finally found happiness, and it was together. That happiness was ruined when Lord Dunovan demanded that she return to Dunovan Castle or her mother would die. Kathleen left me to save her mother. I saw her one last time; she told me Lord Dunovan was forcing her to marry someone else. I left Ireland and came here to England to forget her, and you know the rest of the story."

Edward sat in stunned silence after listening to Michael. He realized Michael carried emotional baggage, but this. He could never in a million years have known that Michael could have gone through this. Edward had watched Michael when he spoke of Kathleen and saw the burning love in his eyes. It almost made him forget about his plans regarding Clara. Almost, but not quite.

"Michael, I am very sorry about your loss of Kathleen, but you must go on with your own life. After all, she did."

"Against her will. She did not want to leave me. Kathleen loved me,"

Michael said angrily.

"Michael, calm down do not get upset. Listen to me. You have become very dear to me, like the son I never had. I want to repay you for your kindness to an old man."

"You do not have to do anything for me. You have sheltered me and fed me. You did not have to take a stranger into your home like you did."

"Michael, I am an old man. You know that I am sick. I see it in your face every time you examine me and so happily lie to me and tell me I am fine. Michael, I know in my heart that I do not have long to live."

Michael remained silent, knowing that Edward told the truth. He just could not admit even to himself that this kind old man was sick and not going to get any better. Michael had lost so many people in his twenty-one years, he did not think he could lose someone else he had grown to love and respect.

"Michael, I want to leave Liverpool House to you along with the title of Duke of Liverpool. I have gotten the permission of London's magistrate; it is all set when I die you will inherit everything. Like a son should."

"Why me?"

"Michael, you are trustworthy, honest, and I know you will use the power I am giving you to help others."

"What about Clara?"

"Clara is my only daughter, Michael. I love her and worry about her. She too has lost much in her short life. Ever since her mother and James, her fiancé, died she has never been the same girl. She's quieter, withdrawn. At only eighteen, she has her whole life ahead of her." Edward paused and dived in, "I want you to marry her."

Michael choked on the liquid he had in his mouth. Marry the cold blonde English bitch who hated him?

"Edward, come on. Clara does not want to marry me."

"Oh she does. She just does not realize it yet." What Edward spoke was the truth. He could tell she was infatuated with Michael. He reminded her of James. Infatuation was a good enough reason to marry.

"I will not marry your daughter, Edward," Michael stated firmly.

"You will," Edward countered just as firmly.

* * * * * * *

172

Alone in the darkened library, Michael recalled how he had finally agreed to marry Clara Worthington so Edward could die in peace. He remembered how surprised he had been when Clara had actually looked happy when he proposed to her. He had bought her a diamond ring, knowing that was what she expected. He wore the ring he was to marry Kathleen with on a fine gold chain around his neck. He had told Clara about Kathleen, and she told him about James. Both knew in their hearts the other was mentally with someone else. They were married as a convenience, nothing else.

They had an arrangement that neither one of them would mention the other's lost love. They attended functions together, and he would stay faithful toward her. On the other hand, he would never force her to do anything she did not want to.

To have rules set up before they married made life much easier for them to accept what their lives had become.

Their wedding had been pleasant but hardly a joyous special occasion. Edward had died one week after the marriage.

Michael sighed and headed up toward the long staircase to the room he shared with Clara. On their wedding night Clara had firmly told him she would only stay with him until they produced a male heir, after which they would have separate rooms. This was fine with him, for he found no pleasure in bedding his wife. Not after having Kathleen. Michael opened the door, determined to make the best of his life and try to forget Kathleen.

Michael made the same vow every night, but never could totally forget about Kathleen. Nor could he make the best of his shattered life.

Chapter Fourteen

The years passed slowly for Michael Fitzpatrick, much to his dismay. They say time heals all wounds, and a lost love will be forgotten only to be remembered with fondness. He remembered his lost love with much more than fondness, especially now that he no longer had a wife. Clara had left him and the world late spring of the year 1802, after giving birth to their son Patrick. He cherished his son more than anything in the world; at least his marriage to Clara had one bright side to it.

Patrick had inherited Michael's black hair and his mother's light blue eyes and pale complexion. Although Clara's coloring had left her looking washed out, Patrick had a special glow to him that made him look like an angel. Everyone Michael met told him that his son was the most well-behaved, polite child. Even Sidney, who had come to respect Michael, although grudgingly, took a special fondness toward Patrick.

Michael suspected that God had granted him this lovely creature to try to make up for all the horrible things that had happened to him. His life as the duke of Liverpool kept him extremely busy and earned him respect from much of the English nobility. He, in all his life, never imagined he would be having dinner with the King of England in the palace. With his power, he was able to help earn more rights for his fellow Irishmen, as well as the lower class English. He learned to realize that he was not the only one who had gone without food and had to work like a dog to put a meal on the table.

Even with all the work he was doing as well as raising a son on his own, he still often thought of Kathleen. Many times he refused to allow his mind to wonder down that well-worn thought, but it snuck up on him. He wondered if she was all right. If she ever thought of him, if her husband treated her well, and if she had any children. It had been over four years since he had seen her. He was sure that she had moved on with her life. Michael vainly wished, as he often did, to see Kathleen once more to make sure she was healthy, well and happy, for that's all he wished, that she was happy.

* * * * * * *

Kathleen was not happy and doing well, much to Ryan's and 2½-year-old Willow's dismay. Kathleen had been sick with pneumonia for many months. Doctors had come and gone with the same diagnosis. They did not know why she was not getting better, and it was as if she had given up on herself and life. She lay in bed, not saying anything to anyone, except every once in a while when she was delirious. Even then, she just had conversations with Michael, when she was happy during those wonderful few months so long ago.

She refused to eat on her own; she would have died from starvation had it not been for Ryan, who hand fed her like a baby three times a day. Ryan knew she did not care if she lived or died, but he did, and so did Willow, who did not understand why her mommy would not come out to see her.

Ryan was losing patience with his wife. He felt she had brought her sickness onto herself, whether it was voluntary or not. After that night so long ago when she had offered herself to him, she withdrew into herself. She started taking long walks alone, never attended any of the many balls the Duke and Duchess of Winchester were expected to be at. She never wanted to host any of the functions that Dunovan Castle held. Kathleen never went near Willow, letting the maids and Ryan handle all mothering duties, except to kiss her good night.

Even the cold-hearted Lord Dunovan and hermit Webster had noticed a drastic change in Kathleen and had stopped needling each other at every opportunity. Ryan had called in yet another doctor from England, trying to find out what was wrong with his wife. The latest doctor had told him that Kathleen was strong enough to get better if she would just help herself.

Ryan chose a night two weeks before Kathleen's twentieth birthday and Willow's third to try to knock some sense into his wife. He knocked softly on the door that led into Kathleen's room. When there was no answer, he went in anyway. As always, Ryan noted, Kathleen lay in bed wide awake, pale, looking up at the ceiling. He walked softly toward the bed, sat down and brushed her hair off her forehead. Kathleen ignored him, still looking at the ceiling.

"Kathleen sweetheart, would you please look at me please?"

Kathleen continued to ignore him, gazing above her unblinkingly.

"Listen to me, Kathleen. You are going to be twenty years old in two weeks. You need to stop acting like a spoiled brat and face facts. You have a child who is almost three years old who needs her mother, not a maid, to take care of her. You are a duchess who has responsibilities and duties. That may not be exciting or fun, but they are important. Willow will someday inherit that title. It is unlikely that we have anymore children, so if her mother ruins her title, it would be unfair to her. You have a husband who loves you more than anything else in the world and is very worried about you."

When Ryan received no response from the motionless figure on the bed, he spoke a little louder, getting angry at her. "What about your father, Kathleen. Webster is old, Kathleen, and grieves over your mother. He missed all of your childhood. He wants to be with you now in the last few years of his life, but you are the one who is denying him now. Kathleen, you need to snap out of this mood you have been in right now!"

Ryan finished off angrily and stormed out of the room with a loud bang.

Kathleen winced at the harsh sound in the silence of the room. She sighed loudly, knowing Ryan was right, that she was behaving poorly, but she could not help herself. She was sick, more than just the pneumonia, more than losing Michael; she had no desire to live any longer. If she would have been allowed to stay with Michael, none of this would have happened to her. Lord Dunovan had finally done what he had always wanted; he had broken her spirit completely, in a way that was so terrible that she had lost all reason to live.

All her life she had always known that Lord Dunovan hated her; it was evident from the way he spoke to her or looked at her. On reflection, she guessed she always knew that he could not be her real father. She never did realize how much his distaste for her was until the day he came to her after she and Ryan had made love together for the first and last time.

Kathleen turned her head to the side, weeping as she remembered the way Ryan had woken her the next morning gently kissing her throat, telling her he had to go to a meeting. Kathleen had groaned, grumpy about being woken up so early, nodded her head and went back to sleep. She did not see anyone until much later when she finally got up and dressed. Emerging from the room in an old black dress with her hair tied back away from her face, she ran into Lord Dunovan.

Lord Dunovan stood in front of her dressed in gray with his arms folded across his chest. "Good day, Kathleen."

Kathleen mumbled an incoherent greeting and tried to walk past him, but failed when he put his arm against the wall to block her passage.

"Is there something I can do for you, Lord Dunovan?" Kathleen asked coldly.

He made her nervous always watching her but never saying anything to her. William stared at her with his unblinking gray eyes. Kathleen began to get nervous when he idly touched her smooth cheek with the palm of his hand.

"What can I do for you, Lord Dunovan?"

"You should know better than anyone, Kathleen," he said, placing his hand on her head and loosening her hair from its bonds.

Kathleen jerked her head away from his touch and said, "Just what do you mean by that?"

"You are so beautiful, Kathleen, much more beautiful than your bitch of a mother."

"How dare you speak of my mother in that manner! She was the kindest most caring person that I knew."

"She was a stuck up whore who got what she deserved, just like my mother. They both are better off dead than hurting others."

Kathleen raised her hand and hit William across the jaw as hard as she could, leaving her palm stinging. He did not even flinch. She wondered if he even felt the blow. William did feel it and grabbed Kathleen by the hair while twisting her arm behind her back.

"You will apologize for striking me," he said calmly.

"I most certainly will not."

William uttered an oath, pushing Kathleen's arm higher up on her back, and shoved her into Ryan's room. Throwing her down on the bed, looming over her, he said, "I know you understand the fact that I hate you too, like your mother and mine. But let me explain to you why."

"Because you are a selfish, cold, son of a bitch," Kathleen whispered harshly into his face struggling to free herself from his grasp, failing miserably.

William laid down on her ignoring her writhing body, placing his arms on either side of her head, effectively trapping her.

"This is true what you say, dear Kathleen, but I have another reason for hating you. Ever since you started to develop and mature from a little girl into the lovely young lady of today, I have wanted you. I knew you would be more responsive than she would, but you have always rejected me. You must have always known that you and I were not related. I knew once your mother had told you who I really was there would be nothing wrong with my having you. Your birthday was the perfect time for you to know of your true heritage. I thought you would be grateful toward me for sheltering you, feeding you and caring for you as a virtual stranger to me. Instead, you were elated that we were not bound to each other by blood. You claimed you were glad, that you hated me. I was so enraged, Kathleen, so I turned you out of the castle. That was my mistake. Kicking you out of the castle cost me what was rightfully mine. You ruined yourself with Irish scum. Like your mother, you sold your body to the Irish for what? A bastard brat. I wonder what dear Willow will say when she learns Ryan is not her father. Or will you keep it a secret, Kathleen. Like all women, I am very sure you are good at keeping secrets. Does Michael know he is the father?"

Kathleen was horrified. Lord Dunovan was crazy, sick in the head. She needed to get away. Struggling, she tried again but failed. "You stay away from Michael. You have already hurt him enough."

William looked down at her and laughed. "Did Ryan tell you about your beloved Irishman? He went to London and married."

"I know," Kathleen said hotly.

"Do you, darling Kathleen. Do you know whom he married? An English duke's daughter, he is a duke now, inheriting the title from her father. Don't you see, Kathleen? I saved you. Michael only wanted you for your money, nothing else," he said cruelly, kissing her forehead.

"No, Michael loved me."

William trailed a finger over Kathleen's throat coming dangerously close to the swell of her breasts. "Did he really love you, Kathleen? Why then did he marry another girl, especially an English one. Tell me, Kathleen," he whispered softly, like the snake in the Garden of Eden.

"I am not sure. Michael did love me." Kathleen was distracted by William's hand moving to cup her breast.

"I really do not care if he loved you or not. All I care about is that he knew your body and I did not. I waited all those years, and he had what I wanted, what I deserved. But we are going to change that right now," he said, ripping her dress at the neck to her waist. Kathleen struggled to get away from him, scratching, biting, and kicking, to no avail.

William laughed cruelly at her. "Try all you want, Kathleen dear. It will not do you any good."

William moved down Kathleen's helpless body, tearing the rest of the dress from her. Kathleen closed her eyes, knowing it was useless to try to get away from him. She tried to block out the assault on her body and to think of Michael. No, she thought, tossing her head from side to side, I can not think of Michael. He married an English duchess, not her. He had forgotten about her. Kathleen finally lost consciousness, releasing her mind and body from the horror of what William was doing to her.

As Kathleen thought back to that terrifying experience, she did not think she would ever get out of bed again.

* * * * * * *

"Matthew, I hope she does not lose her child," Gabrielle Fitzpatrick whispered to her husband.

Matthew glanced at his sister's tiny form dressed in black standing over her husband's grave.

It was a dark gloomy day with clouds threatening to break open with rain on the day Dutch O'Brien was laid to rest. Leaving his wife of four years carrying his sole unborn heir, Dutch had left the earth, dying in a terrible fire.

Beth stood bravely detached from the rest of the mourners trying to keep her promise to herself not to cry until she reached home. She could not believe Dutch had left her. She expected him at any moment to put his hands on her stomach to see how the "little lad" was doing, as he so often did. When she had found out that she was expecting a child, she had never seen him so happy, despite his previous reservations. Dutch has brought her something new almost everyday after finding out – a new dress, built a crib out of the strongest wood, clothes for the baby. He was certain it was to be a boy.

His attitude toward children had begun to change last year when Matthew and Gabrielle had had their son Joseph. He was always around, reporting some new gurgle or tooth that Joseph had acquired back to Beth. The way he doted on that child one would think he was the father.

Beth swallowed, trying to fight back the tears as she thought of Christmas Eve, how Dutch had rocked her in his arms in front of a low fire, telling her how he would always take care of her. His promise turned to be false on New Year's Day when he went to help put out a fire in Aaron Bennigan's stables. Beth had begged him not to go, feeling some strange deep premonition that something bad was going to happen. But Dutch, being who he was, would not let a friend down in his time of need. He told her not to worry, that he had to help. The Benningan stables were what brought in his income; he had to save those horses.

Tears went unchecked down Beth's cheeks as she thought of how the horses were saved but Dutch's life was taken. What a way to bring to bring in the new year of 1804, she thought bitterly. A child on the way and no husband to care for her. Why did everything seem to go wrong at the beginning of a new year when things were supposed to be so perfect and new? Kathleen had come to them half-dead, Michael and Kathleen's child had been born but the father was never to know or see her, and Dutch had died a horrible death. Were they cursed? Was there never to be any happiness for them?

Beth jumped as she felt a gentle touch on her shoulder. She turned to see Matthew and Gabrielle behind her. Gabrielle reached out and held her friend tightly as the tears Beth had so bravely fought back finally burst out like a dam.

"Beth, everything is going to be all right. You can stay with Matthew and me. We will take care of you."

Matthew rubbed his sister's back, thinking God had surely punished his family enough and nothing else bad could happen to them.

* * * * * * *

How wrong Matthew was. Two weeks later, when Beth gave birth to her child, a daughter named Francine, Matthew watched as Michael, who had finally come home, brought the sheet over their younger sister's face. Beth had begged Matthew to send for Michael, knowing in her heart she would not survive the childbirth. She had to see Michael one last time before she died. He had always been her favorite brother, despite his arrogance.

Michael, who had not seen his family or his homeland in over four years, had been happy to have an excuse to go. He had wanted to go so many times, but could not face running into Kathleen.

However, his happiness died the minute he walked into Dutch and Beth's cottage to find his family in despair. Matthew in his letter had failed to mention the death of his sister's husband and the fact that Beth was sure she was going to die in childbirth. He had arrived with gifts for his family that he could never afford before, glad that he could was finally able to bring them everything they deserved.

Michael arrived the day before Francine's birth to be greeted by Matthew, who was shocked at his brother's appearance. Michael had aged harshly over the last few years and still looked sad. Matthew guessed he had never gotten over losing Kathleen.

"Hello, Michael," Matthew had said, quietly taking Patrick and the boxes Michael was weighted down with.

"Matthew, you are looking well. The responsibility of two children looks like it is doing you some good."

"Gabrielle will have another in six months," Matthew said, leading Michael into the cottage.

"Congratulations, Matthew. It looks like you have everything you wanted."

"You did well for yourself, did you not, Michael? A duke and a son is nothing to scoff at."

"Yes, but I would give it all up to see Kathleen once again, but I did not come here to talk about me. Where is my favorite sister?"

"Michael, there are a few things I need to tell you about Beth."

Michael sighed wondering what could be wrong. "What about Beth, Matthew? What's wrong?"

"I did not want to worry you on your trip from London, but Beth is not doing so well."

"What is the matter with her?" Michael asked in alarm.

"Dutch died the first of the year in a blazing fire, saving Benningan's stables."

"Jesus Christ," Michael swore softly.

"Beth is positive that she will not live through the childbirth; that is why I asked you to come home. No matter what a pain in the arse you are, you have always been her favorite. Mine too by the way."

"Where is she?" Michael hoarsely asked.

Matthew led Michael to Beth's bedroom where they found her pale and weak, holding Gabrielle's hand. She looked up with large, pain-filled eyes when Michael entered the room.

"Michael?" she asked, unsure of her eyes, wondering if it was an illusion.

"Aye, little one, it is me," he said, taking over Gabrielle's position on the bed.

"I am not going to live, Michael."

"Beth, it is not nice to lie to your older brother," Michael reprimanded her, though he knew that what she said was the truth. She looked exactly like Clara before she had Patrick. He thought back to the year she was twelve. She had the scarlet fever and almost died from the sickness. It had left her weak. Every time she had gotten ill, she had to take to her bed for days. She just was not strong enough to withstand any sickness, despite the brave way she acted, and she certainly did not have the strength to give birth and survive.

"I need to talk to you, Michael," Beth whispered to him.

Michael turned to his brother and sister-in-law and quietly asked them to leave. They did, mentioning to call on them if he needed anything. After Beth was sure the door to her room was firmly closed, she looked back up at

Michael.

"Michael, you have always been my favorite. Although I love Matthew and Gabrielle, they have two children and another on the way." Beth swallowed. "What I am trying to ask is, would you…Michael, would you take care of my baby and raise it for me? Make him your own?"

"You will not die, Beth," Michael protested feebly.

"Please, Michael, just say yes. Please."

"I would be honored to take care of your child and raise him as mine."

Satisfied with Michael's answer, Beth went into a fitful sleep, only to wake up later to give birth to her daughter, who she named Francine, before she died early the next morning.

Matthew watched as Michael moved away from his sister's body to hold Francine in his arms. Michael looked up and met his brother's eyes and said, "She has asked me to care for Francine."

Matthew nodded, knowing she would. "What are you going to do now, Michael?"

"I would like to stay in Ireland to visit with you for a while. I have not even met my niece and nephew."

"Marilyn and Joseph would love for their Uncle Michael to stay, but are you sure you should stay here so close to Dunovan Castle?"

Michael asked the question he had been wondering about since he came back home. "Is Kathleen still living there?"

Michael and Matthew walked back into the living room and sat down.

"Rumor has it that Lord Dunovan made Ryan Winchester his partner, forcing Kathleen to stay in the castle."

"Why on earth would he do that? He is the one who beat her up and kicked her out of the castle."

"The man is sick, Michael, He makes no sense, but Webster stayed with her. Maybe they made some kind of deal that Webster could stay with her if she remained at Dunovan Castle."

"Have you seen her? Do you know how she is?"

Matthew saw the desperate look on his brother's face, heard it in his voice, but he could not tell him about Kathleen's child who was most likely his. If Michael knew, he was not sure what he would do. Storm the castle for a start, Matthew was sure.

"No, I have no news of Kathleen. She never comes down here. The castle has not had a party in years."

"I hope she is safe and happy." Michael almost sounded convincing on the latter of his comments. He sat gently rocking Francine in his arms, changing the subject by asking, "May I stay here for a while with you? I'll keep a low profile; I will not try to see Kathleen. I'll stay away from the castle. Lord Dunovan would have my head if he knew I was back."

"Of course you may stay with us, and to hell with Lord Dunovan. You are a well known respected duke now, Michael. If he tried to anything, he would be killed so fast, he would not know what hit him. The person to stay away from though is Eva; she is a vicious bitch, Michael. She vowed years ago to get revenge on you and Kathleen."

"It was she and Bartholomew McKnight that told Lord Dunovan that Kathleen was here. It was their fault my Kathleen was taken away from me."

"Michael, you have to get over her someday."

"God damn it, Matthew! Do you not think I have tried? I married Clara and still could not stop thinking about Kathleen."

"I am sorry about Clara, Michael."

"I am too. I made her life hell. She was not Kathleen. I could never love her. But she did not love me either. Her fiancé had died from influenza. She never wanted me. Ours was a marriage of convenience. It was wrong of us to marry; we did it to make an old dying man happy. I think she was happy to die."

Matthew saw the sorrow in Michael's handsome face.

"Matthew, what did we do for God to give us such pain on this earth?"

"I ask myself that same question day after day. I was convinced that after Dutch died things would start to brighten up for us. I had not expected Beth to die."

"Maybe things will be better now."

Blue eyes met brown, and both reflected doubts at Michael's sentiment.

* * * * * * *

It was a dark, cold winter's night, the night Lord Dunovan finally met his death. After ruining so many innocent lives, his was taken from him by Webster O'Leary. Webster had found out that William had abused his daughter, and he stabbed William several times in a fit of rage.

On the night of William's death, Webster had gone to see his daughter, who Ryan said was finally getting better. Although quiet and reserved, she had made an effort for Willow's third birthday. Webster knocked gently on Kathleen's door. When there was no reply, he started to walk away and came back later until he heard weeping from inside. He knocked again and called Kathleen's name. When she refused to answer him, he turned the knob, found it unlocked and walked in.

Kathleen was laying in the fetal position on her bed sobbing.

"Kathleen lassie, what is wrong?" he asked worriedly as he picked her up to hold her in his arms.

Kathleen shook her head, trying to say nothing was wrong, but a strangled sob came out.

Webster refused to listen to her. "Lassie, you have to tell me what is wrong so that I can help you."

Kathleen love you tell me what's wrong so I can fix it. Michael's words floated through her mind. *Where are you now, Michael? Can you fix my problems now?*

"Kathleen, what is it?"

"I can not tell you. I am too ashamed," she said so softly Webster could barely make out the words.

"You have to tell me. I can not stand to see you like this."

Kathleen did, knowing that if she did not she would never be able to live a normal life again. The moment she was finished telling him, she felt relieved, but then she saw the look in her father's face. It was one of rage and fury.

"You can not do anything about it. I feel better now just telling you. Please do not do anything," Kathleen pleaded as he dumped his daughter on the bed and stormed out.

Kathleen ran out after him, grabbing his arm. "Please do not go after him. Do not do anything drastic. Please."

"Kathleen, unless you want me to hit you, I suggest you let go of my arm."

Kathleen released her father and sank to the floor sobbing.

Webster found William in the library drinking by a large fire. "I want to talk to you, Lord Dunovan. Now," Webster said through clenched teeth.

"Why, Mr. O'Leary, you seem a tad upset. What on earth could be wrong?"

Webster grabbed William by the collar of his shirt, lifting him to his feet. "You know exactly what is wrong. This moment has been coming for many years. I have learned something to cause your death."

William was unconcerned about Webster's fury as he asked, "And what have you learned that has made you upset?"

"You raped Kathleen, an innocent girl."

"Ah. So she has finally come out of her silence. I was wondering how long that would last."

"Is that all you have to say for yourself you damn son of a bitch?"

"What do you want me to say Mr. O'Leary. I have always had a fascination with her. I just took what I wanted."

Webster tried to contain his temper as he asked, "You find nothing wrong with what you did?"

"Why should I? She is not my daughter, but I raised her like my own. She owed me."

"You kill Mary, you ruin Kathleen's life, and then you take advantage of her. What kind of man are you?"

"I am a man who does what he must to survive."

Webster released William and moved toward the fireplace, selecting a long golden poker with a sharp point at the end of it. He put it behind his back and walked back to William.

"You have known for years I have hated you. How could you have married Lass when you did not love her?"

"One should not marry for love; love gets you in trouble. You should know. My mother found out that little fact when I killed her too. Irish bitch."

The man was crazy. "You will experience pain, all the pain you have caused so many others."

"You do not think I have experienced pain? My mother betrayed me in a way that is unspeakable. And you are wrong about not loving Mary. I did. How could I let her live when she did not love me?"

"You deserve to die, Lord Dunovan."

"Yes, I suppose I do," he stated calmly. "I guess it is the proper way to die, by your hand."

"Yes, I think it is," Webster said simply, raising the poker high above William's head, ready to strike.

William nodded, accepting his fate. "Before you kill me, realize that you will be hanged for the act."

"At least I will go to heaven, for God will not condemn me for killing you, and I will be with Lass. Go to hell, Lord William Dunovan," Webster said, bringing the poker above his head again bringing it down upon William, ending the life of the man who had caused so much pain and ruin to so many other lives.

* * * * * * *

A year later, Kathleen experienced happiness again, which she thought would never happen after Lord Dunovan's death and her father's hanging. She and Ryan had moved to London, to Ryan's ancestral home, Winchester Manor. Dunovan Castle was closed and, management of the land was placed into Matthew Fitzpatrick's hands.

Kathleen, to her surprise, found London to be charming and loved Ryan's home. After the untimely deaths of Lord Dunovan and Webster, Ryan had sat Kathleen down to tell her it would be best if they left Ireland. There were too many bad memories for her there. He told Kathleen that he loved her always and would always protect and care for her. Kathleen, although she would never forget about Michael, accepted Ryan's love and accepted Ryan as her husband.

Together they had a green-eyed, light brown-haired daughter named Julianne, after Ryan's mother. Kathleen, for the first time since Michael, felt secure and cherished. She prayed to the almighty everyday that nothing bad would happen to her or her family again. And she asked God to take care of Michael too and hoped that he had found joy out of life.

Every once in a while, she did ask to see Michael again, for when she allowed herself to think about him, she missed him very much.

Chapter Fifteen

Sixteen-year-old Willow Winchester put one last stray curl into place before she left her room. In the hall she could hear the sounds of guests and music floating up the stairs. It was January 15, 1817, the day of her presentation to society. It made her nervous just to think about it, being presented to society, to be viewed and judged for the way she looked and behaved. All this just to find a husband that was befitting to her social status. At least that's what her father told her. She had to marry someone of nobility. To confuse Willow even more, her mother had spent many hours on her newly passed sixteenth birthday to tell her to marry for love not money or status, and never, ever to please anyone else.

Willow thought back to how her mother's beautiful face had taken on a faraway look when she stressed the importance of finding love and happiness. It made Willow wonder, as she did many times, if her mother was happy with her father. Her parents never fought with one another, or spoke harshly to each other her or her younger sister, but Willow had a feeling that her parents were not happy with each other. Although her father never yelled at her, he had always treated her differently than her sister, Julianne. There was a distance between them that she did not know where it came from. She had an idea it was because she looked nothing like him and exactly like her mother, except for the eyes. Willow had brilliant blue eyes, as deep as sapphires.

As Willow started to descend down the staircase, her twelve-year-old sister ran up to her agitated with their mother. "Willow, why am I not allowed to go to the party?"

Willow sighed as she looked up at her sister who recently had a growth spurt, inheriting their father's height while she remained petite like their mother.

"Juli," she said affectionately, "you know you are far too young to attend formal functions."

"Willow, you do not seem very happy. Aren't you excited?" Julianne asked, looking at her older sister with wonder. Willow had never liked to attend social functions, preferring to read and stay indoors. She had always been somewhat shy and reserved, although if she truly liked someone, she could be quite charming and even a little flirty. Julianne loved her sister, thinking she was the most beautiful person in the world, next to her mother, and should meet more people instead of spending her time reading. Julianne hated to learn. She was bored with books and schooling; she wanted to spend her time outdoors with her horse, not stuck in doors with dusty old books.

"I guess I am a little scared, Julianne. What if I fall dancing, or I say something stupid and no one likes me?"

"Willow, you are the most graceful dancer I have ever seen. Remember, I am the one who always falls during awful dancing lessons. If you are worrying about anyone not liking you, that is the funniest thing I had ever heard. People love you; you just never let anyone close enough to get to know you. Now go. You look absolutely beautiful," she said, her voice full of admiration.

Willow was dressed in a silk and velvet dress the color of her eyes, a gift from her father for her birthday. The bodice was made of the soft material which left her shoulders bare, with the neckline coming to a V where her cleavage started. The velvet ended at her waist, starting the silk skirt in a lighter blue falling straight to the floor.

She wore her light brown, curly hair pulled away from her face, but flowing down her back. She was still unsure of how she was dressed; she was not used to looking so mature.

"Are you sure I look fine? Maybe I should go find something else to wear."

"Willow, do you want me to hit you to knock some sense into you? You look gorgeous." Julianne kissed her sister on the cheek and gently pushed her toward the stairs. "Now, no arguing, you go on down those stairs and have fun for the both of us."

Willow, about to protest again, received a stern look from her sister, so sighing loudly, she started the long descent down the stairs, hoping no one would notice her. She heard Julianne's door close and thought she should be the one attending this stupid ball not her. Her hopes that no one noticed her were dashed when her father spotted her as she reached the bottom step, "Ah, here she is. The guest of honor has finally made herself present."

"Ryan, leave her alone. You are embarrassing her," his wife dressed in a green and white, hand painted, silk gown chastised him as she watched her daughter enter the room.

"Kathleen, no one that lovely should be embarrassed about anything," he stated with pride.

Kathleen lightly squeezed her husband's shoulder, moving toward her daughter. "You look lovely, Willow darling," she said, kissing her on the cheek.

"Do I? I am not sure about the dress."

Kathleen saw the uncertainty in her daughter's eyes, startling her as she remembered the same look the day Michael had proposed to her. She had never realized how truly blue Willow's eyes were, just like Michael's. She had not let Michael enter her mind in years; she wondered what it was about Willow tonight that made her think of him. She just must be feeling emotional that her daughter looked so beautiful.

"Of course you look wonderful, dear. Now go on, dance with that nice Rodchester boy who has been waiting for you."

"Do I have too?"

"Yes." Her mother firmly pushed her towards a tall, light-haired young man who faintly resembled a Roman god.

Willow sighed and went towards the handsome young man who smiled at her and held out his arm.

* * * * * * *

Two hours later, after being thoroughly bored by David Rodchester, the third, Willow went to the library to hide. One would think that with so much money David could find something else to talk about than his stupid stables. You would think he gave birth to some of those horses. Opening the library door expecting to be alone, she was peeved to find a dark, brooding, blue-eyed man sitting alone in a chair by a fire. She had heard him being announced as the Duke of Liverpool when she was dancing with David. He had arrived late in the evening with his son and niece. Willow smiled as she remembered her sister sneaking down the stairs in one of their mother's old ball gowns and chose the son of this man to chase around the ballroom.

Willow suspected the man had been invited because of his title out of courtesy. His son was too young for her, and his manner was not friendly. She observed her father introduce himself to the Duke of Liverpool, and the short conversation that followed, leaving her father looking disturbed. She had wondered idly where her mother was during this time.

Michael Fitzpatrick looked up, surprised to see a young girl standing in the doorway; he had not heard anyone come in, so deep in thought he was. When Michael had received the invitation to Willow Winchester's coming out ball, he never made the connection to Kathleen. He thought she was still in Ireland, not England. When Ryan Winchester introduced himself, he had realized this was Kathleen's husband, but not seeing Kathleen, he had gone in search of Patrick and Francine. He found them having too good of a time to take them away. So he decided to go to the library to stay away from the crowd. Not seeing Kathleen made him wonder where she might be; he assumed she must be dead. Lost in the silence of the library, he had never expected this lovely girl to disturb him. He stood up and walked towards her, noticing the resemblance to Kathleen.

"Who are you?" he demanded of her.

"Who am I? Shouldn't I be the one who asks that question of you. After all, this is my house," she answered coolly.

Michael had to smile at her. This must be Kathleen's daughter. It was almost a repeat of the conversation Kathleen and he had the day he met her.

"I am Michael Fitzpatrick. I am the Duke of Liverpool."

"You are Irish then, yes?" She was well aware of the rumors of an Irish man becoming a duke and helping those less fortunate.

"Yes, I am," he answered, moving away from the girl toward the door to leave. He had to leave. She looked far too much like Kathleen for his comfort. However, he was stopped when she asked, "Do you not want to know who I am?"

Michael's sapphire eyes met Willow's own and saw the uncertainty in them. Feeling sorry for her, he smiled and said softly, "I would be happy to know your name."

"My name is Willow."

"Ah, the lovely girl who the party is for. It is a beautiful name for a lovely lass."

Willow felt a bond with this tall, dark-haired, good-looking man with the brilliant blue eyes; she wanted to know everything about him for some strange reason.

Trying to stop him from leaving, she said the first thing that popped into her mind, "Have you met my mother? She is part Irish."

Michael swallowed thickly. Kathleen was alive here in this house so close. "Is she?"

"Yes, her father, Webster, was Irish," she began chatting at him, ignoring the look on his face as his story was recited to him through this young girl. "My grandmother, an English heiress, fell in love with Webster when she was young, then forced from him by her father. She had to marry Lord

Dunovan, whom Webster killed years ago. He was hanged for the murder when I was three. We never speak of it. Mother refuses. She never went to see her father before he was hanged. Shortly afterward, we left Ireland and moved here. Sometimes I wish we could have stayed in Ireland. I do not remember much about it, except it was lovely and green," she said wistfully.

Michael reached out to touch Willow's smooth cheek gently. This young girl experiencing so much at a young age made him want to protect her. He had known of Webster's hanging, for he had gone to be with him his last moments on earth. Webster had told him what had driven him to finally kill the evil man that had ruined so many lives. Michael, who long ago thought nothing else could hurt him, had tears in his eyes to learn of Kathleen's pain and suffering. He told Webster he was sorry that he was to be killed for such a justifiable act. Webster had replied that he was glad to die so he could be with Lass again.

"You do not like England, Willow?" he asked, still caressing her cheek; he too felt some unexplainable bond between them. It went deeper than her being Kathleen's daughter; it was almost as if they were somehow related.

"It is not that I do not like England. The royal family is quite nice, and I enjoy the theatre, but I miss Ireland sometimes."

"It sounds to me like you have a great deal of Irish blood in you. They say an Irishman never forgets the land. It is almost like his mother."

Before Willow could respond to Michael's comments, her mother came rushing through the library door with a scowl on her face.

"Willow Winchester, what on earth are you doing alone in the library when you have a house full of guests? With some strange man no less." Since Michael's back was still turned from her, she did not know who he was. Walking toward the couple, she continued with, "And you, sir! Just who do you think you are taking young girls into the secluded library?"

Willow took Michael's hand away from her face, running around him to face her mother. Michael, shocked to hear Kathleen's voice after all these years, stood still unable to move. He wished he were anywhere else in the world but here. He wanted to see Kathleen more than anything, but he did not want to disturb her life. It had been too long.

Willow, unaware of the war within Michael, was trying to explain herself to her furious mother. "Mom, it is not what you think!"

"Well, I certainly hope not. Honestly, Willow, you are still too trusting for a girl of sixteen. The world is full of men who will take advantage of young innocent girls like yourself."

"Mother, I assure you the duke was just talking to me. Is that not the truth, Mr. Fitzpatrick?" Willow asked, pleading for help.

It was the mention of his name that finally caused Michael to turn around.

Kathleen's golden eyes widened at the sight of Michael standing in front of her. She grew dizzy and sat down. Michael stood before her, not saying a word, dressed in black, still looking the same as when she last saw him, except for a few creases around his eyes. But a few wrinkles could not take anything away from his good looks. At close to forty, he was still the best looking man she had ever seen. She put her hand to her forehead, unable to believe after all these years, Michael was standing her in her house talking to their daughter.

Willow watched as her mother grew pale. "Mother, are you all right? You look ill."

It was several moments before Kathleen could answer her daughter, and when she did, it was so low and hoarse she could barely get out the words. "Yes, Willow, I am fine. Willow, I came to find you to tell you to go find your sister."

"Julianne?"

"What other sister do you have? Go find her now."

"What do you want to tell her?"

"Tell her to go to bed, Willow. Make sure she goes to bed before her father finds her."

"Yes, mother." She turned to Michael, held out her hand and said, "It was a pleasure to meet you, Mr. Fitzpatrick."

Michael took his eyes off of Kathleen to take Willow's hand in his, saying, "It was a pleasure for me to meet you, Willow."

Willow spotted the ring Michael still wore on a gold chain around his neck. She could not stop herself as she lifted it up to get a better look at the piece of jewelry. She had seen it before.

"Mother, Mr. Fitzpatrick has a ring exactly like the one you wear."

Kathleen looked down at her right hand to the ring with the carved roses she wore.

"Willow, please leave and find your sister. Tell your father I have business to attend to, and I will be out in a moment."

Willow nodded her head, leaving the library, closing the door softly behind her, thinking her mother was behaving very much unlike herself.

Michael waited until Willow left the room to kneel down in front of Kathleen's chair and take her face into his hands. He forced her to meet his eyes, which were shiny with tears, as he took the opportunity to look at Kathleen up close for the first time in over fifteen years.

Kathleen had grown even more beautiful in the time they had been apart; she had lost the roundness in her face of youth, leaving her with a sculpted beauty that took his breath away. She still wore her hair long, letting it fall in soft auburn curls down her back. He could not believe his love, his Kathleen, was right in front of him after all these years.

He finally broke the silence by saying, "You have a lovely, well-mannered daughter, Kathleen love."

Kathleen answered him with tears in her own eyes by saying, "We, Michael. We have a lovely daughter. And she is only well-mannered sometimes."

Michael swallowed the lump in his throat, gently wiped away Kathleen's tears and said, "Willow is mine? How?"

Kathleen nodded her head and raised her eyebrow. "You know how, Michael. I was pregnant before I came went back to Dunovan Castle. She has your eyes, you know."

"Does she know Ryan is not her father?"

Kathleen shook her head. "She went through so much, Michael. She was the one who found Lord Dunovan's body, with my father standing over it. It has left her more reserved than she should be. That was why I was so furious to find her with a strange man alone in here. She never goes anywhere alone."

"Oh, Kathleen, I am so sorry," Michael whispered, smoothing her soft hair.

"She has had so much pain, Michael. I could not tell her that Ryan was not her father. She knows nothing about you, although I suppose I must tell her. She will be the same age I was when I found out my father was not who I thought he was. I guess history does repeat itself," she said wistfully.

"Kathleen, I did not know it was you when I came here. The invitation I received stated that it was the Duke and Duchess of Winchester requesting the Duke of Liverpool's presence at their daughter's ball. I never made the connection that it was you. I swear Kathleen; it was not until I met Ryan that I knew. I came in here to be alone."

Kathleen looked at Michael, asking quietly, "Did you not want to see me, Michael?"

Michael groaned, burying his face in her hair as he used to. "She asks me if I wanted to see her again. Kathleen, when I did not see you, I thought you were dead. Ever since you were taken away from me, all I wanted to do was to see you again, hold you like I am now. I stayed away. It hurt too much to know you were in Ireland. Then I heard you moved to England, so I moved back to Ireland. I have never stopped loving you, Kathleen, never stopped thinking of you, although I tried. I tried so damn hard, knowing I would never see you again."

"You make it sound like you would never have come to Willow's ball if you knew I would be here."

"If I would have known, I would not have come here, Kathleen. I do not want to ruin your life, Kathleen."

"How could you have ruined my life?" Kathleen asked, bewildered. Had her life not been destroyed already?

"You have a life here, Kathleen, that does not involve me. You have two daughters; you do not need me."

"I do not need you?! How on earth can you say that I do not need you, Michael? All these years, I have missed you so much it hurt. All the times I looked at Ryan holding Willow when she was a baby, knowing it should be you with your daughter. Willow is my favorite child because she is yours. During Willow's birth, the cruel actions by Lord Dunovan, my father dying, I only survived on the hope that I would one day see you again. I love you, Michael Fitzpatrick, and I always will."

Hearing these words, Michael stood up, lifting Kathleen up into his arms and holding her. Just holding with her head against his chest like he used to. He kissed the top of her silky head, feeling the soft mass of hair he thought he would never feel again. "Please do not cry, Kathleen love, please."

Ryan Winchester walked into the library finding his wife of over sixteen years in the arms of another man. Both had tears streaming down their cheeks that went unnoticed, and Michael was still kissing Kathleen's head over and over again.

"So at last you get to meet the elusive Duke of Liverpool, Kathleen," he said loudly, slamming the door behind him.

Kathleen jumped away from Michael, hastily wiping the tears off of her cheeks. "Ryan, I—"

"No, Kathleen, please do not say a word. Go back to the party. Mr. Fitzpatrick, I believe it is time for you to leave my home." Although he said it calmly, Kathleen saw the pain in his eyes and went to touch his shoulder with sympathy. "Do not touch me, Kathleen," he said stiffly.

Kathleen turned red with embarrassment and shame, dropping her hand from Ryan's shoulder.

"Kathleen love…Kathleen, I better go find my son and niece and leave."

Michael turned to leave, but not before he looked at Kathleen one more time. She still loved him, but she avoided his eyes by looking down at the rug, tracing a pattern over and over with the point of her shoe.

Michael went into the ballroom in search of Patrick, to find him talking to Willow. He was so confused to see Kathleen right here and married to someone else. Willow, his daughter, born out of love, had suffered so much already. How would she take it if she knew he was her real father? He peered closely at Willow and realized she did have his eyes and Patrick's. "Patrick, it is time to leave. Go find Francine."

"Mr. Fitzpatrick, may I ask what is going on? Is my mother all right? I told my father she was talking to you in the library, and he stormed out of the ballroom. I have never seen him so angry."

"I do not think he likes me very much, Willow darlin'." He turned away from his daughter. "Patrick, go find Francine so we can leave."

"Francine is with Willow's sister, Julianne."

"Well, go get her, god damn it!" Michael yelled, causing several people to turn around to see what the commotion was about. Michael noticed the party had thinned out somewhat, but there were enough bodies around to start rumors. He gave them a long look that told them to mind their business, but nevertheless lowered his voice saying, "Patrick, go get your cousin, please."

"Mr. Fitzpatrick, it is storming outside, and several of the bridges leading away from our home have been washed out, including the one to Liverpool House. I am afraid you have to stay here tonight. I sent Francine to stay with Julianne, my sister. They seem to have become fast friends."

Michael looked up at the ceiling with hands on his hips and asked silently, *Why God can you not make anything easy for me?* "Perhaps there is an inn close by that we could stay at, Willow?"

"I am sorry. There is not one close by. Come, I will show you to a room that you can stay in. Our home is not that bad, Mr. Fitzpatrick. Patrick, you can share a room with David Rodchester. He is a little boring, but he is nice. He will protect you from my sister also."

Julianne had chased Patrick around the ballroom for the better part of the night. She thought he was dreamy. He thought she was a pain and ruined his chance at a raven-haired beauty that had caught his fancy.

Patrick went to find his roommate for the night, as Michael followed Willow up the long winding stairs.

"Does your father know I am staying the night here, lass?"

"He knows a number of people have to stay here tonight because of the storm. That was the reason he went to look for my mother in the first place." Approaching a room, she unlocked the door, declaring, "This is your room. If you need anything, my parents are across the hall down one door to the right."

Thanking her, he looked down at his daughter, wishing that he could tell her who he really was. He wished he could tell her that he loved her and never wanted to leave her mother. He wondered if his family had heard of her and why they never told him if they had. He wished Kathleen had never been taken away from him. Most of all, he wished he could kill Lord Dunovan all over again himself.

Willow watched as Michael's face took on a faraway look. Feeling weary of him, she asked, "Can I get you anything, Mr. Fitzpatrick? You look ill."

"No, thank you, Willow, I feel fine. Good night," he said, walking in and closing the door behind him.

Willow shook her head, thinking that the night had gotten very strange very quickly, and began to walk back down the stairs. At the start of the storm, many of the closer resident guests decided to leave, so now the ballroom was almost completely empty, except those that had to stay the night. She found her mother and father directing their guest to bedrooms they could take shelter in. Her mother still looked very pale, and her parents avoided each other's eyes. She wondered what had happened between them in the library after Michael Fitzpatrick had left.

She approached her parents to inform them where the Fitzpatrick family was staying, but before she could say anything, her father spotted her and said, "It is after midnight, Willow. Go on to bed now."

"Yes, Father, in a minute. I came down to tell you that the Duke of Liverpool is across the hall and to the left of your room. His son is staying with David Rodchester, and Francine is staying with Julianne."

Kathleen, upon hearing this news, sat down. Michael was in her and Ryan's home. He had to stay the night; she took several slow deep breaths trying to calm herself. Ryan ignored his wife, patted Willow on the head and said, "How nice of you to help them. Willow, thank you."

Willow, looking puzzled, nodded her head, kissed her father's cheek and said, "Thank you for my lovely party. It was fun. Goodnight, Father, Mother."

Ryan waited until Willow and all the other guests had gone up to their separate rooms to turn to Kathleen. In the library he had refused to discuss anything with her about Michael and explaining the situation about the storm. They had not said another word to each other, trying to make their guests comfortable. Now he went to her where she was sitting and rubbing her forehead with her eyes closed. "Do you have a headache, Kathleen?"

Kathleen opened her eyes to find Ryan standing over her. "Yes, Ryan, I do have a slight headache." Slight, was not the word for it; she had a constant pounding that she suddenly feared would get worse.

"I wonder if you would have that pain if Michael were down here. Perhaps he could hold you again?"

"I am going to bed now, Ryan," Kathleen said, ignoring Ryan's remarks and starting for the door. Ryan grabbed her by the arm, forcing her to turn to look at him. She stepped back when she smelled the liquor on his breath; he had been drinking quit a bit that evening since seeing Michael and Kathleen together.

"We need to talk, Kathleen."

"There is nothing to discuss."

"Like hell, there is nothing to discuss!" he yelled, holding her arm tighter.

Kathleen jerked her arm free, saying, "You will wake the guests with your shouting. You will cause a scandal. Please try to calm yourself."

"Calm myself? Just how do you suggest I am to calm myself? Michael Fitzpatrick, your lover, Willow's father, is in my goddamn house. I find the two of you in each other's arms. You tell me how to calm myself."

"You could try to contain your temper until we are in our room and can talk about this rationally."

Ryan tensed his jaw as he followed Kathleen to their room and held the door open for her. She walked in, sitting down on her bed and waiting for Ryan to begin. She watched him sit down on his bed, then get back up again, pacing back in forth in front of her. After Julianne had been born, they had stopped sharing a bed except on special occasions. Ryan still wanted a son. Kathleen felt funny sleeping with someone she did not love.

"You do not love me, do you, Kathleen?"

"I am very fond of you, Ryan, but, no, I do not love you," she answered honestly, "I have never told you that I have."

"That is true, Kathleen, but it is not fair, is it? Life, I mean. I love you so much, Kathleen, more than anything else in the world. I took a child that was not mine and gave her a good name. We have a beautiful daughter together, and yet you still do not love me."

"I do care for you a great deal. I may even love you in a way, but not like…" She trailed off.

"Not like Michael. No never like Michael. I wonder if you would never have met him if you would love me, Kathleen." She watched as he went to pour himself another drink from his dresser before asking one more question, "Do you still love Michael, Kathleen?"

"Yes, I still love Michael."

"I wish you the best, Kathleen," he said, turning his back on her.

"Ryan?" she questioned confused.

"I love you, Kathleen. I want you to be happy. Go to Michael."

"Are you sure, Ryan?"

"Get the hell out, Kathleen! Just get out," Ryan said hoarsely, still not looking at her.

"I will not shame you, Ryan. I will do nothing to harm your social status. I will stay your wife if you wish me to."

Ryan nodded his head, not saying another word as Kathleen left the room. She felt horrible for him. He was such a kind and gentle man. But as much as she knew it was hurting him, it was hurting her not to go to Michael. She left the room, closing the door quietly behind her. She heard a loud crash and growl from within the room.

"I am sorry, Ryan, so sorry," she whispered to the door.

* * * * * * *

Michael lay on the bed on top of the covers with his shirt undone and hanging loosely around him. He looked up at the ceiling, playing with the gold ring around his neck, thinking of what had taken place tonight. He was still in shock to see Kathleen again after all these years. He hoped Ryan was not mad at her. She had not known he would be there. If anything, Ryan should be angry with him. He should have left right there and then when he realized this was Kathleen's home. Why did life have to be so difficult?

All those years he had rejected being Irish, struggling so hard to be a doctor and failing, being forced to be an Irish farmer. Then Kathleen had come into his life and turned it upside down. She made him laugh and realize that life was what you made it. He had fallen in love with her at first sight; then she was taken away from him. And now after all these years, almost two decades, he finally found her again, but he could not be with her.

Michael heard a faint knocking on his door, but ignored it, not wanting to be bothered with anyone. It sounded louder again this time. Sighing loudly, he knew whoever it was, was not going to go away. He got off the bed and ran a hand through his hair, knowing he looked like hell. He certainly felt that way. Expecting to see Patrick or Francine, he was surprised to find Kathleen on the other side of the door. She was still dressed in her ball gown, and although she was not crying, she looked very somber as she stood before him.

"Kathleen?"

"May I come in, Michael?" she asked shyly avoiding his eyes.

"Of course," Michael answered, standing to the side so she could enter, then closing the door behind her, but not before looking out in the hall for Ryan. Seeing no one, he stood in front of her.

"Did I wake you?"

"No."

Kathleen glanced around the room and sat down on the edge of the bed. Michael watched as she opened her mouth to speak, obviously at a loss for words. He went to sit next to her on the bed, thinking of what might put her at ease. She jumped when he gently caressed her cheek.

"Why are you here, Kathleen love?" he asked softly.

"Michael, I—" Kathleen could not express herself, too overwhelmed by the fact that Michael was right next to her.

"Where is your husband?"

"Ryan is in our room. He sent me here, Michael. He says he understands."

Michael swallowed. "What do you mean, Kathleen?"

"I still love you; he knows that. I—" She looked down.

"What is it, love? What's wrong?"

"I still love you so much. I never stopped. I need you, Michael," Kathleen finally said, meeting his eyes.

Michael groaned, pulling her down to lie on his chest. He looked at the beautiful face that he had thought about for so long. Kissing her on the nose, he said, "Are you sure, Kathleen love?"

Kathleen nodded her head. "I have waited so long, Michael, to see you again."

"Me too, love. It seems that I have waited all my life to hold you in my arms again."

"Please, Michael," Kathleen whispered, achingly kissing his chest.

Michael sighed. It was as if nothing had changed. Her body knew even after all these years that it belonged to him. He rolled her on her back, kissing her deeply and removing his shirt.

"Love, do you know how long I have waited for you?" Michael whispered, softly helping her out of her ball gown. "You are so beautiful, Kathleen," he said as he moved to renew their love that had been denied from them for so long.

* * * * * * *

Later that night, Michael pulled the covers over them, moving Kathleen's head to his shoulder. He smiled as she moved closer to him in her sleep. He gently rubbed her neck after moving her heavy mane of hair. Kathleen was more beautiful than he had remembered. His beautiful Kathleen right here in his arms. He placed a soft kiss on her head, holding her tightly, never wanting to let her go.

Kathleen stirred in Michael's arms, smiling sleepily up at him. Michael smiled back, asking teasingly, "You are not sorry, are you?"

Kathleen kissed his chin, letting him know that she remembered that is what he asked the first time they were together. "No, Michael, I am not sorry. Are you?"

"Kathleen, how on earth can you ask such a thing? What a stupid idiotic question," he chastised her.

"What about your wife, Michael?" she asked, pressing her face to his chest, refusing to look at him when he gave her the answer.

Michael sighed, moving off the bed, pulling on his pants. He could hear the clock strike three in the distance. It was late, but he knew this conversation had to be.

"Kathleen, Clara died giving me my son Patrick."

Kathleen sat up in bed, holding the sheet over her chest. "Did you love her, Michael?" she asked, remembering the hurtful words Lord Dunovan had said to her about Michael marrying for money.

He looked at her and honestly said, "No, I did not love her."

"Why did you marry her then?" she asked, fearing his answer.

"Kathleen, the day I saw you the last time was the worst day of my life. You remember, Kathleen, the day in the stables? The day you told me you had to marry Ryan Winchester, I thought I would kill myself. The only reason that I did not was because I hoped to see you again." He reached over to touch her cheek. "I am glad I did not, but the thought truly crossed my mind. I stayed in our cottage that you had fixed up for two days, not drinking, just sitting there. All I thought of was you and how I wanted to kill Lord Dunovan.

I am sorry now that I did not kill him. I know what he did to you, Kathleen love. I was in Ireland at the time, visiting Beth during the birth of Francine her daughter. I saw Webster before he was killed, shortly after Beth died during childbirth."

"Oh, Michael, I am so sorry to hear about Beth. I loved her like a sister."

"She knew she was going to die, so she asked me to raise her daughter on her death bed. Matthew and Gabrielle already had two children and another on the way."

"What about Dutch?"

"Dutch died in a fire on New Year's Day."

"New Year's Day. It seems that nothing good ever happens that day."

"You came to us, Kathleen love."

"Michael, you were not happy to have an English brat in your house. You hated me. How could you marry an English duke's daughter?"

"In the long run, I was happy you came to my home, Kathleen. I fell in love with you the moment I saw you. Anyway, to answer your question, I could not stay in Ireland when I knew you were so close by married to someone else, so I went to London and saved Edward Worthington's life, the duke of Liverpool. We became friends. He gave me the option to marry Clara his daughter and inherit everything. I only married her to make a dying man happy. Clara never loved me; she lost her fiancé the year before. It sounds cruel, but I was relieved when she died. I loved you, Kathleen. I kept the ring we were to be married with as I see you kept yours. To me, it was always a symbol of our love. If I had that, maybe one day we could be together again."

"I am so sorry, Michael. Because of me you had to leave your home, marry someone you did not love. It might have been better if we never had met."

Michael moved to sit in front of Kathleen, holding her face in his hands. "You do not really mean that, do you?

Kathleen shook her head no, crying again. "You know, Kathleen love, you are still the only girl in the world who cries at everything."

Kathleen sat up, hitting Michael on the chest with her fist. "Only with you, Michael. I have not cried this much since we said goodbye."

Michael grabbed her fist, kissing it, asking, "What about Ryan? Do you love him?"

"Yes, Michael, in a way I do, but not like us. He took Willow as his child. He did not have to; he could have made me give her away."

"He seems like a good person, Kathleen love. I am glad for your sake and

Willow's that he was not like Lord Dunovan."

Kathleen shuddered at the name. "Michael, you said you know he...what he did to me. How?"

"Webster. I heard he had killed him and went to him, like I said, before he was hanged."

"How was he?"

"He was very calm and relaxed like, he did not have a care in the world. He was glad his life was over; he had suffered enough. He wanted to be with your mother again."

"Life really has not been easy for any of us, has it, Michael?"

"No. Kathleen love, why did you pick Willow as a name for our daughter?"

Kathleen smiled. "Can't you guess, Michael? You are really smart."

"Tell me, love."

"That first time we made love under the willow trees, it was an appropriate name for our daughter."

"She really is a beautiful girl, almost as lovely as her mother."

Kathleen blushed as Michael removed the sheet and pushed her back down on the bed. "What are we going to do, Michael?"

"Can't you guess, love?" he asked teasingly as he kissed her neck.

"Not that, Michael," she said, hitting him on his back.

"What is going to happen now, Michael?"

"I do not know, Kathleen. But losing you again is out of the question. Everything is going to be fine, Kathleen, I promise. Do you trust me, Kathleen?"

Kathleen looked into Michael's beautiful blue eyes and honestly replied, "Yes, Michael, I do trust you."

Chapter Sixteen

Willow Winchester woke the day after her coming out ball to the sound of arguing outside her door in the hall. It sounded like her sister Julianne. Willow sighed and resolved to get out of bed. As Willow got out of bed, quickly combed her hair, and put on her robe, she wondered what her sister was up to now. She was a little surprised to learn that Julianne had received no punishment for sneaking down to the party last night. Then again, her parents had been preoccupied with something. She was still unsure as to what they were preoccupied with, but it looked important.

She knew it had something to do with Michael Fitzpatrick, and she wondered why her father did not like him. She had liked him very much, and she was ashamed of herself for not curtsying to him, especially after she found out that he was a duke. But he did not seem to mind, and her mother did not reprimand her like she usually would.

In fact, her mother's reaction to Michael Fitzpatrick puzzled her. She had looked at him like she knew him, and knew him well. This could not be, since she Willow had never seen him, and she knew all of her parents' friends. Perhaps her mother had known him when she was younger? But that could not be it either, because her mother always told her that she was not allowed to mingle with the people on her father's land. The issue that her mother had found Webster confused her more. Where had she found him if she was not let out of Dunovan Castle?

Years ago, Willow had given up trying to find out about her mother's history. All that ever came out of her questions were vague answers and, never mind it was grown up business.

Willow sighed and left her room to find Julianne arguing with Patrick Fitzpatrick. She felt sorry for the almost fifteen-year-old boy. She knew Julianne was capable of chasing down a boy until he gave in or hit her. Julianne was known to have many bruises after a ball at Winchester Manor. It was not that Julianne was boy crazy or looking for a boy, it was just that she had it in her mind that her parents were going to force her into an arranged marriage. Willow was never sure where Julianne had gotten that idea. Their mother had always been adamant with her daughters that she would make sure they could choose whomever they wanted to marry. The way Kathleen spoke with such firmness made Willow wonder if her father was her mother's choice in marriage. Of course if she were ever to ask her mother if her father was her first choice in marriage, she would not have received an answer.

Julianne spotted her sister emerging from her room and tried to make a run for it, but was not quick enough. It took Willow two quick strides to reach her sister. "Julianne, do you know what time it is?" she whispered loudly.

"Much too early to be bothering me," Patrick said in a deep Irish brogue. He had only inherited his mother's light eyes and fair complexion. He was like his father in every other way. He wanted to be a doctor, which Michael was wholeheartedly in favor of. Michael's one failure was never to be the doctor he had always hoped to be. He was only glad to be married to Clara so he could have the money to send his son to school.

"I was just trying to ask you a question, Patrick," Julianne pouted.

"And I was just trying to tell you that we will not marry."

"Julianne!" Ryan said, loudly overhearing the commotion in the hall.

Julianne turned red, as her father came out of his room. She knew she should have waited to talk to Patrick until later. Now she was going to get it from her father.

"Julianne, it is six o'clock in the morning. Just what in the hell are you doing?"

"I was talking to Patrick," she said quietly, pointing to the uncomfortable looking boy.

Ryan turned to Patrick, immediately noting the resemblance to Michael, and sighed. The man was forever to haunt him. First, he had come back into Kathleen's life out of the clear blue sky, and now his daughter was infatuated with his son. The worst part of this whole mess was that Kathleen had let him take the place he had left all those years ago. He supposed there was really nothing he could do about it. He had given his permission for her to go, and she went. That really hurt. Even though he knew she did not love him, he felt she owed him something. He had taken on Willow as his own child and never forced her to do anything she did not want to. He loved her; it just was not fair that Michael had come back into their lives, after all these years. Fate had played a hell of a joke on him.

Ryan remembered when they were deciding on who was to attend Willow's ball; it was always touchy who to invite and who not to invite. As always, parties were for the social occasion as well as making business deals. Kathleen was almost never any help deciding whom to invite, but they had both idly wondered who the Duke of Liverpool was. The name had sounded familiar to them both, because there was always a great deal of talk about the man doing many acts of kindness for those less fortunate. Ryan should have been suspicious; no one of nobility helped those who did not have as much as they did. Why should they? But he should have realized this man was Michael. Michael, who did not have much growing up, had felt an obligation to help the poor when he did come into his good fortune.

"Julianne. leave the poor boy alone and let him go back to sleep. I am sorry for my daughter. She is usually well-mannered."

"That is all right, sir," Patrick answered, glaring at Julianne. He did not believe she was well-mannered at all.

"Julianne, have you seen your mother? I seem to have lost her this morning."

"She went riding with the Duke of Liverpool."

Ryan took this bit of information rather gracefully. Nodding his head, he went back to his room, brushing by Willow without a word.

Willow was rather surprised her sister had gotten off so easily, considering the hour she had woken them all up. Willow had a funny feeling her life was about to change.

Back in his room, Ryan picked up a cut glass container, empty now after the long night, and threw it across the room, breaking it into a thousand little pieces. Damn Michael Fitzpatrick to hell for coming back into Kathleen's life and ruining his own.

* * * * * * *

The early morning air was crisp and cool as Michael and Kathleen thundered over the frostbitten grass on matching stallions. They had gotten no sleep the night before, talking, catching up on the long years apart from each other and basking in the warm glow of each other's love.

The storm had stopped when day broke, lighting the room Kathleen and Michael had shared with a warm glow.

Kathleen had winced and hidden her face in Michael's shoulder when the light hit her face. "Are you tired, love?"

"No, Michael, I am not tired."

Michael, playing with Kathleen's hair, smiled at her answer,."You have gray hair now, Kathleen." Kathleen hit him and snuggled deeper into his arms. "Are you happy, love?"

"Yes, Michael, I am very happy. I can hardly believe that you are here. And you have gray hair now too, by the way."

Michael smiled at the wonder in her voice. "Believe it, Kathleen love. I am here to stay; I never want to leave you again."

Kathleen suddenly lifted herself up by placing her hands on Michael's chest. "Let's go riding, Michael."

Michael groaned. "Kathleen, do you realize we have gotten no sleep whatsoever?" She nodded her head happily. "And you still want to go riding?"

"Yes, I do. More than ever," she replied, bouncing off the bed oblivious to her unclothed body.

Michael, however, noticed and could not resist saying, "Love, have you put on weight?"

Kathleen stuck out her tongue at him and went over to tug on his arm, saying, "Come on, Michael! Let's go riding. Please," she begged.

Michael groaned and pulled her down on top of him. Trying to distract her from her intent, he kissed her.

Kathleen pulled away and said, "We are going riding now."

"Are you going to wear your ball dress, Kathleen? Or are you going nude like Lady Godiva? I would not mind, but the horses might."

Kathleen hit Michael on the chest for the former remark and pulled the sheet off of him to cover herself and replied with as much dignity as possible, "Neither. I know exactly what I'm going to wear."

"Would you like my assistance?"

"Get dressed, Michael," she said sternly.

Finally, Michael put on his pants from the night before and grabbed Kathleen. "I love you so much, Kathleen," he said into her hair.

"I love you too, Michael."

"Yes, but, Kathleen, I love you despite your faults," he teased trying to lighten up the mood.

"What faults might those be? Before you answer, remember I know which horse have tempers and which are gentle."

Michael laughed and kissed her head again. "I was just thinking the only fault you have, love, is that you have grown more beautiful with age."

"Michael finish getting dressed. I will be downstairs in a minute. I need to go find clothes."

"Do you have to go into the room Ryan is in to get dressed?"

Kathleen saw the worry on his face that he tried to hide as he asked the question casually.

She placed her hand on his cheek. "No, Michael, I have clothes in another room and will get dressed there."

"Be careful, Kathleen love."

"Do not worry, Michael. Do you trust me?" She repeated the question he had often asked her so many years ago, teasingly.

"Yes, love, I trust you."

Kathleen quietly opened the door and went into a room across the hall after making sure no one was around. Michael finished getting dressed, pulling on his boots and shirt, then going down the long staircase to wait for Kathleen. *Riding,* he thought with an amused smile. *She wants to go riding at five o'clock in the morning after no sleep the night before.* Well, that was Kathleen for you. After all these years…still demanding. And beautiful so beautiful.

Patrick ran down the stairs to find his father at the bottom, gazing up into space with a stupid smile on his face.

"Pa," he whispered, "are you all right?"

Michael was startled out of his thoughts. "Patrick, what on earth are you doing up so early?"

"I could not sleep any longer. Some damn girl was after me. Do you think the cook will make me an early breakfast so we can leave?"

"We are not leaving just yet."

"What? Why not?" He was worried Julianne would come after him again.

Kathleen ran down the stairs, wearing the shirt Michael had given her with the embroidered deer with a long white skirt. Michael's eyes widened at the sight of her. She had not forgotten even after all this years.

"Oh, good morning," Kathleen said, almost colliding with Patrick.

"Good morning, your grace," Patrick replied respectfully.

"Please, you must call me Kathleen."

"Pa?"

"If she wants you to call her Kathleen, you might as well," Michael said, breaking his gaze he had with Kathleen. She had kept the shirt, nearly twenty years, and she still had it.

"Pa, why can we not leave now?"

"The duchess is going to take me riding to show her estate to me. So just calm down and relax, Patrick."

"Kathleen, do you suppose your cook could make me something to eat? Please."

"Patrick has an appetite that rivals my brother's."

Kathleen hid a smile as she thought of all the food Matthew could wolf down and said, "I am sure the cook can find a small cow to feed you."

Michael laughed and waited for Kathleen by the entrance as Kathleen led Patrick to the kitchen, telling him to help himself to whatever he wanted.

She returned saying, "You have a wonderful son, Michael. He reminds me of you in some ways. Except he is nicer than you were."

"He wants to be a doctor. I have the money and name to allow him to have that dream."

"If he is anything like his father, he should be a good one."

"You kept the shirt I gave to you."

"Of course I kept it. I loved it when you gave it to me."

Noticing that Kathleen was at a loss for words, he said, "Come, Kathleen, let's go." Kathleen placed her hand in Michael's, and they ran towards the stables.

As they rode through Ryan's estate, Michael looked over at Kathleen. She looked so beautiful with her long golden hair flowing down her back. He realized her hair was more brown than it used to be, but it still shined and moved with a life of its own. Michael slowed his horse down to a trot and waited for Kathleen to do the same. He looked over at Kathleen's happy face. She looked so beautiful, his Kathleen. Never in his wildest dreams did he think a coming out ball for some duke's daughter could have turned out to be one of the happiest days of his life.

"Kathleen love, we need to talk. Is there a place you know of that we could have some privacy?"

"Follow me. I know of a place just beyond those hills." She gestured with a wave of her hand.

Kathleen led Michael to her place where she had always gone ever since she found it, when she first moved to the Winchester home. The small piece of land had always reminded her of the place that Michael had taken her to so many years ago. She always found peace there, a peace she only felt when she was with Michael or thinking of him.

When they reached the woods, Michael gracefully swung his tall, lean body off of his horse and went over to help Kathleen down from her horse. Once she was on the ground, he drew Kathleen close and kissed her. She wound her arms around his neck and kissed him back. Michael gently broke away from her and looked down at her face.

"Kathleen, my love, my life. You have always been my only love. How on earth did I survive without you?"

"Michael, we need to talk. We have a lot to discuss."

Michael sighed loudly. He knew what they needed to discuss, and he did not want to. He tried to distract her from her thoughts by kissing her again, but she stopped him by placing her hands on his chest and pushing him away.

He resigned to her wishes. "I will tie up the horses. You find a clearing where we can sit and talk."

Kathleen went by the lake to sit down, staring into the depths, looking for answers to questions she was not even sure about.

Michael joined her several moments later, taking her hand in his, looking in the water at their image. They sat in silence for a long while, neither knowing what exactly to say to the other. Michael finally broke the uncomfortable silence, saying softly, "What did you want to say, love?"

Kathleen hesitated, not knowing how to start. "Michael, I...I really do not know what to say. I just know something has to be said."

"Tell me how you feel, Kathleen love."

"I feel happy, Michael, because you are here with me. I never thought I would see you again."

"But?" he prompted seeing that she was faltering.

"But I do not know what we are going to do. I want to be with you always, Michael. That's all I ever wanted. But now there are so many other people involved. We are older. I have a husband and two daughters."

"One of them is mine," Michael reminded her gently.

"She does not know, Michael. Willow believes Ryan his her father, and in reality, he is. She loves him, and he loves her, even though she is not his daughter. I have to think of my children. I can not harm them. You must think of Patrick. He is going to have a lot of responsibilities being your only heir. A scandal could ruin many lives."

"What about us, Kathleen?" he asked in a voice filled with emotion. "We have been apart for so long. Was that fair to us? Did we ask to be separated?"

"No, but, Michael—"

"No, Kathleen! You listen to me. We were happy sixteen years ago; we were to be married. If we would have stayed together, Willow would have been raised as my daughter like she should have been. Ryan and Clara would never have had to been involved with us. They would never have been hurt."

"Then Julianne and Patrick would never have been born."

"Would it really matter to you, Kathleen, if we were together? You talk of scandal? It was scandalous when your father killed Lord Dunovan, when an English Duke made an Irish farmer his son-in-law and heir. I know that if we were married, nothing would matter because I would have you."

"Michael, you know I would go with you in a heartbeat if I could. But—"

"Kathleen, then you left me because of your mother, I know. Now there is nothing that can stop us. Ryan knows you love me; the children are almost adults."

Kathleen stood up away from Michael; she had to make him understand. She could not just leave her husband; he had always cared for her and loved her and her daughter. And what of Julianne? "Michael, you have always thought about yourself and not anyone else."

"Are you calling me selfish, love?" he asked, putting his arms around her waist from behind her.

"Somewhat. You just have to understand. We have responsibilities now, and our own lives we have changed, Michael."

Michael turned Kathleen around in his arms and studied her face. "Have we changed that much? I know that I love you more than anything else in the world."

"I love you too, but—"

"But nothing, Kathleen. All my life I have waited for you. I will not be separated from you ever again."

"Michael, the consequences."

"To hell with the consequences. So we become the talk of the British Empire; it will be an interesting story for years to come. You are my love, my life. You belong to me, Kathleen, and no one else."

At these words, Michael drew Kathleen closer to him and kissed her roughly, shoving his hands in her silky mass of golden hair.

"Everything will be fine, love, I promise. Trust me."

Kathleen wanted to believe him, but in the back of her mind, she knew something bad was going to happen to upset their happiness.

Chapter Seventeen

It was Willow Winchester's eighteenth birthday when she boarded the ship that would take her to France and away from her family and home. She stood alone at the ship's railing, wearing a long gray cape, waving to her mother and sister. Her father, at least the man who she knew raised her, was no where to be seen. She was still in shock over what she had learned just two nights ago at her birthday party.

As the ship began to move away from the shore, she could no longer see her sister and mother. Willow began to let the truth about her family sink in. The night of her ball she had been dancing with Patrick Fitzpatrick, who had just confessed that Julianne was not as bad as she used to be, when her mother asked to speak with her in the library. Willow sighed. The library, all major discussions happened in the library. She wondered what was wrong now. Someone must have complained that she did not dance with him.

As she entered the room, she was surprised to find her mother and Michael Fitzpatrick waiting for her. Michael, as he insisted she call him, seemed to always be around. Ever since her coming out ball, Michael Fitzpatrick seemed to be attached to her mother. She knew something had happened with her mother and him and was happening now. Her father was never around when they were together; the fact of the matter was, that in the past two years she hardly ever saw her father. Her father was always out of town on "business." She thought it had something to do with Michael.

When she walked in the room, Michael got up out of the chair he was sitting in facing her mother and indicated that she sit. Willow obeyed, noting that he got up to stand behind her mother with his hand on her shoulder. She raised her eyebrow at her mother, but said nothing, waiting for her to begin.

Kathleen sighed when she saw Willow's expression at Michael's intimate gesture. How on earth was she to begin? She thought back to the disastrous scene so long ago on her own birthday when Lord Dunovan had forced her mother to tell her of Webster O'Leary. But Ryan had only suggested that Willow was old enough to know the truth, especially since rumors were starting to spread about them. After talking over the matter with Michael, she had agreed that it was time to tell Willow. But how, how was she to tell Willow that her whole life was based on a lie? How would Willow take it?

Kathleen felt Michael squeeze her shoulder as if he knew what she was thinking.

"Willow...I—" Kathleen stopped unable to continue.

Willow looked at her mother's pale face, wide brown eyes, and got nervous. "Mother, what is it? What is the matter?"

"Nothing is the matter, Willow. I just need to tell you something. It is rather important though."

"Did something happen to Father?" Willow asked in alarm.

Kathleen grew paler at the mention of Ryan's name. Nothing had happened to him yet. "No, Ryan is fine."

"Then what is it? You are making me very nervous, Mother. Just tell me."

"Do you remember your grandfather, Webster?"

Willow winced as she remembered walking in on Webster standing over Lord Dunovan's body with the fire poker. She had tried to block out the scene from her mind for years. Why was her mother bringing it up now? She nodded her head in answer to her mother's question.

"You see, Willow, he was your real grandfather. My mother had me with him illegitimately, one summer she had spent in Ireland. They fell in love, but were not be able to be together. She was forced to marry Lord Dunovan and live in Ireland at Dunovan Castle. I found out the story of my mother on my sixteenth birthday. I rebelled. I told Lord Dunovan I was happy he was not my father. He beat me within an inch of my life and threw me out of the castle. I ran and ran until I finally collapsed in front of a cottage and lost consciousness.

"I woke the next day to remember the beating, but not how I got to the cottage. I came to meet a rude individual who yelled at me. He was the most ill-mannered man I had ever met." Kathleen smiled with fondness.

Michael smoothed her hair and smiled at her remembering the morning.

"He was also the most handsome man I had ever seen. I stayed with his family even though he had a fit over having an 'English brat' staying at his home. I became very close to his family despite this; his mother and father treated me like another daughter. I soon became close to his sister and his brother's fiancée."

"And the man who was rude?" Willow prompted.

"He wanted to be a doctor; he was very intelligent. His family did not have the money to send him to school, and he blamed this on Lord Dunovan.

Lord Dunovan owned the land they farmed on, leaving them with nothing of their own. He knew who I was, so his hatred turned on me too. He treated my wounds and nursed me back to health, but he never wanted anything to do with me. From the moment, I regained strength, he told me to leave. Sometimes, though, I saw him looking at me with interest, but he always shied away from me.

I was hopelessly in love with him, despite that fact he could not stand me. I loved him because he was kind and caring; he would have made an excellent doctor. He never shared his feelings for me until the day I told him the truth about myself. He told me he loved me. He took me to his sister and brother's wedding. The wedding was the day I met Webster, my true father, for the first time. That night was officially the first time the man I fell in love with asked me to marry him."

"Then what happened?" Willow asked intrigued.

"Elizabeth, his mother, got sick, and he blamed me. He blamed me again for not being able to be a doctor and saving his mother. He never truly realized until after she died that it was not my fault. On May first, we finally were able to put our past behind us and expressed our love for each other for the first time. From this experience, I got pregnant, although I would not realize it until much later. He asked me again to marry him, and I said yes.

We never did get married. During the months I stayed with him, Lord Dunovan had been searching for me, and he finally found me and forced me to come home. I was forced to marry Ryan Winchester."

"What happened to the baby?" Willow whispered.

"I had a baby girl – you, Willow."

"You mean my father is not my father, and I am more Irish than anything else?"

Kathleen nodded her head tired after telling her story.

"What about my real father?"

Michael, who had been silent throughout Kathleen's speech, got down on his knees in front of his daughter. "I am your father, Willow."

"But...I...Why did you not tell me before? When you met me?" Willow was stunned and confused.

"Your mother and I thought you had been through too much to learn the truth when we met."

"Ryan thought it would be best if you knew. You are eighteen now. You need to start thinking about finding a husband."

"Husband? I don't want to get married."

At Willow's indignant cry, Ryan Winchester walked in. "Willow, baby, you know I love you. I always have, but if you look deep into yourself, you know that there has been a distance between us. It would have been better for your parents to stay together and raise you. I tried to be a good father to you. I really did."

Willow stood up and hugged the man who had taken care of her for eighteen years. "I do love you."

"I know you do, Willow. That is why I am sending you to France. You need to find a husband."

"France? Why do I need to go to France to find a husband?"

"Willow, you will never be happy here in Ireland or England. Your mother and Michael, although they have been discreet, are being talked about all over the British Isles. You will not be accepted by either country completely. I am going to send you to stay with old friends of mine, Pierre and Paulette DuBois. The French are more accepting about these things. They are lovely people and are happy to have you."

Willow's new life was all settled; she had nothing to say about it. Nor did Michael or Kathleen. What could they say? Ryan was right; they were being gossiped about all over Britain. They could not stand to ruin their daughter's life.

So two days after her eighteenth birthday party, after learning the whole truth about herself, she set sail for the two and a half week voyage to Chateaux DuBois in the heart of wine making country, Champagne.

* * * * * * *

Kathleen, after explaining to Julianne that she was in no way related to Michael's son Patrick, was summoned to the library by Ryan. It had been a month since Willow had left them, and she had not seen or heard from Michael Fitzpatrick. In fact, Kathleen had not seen her husband for almost as long, despite the fact they lived in the same house. So when he did call her on that rainy day, she was apprehensive about seeing him.

She walked in to find Ryan in rumpled clothing, unshaven, and uncombed hair sitting by the fire drinking.

"Hello, wife. Please come join me. We need to have a nice little chat."

Kathleen sat down wearily. By his choice of words, Ryan seemed to be drunk, but he was clear-eyed and his hand was steady as he poured more liquid into his glass.

214

"How are you, Kathleen darling?"

"Fine."

Ryan nodded his head. "I am glad to hear that. That is really good, Kathleen, that you are fine. Would you like something to drink?"

"No, thank you. Ryan, is something wrong?"

"No, Kathleen, in fact everything is wonderful. Have you seen Michael lately?"

"No."

"Good. I told him to stay away, so there would not be any talk about you and him after it happened. There have been enough rumors lately."

"After what happens Ryan?"

"Kathleen, I have lived a long life. It has been good, for the most part; I had a wonderful wife for almost twenty years, who gave me two beautiful daughters. I say two because Willow is my daughter. I raised her and gave her everything she ever needed. I loved her like my own. I had a beautiful wife who I love more than anything else in the world. Alas, you could never love me, Kathleen. Oh, I know you care about me, but I just can not stand to see you suffer any longer. You need to be with Michael. Without him, you just are not whole. I see that now. My life is over."

"Ryan, what are you saying?" Kathleen asked in alarm. "No, Ryan, I'll stay with you, please. You are my husband."

"Not in the way I to be. I have no reason to live."

"Julianne."

"Julianne is in love with Michael's son. I really can not stand another of my girls going off with a Fitzpatrick."

Kathleen slowly approached Ryan. "What are you planning to do, Ryan?"

Ryan took a swallow of the amber colored liquid in his glass and looked steadily at Kathleen for a few minutes. He showed her a silver-colored pistol.

"Ryan, no, please," Kathleen cried, lunging at him, trying to stop him.

"You know, Kathleen I really did love you, maybe more than Michael does."

Kathleen fainted as he brought the gun to his head and ended his life.

* * * * * * *

Willow read the ten-page letter from Michael two months later describing his and her mother's wedding. She was heartbroken that Ryan had ended his life in such a way. She was thrilled for her mother and Michael though. After such a long time apart, they were finally happy and together. There was also a blurb about Julianne and Patrick. They were in love and trying to hide it from her mother. Everyone seemed to be happy and in love except her. She was in love all right, but with a person who could never love her back.

Jean-Claude DuBois was the only son of Pierre and Paulette DuBois. Light brown hair, sea-colored eyes, a physique to make gods jealous, Jean-Claude was gorgeous. Willow had never felt this way before; he was nice, kind, caring. At twenty-five, he was extremely popular throughout the high society class the DuBois family belonged to. Willow felt out of place at such functions. She had avoided all the generous invitations bestowed onto her by the DuBois family and their friends.

Now sitting alone in the sunny kitchen at Chateaux DuBois, she thought of Jean-Claude and all of his female admirers. He was the most eligible bachelor in France with his good looks and wealth, and sought after by many different women with one thing on their minds. Marriage. She thought of lovely Lady Isabelle from Spain. With light green eyes like a cat's, raven hair dark as night, and warm brown skin, Willow was not surprised Jean-Claude was taken with her. She was sure they would marry.

She had meet Lady Isabelle a few nights after she had arrived. At twenty-one, Lady Isabelle knew she was beauty and how to use it to her best advantage. Dressed in a red gown that accentuated her height and coloring, she swept into the chateaux. She kissed the air next to Willow's cheek exclaiming that she was so happy to meet her and that she must visit her at her home. After the first initial greetings, she had clung to Jean-Claude for the whole night. After dinner, Jean-Claude invited her to go for a carriage ride, not returning until the early morning.

Willow sighed loudly and played with her bowl of fruit a maid had set out for her breakfast. Jean-Claude had always been really nice to her but distant, not really getting to know her. She supposed she just was not as beautiful and glamorous or sophisticated as Lady Isabelle was.

"Well, top of the morning to ya."

Willow turned to the cheerful voice to find the image of her daydreams come in and sit across from her.

"How did you know I was part Irish?" Willow asked blushing.

"My parents told me you had a little Irish in you. Besides, you have red hair. Don't all Irishmen have red hair?"

"Mine's not really red," Willow protested taking a strand of her hair and examining a golden curl.

Jean-Claude gently reached over and touched the lock of hair saying, "No, it is just the color of the rising sun."

Willow blushed at his flattery, telling herself he was just being kind, and bent her head to avoid his eyes.

"Willow, tonight is the Lancômes' Ball. Are you going?"

"I really had not thought about it, but I suppose not."

"How old are you, Willow?"

Willow looked up at him and asked, "Why do you want to know?"

"Because someone as young and pretty as you should not always stay home alone. You should be out having fun meeting people."

"I really do not feel comfortable around large crowds."

"What about if I took you to the ball?"

"What do you mean?"

"Just what I said. I will take you to the ball."

"What about Lady Isabelle? You usually take her to society functions."

"Lady Isabelle and I are only friends. She is going with someone else."

"Really?" she asked hopefully.

"So how about it, Willow. Will you go with me?"

Willow looked into his sea-colored eyes and said, "Aye, I would be happy to go with you."

* * * * * * *

Later that night, Willow stood outside alone on the balcony of the Lancômes' home crying. Jean-Claude had kept his word and taken her to the ball, but as soon as he got there, he left her alone with his mother. He went straight to Lady Isabelle and asked her to dance. Why on earth had she agreed to go? Why had he asked her – to humiliate her? She should have just stayed home and read like she always did. She never should have borrowed the peach-colored, satin dress from Jean-Claude's mother.

After leaving her to dance with Isabelle, Jean-Claude's mother had asked one of his friends to dance with her. Never in her life had she been so embarrassed. The young man said no, claiming that she had come with Jean-Claude and it would not be fair to him. What in the hell did that mean? Was it not obvious that Jean-Claude was not interested in her? Willow left the ballroom and went outside to be alone.

Willow was lost in her thoughts when she heard a noise behind her and jumped around startled.

"So this is where you ran off to." Jean-Claude dressed in royal velvet came out of the ballroom, closing the door behind him.

Willow turned around, ignoring him. Jean-Claude moved beside her to ask, "Willow, why are you out here alone? Everyone is looking for you."

Willow wished he would go away, leave her alone, and not act like he was concerned about her. She shrugged her shoulders, refusing to answer him or look at him.

"Are you all right?"

She nodded her head and felt the tears rise again in her eyes.

Jean-Claude gently turned her face around to look at him. She kept her head down as he touched the trail of tears on her cheek.

"Willow, look at me. Tell me what the matter is."

"I thought you liked me. I thought you wanted to take me to the ball."

"I do like you, Willow. I did want to take you to the ball. You took off and hid from me," he answered softly, playing with her hair and loosening it to fall in soft curls around her face.

"You can not like me. You asked me to the ball, and then you ignored me."

"I am sorry, chere. I had to explain to Isabelle about the upcoming wedding."

Willow looked up at him. "Are you getting married?"

"Yes, I am, hopefully soon."

Willow moved away from him. "I hope you will be very happy."

"I plan to be. I am marrying the most beautiful girl in the world."

"Good for you," she said with a touch of sarcasm.

"Would you like to know who I am going to marry?"

"Isabelle."

"No, Willow, not Isabelle. I told you we were just friends. I am going to marry a tiny doll-like girl with hair the color of the rising sun. She is kind of shy, reserved and very, very angry at me."

"What on earth are you talking about? You are being stupid."

"I want you to marry me."

"But I...we hardly know each other."

"I know that you are the only girl I want to marry. I have loved you ever since you came here. I have left you alone because I know about your family, and you needed to heal."

"You know about my family?"

"I do. Ryan wrote to my family when he sent you here."

"And what do you think?"

"Two special people had one special daughter who was raised by a kind, loving man."

"You do not mind?"

"Well, it is a little unorthodox, but you should hear about my mother's family sometime. Will you marry me, Willow?"

"Yes," Willow said smiling.

Jean-Claude lifted her face, gently kissing her. Willow was the happiest girl in the world.

Chapter Eighteen

"Michael, have you explained to Patrick about us?"

"Yes, love," Michael said wearily for the thousandth time since they married.

"And you are sure he does not think badly of me?"

"He better not, if he knows what's good for him."

"Michael!" Kathleen exclaimed, hitting him on his shoulder.

"Love, you really have to stop beating me. I am black and blue."

"I will think about it. Have you seen Patrick and Julianne?"

"They should be around here somewhere."

Michael and Kathleen were watching the ocean on a moonlit night before they were to dock in France for Willow's upcoming wedding. Kathleen still could not believe Willow was going to be married. She seemed so young and fragile. In her letter to Michael and Kathleen, she sounded ecstatic though.

Finally, there would be some happiness for her family. Kathleen was still amazed how much her life had changed in the past two and a half years. Willow met her father, who was going to give her away to Jean-Claude. Julianne was sixteen and in love with Michael's son, although they tried to hide it from her. They would sneak off, like now, to remote little corners to share a few kisses and embraces when no one was looking. Of course the biggest change in her life was that she finally was married to Michael.

"What are you thinking of?" Michael asked, wrapping his arms around Kathleen's waist and bringing her body back to rest against his.

"How happy I am."

"Are you happy, love?"

Before Kathleen could reply, Julianne and Patrick interrupted them.

"Mother, what time is the ship docking?"

"Around noon. Julianne, it is late. You should be in bed."

"I am going. Patrick and I were taking a walk before we went to bed."

"Well, Patrick can take you to your room now," Michael said.

Kathleen waited for them to leave before turning to Michael. "Michael, I am worried about them."

"Why?"

"They are in love, Michael. I know you know they love each other. You help them try to hide it from me. What will people say if they got married?"

"I hid that from you because you worry too much, Kathleen, and you have gone through too much this year. As far as them getting married and people talking about them, well, people talk no matter what. If they love each other, then it is right for them. People talked about us when we married. We did marry despite that, because we loved each other. People will talk until something better comes along, love. They hardly even remember you were married for so long to Ryan Winchester."

"But, Michael."

"Kathleen, let what happens happen."

"I still worry so much about everything, Michael. I just want to be happy."

Michael pulled Kathleen back into his arms and kissed her forehead.

"There is no need to worry when you have me. I will never let anything happen to you or to the ones you love. Trust me, Kathleen."

* * * * * * *

The night before her mother and father were to arrive from England, Willow sat outside in the DuBois garden alone. She loved the garden with the little swing under a bridge of flowers where she sat now. She had fallen in love with the floral paradise the minute she saw it. It was her mother-in-law-to-be's greatest achievement next to Jean-Claude. She often went there when she had problems to think about to try to sort them out.

However, the night before her wedding, she had not problems or worries to sort out. She was so much in love with Jean-Claude, she felt she would never have any troubles again, although she was a little worried about Pierre and Paulette meeting her parents. She knew Ryan in his first introduction letter had explained to them about her parents, but she was not sure what they thought about it. It was a rather sordid tale.

Willow turned around startled when she heard a rustle in the leaves. She stood up when she saw Jean-Claude.

"Chere, what are you doing out here all alone?" he asked softly, coming to stand by her.

Willow sat down and looked up at Jean-Claude. Every time she looked at him, she caught her breath; she loved him so much it hurt.

"Willow, is everything all right?"

"Oh, Jean-Claude, I am so happy."

"I am glad, Willow. I want to make you happy for the rest of your life."

"What about your parents? What do they think of me? Of my family?"

"Is that what you are worried about?"

"It is very important to me that your parents like me."

"Willow, if my parents did not like you, you would have been back in England a long time ago."

"What about Isabelle? Wouldn't she be a better choice of a wife for you?"

Jean-Claude pulled Willow off the bench and into his arms. Looking down into her face, he shook his head and said, "My parents want you as their daughter-in-law, and I want you as my wife. Even if they did not want you, it is my life, not theirs. What about me? Do you think your family will like me?"

"I am sure they will. They would be crazy not to."

"And what if they do not?"

"Jean-Claude, I refuse to end up in a loveless marriage like my grandmother and mother. They always wanted the one they fell in love with but could not have them. My mother wasted almost twenty years of her life away from my father. I will never let that happen to my children or me. If we have a daughter and she wants to marry an Egyptian, then we will have exotic grandchildren."

Jean-Claude smiled at the determination in her voice, but when he saw the seriousness in her eyes, he stopped and said, "We will get married tomorrow and be happy for the rest of our lives." He brought up the back of his hand and rubbed her smooth cheek. "You are so beautiful, Willow." He whispered before bringing his mouth down to hers, "I love you so much, Willow. You are the best thing to come into my life."

"That is were you are wrong, Jean-Claude. You are the best thing to happen to me. My life has not always been easy, even though we had money. I have memories that will not go away."

"Willow, I will help you erase all the sadness in your life. You will be safe and happy with me. I will never let anything bad happen to you ever again. I love you, Willow."

"I love you too, Jean-Claude," Willow whispered softly before Jean-Claude gently kissed her. In that kiss, Willow felt for the first time happiness within her grasp.

* * * * * * *

The night of Jean-Claude and Willow's wedding, Kathleen was amazed at the change in her daughter. Gone was the shy, reserved girl who always stayed in the background watching with her large, sapphire-colored eyes. Instead, Willow was out celebrating with everyone and having a wonderful time. She saw her mother-in-law embrace her and kiss her cheek. Perhaps Willow had finally forgotten all the horrors she had witnessed. Kathleen knew her daughter had never been happy in England. Maybe the change of scenery had been good for her. She seemed to belong in France.

Or more likely, the change in Willow was caused by the very handsome, very charming Jean-Claude. Kathleen adored him and was overjoyed that her daughter had found someone who was worthy of her. Even Michael, who was still weary of wealth, had taken a strong liking to their daughter's new husband. Michael thought he was a fine gentleman and was learning about the winery business from him.

Kathleen waved to Michael and Willow dancing together, then turned to look for Julianne. She was going to beat that girl. No matter what Michael said, she still worried about gossip that was already starting about Julianne and Patrick. Julianne was simply behaving with absolutely no decorum, always taking off with him.

"A pretty lady such as yourself should not look so worried."

Kathleen turned around to find Jean-Claude standing next to her. "Hello, Jean-Claude. Have you seen Willow's sister?"

"She went off with Patrick somewhere." Jean-Claude saw the frown on Kathleen's face deepen. He held out his hand to her and led her to the dance floor. "Do not worry so much, Kathleen."

Kathleen looked up at him with amusement. "Have you been speaking with my husband?"

"I have, and he worries about you. He thinks you should relax."

"Who worries about you, Kathleen love?" Michael asked, twirling Willow next to them on the dance floor.

"Only a much older annoying pest I see sometimes."

Michael gently swatted Kathleen's bottom and pulled her into his arms. "Do not talk to me about old. You are the one who found two gray hairs this morning."

Kathleen punched Michael in the chest. "It is not everyday your daughter gets married. It is bound to make one feel their age."

"Love, you do not look a day over two hundred," he said, laughing as

Kathleen took a swat at him again.

"Michael, Kathleen seems to hit you an awful lot. Will I have to worry about Willow?"

"Yes, you see it is a family trait. Kathleen inherited from my sister and sister-in-law."

"Julianne has the same trait, you know. I saw her hit Patrick many times," Willow remarked, grabbing hold of Jean-Claude's hand.

"Have you seen your sister, Willow?" Kathleen asked, remembering she had been looking for her.

Willow looked into her mother's eyes and saw the worry in them. She knew where her sister was, but she would rather not tell her mother. "She is with Patrick somewhere." That much was true at least.

Michael felt the tension in Kathleen and gently kissed her forehead. "She is fine love," he whispered to her softly. He would have a talk with Patrick later on about his behavior.

* * * * * * *

Julianne was more than fine as Patrick kissed the side of her neck upstairs in a long forgotten room of the DuBois Châteaux.

"Patrick," Julianne gasped as he gathered her up in his arms and laid her down on the bed. Julianne tried to move away from him as he began to undo the ties at her bodice, but he kept her firmly under him. She tried once again to move away from him when she felt his manhood throbbing against her leg. "Patrick, please stop."

"Julianne baby darlin', I love you," he whispered urgently as he stripped away her dress and removed the rest of his own clothing.

At nineteen, Patrick was truly in love with the sixteen-year-old daughter of his father's wife. To him, it did not matter that by marriage she was his stepsister. They were not blood related. To hell with what others thought. He loved her and would marry her.

"Patrick, please we can not do this. It is not right."

"I love you, Julianne. There is nothing wrong. You are going to be my wife."

"Your wife?"

"Aye, my wife, darlin'."

Julianne wound her arms around Patrick's neck and kissed him. It was right, this love between them.

"Patrick, I do love you."

224

* * * * * * *

"Willow chere, ever since I saw you, I wanted you. I wanted to touch you, make you mine," Jean-Claude whispered to Willow as he lay on top of her.

Willow was amazed how fast he had whisked her away from the party and had her stripped and wanting him.

"Jean-Claude, I love you."

"Willow."

Willow writhed under Jean-Claude's exploring hands and mouth as he kissed her, moving down her body, finally taking her breast into his mouth. She moaned. She never knew anything could feel this good. This is what it felt like to love and be loved back. This was how it was between her mother and father; she knew it. No wonder they could not forget about each other.

"Willow?" Jean-Claude questioned when he saw the faraway look in her eyes.

"Jean-Claude, be gentle," she whispered before kissing him.

* * * * * * *

"What are you thinking of, Kathleen love?" Michael called from bed as he watched Kathleen brush her hair in front of the mirror.

"Life, Michael."

Michael sighed and put down the book he had been reading on grapes and which were the best for wine making. Kathleen was in one of her philosophical moods.

"What about life?"

Kathleen studied her face in the mirror and noticed a tiny line next to her eyes. She thought of her life and all that had happened to her. Living in a home without the love that she needed, being kicked out of Dunovan Castle, finding the love of her life and being taken away from him. Then the fact that she had Willow, then Julianne, spending eighteen years with a good kind, caring man whom she could never truly love. Finding Michael again and the tragic end to Ryan's life. Now Willow was married, and her other daughter was in love with Michael's son. What a tangled web life was.

"Love?"

"Life is strange, is it not, Michael?"

"Strange in what way?"

"Full of surprises. The way everything has happened to us, to our children, to our families. Despite all the tragedy, things seem to be on the right track finally."

"Did I not tell you they would? I told you to trust me."

Kathleen finished braiding her hair and went to lie down beside Michael. "I have always trusted you, Michael. I just had my doubts, concerns, worries."

"You would not be human if you did not," he said, stroking her back.

"Is that what is wrong with me? I am human."

"Well, love, sometimes I wonder if you are human or some ethereal creature that came to me and turned my life upside down. You are the best thing that ever happened to me. You know that, right?"

"Michael." Kathleen sighed, lifting her head up for his gentle kiss. Michael moved Kathleen so that her head rested on his chest. He played with her braid while he read his book.

Thinking that she had fallen to sleep, he was surprised when he heard her mumble something about Julianne.

"Love, what about Julianne?"

"I spoke with her a while ago."

"And?"

"She and Patrick are to be married."

"How do you feel about that?"

"They are in love, Michael. They better get married, the way they have been carrying on. I do not want to be the cause of ruining their happiness."

"You still have doubts about the two of them?"

"Not like I did at first. Patrick is a wonderful man, Michael. He asked me for Julianne's hand in marriage."

"What did you say?"

"I said yes." Kathleen waited for Michael to say something. When he did not, she looked up at him to see a faraway look in his eyes.

"What are you thinking of, Michael?"

"The day I asked Webster for your hand in marriage."

"What did he say to you?"

"Yes, of course. He probably saw the look in my eyes if he would have said no."

Kathleen laughed. "What kind of look was that?"

"The look that said he would not live very long if he would have refused me."

Kathleen smiled and went to hit Michael, but he caught her hand and kissed it instead. "Isn't this better than hitting me, love?"

"Better for whom?" Kathleen teased before kissing him again.

Michael rolled Kathleen on her back, kissing her deeper. Kathleen jumped when she felt the book under her back. She reached under her and waved it at Michael.

"You never did teach me how to read. Michael." she accused him.

Michael took the book away from her, throwing it on the floor. He continued to kiss her.

Kathleen broke away from him. "Michael," she said sternly.

"Kathleen love, this is so much more fun than reading. Trust me."

"Michael, do you realize that I do not even know what you said in that letter you wrote me so long ago?"

"Did you keep that, love?" Michael asked with surprise in his voice.

"Of course I kept it, and your Hamlet book."

"So that is where my book went."

Kathleen had kept everything that he had ever given her. She really was special, his Kathleen. Thank God he was with her.

"So will you teach me how to read, Michael? Like you promised."

"Tomorrow. Tonight we finish what we started, love."

"I was hoping you would say that."

* * * * * * *

The first year of Jean-Claude and Willow's marriage passed without much eventfulness. The peace in their lives was more than they could ask for. Willow thought she would never know such happiness as she did with Jean-Claude. Married life was not what she had expected though. She thought she would miss her family much more than she did. Although she did miss them, she knew her place was by her husband in France.

"Willow, come to bed, chere," Jean-Claude called from the bedroom as Willow prepared herself for bed.

"Coming," Willow called, running a brush through her hair quickly and going into the room she shared with Jean-Claude. She climbed into bed after shedding her robe. She was a little astonished how quickly she had lost her shyness around him.

"Willow, have you gained weight?" he asked, gently rubbing her stomach.

"I feel like I eat more and more, Jean-Claude, but every morning I get sick. I am thinking of going to a doctor next week. I would hate to have some kind of virus that you could get too."

Jean-Claude smiled, kissing her smooth cheek, thinking she was still so innocent. "Willow, I do not think what you have I could get. I think I caused it though."

"What on earth do you mean?" Willow asked with wide round eyes. Did she have some kind of disease?

"I think we have been blessed with a miracle."

"My being sick is a miracle?"

Jean-Claude was confusing her; maybe he had too much wine at dinner.

"Willow, I think you are going to have a baby DuBois very soon."

Willow sat up and looked at her husband. "A baby?"

"Oui, chere."

"A baby," Willow whispered to herself, touching her stomach gently.

Jean-Claude pulled her into his arms and covered her hands with his own. "How do you feel?"

"Happy, Jean-Claude, very happy. What do you think it will be?"

"A beautiful girl like her mother, with hair the color of sunset and big blue eyes like sapphires."

"Do you not want a boy?"

"I will take whatever you give me, but mark my words, it is going to be a girl. You come from a long line of red-haired girls, and that is what our child will be."

* * * * * * *

Jean-Claude gloated on the warm spring day in 1823 as he carried the baby girl that Willow had given birth to early that morning after keeping the whole house awake the night before.

Willow laughed when Jean-Claude came in and said, "See, what did I tell you? A beautiful baby girl."

"It is not nice to brag, Jean-Claude," she scolded.

"I was right though – a girl with red hair and blue eyes."

"Her hair is more golden brown, and she has your sea-colored eyes."

"What do you want to call her, chere?"

"Marie."

"Marie," he whispered to his daughter who gurgled in response and went to sleep. "She seems to approve. We can name her Marie."

"Are you planning on spoiling her?"

"Of course. I have to win her love, do I not?"

"If she is smart, she will love you because you are you."

"Do you love me, Willow?"

"Yes, I love you. What are you thinking asking a stupid question like that?" Sometimes she wondered about him. He just said things that did not make sense.

Jean-Claude handed Marie to a nanny and went to sit by his wife. He knew she had had a hard time giving birth, but she never complained. She had lost a lot of blood and was awfully pale, but the doctor thought she would be fine. He smoothed her hair off her white face and asked worriedly, "Are you feeling all right, chere?"

"Well, honestly, I have felt better, but I will be fine. I am a little tired. Why did you ask me if I still loved you?"

"I know the birth was not easy, Willow. I wanted to be sure you were not mad at me for causing you so much pain."

"Marie was a miracle that I wanted very badly. I did have something to do with her being here, by the way." Willow accepted his gentle kiss before asking, "Are you happy with her?"

"Happy? Now who is asking stupid questions? I am more than happy with her; she is a beautiful baby." He kissed her forehead before reaching over her to his nightstand and gaving her a black velvet box. "This is for you, chere. I had it made when I knew you were pregnant."

Willow looked at Jean-Claude and took the box from him. "Jean-Claude, what is it?" she asked, rubbing the soft velvet.

"Just open it."

When she finally did open it, inside she found a lovely necklace with sapphires and diamonds altering back in forth until meeting in the center with a large heart shaped sapphire.

"Do you like it?" he asked when his wife just sat there staring at it.

"Jean-Claude, you really should not have bought such an extravagant piece of jewelry for me."

"Why not?"

"You have already given me so much. This necklace is beautiful."

"You are a beautiful girl who deserves beautiful things. Besides, it reminds me of your eyes."

"Jean-Claude, I love you so much."

"Me too, Willow. I love you too," he said, tucking her under the blanket as she fell asleep.

Willow was so lovely; he would die if anything were to happen to her. He had been scared to death last night when he heard her screams. He was so worried, he had to leave the châteaux to go to the family church to pray.

Jean-Claude knew Willow was fragile. All she had been through and her family history certainly did not help matters. He worried about her a great deal. He wanted to give her whatever she wanted to make her happy. She never did ask for anything; she was just happy being with him.

He watched her sleeping for a long time before leaving to go back to church to thank God for saving her.

* * * * * * *

It was several weeks after Marie was born that Kathleen received the letter from Jean-Claude telling her about the birth. She ran into the sunlit dining hall of Liverpool Manor waving the letter in front of Michael, who was having breakfast with Patrick.

"Michael!"

"Kathleen, calm down. What on earth is the matter with you?" Michael asked, looking at the bright-eyed woman who looked like the Kathleen he knew when he had first met her.

"Willow…baby." Kathleen took a deep breath. "Willow had her baby, Michael. A beautiful legitimate baby girl named Marie."

"How do you know, love?" Michael asked.

"Jean-Claude wrote us a letter, and I read it, Michael."

He smiled at Kathleen. She looked so proud of herself, like the day he had come home from the fields and she had been cleaning.

"I can read, Michael. Thank you. Do you think Marie will be different since she is the first girl in a long time to be legitimate?"

"She'll probably be better mannered than the rest of you."

Kathleen raised her fist, but Michael caught it and kissed her hand.

"See, love, nicer."

Patrick saw the look pass between them and coughed loudly, letting his presence be known. Kathleen blushed and looked over at Patrick.

"Where is Julianne, Patrick?"

"She went off somewhere with Francine."

"Up to trouble again, I suppose," Michael said, going back to eating his breakfast.

"Kathleen, Pa, Julianne is going to be eighteen soon. I was wondering if we could marry on her birthday? We have waited like you wanted us to."

Kathleen looked at Patrick. No wonder her daughter loved him. He looked more like Michael everyday, except for he was very fair. That must be from Clara. She thought back to the time many months ago when they first learned that Willow was with child. She had been about to fall asleep while Michael read to her, when Patrick had come knocking on their door. Kathleen had groaned and pressed her face deeper into Michael's chest.

"Come in," Michael called.

Kathleen remembered how Patrick had come into their room looking very worried.

"Pa, could I talk to you? Alone. Please."

Michael gently moved Kathleen off of him and went out into the hall to talk to his son.

When he returned Kathleen stirred and mumbled sleepily, "What is wrong, Michael?"

"Patrick wanted to know how easy it was to get pregnant."

Kathleen groaned and asked, "Is Julianne pregnant?"

"No, love, they have only been together once. The night of Willow's wedding."

Kathleen groaned again saying, "They are too young, Michael."

"Do not talk to me about being too young, Kathleen. I seem to remember a very young, inexperienced girl…"

"Good night, Michael."

"Good night, love," he answered, laughing softly.

"Would it be all right if Julianne and I married on her birthday?" Patrick asked, bringing Kathleen to the present once again.

"I think that would be a lovely idea, Patrick. You have waited long enough."

"Pa?"

"It is fine with me."

"Patrick, wait," Kathleen called as he got up to try to find Julianne.

"You love my daughter?"

"Yes."

"I want you two to be happy. I want you to ignore all the old gossip and prejudices. I want you to be together and have a happy life."

"Thank you, Kathleen."

"For your wedding gift, I am giving you and Julianne Dunovan Castle. She loves Ireland, and she has always been fascinated by the castle."

"Love?"

Kathleen ignored Michael and looked at Patrick. "Will you accept my gift to you?"

"Kathleen, I am really not sure what to say?"

"Say yes."

"I will say thank you, Kathleen, on behalf of Julianne too. Kathleen, I never knew my mother, but I had you. You are the closest thing I have, and I love you."

Kathleen felt the tears in her eyes as Patrick bent over and pulled her to her feet embracing her.

"I love you, Patrick."

"I am going to find Julianne and Francine."

Kathleen sat back down after Patrick left, staring outside, letting the tears fall down her cheeks unchecked.

"That was a very generous gift, love."

Kathleen nodded, not saying anything. "What is it?"

"Michael," she cried, throwing herself into his arms sobbing.

"I am so happy, Michael."

"Yes, I can see that," he said sarcastically.

Kathleen laughed and hit him on his arm.

"Now, Kathleen, I thought we agreed on not hitting me."

"No, Michael, you agreed."

"Love, why did you give Dunovan Castle to Patrick and Julianne?"

"Julianne does like the castle, and I thought someone should find happiness in that castle, Michael."

"You do not want to go back to Ireland? We have been a way for so long."

"Maybe to visit Matthew and Gabrielle."

"You really want to?"

"Yes, I miss them."

"Me too. We will make plans to go later today."

"Would you want to move back to Ireland, Michael?"

"Kathleen, I do not care where we live as long as I have you."

"You are not mad at me for giving away the castle, are you?"

"No, Kathleen, if we were to move back to Ireland, I would never live at Dunovan Castle, and I know you could not either."

"Thank you, Michael, for understanding."

"I love you, Kathleen."

"Me too," Kathleen said, standing up and grabbing his hand. She tugged on his arm causing him to stand up.

"What do you want, Kathleen?" Michael asked as she circled her arms around his neck.

"Guess, Michael."

Michael lifted her up in his arms and carried her up the stairs.

* * * * * * *

The next year passed with two great events. Jean-Claude and Willow DuBois had their second child, a son Charles, a blond-haired, brown-eyed boy who Jean-Claude was sure was going to be exactly like him. The birth was harder on Willow, and the doctor told Jean-Claude that Willow should not have anymore children if it was possible.

Willow was disappointed that her parents were unable to travel to France for Charles' birth, but she understood why they could not, for Julianne and Patrick finally got married. It seemed impossible for Willow to think of her younger sister married. But nineteen-year-old Julianne finally got the boy she had been after for years.

Willow read the letter her mother wrote her describing how happy Julianne was on her wedding day. Her mother also mentioned that she and Michael were planning a trip to Ireland to visit Michael's brother Matthew. After their visit, they would come to France to see their grandchildren.

Willow smiled at how happy her mother seemed, and all because of Michael. It seemed happiness had finally come to her family. Her mother had Michael, she had Jean-Claude and two beautiful children, and Julianne had Patrick.

Maybe their family had paid their debt to God, and the horrors of the past were finally over.

Chapter Nineteen

It was a dark, rainy day when Matthew and Gabrielle Fitzpatrick, along with their youngest son Gerald, went to Dunovan Castle to see Patrick and Julianne. Although the weather provided a dark atmosphere, the occasion was a joyous one. After being married a year, Julianne had given birth to twin boys, Frederick and Robert, the cold February morning in the year 1826.

The morning Julianne had her twins was the first time in over twenty years that Matthew would see his brother, who had come back to Ireland for his grandchildren's births. Kathleen and Michael had always meant to come back to visit, but as always, something came up to stop them. They had kept in touch throughout the years by letter, so Matthew knew about Kathleen, Willow, and the fact that Patrick and Julianne were stepbrother and stepsister. Matthew sighed as he drove the wagon through the woods that led to Dunovan Castle, thinking that the Fitzpatrick family was finally blessed with happiness.

"Pa, what does Aunt Kathleen look like?" twenty-year-old Gerald asked.

Gabrielle looked over at her youngest child warily. Joseph and Marilyn were both married and settled down, but Gerald…Gerald would not settle down. Gabrielle knew the problem. He loved women much too much. He had a job working as an overseer on Dunovan land, which Matthew was the head of now. Many nights Gerald had come home late from work to be yelled at by Matthew. Instead of doing his work, Gerald had snuck away with some young village lass to lie in the grass.

Gerald often reminded Gabrielle of Michael; both were always looking for something else. Although, Michael had wanted to be a doctor to better himself, while Gerald wanted to bed every girl that crossed his path. Gerald even resembled Michael a little, tall, dark and brooding, except he had holly-colored eyes instead of blue.

Gabrielle shook her head at her good-looking son; she wished Gerald could find someone like Kathleen. Kathleen had done wonders for Michael; he had been changed completely by her. He had settled down, relaxed, been happy. Gerald needed someone that would help him settle down.

"Ma, was Aunt Kathleen truly beautiful? I have always heard that she was."

"Kathleen was the loveliest person I have ever met, as well as being one of the nicest."

"Uncle Michael is also a mystery to me. I know he became a duke by marriage somehow, but what was he like when he was young?"

"I will try to explain the young Michael I grew up with to Gerald, Gabrielle. Michael is my older brother, who growing up, gave me a pain. He always wanted more than we had. He was rude and selfish."

"Matthew!" Gabrielle exclaimed, shocked.

"I was only teasing, somewhat, Gabrielle. You know Michael was an arrogant son of a—"

"Matthew, stop that."

"Sorry, sweetheart."

They rode in silence the last few moments of the journey to Dunovan Castle. The castle, as always, looked forbidding as they came upon it, rising out of the late day mist. Matthew pulled the wagon to a stop, helping Gabrielle down while Gerald leapt to the ground, pulling presents for the new infants out of the back.

"Matthew, no fornicating on Dunovan Castle grounds." A deep voice startled them from behind.

Matthew turned to see Michael standing behind him with his hands on his hips. The two brothers stood staring at each other. Michael was still disgustingly handsome, thought Matthew.

"Michael!" Gabrielle cried, throwing herself into Michael's arms.

"Gabrielle darlin'! You are still lovely and still married to my cow of a brother. You know I had to send extra food to Ireland just to satisfy my brother's appetite."

"Michael, be nice. You know there is no one else who would have taken Matthew on. I had to stay married to him. He would have starved or driven some other lass senile."

"Gabrielle," Matthew said threateningly.

Michael let go of Gabrielle and moved toward his brother once again.

"Matthew, you look really good. Gabrielle must be taking good care of you. I suppose being a farmer was your call in life."

"Michael, you do not look half bad yourself." The two brothers embraced each other. Matthew was the one who broke free first, seeing Gerald heading towards the castle. "Michael, you have to meet my youngest. Gerald, come over here and greet your uncle properly."

"Hello, Gerald. I am very pleased to meet you," Michael said, shaking hands with Gerald.

"I am very happy to meet you too, Uncle Michael."

"Michael, it's all well and good that we see you. But you know the main reason we are here."

"She's in the castle, Gabrielle, with Julianne and Francine and—"

"Francine is here too? How is she?"

"A beautiful young lady like her mother. And just as independent."

"I bet she's like Beth," Matthew mused.

"Ma, let's go meet Kathleen and the others," Gerald whispered, sensing the somber mood set as they thought of the loss of Beth.

"There is another surprise in the castle waiting to meet all of you," Michael said with an air of mystery.

"Oh really? You have the English royal family in there or something?" Matthew asked teasingly.

"I think not, dear brother. I have not changed that much. Willow, my daughter with Kathleen, is here with her husband Jean-Claude and their two children. They came from France to be with Julianne. Willow was getting a little mad at us too, since we never get to travel to France much."

"Michael, how wonderful."

"It is, Gabrielle. It really is. Come meet my family."

"Wait, Michael. Could I speak with you for a little while? It has been so long since I saw you, and letters, well, they just do not mean the same," Matthew asked.

"Of course. Gabrielle, Gerald, you all go on into the castle. I am sure someone in there can find you something to eat or drink."

Matthew waited until his wife and son went toward the castle doors to turn to his brother. "Come, Michael, let's go for a walk."

The two brothers walked in compatible silence through the emerald green hills of Ireland away from Dunovan Castle.

Michael looked at the green grass, clear blue sky and realized how much he missed his homeland. He was ashamed that when he was young; he never appreciated how beautiful his homeland was.

"How does it feel to be back in Ireland, Michael?"

"It feels rather odd after all these years. I have been so close, yet so far away. I have missed it; London is gray and depressing. The people here are friendlier; the people in London are kind of cold. And the food! Tea every afternoon, slop for dinner. I miss corned beef and cabbage. Some of the food they eat, we gave our hogs."

"Do you want to move back to Ireland, Michael? We would love to have you close to us again. We are not getting any younger."

"I would like to maybe, but I have left the decision up to Kathleen. We could not live here in the castle. I could not, and Kathleen has too many bad memories of it."

"The castle has totally changed now though, since Lord Dunovan's death. Kathleen has given the people the land they have worked on for many years, and Julianne and Patrick live in the castle. They have parties and balls for everyone, not just the wealthy aristocrats."

Michael was silent for a moment. He wondered if he should tell the whole truth about Kathleen. It hurt him to even think about it. But his brother did have a right to know.

"Matthew, I am going to tell you something about Lord Dunovan and Kathleen. You cannot tell anyone, not even Gabrielle, and do not tell Kathleen I told you."

"I swear, Michael, whatever you tell me goes no further."

"Kathleen could never live at Dunovan Castle for reasons hard to explain, no matter how much it has changed."

"I know Lord Dunovan beat her up, killed her mother and forced her to marry Ryan Winchester, then live here for years. I know all that, Michael. She really should be over that by now."

"Matthew, listen to me. Kathleen has the memory of the beating and killing her mother, but there is something much, much worse he did to her."

"Like what? What could be so bad that she could not live here?"

"Lord Dunovan raped her one night. Webster found out and killed him. Webster stayed with his daughter even after the death of Lady Dunovan because she needed him. But when he violated her in such a way, he could not take any more from the man, so he killed him."

"Michael, I am so sorry. I had no idea. You never wrote about it, but then again, it is not something you write in a letter. Of course you could not live here, but there are other places."

"Well, Kathleen would like to see you and Gabrielle more. She knew you such a short time, but became very attached to you."

"How is Kathleen, Michael?"

"She is fine and beautiful. She has me now; that's all she ever wanted."

"Still conceited after all these years, uh, Michael?"

"Of course I am. You cannot change everything, Matthew. Besides, after living in London, I have learned a thing or two about being stuck up."

Matthew punched Michael lightly on the arm.

"Matthew, please, Kathleen hits me more than necessary."

"Are you getting so old, Michael, that you cannot take a punch from a girl?"

"I am only two years older than you, Matthew."

"Those two years mean a lot, dear brother of mine. Seriously though, how is Kathleen handling everything? It seems like she took many rough punches throughout her life. She seemed so tiny, so fragile, when we knew her."

"Matthew, believe it or not, Kathleen is a very strong person. Everything that she has gone through, she has taken and tried to make the best of it, although she is a tad emotional. She cries at almost everything," Michael said with a smile.

"What is Willow like, Michael? I always suspected she was your child when Kathleen had her. It just seemed too soon that she would have one after being married to Ryan Winchester."

"She is mine all right. She's beautiful. She has my eyes, but the rest is Kathleen. Except we worry about her. She is the one who is fragile. She was the one who found Webster over Lord Dunovan's body."

"My God."

"No, Matthew, that is not all either. Physically, she is not strong. She should not have any more children, but she loves them. Kathleen and I suspect she wants more and is trying. It would crush Kathleen if Willow died. She is our favorite child."

"What about Patrick and Julianne? It is amazing that your son and Kathleen's daughter got married."

"Patrick is a wonderful son, Matthew. He is everything that a father would want in a son. Julianne is a sweet girl. I am happy they found each other. Kathleen was the one who was worried about the gossip regarding the two of them. I always knew they would wind up together. She has finally accepted the fact that people will talk about us no matter what. We have been a very intriguing story for Great Britain. She gave them Dunovan Castle, hoping they would find some joy in it. Julianne loves the castle, and now a new generation of Fitzpatricks is going to grow up in it. Can you believe the Irish are living in Dunovan Castle? The Dunovans must be rolling in their graves."

"Talk about old, Michael. You are a grandfather."

"You are too, Matthew. How are your children?"

"Joseph and Marilyn are fine. It is Gerald we worry about."

"Why?"

"He is restless, like you always were, looking for something else than what he has. Except you had always had a goal. You wanted to be a doctor. Gerald just wants to bed every girl this side of Ireland."

"How is he at work? Kathleen tells me he's an overseer."

"When he shows up to work and stays, he is a great worker. He just always seems to find a girl to play with instead."

"Maybe you should try to give him some added responsibilities, not do his work for him if he does not show up."

"I am not sure if that would work."

"It would not hurt to try."

"I guess not. I will give it a try. Kathleen does not have any other children roaming around, does she? I think a girl like her would be good for Gerald."

"Nope, she just had two, and they are both spoken for. Gerald will be fine, Matthew."

"Uncle Michael!" a young, black-haired, blue-eyed girl called from the top of the hill.

"Michael, 'tis Beth?" Matthew said unthinkingly as he watched the girl run down the hill to them.

"Close, but no, it's Francine," Michael said to his brother who honestly looked like he had just seen a ghost.

"Francine, what is it?"

"Aunt Kathleen and Aunt Gabrielle sent me to tell you that if you want dinner you had best get back to the castle now or Gerald and Patrick will eat all the food."

"Francine, you do not remember him of course, but this is your Uncle Matthew."

Matthew shook his niece's hand and kissed her cheek. "You look exactly like your mother."

At a loss for words when she saw the tears shining in Matthew's eyes, she simply said, "Thank you."

When Michael, Matthew and Francine finally arrived at the castle, Kathleen did what she usually did when she was irritated with Michael; she hit him and scolded him.

"What is the matter with you, love?" Michael asked as he pulled her into his arms.

"It would have been nice to let me see Matthew too, Michael, before monopolizing all his time when he had not even met the rest of his family."

"Love, it was Matthew who wanted to talk to me. Do not blame me," Michael protested.

Kathleen, thinking that Michael was lying to her, hit him again while Matthew laughed.

"Matthew, stop laughing and tell this wench who forced me to marry her that you were the one who wanted to speak with me."

"Kathleen, it was I that asked Michael to speak with me. I did not mean to get him into trouble."

Kathleen kissed Michael on the cheek and apologized, then hit Matthew.

"Kathleen love, I did not mean to," Matthew protested in perfect imitation of his brother.

"Hey, Matthew, only I call Kathleen that."

"Matthew, would you please leave Kathleen and Michael alone?" Gabrielle said coming from the dining room hearing them arguing.

"Gabrielle, I swear it is all Michael's fault. He always starts the fights."

"I am waiting for food," Patrick called from the dining room.

"Would you listen to that, Kathleen? A Fitzpatrick if I ever heard one," Gabrielle said.

Kathleen nodded in agreement. "Sounds like Matthew."

"Patrick, do you or do you not have two hands of your own that you can get up and get your own food?" Willow asked.

"Michael, that must be Kathleen's daughter," Matthew said smiling when he heard the young voice.

"Yes, that would be our Willow, as bossy and demanding as her mother ever was. I am surprised her husband puts up with her."

Kathleen glared at her husband and raised her hand to hit him but was blocked by Michael grabbing her fist.

"Now, love—" he began.

"Do not 'love' me, Michael Fitzpatrick. You say you're sorry for that remark."

Willow came in announcing dinner when she heard her parents arguing.

"Willow, this is Matthew. Your uncle."

Willow raised an eyebrow at her father, who in turn grinned sheepishly at her and said, "Of course you know he is your uncle."

"It is a pleasure to meet you, Uncle Matthew."

"Why, if you are not the spitting image of your mother, I do not know who is," Matthew said, kissing her cheek. "Your eyes are Michael's though; that is for sure. But that red hair, that is Kathleen's."

"Mine is not really red," Willow protested.

"No, like I always say, it is just the color of the rising sun," Jean-Claude said, coming to stand beside his wife and kissing her blushing cheeks.

"Jean-Claude, this is my Uncle Matthew, my father's brother."

"Younger brother, lass, always remember younger. Jean-Claude, I am very pleased to meet you. I hear you two have children. I would enjoy meeting them."

"I am sure they would love to meet you too."

"The oldest, Marie, is three and very independent. She has a mind of her own. I am sure she is around here somewhere harassing the animals."

"Let me take a wild guess. Marie is a redheaded girl."

"Of course she is. What else would Willow have as her first child?"

"Uncle Matthew, please do not get him started on that subject. I have already eaten my words many of times."

"Whatever do you mean, Willow?" Gabrielle asked, sitting down at the table.

Willow waited for everyone to settle down in their seats before saying, "Jean-Claude informed me when we knew I was pregnant that I came from a long line of red-haired girls and that is what I would have as my first child. He actually gloated when Marie was born. It was rather shameful."

Gerald came in, sitting down and heaping a pile of food on his plate, announcing that Julianne was asleep and would meet with her Uncle Matthew tomorrow.

"Why is it that you never come up to the castle, Uncle Matthew?" Patrick asked, shoving a large piece of ham into his mouth.

Matthew was also chewing when he answered, "I have had too much work to stop by for a visit, Patrick. Honestly, I really never have enjoyed barging in without being invited."

"Invited? But you are family. You are always welcome here."

Silence greeted Patrick's statement, as each person looked at everyone else. They were family, strange as it was. They would always share a special bond.

Kathleen cleared her throat. "Who would like more food?"

Immediately Matthew, Patrick and Gerald said they would. Gabrielle in turn replied that they could go into the kitchen to get more.

Kathleen looked at Michael and smiled. He took her hand and squeezed it gently. Who would have thought on that rainy night so long ago that she, Kathleen Dunovan, would have happiness after Lord Dunovan kicked her out of the castle? But happiness is what she did find and all because of one man, Michael Fitzpatrick.

* * * * * * *

Later that night, in the silence of early morning, Kathleen stirred in her sleep to feel something moist and warm under her ear. She opened her eyes when the wetness moved down her shoulder.

"Michael?" she questioned sleepily.

"Aye, love. Were you expecting anyone else?" he whispered before kissing her mouth.

"What time is it?"

"Time to go for a ride, Kathleen," he said, rolling away from Kathleen's warm body and getting off the bed.

"Michael, it must be after midnight."

"One-thirty, love," he replied, getting dressed.

"Why are you awake?" she groaned, rolling over on her stomach, burying her face in her pillow.

"We are going for a ride, love," he declared gently, tugging on Kathleen's hair.

"You have a mental problem if you think I am going riding with you at one-thirty in the morning, Michael Fitzpatrick. We can go tomorrow, during daylight. I am tired."

"Come on, Kathleen. I have something to show you."

"Show me tomorrow please, Michael," she pleaded.

"The Kathleen I fell in love with would go with me anywhere anytime I asked."

"The Kathleen you fell in love with was a good twenty-five years younger, and did not need as much sleep."

"Please, Kathleen, it is important to me," Michael implored, turning Kathleen around and fixing his gaze on her.

Kathleen looked up into Michael's beautiful eyes pleading with her to follow him and exhaled loudly. When he looked at her like he was now, she could deny him nothing.

"All right, Michael, I will go, but in the future, when you get this desire for a midnight run, let me tell you—"

Kathleen's lecture was cut off by Michael gently kissing her. "Kathleen, I want you to wear this," he said, holding up the shirt he had given her so many years ago.

"Seems like you have everything planned," Kathleen said more awake now.

"Aye, love."

After dressing in that shirt Michael had given her and an old skirt, Kathleen followed Michael out to the stables. She paused as a feeling of nostalgia took over her, remembering saying goodbye to Michael in these very stables. Michael reached a black horse before he realized Kathleen had paused at the entrance to the stables.

"Kathleen, are you feeling all right?"

Kathleen nodded her head, walking into the stable. "Michael, I am really tired. Must we go riding now?"

"Please, Kathleen, you are a wake now. It is important to me."

"Fine, Michael."

Michael swung up on the horse and reached down for Kathleen. Kathleen hesitated before reaching up for Michael, who pulled her up without effort and held her in his arms.

"Michael, I still do not think it is proper to go riding in the middle of the night."

"Since when have you ever done anything proper, love? Besides, I am going to take you somewhere special. You will be fine. Do you trust me, Kathleen?"

"Yes, Michael, I do."

Michael and Kathleen rode out into the dark early morning to a special place to both of them. It was the paradise they had first shared many years ago. Nothing had changed; it was as if time had stood still in this one perfect place. Being there once again with Michael made Kathleen feel sixteen years old, but this time she had not a care in the world.

* * * * * * *

Francine O'Brien was also awake and not in bed like she should have been. She was outside by a tree waiting for Timothy O'Leary beyond the walls of Dunovan Castle, when she spotted a dark horse with a couple gallop by. It must be Uncle Michael and Aunt Kathleen, she thought to herself, as she pulled her dark cape closer to her, trying to gain more warmth from it.

She wished she could meet Timothy during the day, instead of sneaking out late at night, but that was impossible.

What would Uncle Michael say if he knew? Aunt Kathleen would hate her forever if she knew that her niece was in love with the son of the man who ruined her mother's life.

Francine had fallen in love with the son of Webster O'Leary's brother Aaron. She sighed loudly, as she thought of the old gossip she heard when she was a child. Things that had happened over forty years ago were spoken as if they had gone on yesterday.

Timothy O'Leary was different than his father. He was kind and gentle and caring. She loved him very much. He could never hurt her, nor would he want to. She was convinced he truly loved her, so if someone would have told her he was not meeting her because he was bedding Eve McKnight, daughter of Bartholomew and Eva, she would deny it until she was blue in the face.

They were to be married; he would never go with someone else.

* * * * * * *

Gerald Fitzpatrick was in shock, he realized several weeks later. Of all the impossible things, he had fallen in love. How on earth had it happened to him of all people? He bedded all the prettiest girls in town, but he did not fall in love. Except now he knew he had. It had been over a month since Fredrick and Robert were born, and he still could not stop thinking of Julianne's strawberry blonde maid. Her name was Siobhan Gangler, and she did not like him very much. When he had tried to make conversation, she had told him to go to hell and stay there.

Gerald had been shocked. Never had a girl refused his advances. His mother thought him to be conceited, but he was well known to get any girl he wanted. He got bored quickly with them though, so his relationships never lasted long. He had been with every type of girl imaginable – older, younger, blonde, brunette, wealthy, poor. He loved women, and they loved him. He just never stayed interested enough to settle down. He always remained their friend afterwards, however, and treated them with respect. His best friends were girls.

But this girl, this maid, had refused any advances toward her made by him. At first he thought she was married, but after asking Patrick, he found out that was not the case either. She was very shy, reserved, but he did find out from Julianne that she went to the village every weekend to see her family. Julianne loved her as her maid. She was good with the children. She would never let her go. Gerald became a frequent visitor to the castle, always making an excuse to go after work, just in time for dinner and to see Siobhan.

Gerald was not even sure what about her intrigued him so much. She was lovely, but no great beauty. There had to be something else about her that he could not describe. His father had suggested that it was because she ignored him that he wanted her more, due to the fact he was not used to being rejected. Maybe that was the reason, he decided. Whatever it was, all he knew was that he had to see her again. He had to get her to talk to him.

It was the next day, a sunny Saturday afternoon, that Gerald got his wish.

"Gerald, lad, would you go into town and fetch some fabric for your mother?"

"Pa, don't you think getting fabric is a woman's job?"

"Matthew Fitzpatrick, so help me God, if you answer that boy's question with a yes, I will beat you with my broom!" Gabrielle yelled from the kitchen.

"Temper, temper, Gabrielle darlin'," Matthew called back laughing. "Gerald, go get some nice fabric for your mother before she comes after you with her broom."

"Yes, Pa," Gerald said with a twinkle in his eye

It never failed to get his mother riled up when he said something like that. It really was amusing to see her upset, sometimes. That broom though, that hurt.

"Matthew, I wish you would learn to control your son."

"My son, sweetheart? I could have sworn you had something to do with him."

"Selective memory."

"Ah. It seems Michael has the same thing when it comes to who is older. You know he wrote the other day to let us know he and Kathleen were going to move to France for a few years to help Willow. It seems that Willow is going to have another child."

"I thought she was not supposed to have any more children."

Matthew shrugged. "I am sure she will be fine."

"I hope so. This family could not take another tragedy."

"Gabrielle, why did you send Gerald to get your supplies?"

"I received word from Julianne that her lovely maid goes to town every Saturday to get medicine for a member of her family."

"Matchmaking are we, darlin'?"

"Aye, Matthew."

* * * * * * *

Gerald stopped dead in his tracks when he saw the beautiful maid drop the bundle she was carrying not five feet in front of him. Before she could do anything, he swooped down in front of her to help her gather her things.

"Do you mind?" she said, snatching back her packages and hurrying on away from him.

Undaunted, Gerald followed Siobhan and took the packages again as they began to slip away from her.

"Just what do you think you are doing?" She turned toward him, her blue eyes flashing at him.

"You need help, so I am helping you."

"I do not need help or anything from anyone else, especially you," she spat out. "Now give me my packages back."

"Look, I am not sure why you hate me so much, but you need help and that is what I am here for."

He looked down at her, waiting for her to tell him off again. Siobhan sighed. She really did need help, and she did like Gerald. She always had, but when she was young, he had ignored her because she had been rather plain. Now when he was interested in her, she could not return the feelings because of her father.

Ross Gangler was dying of lung disease. With her mother and brother dead, Siobhan had no time for romance. She did not know what she was going to do though. The look in Gerald's eyes was unmistakable, and she felt the same way.

* * * * * * *

Two years later, on a warm autumn day, Siobhan had finally made up her mind. She wed Gerald after a long serious courtship. Her father had died the year before, and Gerald waited patiently for Siobhan to mourn her loss. He had really settled down, much to Gabrielle's relief, and was training to take over his father's job one day.

That year also brought the final child to Jean-Claude and Willow DuBois – a beautiful girl with violet eyes and red hair, different than anyone else's in her family. Jean-Claude had been so happy that Willow had survived that he built her another chateaux in the south of France, with a winery for their son Charles to take over one day.

Brigitte, even at a young age, showed a great fascination for the grapes, always pulling them off the vine. She would go outside and just crawl around in the dirt, smelling the air like her father and all great wine connoisseurs.

Francine finally told Michael and Kathleen of her love for Timothy O'Leary, and after much yelling, she convinced them that Timothy had nothing to do with his father. They were married that summer in France.

They returned to Ireland, ready for a grand new life.

After Francine had won her love, she was not sure that it was he that she wanted. The rumors of Timothy and Eve McNight followed her everywhere. Other gossip of more girls and other affairs were whispered behind her back, but no one ever told her to her face. She trusted him completely, but she did have a feeling that maybe the rumors were true. She just did not know how to approach the subject with him.

Chapter Twenty

It was a dark day for three countries the day the news came, and an even darker day the funeral was held. The funeral was held on a beautiful piece of land some referred to as Eden. This perfect place was the only place the family of Michael and Kathleen Fitzpatrick could bury the beloved couple. Matthew, dressed in black, watched at twin pine coffins were lowered into the ground.

Matthew could hardly believe his brother was dead, his wonderful, arrogant, handsome brother. He never told anyone, but he had always been a little envious of him. No matter where he went, he had always been loved, despite his aloofness or maybe because of it. Michael had always had something special that few people possessed. He had become an Irish duke, unbelievable, but he had gone and done it.

Matthew had always admired Michael's strength. He had overcome self-pity, a loss of his love and getting her back. Kathleen was the one who had changed his brother. The small lovely girl who had come to them on a stormy, cold night had been brave enough to stand up to his brother and won. She had told him what an arrogant fool he was, that he had the choice to change is life.

Matthew had a lot of respect for the girl who had captured his brother's heart – the tiny, golden-red-haired girl who had seemed so fragile but had turned out to have a spine of steel. Both were gone now. At least they had gone together. Neither would have survived without the other. He reached for Gabrielle's hand, needing to feel her close to him. She was all he had left in the world now. Of course he had children, but they were gone and married.

He crossed himself before he threw the dirt over Michael and Kathleen's grave, wiping away tears as he walked away.

Gabrielle watched as her husband swallowed painfully as he looked at the two coffins now covered with dirt. Gabrielle had loved both Michael and Kathleen; they were her family too. Kathleen was like a sister to her like Beth had been. Kathleen had been so good for Michael; she had made him see that he was good enough for her, an English aristocrat. Kathleen, the

248

daughter of Lord Dunovan who learned to scrub clothes, cook, showed Michael that it was not where you came from, but what you could do. Gabrielle looked over at Willow, who was as white as a sheet as she hung onto her husband's arm.

Willow gripped Jean-Claude's hand as she watched her mother's and father's coffins being covered with dirt. Her beautiful mother gone forever. Her parents, who had only gotten to spend fifteen years together instead of a life time, had died tragically because of her. If she had not asked her parents to come stay with her, they would never have been on the ship that had sunk in that terrible storm.

Jean-Claude felt Willow shudder next to him. He knew she blamed herself for their deaths. The guilt she heaped upon herself for everything that went wrong had always astonished him. The responsibilities she took upon herself were too much for her. Since the death of her parents, Willow had all but stopped eating.

Jean-Claude felt just as sad about his mother-in-law's and father-in-laws's death as his wife. If, he thought, Willow was not so sick, he would never had asked them to come live with them in France. After that last trip to see her sister Julianne, and then the baby, Willow had been ill. Jean-Claude was afraid she might have consumption and was afraid he would soon lose her.

Then she had gone and had another child and almost died. He had asked her what she wanted most, and she had said her mother. He wrote them, hoping that they would come, and they died on their way over. He was to blame, not his beloved Willow.

Francine O'Leary stood alone with her two children, her husband no where to be found. He was off with his new mistress, she just knew it. He did not even have the decency to show up to a family funeral, the son of a bitch. She should have listened to her uncle and stayed away from him. She threw her clump of dirt over her uncle and aunt and gathered her children to head back to the castle.

Julianne moved to put the last fistful of dirt on her mother's grave. Gone was her perfect mother, who seemed ageless, and the good, kind, gentle man who loved her. She would miss them both more than words could say.

Patrick led the way to Dunovan Castle to have the wake for his father and the woman he had grown to consider as his mother. Why had God taken them away now? Now, when they had happiness and love, they were gone from earth forever.

The family entering Dunovan Castle was somber and quiet as they walked slowly toward the library. Matthew stared at the long, solemn faces of the members of his family. The traditional Irish wake was to speak of the deceased, of what they meant to them. Matthew knew it was what his brother and beloved wife would want. He decided it was his duty to begin. Kathleen and Michael would want them to be happy that they were together forever.

"Willow lass, have you ever heard the story of how your mother and father met?"

"Matthew, I hardly think this is the time for that," Gabrielle scolded him as she saw the blank look on Willow's face.

"Gabrielle, I know what I am doing. Anyway, I am sure you have all heard the story, but let me tell it again. One stormy New Year's Day, a lovely lass arrived on my family's doorstep. Michael took one look at her and fell in love, but, being stupid like he usually was, decided to hate her. Well, Kathleen did not put up with that and told him that he was an arrogant cuss. They fell in love, got split up, both marrying someone else, and got back together. They will be surely missed, but remember, they would not have wanted to be apart from one another. So, let us look on this day as a gift from God. He finally let them be together forever. We should all be so lucky to stay with the one we love forever."

* * * * * * *

Life, of course, went on for the remaining members of Kathleen and Michael's family. Matthew and Gabrielle watched as their grandchildren grew and Francine went about her revenge on her husband for cheating on her. Willow and Jean-Claude returned to France to raise their children and experiment with new winery techniques. Julianne and Patrick decided to stay in Ireland at Dunovan Castle.

Dunovan Castle, the large stone structure that had been a constant presence in the continuing saga of the Fitzpatricks lives, would always remain a reminder of the two special people that had given much joy to many people, for without Dunovan Castle, in spite of all the tragedies that had taken place there, Michael and Kathleen would never have met, and their children and grandchildren would not have existed to carry on the story begun almost half a century ago.